Kiss the Girl

What Reviewers Say About Melissa Brayden's Work

WAITING IN THE WINGS

"This was an engaging book with believable characters and story development. It's always a pleasure to read a book set in a world like theater/film that gets it right…a thoroughly enjoyable read." —*Lez Books*

"This is Brayden's first novel, but we wouldn't notice if she hadn't told us. The book is well put together and more complex than most authors' second or third books. The characters have chemistry; you want them to get together in the end. The book is light, frothy, and fun to read. And the sex is hot without being too explicit—not an easy trick to pull off."—*Liberty Press*

HEART BLOCK

"The story is enchanting, with conflicts and issues to be overcome that will keep the reader turning pages. The relationship between Sarah and Emory is achingly beautiful and skillfully portrayed. This second offering by Melissa Brayden is a perfect package of love—and life to be lived to the fullest. So grab a beverage and snuggle up in a comfy throw to read this classic story of overcoming obstacles and finding enduring love."—*Lamda Literary Review*

"Although this book doesn't beat you over the head with wit, the interactions are almost always humorous, making both characters really quite loveable. Overall a very enjoyable read."—*C-Spot Reviews*

HOW SWEET IT IS

"'Sweet' is definitely the keyword for this well-written, character-driven lesbian romance novel. It is ultimately a love letter to small town America, and the lesson to remain open to whatever opportunities and happiness come into your life."—Bob Lind, *Echo Magazine*

"Oh boy! The events were perfectly plausible, but the collection and the threading of all the stories, main and sub plots, were just fantastic. I completely and wholehearted recommend this book. So touching, so heartwarming and all out beautiful!"—*Rainbow Book Reviews*

By the Author

Waiting in the Wings

Heart Block

How Sweet It Is

Kiss the Girl

Kiss the Girl

by

Melissa Brayden

2014

KISS THE GIRL

ISBN 13: 978-1-62639-071-3

This Trade Paperback Original Is Published By
Bold Strokes Books, Inc.
P.O. Box 249
Valley Falls, NY 12185

First Edition: July 2014

Credits
Editors: Lynda Sandoval and Shelley Thrasher
Production Design: Susan Ramundo
Cover Design By Sheri (graphicartist2020@hotmail.com)

Acknowledgments

I love New York City. I always have. There's something about it that's just so alive. The energy in the city is palpable, and there's a feeling of such possibility. Over the years, it's become a home away from home, and I had a great time further exploring its nooks and crannies in the research for this story. I couldn't imagine a better backdrop.

Working on this book didn't much feel like work, and I think that is a testament to those who were on this journey with me.

Lynda Sandoval, you are a smart and witty person. Editing this book with you was an enjoyable ride. You understood where I was going and worked hard to enhance that vision. I felt supported, cheered on, and learned a lot from working with you. You're everything a unicorn should be and more.

Shelley Thrasher, I think it's safe to say that you are a master of sentence structure and make me sound better than I really do.

Radclyffe, Cindy Cresap, Sandy Lowe, Sheri, and all of the Bold Strokes associates, authors, and proofreaders, you make me happy to be a part of this team. Thank you for doing all of the hard stuff so I can stare at walls and dream. I'm very lucky to have you.

Alan, you've shared more New York trips with me than I could ever count. Blizzards. Late night theater debates. Wine bars in Hell's Kitchen. Reading books in the park. Jazz at Birdland. Ticket missions. Writing words at coffee shops. And surely lots more to come.

As for The Triumvirate, what would I ever do without you guys? It's really nice to have somewhere to turn. What a happy accident we were…

Lastly, thank you to the readers who have been so wonderful to me. I hope this is a long relationship. As long as you're willing to read, I'll try to have more stories to tell.

Dedication

For The Lady
(the most awesome mom a person could have)

PROLOGUE

It was September in New York and that meant the start of something new. The NYU campus was alive with the hum that only back-to-school week brought with it, and the excitement was palpable. The bookstore was crowded with students, Starbucks had a line out the door, and copious numbers of coeds were playing ultimate Frisbee in Washington Square Park. Academia was in the air and the world felt fresh, exciting.

And Brooklyn Campbell was ready.

With her sophomore year stretched out in front of her like a clean slate, she could be anyone she wanted to be. The possibilities were endless, and she planned to, once and for all, take advantage of them. True, she'd laid low her freshman year, not really venturing outside of her schoolbooks much. As a result, she hadn't made a ton of friends, but the decision had been purposeful. When you've been burned as many times as she had in life, you learn to live cautiously, depend on yourself.

But it was time for a change.

She stared up at the nondescript brick building in front of her and blew out a breath. She checked her outfit out of nervous energy, as she couldn't really do anything about it now. Faded jeans, a white scoop-necked T-shirt, and navy fringe scarf. Casual but trendy. She'd pulled her blond hair into a ponytail that day because somehow she thought that would trick her inner self into thinking she could take on the world.

In good news, the plan seemed to be working.

The interest meeting was set for three o'clock. She was late, but only because she'd taken time to enjoy the walk through campus. Brooklyn tended to operate on her own schedule. It was a problem she was working on.

Upon entering the room, she didn't find it nearly as daunting as she'd imagined it would be. She looked around at the fifty-or-so minglers and blew out a breath. Actual gay people, congregated in one spot. It was a new concept and what could be an exciting new chapter of her life. As she strolled farther in, a couple of heads turned in her direction from the rows of chairs that were set up. Then a few casual smiles from the refreshment table, with some nervous glances thrown in, reminded her of how she was also feeling, which was, you know, encouraging.

She could totally do this.

Just as she took her seat in the fourth row on the aisle, a striking brunette stood and addressed the assembled students. She looked pressed and polished in a gray tapered blazer, medium-heeled boots, and a rather complicated French braid. Impressive.

"Welcome, everyone. I'm Mallory Spencer, this year's president of the LGBT Student Interest Group. I hope we have a fantastic year ahead of us. In fact, I know we do." Brooklyn exchanged a smile with the boy sitting next to her and exhaled slowly.

For the first time in a long time, she was exactly where she was supposed to be.

"It's our goal to make this group a home for LGBT students and their allies. A place where our members can connect with one another socially and academically, and generate awareness around campus." She held up a hand. "Don't worry. We also plan to have a lot of wild parties you could get arrested for." This generated a few laughs and knowing high fives.

"Later, you'll have the opportunity to sign up for a committee, and we hope you'll take us up on that and volunteer your time to make NYU a more diverse campus."

As Mallory continued, Brooklyn took in the room. The group was fairly evenly made up of male and female students, who looked just as excited to be there as she was. Some sat in groups who shot each other inside glances as if they'd been friends for a long time. She couldn't help but feel envious of that friendship, their histories. Others sat on their own, taking notes on everything Mallory said. She felt the butterflies in her stomach again, the same ones she'd experienced when she'd set out from her dorm room.

The truth was, she'd been aware of her sexuality since she was in her mid-teens; she'd just never been inclined to act on it. A big coming-out announcement hadn't been necessary, as she didn't really have anyone in her life to come out to. Just herself, really, and she'd done that.

After Mallory's address, the meeting shifted into a more casual atmosphere as the students mingled, drank coffee, and snacked on the requisite cookies and raw vegetables. Brooklyn sipped from her Styrofoam cup, taking note of the fact that coffee, which she'd never really tried, wasn't half bad. She might have to pick up the habit.

"Hey, I don't think we've met." Brooklyn turned and accepted the hand that was offered to her. "Samantha Ennis. Sam, actually." The spunky girl looking back at her smiled brightly. She was several inches shorter than Brooklyn and had deep-auburn hair that she wore in a headband. Her eyes were green and luminous, pretty.

"Nice to meet you. Brooklyn."

"Cool name."

"Oh. Thanks. I think it's a birthplace kind of a thing."

"You think?"

Brooklyn lifted a shoulder. "Well, I was given up for adoption so I don't really know for sure." Okay, that was maybe too much information. "Sorry. I didn't mean to lay my life history on you in the first sixty seconds."

"Got it and no worries. Cool names don't require explanations anyway, as far as I'm concerned. Have you been to one of these things before?" Something about this girl spoke of kindness. She seemed entirely nonthreatening.

"Never. You?"

Samantha reached across her and snagged an Oreo, which she promptly began to disassemble like a pro. "I started attending last year. Everyone's pretty great, but I told myself that I'd get involved this year. I've volunteered to work with Mallory on the film series we're launching next month. We're thinking of setting up one screening each month."

"Really? That'd be awesome. I'm kind of a film buff so I'll be sure to check that out."

Samantha slid her a sideways glance as an idea flashed across her face. "I don't know if you've signed up for a committee yet, but we're looking for some extra help."

Plans with people. Yikes. Her first instinct was to come up with an excuse, tell Samantha she didn't have a lot of extra time in her schedule, because really she didn't. Plus, it was the safe way out. But she was supposed to be pushing past that tendency. New-leaf time, she reminded herself. *Turn some leaves, already.* "Um, sure. What can I do?"

"We're meeting at Barry's tomorrow night at eight to start planning. It's a little coffee shop on Mercer between Third and Fourth. Can you make it?"

Brooklyn took a deep breath. An opportunity to try out her aspiring coffee habit? How could she say no? "I'll be there."

Barry's Coffee House was one of those ultra-hipster spots that made Brooklyn feel like she was infinitely smarter just for being there. It had a brick interior with lots of red leather couches and overstuffed brown chairs arranged in loose little seating conglomerates. Students with laptops and journals sipped lattes as quiet jazz music slipped in through the speakers.

She'd located Samantha and Mallory easily enough, and after snagging a cappuccino, which she was a little unsure about, she settled in across from them.

"Hi." Mallory smiled as Brooklyn sat down. "Mallory Spencer."

"I know. I enjoyed your speech yesterday. You're really great in front of a group. Brooklyn."

"That's nice of you to say and it's nice to meet you." She opened the leather-bound folder that said she meant business and pulled out an agenda. An *actual* agenda. "So, let's get you caught up. Sam and I have some ideas in the works for the film series, but we could definitely use help finessing them."

"And here comes more of that said help." Samantha inclined her head in the direction of the door as a stunning girl with jet-black hair and a messenger bag walked in. She stopped at the coffee bar and kissed the cheek of the smiling barista, who whispered something in her ear. Looked cozy.

As the striking girl strolled over, Brooklyn took in her exotic look. Perhaps she was of Hawaiian descent? Either way she had the most gorgeous hair and soft brown eyes Brooklyn had ever seen. She obviously didn't have to put much effort into her appearance because she'd look great in whatever she wore, however she did her hair. Right on cue, the girl tossed her hair out of her eyes and it fell in perfect haphazard layers. Damn, it was an impressive move. She eased into the chair next to Brooklyn and smiled, a dimple present on her left cheek.

Samantha tossed her a glance. "Brooklyn Campbell meet Hunter Blair. Hunter's in my psychology class and offered to help with the film series. Oh, and she's a consummate flirt. Don't let it offend you."

"I've seen you somewhere before," Hunter said, studying her.

"I think I would remember." Brooklyn definitely would have.

"The library. Second floor. You're there for hours most nights."

Brooklyn turned to her playfully. "Then you must be too."

She smiled. "I like it there. The quiet. The people-watching."

Mallory rolled her eyes. "Hunter's into smart girls."

"Hunter's into *all* girls," Samantha said.

Brooklyn laughed and Hunter nodded in total, unapologetic agreement. This girl definitely had charisma.

"We should get started." Mallory passed around a handout. "This is a list of twenty possible films. We should select nine. The idea is to start with a crowd-pleaser, nothing too heavy. Then we can segue into meatier, artsy stuff down the road once we've developed a following on campus."

Samantha glanced up from the list. "That new movie, *Flutter,* might be available to screen. It's light, comedic, and not too controversial. Plus, the villainess is hot."

Hunter leaned forward. "If you say she's hot, I second the motion."

Brooklyn had a thought. "What if we did a talkback afterward? Movies are great, but people can see movies whenever they want. We're in New York City, so chances of securing someone from the creative team shouldn't be crazy hard. A writer, director, or even an actress."

"Huh," Mallory said, already scribbling notes. "I like this."

"You think we can really make that happen?" Samantha asked, hopeful.

Brooklyn studied her. "There's a good shot. I don't mind making some calls to find out. Just have to figure out who handles the PR for these studios. They could point us in the right direction."

"So are we thinking posters for advertising?" Hunter pulled out a laptop from her bag and flipped it open. The cover was adorned with all sorts of stickers—traffic signs, peace symbols, and random shapes and colors. It was a work of art all on its own.

"Posters for sure," Mallory answered. "And maybe some miniature circulars we can hand out or toss around on tables in the student center."

"On it," Hunter said, already dropping and dragging things across her screen at record speed.

Samantha studied a small ledger. "We have roughly fourteen hundred dollars from last year's fund-raiser available, which comes out to about a hundred and fifty per showing."

"We can get by on that," Mallory said.

Brooklyn had another idea and hoped she wasn't overstepping her bounds. "What if we had some sort of fund-raiser at the events themselves? Maybe a raffle of some sort? Movie posters, DVDs, scripts, or props. Whatever we can get our hands on in advance. We could bundle them."

Mallory sat back in her chair and smiled. "Geez, Brooklyn. You're kind of full of great ideas."

She couldn't have hid the smile that comment inspired if she'd tried. "I am?"

"You kind of are," Hunter echoed as she typed.

Samantha held up a hand. "Has anyone else noticed that the barista has yet to take her eyes off Hunter?"

"I think she hearts you," Mallory said.

Hunter shrugged and flashed a killer smile, dimple and all. "It happens."

Brooklyn laughed.

They went back to work snowballing one concept into another until they felt confident they were heading in an exciting direction. But outside of the symbiotic way they worked together, Brooklyn noticed they also had a lot of fun doing it. She hadn't relaxed around a group of friends in, well, ever.

It was past eleven by the time they finished. They packed their stuff and walked out together. As they spilled onto the sidewalk, Samantha turned to them. "I'm starving. You guys want to chill out over some waffles? They have chocolate ones over at the Cornelia Street Cafe."

Brooklyn inclined her head. "I'm sorry. Did you just say chocolate waffles?"

Samantha nodded. "I did say that. Chocolate waffles. Said it again."

"Chocolate waffles could be intriguing."

"Understatement," Hunter said. "They're amazing. Let's go. You're buying."

Mallory shrugged. "Um…I have kind of an early morning class tomorrow and an incredibly long to-do list before then."

Samantha nudged her shoulder. "*Chocolate* waffles, crazy. *Chocolate* waffles."

Mallory nodded decisively. "Right. Sold."

As they walked, chatting away, Brooklyn smiled to herself, because even though she couldn't put her finger on it, this felt like the beginning of something important.

Chapter One

Ten Years Later

"License and insurance, please."

Brooklyn sighed at the familiar police officer peering into her window. "Seriously, Paul? You know who I am. You know I'm incredibly sorry. You know I'll never do it again." She offered him her most pitiful face because it'd always worked in the past.

He dropped the pad. "Not true. I don't know that. You cut me off at the intersection while doing forty-seven in a thirty just now. Tourists were racing for the curb as you rounded the corner. Foam cutouts of the Statue of Liberty fell to the street. You're a menace to the city and I'm giving you a ticket this time. New York City will thank me."

"Fine, but make it fast. I have to get back to work."

"I'll see what I can do."

"You're a peach, Paul."

She shook her head in annoyance. There went her record. Six warnings in a row, and now Officer Uptight had gone and blown her streak. If the rest of the city would learn to drive, she wouldn't have to break the traffic laws to circumvent them all.

This was so not her fault.

When Brooklyn rolled into the Soho Savvy office, she already had a black cloud over her head. The office was her safe haven, however, and one of her favorite spots on the planet. When she'd gone into business with her three best friends seven years prior, they'd chosen the sixth-floor loft in Soho for its wide-open space and fourteen-foot ceilings, which were perfectly conducive to collaboration. A must for an advertising agency. Plus, something about it just felt creative, and you shouldn't ignore those kinds of signs.

They'd put down a sizable deposit immediately. Without Mallory's inheritance, which was substantial when you came from a family like hers, they never could have afforded this piece of prime real estate, which they'd continue to pay on for years to come. Soho was trendy and that meant expensive.

But the loft was theirs. All nine hundred and eighty-five square feet of exposed brick and beautifully stained concrete floors. Several large pipes ran parallel to the ceiling, giving the place an industrial vibe that worked. They'd outfitted it with no-fuss contemporary furniture, opting for the minimalist approach.

Rather than partitioning off the space into four separate offices, they'd arranged their desks into distinct working spaces but kept the room entirely open. This made it easy enough to work independently but convenient enough to cross-talk whenever they needed collaboration. And they collaborated a lot. To the far left of the metal sliding door stood a conference table for meetings that backed up to an open kitchen, complete with granite countertops and stainless-steel lighting fixtures.

And what was better, it was only five floors below her own loft that she shared with Samantha.

She stood in the center of the room and regarded her friends.

"Cheer me up immediately or I may not make it."

Mallory looked up from her desk in the center of the room. "Well, that's super-dramatic, but okay."

"Completely called for." She held up the speeding ticket and fell backward onto what they called the comfy-couch for fun, because it was really anything but.

"Ohhh, they finally got you," Sam said from the kitchen where she poured a cup of coffee. "Busted. Have you finally learned your bad-motorist lesson?"

"No," Brooklyn answered meekly. Then she sat up. "Wait. What's the lesson again?"

"That you're a horrible driver and should stick to the subway at all costs. We live in New York City, Brooks. This isn't rocket science. They invented mass transit for a reason."

"But I love my little Bug. It's so cute."

Samantha sat down next to her and regarded Brooklyn seriously. "You know what's not so cute? Traffic jail. I'm not thinking orange is your color."

"No, it's not," she answered solemnly. "Would rather steer clear of traffic jail. If that's even a thing."

"Then listen to reason. Sip?" She offered Brooklyn her cup, which she wholeheartedly drank from before handing it back.

"Thank you. That helped."

"I know. Caffeine tends to make the world better." And Sam was off to her desk as Brooklyn studied her thoughtfully.

"Hmm. You're wearing your numbers glasses and your hair's in the serious ponytail. The serious ponytail matters. What gives?"

Mallory swiveled in her chair. "She's finalizing the budget for the Foster Foods pitch. We're not supposed to bother her until she's done."

"Sorry," Brooklyn whispered.

"It's okay," Samantha whispered back. "But I'm going into my numbers tunnel now." And with that she popped on her headphones.

"Any luck with the endorsement deal?" Mallory asked.

"That's the good news I was waiting to spring on you. Jimmy St. Romaine is in, and we didn't even have to counter. He accepted our first offer."

Mallory beamed and clapped her hands once in victory. "You're awesome, Brooklyn. This could make all the difference in the pitch."

"Wait, isn't he a football-coach guy?" Samantha asked, pulling one headphone out.

"He's *the* football coach guy, Samantha. Wait, you're in the tunnel."

"I'm out of the tunnel. Catch me up."

"Jimmy St. Romaine is like the king of football-coach guys, and he's agreed to shoot a commercial for Foster's new maple-flavored bacon. Well, provided we land the account he is. But he's now officially a part of our pitch. We can safely sell him to Foster. A done deal."

It was a major score for them.

In less than a week, they'd be pitching their ideas to Royce Foster and the Foster executives. If they impressed them enough, the Foster account would be theirs. Huzzah! And that would mean a ton of business, a major coup for a boutique agency. As in pop-the-champagne-and-hire-more-staff caliber.

It was the big break they'd been waiting for, and as a consequence, they'd all been working major overtime to make sure the account would go to them.

Mallory checked her to-do list, something Mallory often did. "So as soon as Hunter's back from the printer, you two should sit down so she can storyboard your fleshed-out concept. Meanwhile, I'll get the slides for the presentation ready while Samantha—"

"Makes this budget her bitch," Sam added, a playful gleam in her eye.

Mallory nodded. "Right. What she said."

It was a testament to why the company ran so smoothly and was slowly moving into the who's who of ad agencies. They all four had their own strengths and specific roles within the business. Mallory ran everything, organized everyone, and was the face of the company. Brooklyn was the idea girl and handled most of the creative. Samantha was in charge of the finances and anything that had to do with numbers or money. And Hunter handled all the art and graphic design. They hired assistants on a job-to-job basis but for the most part had it covered.

Yes, Soho Savvy was a small firm, but they offered a hands-on approach that the bigger companies just couldn't.

It was four-way chemistry at its finest.

The loft's sliding door opened and Hunter eased in. Her hair was in a French braid, and she wore an open plaid shirt, lip gloss, and motorcycle boots. She was a walking contradiction in a way that only she could pull off. "Printer didn't have our order ready. He said another two hours tops. Fruitless trip."

Brooklyn turned. "Unless you stopped at the deli on the corner to chat up the counter girl. Fifty bucks says you did."

"Fruitless might have been too strong a word," she said reflectively, a gleam in her eye.

"Wanna play storyboard with me instead?" Brooklyn asked.

"Desperately. Let me get my laptop."

Brooklyn settled in with Hunter at the table and went to work. Over the next forty-five minutes, they constructed the beginning stages of the storyboard for the promo spot. Just as they were finalizing a color scheme, her phone buzzed in her back pocket. Annoying. She checked the readout but the number was unfamiliar.

"This is Brooklyn," she said absently, trying to stay in the zone.

"Brooklyn Campbell?" the woman's voice asked. Official sounding. She hoped it wasn't traffic jail calling. She pointed at the second option Hunter had on the screen and nodded to her, trying to do two things at once.

"Yeah. What can I do for you?"

"I'm calling from the Reunion Registry of New York. Several years back, you placed your information in our registry in the hopes of reuniting with your birth mother. Is that correct?"

Whoa. What was this? She played back the sentence. An unfamiliar tension entered her body and her heart rate skipped. Somehow, she found her voice. "Right. When I turned eighteen."

"This is a courtesy call to let you know we've received a hit. Your birth mother is seeking contact."

The world tilted and Brooklyn had to blink several times to let the words sink in. A chill shot through her. She'd signed up with the registry on a whim but never really thought anything would come of it.

"Yes, sorry." Hunter placed her hand on top of Brooklyn's knee and looked at her questioningly. Brooklyn waved her off as if to say "no big deal." Only it was. It was the biggest deal. "Okay. So what happens now?"

"I've been authorized to provide you with her name and phone number, if you'd be interested, that is."

It was the million-dollar question. Was she interested? This was the woman who had given her up on the day she was born, who hadn't wanted her, who'd set her on a course to a very difficult childhood.

But it was her *mother*. And she'd never had one of those.

Back when she'd added herself to the reunion registry, she'd felt like she had no one in her life. She'd just turned eighteen and was old enough to move out from under the care of the state. It had been a time when reaching out to her birth mother seemed like a possible next step, like she was taking control of her life. So much had changed since then.

But she had to admit, she was curious.

"I'm interested," she blurted. On a purple Post-it, she neatly wrote the name, Cynthia Mathis, followed by a phone number. She stared at the name and ran it through her mind several times. *Cynthia Mathis. Cynthia Mathis. Cynthia Mathis.* It felt strange to actually know her mother's name. It was as if she didn't comprehend how to process the information. She carefully folded the Post-it in fourths and placed it delicately in her pocket.

"Who was that?" Hunter asked once she'd clicked off.

"Oh, um, a referral for a stylist. I'm looking for someone new to cut my hair." A lie. And it felt horrible.

"Oh, keep the layers though. They're sassy, like you. And you need to stay blond, whatever you do."

"Opinionated. I'll keep that in mind."

So she'd sidestepped the truth. It wasn't like her at all. Brooklyn trusted her friends with everything, right down to the smallest details of her life, her innermost secrets. Well, most of them. Yet somehow, this was different. She wasn't ready to share the specifics of the phone call with anyone quite yet.

However, no matter how hard she tried to push it to the side and finish her day, it wouldn't stop tugging at her. Her mother's name. Cynthia Mathis. The purple Post-it burned from within her pocket.

She did everything in her power to focus on the storyboard in front of them, but her mind was no longer working. After twenty minutes of vamping, which only earned her several curious though patient stares from Hunter, she had to get out of there. Take a break and clear her head.

"Hey, I could use some air. How about I pick up the print order for you?"

Hunter sat back in her chair. "Really? That'd be awesome. Thanks."

"No problem."

Mallory eyed her suspiciously from across the room. "Brooklyn is volunteering to run errands. Is the world ending? Has anyone checked the sky recently?"

"It just so happens that I'm just an incredibly helpful person," she shot back with a smile. "I mean, look at me."

"Could be that," Samantha said in contemplation. "But probably Mallory's thing."

Brooklyn offered her most impressive eye roll. "Then enjoy it while you can, you guys. I'm off."

Once she was alone, the full brunt of the afternoon hit her. To be honest, it was a day she never thought would come; yet here it was.

She gripped her steering wheel harder than usual to stop her hands from shaking. She wasn't getting the kind of air she should either, which had her reaching instinctively for her inhaler and taking a couple of hits. It'd been months since her asthma had acted up, but stress was a trigger.

What helped, though, was the drive.

Despite it all, she was able to zip from Soho to Greenwich Village with excellent precision, if she did say so herself, delayed only by end-of-the-day work traffic and lumbering tour buses.

She found something gratifying about fighting the traffic and winning.

The sun was low in the sky and just about to dip below the tall buildings of NYC as she pulled her car into the snug space along the curb in front of the printer. The line inside was longer than you would have imagined for a print shop, but she waited patiently to retrieve the magazine mock-ups for the Newhouse Bottled Water campaign.

All the while, her mind raced.

When she finally received their order, she headed back out onto the street, darkness now in full effect, only to find a tow truck driving off with, dear God in heaven, her car attached to the back! No, no, no. She'd seen the NO PARKING sign and should have paid attention to it, but she thought she'd be back quick enough. *Damn that line. Damn the printer.*

"Wait!" she yelled as the tow truck turned the corner. But it didn't.

She started to run.

It was possible she could catch him if the light changed to red. Pedestrians grumbled at her as she pushed past them. But she wasn't deterred. She rounded the corner, gaining ground just in time to hear the snap from the heel on her left shoe, which, horror of horrors, was her favorite pair. The ones she received all the compliments on. And now the left one was heel-less. Maimed. Needless to say her progress was now stunted. She limped along helplessly and watched the tow truck drive off into the night. With her car.

Damn it all to hell.

This was a day for the record books. Seriously.

She hobbled back to the print shop and contemplated her next move. She could call Mallory to come pick her up, but how embarrassing would that be? Especially after they'd just ribbed her for the speeding ticket. Better she just limp her way to the subway.

But look at that. Across the street, a fluorescent sign for what looked to be a little wine bistro caught her attention. Puzzles, the place was called, and it looked quaint.

Plan B was in order. Because a drink to calm her nerves would be killer right now.

Chapter Two

Jessica Lennox didn't frequent bars. But this place was one step up from that. She'd passed the small establishment nearly everyday on her way home from her office on the Upper West Side but until today had never set foot inside.

She didn't know why, but she was in the mood for a change of pace. Her day-to-day could use a little spicing up, and why not try out the little place on the corner? Unwind from the stresses of her week.

Work had been murder lately, and the long hours were beginning to take their toll. She glanced around the small wine bar, liking what she saw. It was a narrow space, with an upscale bar to the right and a handful of petite tables under sleek, dim lighting fixtures. Large wooden bookcases lined the back wall. It was like drinking in a swanky library. After a quick perusal of the menu, she'd selected a Spanish-red blend and ordered a glass. She'd sip it for a bit as the world came and went, then head home for the night.

As the piped-in music shifted from jazz to classic guitar, a blonde made her way inside and paused in front of the bar. Something about her pulled Jessica's attention. The woman was younger than her, and definitely beautiful. Her hair was down and fell past her shoulders in those flirty layers from the shampoo commercials. Her designer jeans had a singular rip across the thigh, clearly on purpose, and the turquoise top had similar rips perpendicular to the shoulder seam. The effect was the briefest glimpse of the skin beneath. It was a complete look, one *she* could never pull off, but this woman had it down.

"Sterling Chardonnay, please," the woman said to the bartender, who nodded and poured the white wine into an oversized globe.

"Shall I start a tab?" the bartender asked.

"No. I think one will be enough."

"Nine fifty."

The woman's hand went to her side and froze there. Something dawned on her and she closed her eyes. "My wallet is in my car. And my car is on its way to God-knows-where. I have nothing to pay you with." She handed the glass back to him. "Sorry. It's just been one of those days, you know?"

Jessica raised her hand and signaled the bartender, unable to stand it. "On my tab."

The woman turned at the sound of her voice and held out a hand in protest. "Oh, no. You really don't have to—"

"Except I insist."

Brooklyn was struck by the woman sitting at the small table near the bar. Ultrachic was probably the best description. She wore a slim-fitting, cream-colored business suit and killer heels. But her eyes held warmth.

"Thank you," she said, and nodded once. "I don't know if you've ever had one of those days where it feels innately like the universe is conspiring against you. It seems like I can't catch a break. Well, until now." She raised her wineglass in punctuation.

Her benefactor held her eyes a moment and seemed to make some sort of assessment. "I have an extra chair. And lucky for you, I don't intend to conspire. You're welcome to sit."

Brooklyn inclined her head, her interest piqued. "Tempting. But not if you're busy, or expecting someone."

"Nope. Just me and my solitary self tonight."

Okay, now that she looked closer, this woman was incredibly attractive. What was she doing alone? Long dark hair, deep-blue eyes, and yep, perfect cheekbones. She probably worked for some sort of modeling agency. High fashion, perhaps. It's not like she could walk away from a woman like that. Plus, it would be impolite, and that wasn't her style. Uh-huh, that's what she was going with. Manners.

Brooklyn eased into the chair across from her. "All right, but if you get tired of me or want your chair back, don't be shy."

"One thing I've never been mistaken for. It's unfortunate."

Brooklyn laughed. "Good to know. Well, my new non-shy tablemate, do you have a name?"

"In shocking news, I do. It's Jessica." She tilted her head from side to side and smiled. "Jess."

"It's nice to make your acquaintance. I'm Brooklyn."

"Let me guess? Born and raised."

She winced at the frequent assumption that sliced through her on a whole new level today. "Something like that."

"Complicated?"

"Yeah. I'd rather not be, though." She decided to change the subject. "So, Jessica-Jess, what do you do when you're not rescuing women in wine bars?"

"Tell you what." She leaned forward. "I won't ask you about the origins of your name, if you won't ask me to talk about work. The point of tonight was kind of a leave-it-all-at-the-office kind of a thing."

Brooklyn nodded. "We can do that. But I did take note of the fact that you used the word 'office.' That's partial information."

She winced and it was adorable. "I was never good at secrets."

"That's okay. I suck at yoga. You should see my tree pose."

"Really?"

Brooklyn held up her hand solemnly. "On my honor. I failed entirely at downward dog. Was expelled from the class altogether when I pointed out that the instructor just wanted to check out my ass."

"That's enjoyable."

"He didn't think so."

Jessica sipped her wine, an amused glint in her eye. "Somehow I feel better."

A silence. But the comfortable kind, which was kind of nice. Brooklyn decided to enjoy it and the wine. Already she was feeling infinitely lighter as the stress from the day ran off her. She sat back in her chair and traced the rim of her glass. "So do you live around here?"

"Just around the corner actually."

"With your very handsome husband?"

Jessica met her eyes. "Negative."

"Boyfriend then."

"Yikes. Not since early college."

Brooklyn caught the implication and whoa; this shifted things a bit. With this new information, her intrigue level shot up a thousand percent. "This just gets more interesting as it goes."

"Doesn't it? What about you? Madly in love with your doorman?"

Brooklyn shook her head and almost had to laugh at the thought of her and Sly. "He's a nice guy, but no. I haven't dated anyone since my last girlfriend broke up with me eight months ago. I wasn't, as she put it, 'emotionally present in the relationship.' It's something I'm working on."

Jessica's lips parted almost imperceptibly when she said the word girlfriend, and now there was this little gleam in her eye. Yeah, they were so on the same page.

"We should eat something," Jessica said, seeming to shake herself back into the conversation. "It's pretty much dinnertime, and this wine will go to our heads without food."

"Well, I hate to point it out again, but my wallet is woefully absent. It's embarrassing but true."

"No worries. I'm aware of your down-and-out status in the world. I think it makes our meeting all the more dramatic, don't you?"

Brooklyn thought on this. "Well, I can't say I've ever met anyone under these circumstances before."

"See?" Jessica picked up the small menu and studied it, biting her bottom lip in a way that transfixed Brooklyn. "What about a cheese-and-bread plate? Chevre, Vermont cheddar, and, hmmm, a Cashel Blue? Oh." Something seemed to have occurred to her. "Unless you have somewhere to be. Sometimes I'm presumptuous and think the world is on my schedule."

"And I'm grateful for the thought, but I have nowhere to be. Plus, how can I say no to Cashel Blue? Whatever the hell that is." And really, there was no way on earth she could. This woman, she was finding, was smart, funny, sophisticated, and okay, let's be honest, flat-out gorgeous. This was a rare find in combination, and therefore she wasn't going to head home early.

They placed their order and Jessica splurged on a bottle for them to share. The traffic at the bistro picked up considerably over the course of the next hour as the locals got off work. It was easy to see that the charm of the place wasn't lost on the surrounding neighborhood.

"Do you think you'll come back here after tonight?" Brooklyn asked.

Jessica inclined her head. "Will you?"

She smiled. "You know, I think it's a definite possibility."

"So you live in the city?"

"A Soho girl."

"Trendy."

"Oh please, Miss West Village."

Jessica shrugged. "You got me. So what's gone wrong in your day today, Brooklyn, besides the whole wallet fiasco?" She seemed genuinely interested.

Brooklyn nodded once. She didn't mind divulging the basics. "Okay, well, the most recent hit was my car getting towed from right across the street over there." She went on to explain the long line at the printer, chasing the tow truck, the broken heel, and even backtracked to the speeding ticket earlier in the day. Then for whatever reason, she took it one step further, shocking even herself. "But the part that really messed with my head was a call that, drumroll, please, my birth mother wants contact."

Jessica took a minute, her expression sympathetic. "Wow."

"Yeah."

"So you've never met your mother?"

Brooklyn shook her head. "I was given up for adoption the day I was born."

"Oh." She was silent for a moment. "Do your adoptive parents know about the call?"

"Oh, well, I don't have any of those. I lived in six different foster homes until I was fourteen and then finished out my time with the state in a group home."

"A group home. As in an orphanage?"

"Well, they don't really have those anymore, but yeah, I guess this would be a modern-day equivalent."

Jessica rested her chin on her hand. "Then what happened?'

"I graduated from high school, set out on my own, and never looked back."

She shook her head slowly. "I have no idea what to say. It doesn't sound easy."

"No. I wouldn't recommend it. It wasn't a great way to grow up."

Jessica seemed like she couldn't quite wrap her mind around it. "But I don't get it. There are waiting lists for infants. I thought everyone wanted to adopt a baby."

"Oh, they do. Unless the baby has severe asthma and turns out to be more trouble than you ever bargained for. Then you give her back after close to a year and so do the next people. It's gotten better as I've aged, the asthma, but it was a hassle when I was young."

"I'm so sorry."

"Don't be. And I really don't mean to be a downer." She smiled to show Jessica she was fine. "Life's good now. I love my job. I have the best friends a person can ask for, and listen. I have ice-cream sandwiches in my fridge right now, which is a mega bonus."

Jess laughed. "Ice-cream sandwiches, huh?"

"They're the best."

"They are."

Jessica was captivated. She'd spent only part of an evening with Brooklyn, but she already knew there was a lot to this woman. And it was enthralling to talk to her. She was guessing Brooklyn was eight to ten years younger than she was, but she had this effervescence that was contagious. She met Brooklyn's gaze and her stomach fluttered a tad, a new feeling. Plus, she had these light-blue eyes that just begged a person to stare into them. And Jessica didn't require too much begging. Something about Brooklyn really, well, drew her in. She poured them a second glass.

"I like talking to you."

Brooklyn nodded. "I know." Then her eyes widened and she popped herself in the head. It was pretty cute. "No. God. That came out wrong. I mean, I've enjoyed your company too." She sighed. "I'm a total dork sometimes. You should know."

Jessica laughed. "You are not. So are you going to do it?"

"Do what?" Brooklyn said, absently staring at her. Yeah, there was definite chemistry here.

"Contact your mother."

She sat back in her chair, pensive. "Right. Um, I really don't know that part. Things are right where I want them to be in my life. Why disrupt all of that because some woman who gave me the brush-off once, now wants to check in?"

"You shouldn't. Unless, of course, this matters to you. I would imagine it might. You don't have to beat yourself up for being curious."

Brooklyn nodded, suddenly looking very serious. "And it feels like that's what I'm doing, beating myself up a bit. I just wish I didn't want to know so badly. It's annoying me to no end that I do. It makes me feel…weak, which is the one thing I've never allowed of myself. Ever."

"Just my opinion, but I think you're entitled to feel however you want to feel on this topic. And it doesn't make you weak in the slightest. And trust me, I'd tell it to you straight."

"You would, wouldn't you? I kind of get that feeling."

"It's what I'm known for." If only Brooklyn knew.

Brooklyn snagged a cracker and took her time eating it, as if it were just too important to rush. The play-out was endearing, as if each little tiny bite were like a precious find. She glanced up and caught Jessica watching her, which prompted her to break into a grin. "Tell me something about you."

"As in?"

"Anything. A random fact. Something most people don't know about you."

Jess thought for a moment. "Okay. But you can't tell anyone."

Brooklyn held up three fingers in scout's honor, her face extra-reverent to match.

"I love to watch TV. If I had more time, I'd camp out on the couch with a whole list of shows and let them entrance me. Alas, I stick with the couple I can fit into my overbooked schedule."

"Really?" Brooklyn seemed to be enjoying this. She smiled, and it made her eyes shine.

"Really. But if word of this gets out, my reputation is done for."

"Oh, I think you have to explain this reputation."

"Ah, well, it's complicated. A few business moves I've made have prompted people in my field to peg me as a ballbuster. So I do what I can to live up to it. It seems to work. A win-win."

"But really you're secretly at home watching *Dancing With the Stars* rather than preparing for your big trial the next day."

Jessica tossed a cautionary glance to the table next to them, leaned in, and whispered slowly, "I love *Dancing with the Stars*."

"Oh, I can tell."

"But I'm not an attorney."

"Damn it." Brooklyn blew out a breath. "Strike one."

Jessica laughed. "Now you go."

"Okay." Brooklyn stared skyward in contemplation. "I'm incredibly superstitious."

"Hmmm. As in walking under a ladder would be bad luck?"

"The worst luck. You should avoid it at all costs. But it doesn't stop there. I'm in deep. Breaking mirrors, finding horseshoes, opening umbrellas inside. These are all major things."

Jessica sat back, struck by how much the quirky confession just seemed to fit, no, *enhance*, the Brooklyn she'd gotten to know over the last hour. She shook her head, incredulous. "Where did you come from?"

Brooklyn seemed to understand it was a compliment. "Right back at you."

Jessica glanced down at the bottle. She'd settled the tab as they'd talked, but they'd had yet to finish the wine. "There's a little left. Interested?"

She hesitated. "Better not. I think two and a half is my limit. Now, I just have to figure out how I'm getting home." Brooklyn pulled on her green-and-white plaid coat and belted it. It was a great look.

"While I'd offer to drive you, I don't drive in the city."

"A total shame. City driving's the best. My favorite kind driving, actually."

"Says the girl with a speeding ticket and a towed car all in the same day."

"Right. There's that." She held her thumb and forefinger close together. "Minor details."

They walked out together into the brisk night air. Autumn was in full effect in New York, and the cooler temperatures signaled that. "But I'll do you one better than driving you," Jessica said. "I'm the best cab hailer this city's ever seen, and if we walk to the end of this block, our chances grow exponentially. That part comes from valuable experience. And before you say anything, the ride's on me."

Brooklyn hung her head. "I feel horrible. You've paid for everything tonight. You should know that I'm not some grifter preying on the generous. I promise. And to prove it," she raised a finger, "I plan to pay for everything next time."

Jessica stopped walking and turned to her in sincerity. "So there will be a next time?"

"It might be presumptuous of me, but I hope so."

"Me too. I won't lie and say I have a lot of spare time, but yeah… me too."

"Not a lot of time because of all the *stocks* you need to trade?"

Jess smiled and scrunched one eye apologetically. "Strike two."

"I'm going to crack this if it kills me."

They stood beneath a street lamp on Bleecker Street. Light danced around Brooklyn's hair in a delicate halo, and Jessica could have stared at that visual all night. She held Brooklyn's gaze as the air crackled between them. In a move that was so unlike her, she stepped in and did what felt right, inclining her head and capturing Brooklyn's mouth with hers. It was bold. It was impulsive. It was amazing.

And when their lips met, all bets were off.

She'd meant it to be a simple kiss, but the result was too spectacular and she sank further into it. Into the warmth, the wonder. Her body buzzed in a way it hadn't in years, correct that, maybe ever.

Brooklyn had been kissed before. Lots of times, actually.

But this was different. This kiss was electric in a toe-curling kind of way. The effects of it shot through her body with thrumming determination. Her lips clung to Jessica's, holding on to the last lingering moment of what had been an end-all kind of kiss. All parts of her were fully engaged, and she wasn't finding the necessary access to her brain cells. When their lips parted, she found Jessica's eyes. "Whoa," she said quietly.

Jess nodded. "Yeah."

"What if I never see you again?"

"You will. But I'll need your number."

Brooklyn took Jessica's phone and typed it in, just as a cab stopped in front of them. "Told you I was good. Your ride." Jessica paid the cabbie in advance, then held the door open for her. "Good night, Brooklyn."

"Good night, Jessica-the-mysterious. I hope the fashion show you're styling tomorrow goes well."

"And that's three. Sweet dreams." With a soft smile, she closed the cab door, and Brooklyn rode off into the night, alone with her very active thoughts. "What the hell had just happened?" she asked the backseat of the cab as a smile tugged on the corners of her mouth. "I mean, seriously."

It was an encounter like no other, and the beauty of it was that it had been so unexpected. Things like this didn't just drop out of the sky, did they? Women like Jessica didn't just show up in the middle of your bad day and make everything so much better. But she had no other explanation for what had been the most amazing, albeit impromptu, date.

She decided not to analyze it and enjoy the experience for what it had been. Perfect.

❖

"You are way past curfew," Samantha said from the sofa when Brooklyn arrived home to the small loft they shared. Five floors above the office, it was nine hundred square feet of home, divided into Samantha's organized elegance and Brooklyn's haphazard clutter. Samantha's room was to the right, Brooklyn's to the left, with the joint living room and kitchen serving as common space.

Mallory lived four floors up in her own, much-fancier apartment but popped in whenever she felt like it. Hunter, on the other hand, needed a little distance from where she worked and had a studio to herself in the Meatpacking District.

"I didn't realize I had a curfew. But it's nice to know you care."

Samantha was tucked under a blanket on the couch, clearly in for the night and cozy. Her hair was down, glasses off, a sharp contrast to the serious-looking Samantha she'd left back at the office. It was one of her best tricks, the duality. She was a girl who kept you guessing. "If this *I Love Lucy* marathon wasn't on, I'd be highly annoyed at you right now. Lucky for you, Lucy has been a great opening act and padded your delayed entrance quite a bit."

"A. You don't have to wait up for me, and B, which episode is it?" Brooklyn hung up her coat on the vintage coatrack they'd found at a secondhand store when they'd decided to get the apartment together. Samantha had insisted it had to live with them, and Brooklyn knew when to listen to reason. Sam was, after all, the more grown-up of the two of them.

Sam pushed herself into a seated position, obviously about to make a point. "When you head to the printer at six and don't come back until after ten, I tend to worry. It's kind of my job. So what gives? Where have you been? Oh, and it's the episode where Ricky brings home the mink coat."

"Ohhh," Brooklyn said, slipping under the blanket next to Sam. "I love this one. He should just let her keep the coat, you know? He's *never* fair to her."

Samantha glared and muted the television. "Stalling. I know all of your tactics." She pointed the remote at Brooklyn and moved it in an accusing circle. "Where did you run off to? This is all very suspect. And why are you all glowy?"

Brooklyn couldn't hide the smile. "I met someone tonight."

Samantha stared at her. "At the printer?"

"The little bistro place across the street. My car was towed. My heel was broken. I was down-and-out. It was all very tragic. Then, there she was. This woman, this kind, articulate, beautiful woman. And there was kissing."

Samantha gasped and sat up, suddenly energetic. "Start from the beginning. No detail will be spared."

So she did. She recounted the entire tale all the way to the kiss under the lamplight. "It was the most perfect kiss moment ever."

"A Cinderella-kiss moment?"

"A *sexy* Cinderella-kiss moment."

"Oh, my. That is good. Now you just have to figure out who she is. An heiress. A rich royal from Monaco."

"Could be. But the mystery makes it all the more exciting in a way. If we ever do see each other again, I'm sure I'll find out."

Samantha slammed down the remote. "I call disparity. Nothing like this ever happens to me."

"Aww, Sammie-Sam," Brooklyn said, giving her ankle a squeeze. "You'll meet your Cinderella one day." She raised an eyebrow. "Or, in a more mundane scenario, your Prince Charming."

"Is that a bisexual dig? That sounded like a bisexual dig."

"I would never." She bopped Sam on the head before standing and stretching. "I'm off to bed to get my much-needed rest. I'm pretty sure the rest of this week is going to make me its bitch, so I should prepare accordingly. Not even close to being ready for Foster Foods, and I want this one."

"Sleep while you can."

"You staying up?"

Samantha smiled like a kid. "For one more episode. Or, you know, three."

Chapter Three

The office was deserted when Jessica arrived to work the next day. But then it always was at six a.m. The rest of her team didn't arrive until closer to eight, which was perfect for her. She set her attaché next to her desk and went to work, enjoying the two-hour jump she got on the rest of the world.

Hard work was her best friend and had gotten her to where she was today. Growing up in a family with very little money, she'd never had anything handed to her, and she was proud of that. What she'd accomplished, she'd done with long hours and shrewd business moves.

"Hey, Boss."

She glanced up, realizing how quickly time had passed. Her assistant and most valuable employee stood in the doorway with a file in his hands. "Morning, Bentley."

"I have that copy Jasmine wrote up. Want to take a look?"

"Yes. But later. I'm in the zone."

"Gotcha. Coffee?"

"Double espresso. Black."

"On it. Then we need to prep for your ten o'clock."

He headed to the office kitchen. Bentley Fox had been her assistant since she'd started the company thirteen years prior. He was tall and handsome and chased anything in a skirt. Well, except her, for obvious reasons. They worked remarkably well together. Bentley got her and was the glue that held her together. And okay, over the years, he'd also become her friend. And she didn't have a lot of those. Who had the time?

"Ms. Lennox?" Scarlet, her less-than-stellar account executive, poked her head in her office. "I got an e-mail that you wanted to see me?"

She sighed. "Come in." She waited until Scarlet sat in the plush chair across from her desk to begin. "I talked to Jim Culvers over at Dell. They're not happy with the direction your team is taking them. He feels the campaign is too conservative, which is what I've told you all along. They're looking for new and fresh. You were aware of this going in, so I don't understand the disconnect."

"Hmm. Okay. Let me talk to him and see if I can better clarify—"

"No. I've already smoothed things over and told him you'll have new print layouts and campaign concepts for him by the end of the week. Do not contact him until you do." She stood and strolled to the picturesque window overlooking Central Park. "I shouldn't have to do your job for you, Scarlet. This is an important account, and if you can't get it together, I'm giving it to Tina."

"I understand."

"I hope so. Because this isn't the first client that's had issues with your team."

"It's the last time."

"Excellent. So we're clear?

"We are."

As she exited, Scarlet passed Bentley on his way back with her coffee. He set it next to Jessica on the desk and strode confidently to the door, closing it behind Scarlet. "Heads up. Tina's on her way in here and she wants the Dell account."

Jessica sighed. "Of course she does. She's on a one-way ambition train lately. She reminds me of me when I got started, but she needs to dial it down a notch."

"Tina and 'dialing it down' have never inhabited the same sentence."

"You're not a fan. I get it. But she's responsible for a lot of our revenue over the past two years." She sighed. "I had to lay into Scarlet a little. I was pretty harsh." She rubbed the spot just above her eyes where a headache was starting.

"It's what executives have to do sometimes."

She returned to her chair in defeat. "I know. But I don't relish it the way I used to. Maybe I should have been a zookeeper."

He sent her a curious look. "Random. But okay."

"I watched a special on *Animal Planet*. Sometimes I just wish it was more about the work and less of it required me to, I don't know, always be in charge."

Bentley perched on the corner of her desk. "I can't believe I'm hearing these words. That's what Jessica Lennox is known for." He was right. Over the years, she'd developed a reputation for her cool demeanor and hardhearted personnel decisions around the office. Originally, it stemmed from her younger years and the overcompensation that came with trying to be what she thought a high-powered businesswoman would be. And it had worked. Everyone listened to her and doors started to open. Little guys had been stepped on, but they'd recovered. All is fair in love and business.

"Sometimes I feel like I'm playing a part just to keep up with the big boys."

"And has that worked?"

She blew out a breath. "I think that's an affirmative." Because it definitely had. By age thirty-eight, she'd started her own company, watched it ascend the ranks of the advertising world, and had been named three times to the Who's Who List of Executives Under Forty. She loved what she did. She thrived in the creative, fast-paced world of advertising. She just wished she could find a way to be successful and have a life at the same damn time.

"Then you're doing something right. Don't second-guess yourself so much. The fact that you actually have a heart is a secret that's safe with me."

"Gee, thanks."

"And I was proud of you for leaving a little early yesterday. You've been killing yourself unnecessarily. That's why you have a slew of account execs, by the way."

"I just want to be sure everything goes well this week. It's a big deal." She reached for her coffee and felt the smile tug at her lips. "But I did enjoy the downtime."

Bentley turned his face and stared at her out of the corner of his eye. "What's with the look?"

"What look?"

"The smirk. The happy little smirk that shot across your face when you referenced yesterday and your time off. Something's up."

She met his eyes and crumbled because it wasn't like she could keep anything from him. They spent far too many hours together and he knew her too well. "I met someone. I mean, I think I did."

"When you say someone, do you mean a chick?"

She passed him a glance. "Don't be such a guy. I met a *woman*. At this little wine place near my apartment. I still don't know what made me stop in there. That's kind of the cool thing about it. It never should have happened. But it did. And we spent the evening talking about anything and everything."

"Yeah, yeah. Great talking. What happened after that?"

She shook her head at his one-track mind. "There was a rather remarkable kiss and I put her in a cab. Anyway, we should go over the marketing materials for the Foster pitch."

"No. We haven't finished here. Are you going to see her again?"

Jessica hesitated because, as much as she enjoyed her time with Brooklyn, in the clear light of day, she knew it probably wasn't a good idea. She didn't date that often, for a reason. But she'd be lying if she said she didn't want to see her again. And soon. "I don't know." She held up a hand. "Let me get through this presentation first. I can't think about anything else at this point. One thing at a time, you know? I have to stay realistic, Bent. I don't have much of a love life because I don't have time for the drama. I'm married to this company."

Bentley opened the door and glanced back. "Even some of the best marriages end with a little action on the side. Do you really want to die alone?"

That one got to her. "Geez. You have a mean streak, you know that?"

"That's why you hired me. Don't forget your conference call with Folgers after lunch. And Tina's on her way in."

She glared at him just in time for Tina to appear in her doorway. She was slight, with dark hair, glasses, and a severely slicked-back ponytail. There was an edge there and always had been. A Yale grad, Tina meant business and looked like it. "Jessica, can we talk about the Dell account and why it should be mine?" Jessica exchanged a wary look with Bentley. "Sure. Come on in."

She returned to her workday then and dodged the obstacles that were hurled her way like some sort of Asteroids video game, pausing only briefly during her working lunch to think about a blond-haired, blue-eyed distraction.

❖

"Advantage, Starbucks." Mallory walked in and slid the door to the loft closed in defeat.

Brooklyn looked up from her desk. "Uh-oh. What happened this time?"

"I ordered a skinny latte and was rewarded with a chai tea I didn't discover until I was already on the elevator. This brings me to two points. Life is unfair and Starbucks is out to get me."

"There was a time when I would have argued that second point, but Starbucks does seem to have your number."

"They *hate* me."

Brooklyn held her hand out, palm up. "Yet, you continue to go back."

Mallory shrugged. "I'm aware I have Starbucks issues. I'm working through them. I don't need you to point them out."

"Who has issues?" Hunter asked as she rounded the island in the kitchen. She was wearing one of her off-the-shoulder T-shirts that would have her fan girls drooling. Hunter's shoulder was a hot commodity in Manhattan. The dress code around the Savvy office was fairly casual, unless a client meeting was involved. Then they brought their fashion A game.

"Mal has issues. She and Starbucks are breaking up. High drama this a.m."

"You know what? I think you're right. We are breaking up," Mallory said with a newly realized confidence.

Hunter edged her hip against the table. "Unlikely. Starbucks is like your abusive girlfriend, and you just keep going back for more."

"I keep thinking she'll change," Mallory said meekly.

Brooklyn laughed. "While I'd love to delve further in this Mallory-Starbucks therapy session, I happen to have a major presentation to give tomorrow. And might you remember that I've never given one of those before." She looked to Mallory. "I'm the idea girl. You're the pitch person. I'm not sure deviating from our proven formula is the best plan after all. You should do this one on your own."

Mallory joined her at the desk, her expression sincere. "Hey, you're going to do great. I've been trying to pull you into this part of things for a while now. The thing is, no one explains your amazing Brooklyn-ideas better than you do. You have this way of lighting up when you talk about them. And tomorrow, Foster Foods is going to get to see that firsthand. And I'll be there to handle all the rest. "

"So you'll handle opening and closing. I just have to—"

"Wow them in the middle. And you will wow them."

"You will," Hunter said. "Or we'll lose the biggest account we've ever been up for, and no one will ever speak to you again."

At Brooklyn's stricken face, Hunter relented. "Kidding. I just love it when you get that shocked-puppy look. You'll do an amazing job, Brooks. Don't freak out about this."

"What's she freaking out about now?" Samantha asked, hurrying in. "Sexy Cinderella kissing? She finally spilled her guts? Damn it, I overslept and missed the retelling."

Hunter whistled low and Mallory turned to Brooklyn, her mouth open. "Strangely, she hasn't mentioned *any kind* of kissing. Has there been kissing? And more specifically, sexy Cinderella kissing?" Mallory regarded her expectantly, but she didn't get a chance to answer as Sam beat her to it.

"There has been. She met a beautiful woman last night, and I have to say, she seems a little smitten."

Brooklyn held up a finger. "First of all, *smitten* makes me sound like I'm seventy. Give me some cool credit, people. And it wasn't that big a deal. Yes, an amazing kiss with a really hot woman was had, but I doubt anything will come of it. She has my number. We left it there."

Hunter eyed her. "You're downplaying. Describe the sexy kissing."

Brooklyn relaxed into her chair, remembering, and it took her right back there. "It was good. Really good. The kind of kiss that's soft at first but then pulls you slowly in until your toes scrunch up and your body does that all-over tingly thing and you just want to keep going and going and going."

Mallory nodded seriously. "That is a sexy kiss. I haven't had one of those in a while."

Brooklyn gave her head a little shake. "Stop making me think about it. I have so much work to do that it's insane. Sexy Cinderella kissing cannot get in the way of this presentation."

Samantha turned on her heel. "This is true. Leave her alone, guys. She needs to focus. We're not losing another one to The Lennox Group."

Mallory stalked back to her own desk. "No, we're not. And don't get me started on Little Ms. Lennox herself. If I have to see that superior look on her face again, I probably won't make it. Did I mention that I can't stand that woman? Because I can't. That fake smile, the one that secretly says *you're going down*, is beyond infuriating. It's like she knows how to get inside my head without even trying. You should be lucky you haven't gone out on these pitches before, as you haven't had to deal with running into her."

"Yikes." Brooklyn had never met anyone from The Lennox Group or their much-talked-about CEO, but she'd heard enough chatter out there to know the woman was no joke. She meant business and was clearly a royal bitch. The world seemed to be in agreement on that little detail. "Okay. That freaks me out a little. Now I remember why I let you handle these meetings. Is she really that bad?"

"Worse, from what I hear." Samantha heated the water for her tea. "The rumor I heard is that she's married to some billionaire who financed the whole company for her. The Lennox Group gets so many jobs because of his business connections."

"So unfair," Hunter said.

"Not this one. She's not getting this one," Brooklyn muttered, more determined than ever to nail this presentation and seal this account for Savvy. "Lennox is going down."

CHAPTER FOUR

So it was possible that the Foster Foods executives were in some sort of competition with the Eskimos. It was freezing in the waiting area, and Brooklyn found that it only made her tense up more. To say she was nervous about giving this presentation was an understatement. The high ceilings, the opulent furniture, and the high-end coffee station in the corner with all the flavor varieties displayed on a carousel reminded her that this was, in fact, the big time.

Sucking in a deep breath, she reminded herself that the campaign was good. Because it really was. It was quite possibly her best, but the notion that she could single-handedly screw up the *communication* of her ideas had her in a tailspin. She didn't do "in front of people." That's what they had Mallory for.

All they needed now was just a little bit of luck. She reached into her pocket and found the four-leaf clover she'd mounted and sealed when she was in high school. She carried it with her whenever she needed an extra shot of help. She ran her thumb across it now and made a silent wish. And seriously, could they not raise the temperature in here just a few degrees? This was insane. Or at least hand out parkas to all those who entered the office? She was considering lighting a fire in the trash can to warm her hands. Drastic times…

As they waited, Brooklyn stole a glance at Mallory and was not at all surprised to see her in typical game mode and totally in her element. After all, this was the kind of thing Mallory lived for. It was like she was born with this incredible amount of finesse and polish. It wasn't fair. "Look at you. You're a total cucumber over there."

Mallory inclined her head. "Cool, calm, and collected. That's how you get things done."

Cool, calm, and collected. It sounded like a winning combination. She would try it and hope her false sense of confidence would beat to hell the butterflies racing around her stomach. Miraculously, over the next few minutes, that's what seemed to happen. She felt herself relax. She imagined the presentation playing out perfectly and told herself that she had this. That's when the door to the conference room opened and a group emerged.

Showtime.

She was ready to knock this thing out of the park.

They stood as the agency that had presented before them exited with the Foster people.

"Lennox Group," Mallory murmured to her quietly, indicating the two women and one man who stood on the other side of the room chatting with Royce Foster, the new CEO of Foster Foods.

"Got it," she whispered back.

Royce shook hands with the three of them and took a minute to speak quietly with the well-dressed brunette. Her back was to Brooklyn, but she seemed to be the one in charge. This had to be Lennox herself. Finally, the brunette placed a hand on his arm. "Thanks so much, Royce. Today was a pleasure. I'll look forward to your call." As she turned, the brunette's focus seemed to fall on Mallory. She smiled conservatively as she approached them, and that's when Brooklyn felt the color drain from her face.

"Hello, Mallory. How are you?"

"Jessica. I'm well. I'd like to introduce you to my colleague, Brooklyn Campbell. Brooklyn, this is Jessica Lennox."

Stunned.

That's how she felt and that's how Jessica looked as she turned to her, pausing for what felt like an eternity. "Brooklyn," she finally said, extending her hand. "It's wonderful to see you again. We think a lot of Soho Savvy."

Brooklyn swallowed and forced herself into action. She took Jessica's hand and managed a reply. "You too."

"This is my assistant, Bentley, and one of our account executives, Tina." Brooklyn shook hands with Jessica's employees, but she can't say she was exactly present in the moment. Her brain was racing to catch up. Jessica's voice interrupted her thoughts. "If you'll excuse me, I have a pressing lunch appointment. Best of luck in there." She smiled, rejoined her colleagues, and in a flash, they were gone.

Brooklyn was reeling. Mallory shot her a questioning look, which she shrugged off. This wasn't the time to explain.

But as they headed into the conference room, her head didn't agree, because how in the world had this happened? Jessica Lennox was Jess from the bar, and she had somehow missed it? And had Jessica known who Brooklyn was that night? These were the thoughts that were darting in and out of her head as she was introduced to Royce Foster. She only hoped to God she didn't look as confused as she felt.

They set up briefly for their presentation and within minutes it was underway. Mallory was a pro. She opened with poise and power and had the executives nodding and smiling in all the right places. "And now, I'll invite Brooklyn to walk you through the promo spot we have in mind. Brooklyn?"

That was her cue.

She stood and offered the six pairs of eyes staring back at her most winsome smile. "Thanks, Mal. Mallory." *Damn it all.* "Foster's maple-flavored bacon is down-home. It's the crux of every family's breakfast, but it's also a new product, and the commercial spot should reflect that edge." And in that briefest of moments, she lost her train of thought. Wait. What had she been saying? Oh, no. Not now. Not right here. She'd been nervous about the presentation to begin with, and the run-in with Jessica Lennox—correction, her Jess—had only tripled that effect. And while this was the moment she should be speaking, she was instead inside her own head investigating the cause of her distraction. Double damn it. She was going to advertising hell.

Mallory flashed her an encouraging, albeit terrified smile. And Brooklyn picked it up as best she could. The glaring silence hadn't been that long, had it? "Um…Right. So I'll direct your attention to the storyboard. We start with a series of quick shots. Pine trees, a bird chirping from a branch, the natural sounds of the environment are acutely sharp, showcased in fact. We next hear the sounds of play fade in slowly. We see a cabin and four boys engaged in a game of tag football with their grandpa. But it's not just any grandpa. It's Football Hall of Fame coach, Jimmy St. Romaine, who in a brief montage calls plays, throws the ball, and laughs with his grandsons. This is followed by a shot of them walking back to the cabin, Jimmy ruffling the hair of the littlest guy, who looks up at him like he hung the moon. We end with the five of them sitting down to a hearty breakfast they've been craving after the active morning. Jimmy picks up a crisp piece of bacon and the light crunch is audible. The little guy, wanting to be just like his grandpa, mimics the action, a second hearty crunch, as we crosscut to Foster's logo and a voiceover says, "Pass on what you know. Foster's Maple Flavored Bacon."

Mallory joined her. "It's an homage to those commercials we grew up with in the seventies and eighties, only with the natural sound in the forefront, the jump cuts, it has a modern, sleeker approach accomplished through editing. The best of both worlds."

As Mallory went on to outline the rest of the campaign, including print, radio, and an Internet push, Brooklyn watched the faces of the Foster execs. They genuinely seemed into the concept, but in her heart, she knew she'd botched her part of the presentation and hoped it hadn't hurt their chances. She'd completely lost focus and made them look less than professional up there. Thank God for Mallory and her ability to finish strong.

Instead of the subway back to the office, they splurged on a cab. After riding in silence, she sent Mallory an apologetic look. Plain and simple, she felt guilty and thought she should explain. "Sorry about my blank-out in there."

Mallory stared back, but her expression was serious. "A minor blip. It happens to all of us."

That wasn't true. "It's never happened to you in your life, and you know it."

"You were nervous."

"And blindsided. Apparently, a killer combo. You want to hear something crazy?"

Mallory studied her curiously. "Try me."

"Remember the sexy Cinderella kissing?"

"How could I forget?"

"So I found out a little more about her, and it messed with my head a little bit."

Mallory seemed to like this. "In a good way?"

"More like in a shocking, I-never-saw-this-coming kind of way. Mal, it was Jessica Lennox."

Mallory stared at her a moment, her eyes widening and her lips parting in shock as realization hit. "Shut up."

"I'd like to shut up. Really, I would. But I can't, because it's true. She's the woman from the other night."

"The woman you were so into?" Mallory held her hands in front of her and closed her eyes. "Wait. Hold the phone. Let me make sure I'm getting this right because this is really important. You're telling me you made out with Jessica Lennox, the *Jessica Lennox*?"

She considered the question. "Yes. That's what I'm saying."

"How is this even possible?! How could you not know who she was?"

Brooklyn lifted her hands in helpless exasperation. "I knew her name was Jessica, but there are a million Jessicas in New York. It's a pretty common name. Hell, another one lives two doors down from me. If we yelled 'Jessica!' out of this cab window, someone would turn around. And I had never seen Jessica Lennox before today."

Mallory seemed to still be trying to make sense of it all. "So Jessica Lennox is a lesbian?"

Brooklyn tilted her head to the side. "Based on the evidence, I'm gonna have to go with yes."

"Since when exactly?" Mallory was practically yelling now, and Brooklyn, for whatever reason, felt the need to match her.

"I don't know! Always? I don't have these answers, Mal. I'm still piecing this whole thing together."

Mallory paid the cab driver, bringing their conversation to a brief pause, and they walked the final block back to the loft. The October chill was in the air and seemed to calm them both. They walked a bit in silence, adjusting to the curveball that had just been thrown their way. Finally, Mallory turned to her. "You're not going to see her again, are you? Brooks, this is Jessica Lennox we're talking about."

"First of all, stop saying her name over and over again, and second of all, of course I'm not going to see her again. I'm not certifiable."

"Thank God for that. Because there are plenty of women out there who don't happen to be our biggest rival and have ice water running through their veins."

"Agreed. It is a shame, though. You have to admit she's hot."

Mallory sighed. "Makes me hate her even more."

When they arrived back at the loft, Samantha stood in anticipation. "So, how'd it go? We've been dying here. Were you dazzling? You were dazzling, weren't you?"

"It went fairly well," Mallory said conservatively as she set her briefcase on the table.

Brooklyn fell onto the couch. "She's being kind. I had a blank-out moment during the presentation. I recovered, but it wasn't as slick as it could have been."

"S'okay, guys," Hunter said from behind her laptop. "They're not hiring us to give presentations. They're hiring us for our ideas and execution."

"Still." Brooklyn let out a breath. "I was hoping it'd go smoother."

Mallory grabbed a bottle of water and sat down at the table next to Samantha. "That wasn't the most interesting part of our afternoon, however. Oh, no, it wasn't. Are you going to tell them?"

Brooklyn covered her eyes. "Oh God, kill me now. I can't do it. Go ahead, Mal."

Mallory turned to Hunter at her desk across the room. "I think you're gonna want to come in here for this."

With eyebrows raised, Hunter abandoned her laptop and perched on top of the kitchen counter instead. "Appropriately attentive. Shoot."

"We ran into Jessica Lennox in the lobby." She paused dramatically, and Brooklyn closed her eyes in total embarrassment.

"Okay," Samantha said, drawing out the word. "Was there an altercation? Ad-agency rumble?"

"Not even close. It seems our friend here found some common ground with Ms. Lennox in the form of a hot-and-heavy lip-lock the other night. One word. Cinderella."

It took a minute to settle, but then it did.

"No!" Samantha covered her mouth. "God, no. As in seriously? Lennox is the sexy Cinderella kiss?"

"Hot damn," Hunter said, grinning and walking to the couch. "Little Miss Brooklyn."

Brooklyn pointed at Hunter. "No. There is to be no congratulating, or mocking, or amusement of any kind. It was one night, and now that I'm fully informed, it will never happen again. So we're all going to pretend this didn't happen and go about our lives and wait to hear from the Foster execs while we continue to service our other clients and drink coffee and take lunch breaks and everything else we do!" Okay, so that came out a bit more intense than she'd planned, but it felt good.

In response to her miniature outburst, her friends straightened up pretty quick and did their best to hide their smiles as they retreated to their individual workstations. Mallory blew out a breath. "Probably for the best we let her off the hook. I have a lot of work to do anyway. I'm gonna be here late as it is."

"Just make sure you're home by *midnight*," Samantha offered, which inspired a whole new round of laughter from the other two.

Brooklyn picked up the stuffed bear that resided on the corner of her desk and threw it across the room at Samantha, whom she shamefully missed. "Not funny." But the smile had already broken through, and she relented. "Okay, maybe a little."

The day had practically eaten Jessica alive. It was almost ten that night when she finally made it back to her third-floor apartment in the Village. She was half inclined to throw herself on the floor in gratitude just to be home. She wanted a glass of wine, badly she did, but she promised herself she'd try to be healthier and opted for a cup of tea instead. She was only a few years away from turning forty, and it was time she started taking better care of herself.

She slipped out of her heels and sighed in submission at just how amazing it felt to be free of them. She wiggled her toes against the coolness of the hardwood floors in quiet celebration. Fashion took a lot of work, and the truth was, she was most relaxed in a pair of jeans and a T-shirt.

On that note, she changed into a pair of pajama bottoms and a tank top and snuggled into her extra-soft couch, tea in hand, to marinate on the happenings of the day. It was her nightly routine.

The Foster meeting had been an out-and-out success, and she felt pretty damn good about that. She'd worked hard on that presentation, and it had paid off. She had the group in that conference room eating out of the palm of her hand, and she had to say that Tina was pretty impressive herself. She was one to watch, clearly on her way to world domination. If The Lennox Group didn't get the account, she'd be utterly shocked. Inevitably, her thoughts then drifted to the surprise meeting in the waiting area following their presentation.

Seeing Brooklyn, whom she'd thought about on multiple occasions throughout the week, standing there in front of her had been more than surreal. Mostly because she was so very far out of context. Talk about a plot twist.

It was definitely an interesting development to find out she was a competitor. And it wasn't like Jessica was sold on the idea of pursuing anything further with Brooklyn to begin with, but this new scenario definitely nixed the possibility. Too complicated and a total conflict of interest.

But the whole thing tugged at her a bit.

She'd genuinely had fun that night. She liked Brooklyn, and this was the first time in a while someone had captured her attention. If she was honest with herself, it was a disappointing end to it all.

She corrected herself. Because in actuality, it probably wasn't the end. And that could make things more cumbersome, which she wasn't a fan of. Working in the same industry, they would likely see each other from time to time. If nothing else, they should be able to be polite, friendly with one another. She'd just have to find some way to smooth out the awkward first.

An idea sparked.

Before her logical side could overrule the impulse, she grabbed her phone. Too late to call, though. A text might be an acceptable form of communication, however. She typed out what she hoped would break any possible tension.

So it turns out, I'm in advertising.—J.

She waited a few moments, staring at the screen for any sort of reply. But there was nothing. It was deflating, she had to admit. She shook herself out of the land of rejection and headed to the kitchen to rinse out her cup.

It had probably been a dumb move to contact Brooklyn, one she was already regretting big-time. She hated feeling like a loser, and this was shaping up to be one of those times.

That is, until she heard her phone vibrate on the table. Whoa. Not yet a loser. She strolled back to the couch at a carefully controlled pace, because, come on, she was an adult and didn't get a rush of excitement from a text message. She glanced at the readout as casually as she could muster.

Was my next guess.

She exhaled slowly as she typed her response, fighting the smile that threatened. This was a tactical move.

Just wanted to make sure there were no hard feelings.

Question first. Did you know who I was?

Not a clue. Honest truth.

She wondered if Brooklyn would believe her and if it even mattered. She exhaled. Yeah, it kind of did.

It's cool. We can be adults about this.

Agreed.

But probably no more kissing.

Jessica smiled, and a jolt of something powerful moved through her at the memory.

Right.

So I'll see you around.

Take care.

She'd accomplished what she'd set out to do, gathered a little closure, and put things back in place in the event of any future run-ins.

It was a win-win.

Now to grab her six hours before heading back into the office.

❖

It was close to midnight when Brooklyn stepped into the shower. She let the hot water run across her body and work its wondrous magic. God, it felt fabulous. The effects of the highly stressful day began to fall off her slowly but surely. But her mind wasn't quite to that parallel state of Zen. Instead, she was preoccupied with a lot of things. Work. The purple Post-it, the text exchange with Jessica. What had prompted that exactly? Was there some sort of ulterior motive she should be on the lookout for? Because that first message had completely blindsided her.

Then again, that seemed to happen a lot where Jessica was concerned. Why would she expect anything less?

In all fairness, it had seemed like a good-faith effort to smooth things over between them, which was somewhat out of character for the woman her friends described. But not so much for the woman she'd gotten to know that night at Puzzles. Maybe the truth lay somewhere in between.

So they'd be cordial, at least on a professional level. She could handle that. As foolish as she'd felt earlier that day in the face of her best friends, a part of her had wondered about Jessica's take on the whole thing. She claimed no knowledge of Brooklyn's Savvy affiliation the night they met, and she would give her the benefit of the doubt.

As she slipped into a T-shirt for bed, her gaze fell to the purple square that sat atop her dresser. Cynthia Mathis and that little Post-it note weren't going away no matter how much she wished they would. The concept of whether to contact her mother had weighed heavily on her the past week, despite her busy schedule.

Yet, she'd still told only one person about the phone call.

She touched the paper, somehow needing to feel it in her hand. She carried it reverently to bed with her and set it next to her on the bedside table.

As she drifted off to sleep, Jessica's words echoed in her head.

"You don't have to beat yourself up for being curious. And it doesn't make you weak in the slightest."

Chapter Five

"Grab whatever you need. We're headed back to Foster's," Mallory called out, intercepting her the second she arrived at the office.

"Huh? I haven't even had any coffee. People can die if they don't have coffee."

"We'll hit Starbucks on the way." At Brooklyn's admonishing stare, she amended that thought. "Dean and Deluca on Prince Street, then. But we have to hurry. They're expecting us at nine, and Savvy is never late for an appointment."

Brooklyn followed Mallory back to the elevator, offering Samantha and Hunter a wave and a curious look as she left. They would have to cover the rest of the morning's client calls. Good thing she'd dressed the part. "I don't understand. Why are we going back exactly?"

Mallory shook her head slightly. "They want to speak to us again. That's about all I got."

"This has to be good, right? They don't set up an entire meeting just to tell you that you didn't get the gig."

She flashed a smile. "That's what I was thinking. Things are definitely looking up."

But they seemed to be anything but when they arrived in the Foster lobby a short time later to find The Lennox Group waiting there too. The same three as the first time, and Brooklyn deflated a little at the sight. Mallory, on the other hand, didn't miss a beat. "Jessica," she said, and strolled over to her. "We didn't expect to see you here this morning."

Jessica shot the good-looking guy next to her, Bentley something or other, a questioning glance before standing to meet Mallory. "Likewise."

"You were invited?"

"We were."

"Fabulous."

"Isn't it?"

Yikes. All kinds of unspoken tension filled the room, and Brooklyn found it wildly uncomfortable. She interjected. "Why don't we all take a seat and wait for further details?"

Jessica smiled at her conservatively and nodded once in acquiescence. They sat in silence, the five of them, as time seemed to crawl by. Brooklyn did what she so often did when left on her own with little to do; she studied the room, taking note of a lot of things. Spacious. Maroon wallpaper with tiny flecks of gold. Impressive crown molding. Oh, and look at that. A formal portrait of an old guy. She'd bet fifty bucks his last name was Foster. Her gaze shifted. The receptionist tic-tacked away on her keyboard to the right. Geez, she could type fast. Her eyes continued their drift. Jessica was wearing a killer pantsuit. She was guessing designer. Prada, probably. Her eyes moved upward to the pink dress shirt beneath the tapered jacket. She'd left the top two buttons open, and the olive skin peeking out looked flawlessly smooth. She wondered what it tasted like. How warm it would feel to the touch. Her gaze dipped lower, and her breath caught at the perfect curvature of Jessica's—

"Good morning, ladies and gentleman. Thank you so much for joining us. If you'll follow me to the conference room, we have an array of beverages and breakfast pastries for your enjoyment." Like a loud record-player scratch, she was pulled abruptly from her decadent thoughts at the sight of Royce Foster. *It seems someone's had his coffee today.* She stood along with the others, letting The Lennox Group go first. But Jessica lingered a beat longer than the rest and tossed her an amused stare as she passed.

Busted.

She felt the color hit her cheeks but stared straight ahead, following the rest of the group into the conference room. Play if off, she told herself. No naked fantasies happening here. No, sir.

Once they were seated around the table, Royce invited his colleague, Jasmine Huntington, to address the group. Brooklyn remembered her from the presentation. She'd seemed responsive to their pitch.

"You're probably quite curious as to why we've invited both groups back today." She smiled at the collective nodding. "Quite frankly, we met with more than a few agencies looking for that perfect fit. Soho Savvy and The Lennox Group were our top contenders. Both came in with impressive presentations and exciting credentials. In all honesty, you each have a portion of what we're looking for, but we're not ready to make an exclusive decision just yet. As you know, whichever agency receives our business will be handling the advertising for a large number of our products and will be working very closely with our executive staff. We need to be sure the fit is there."

Brooklyn hoped Mallory understood where this was going, because honestly, she had no clue. Royce Foster was known for irreverent practices. Some called him an innovative businessman, which left the door standing wide open for whatever he was about to say. She held her breath.

"In response to what we've seen, we'd like to offer you each a three-month pilot contract with us. In essence, both groups would work with our in-house staff on ad campaigns for a variety of products and go head-to-head, in a sense. You'll be fully compensated for the work you do. And at the end of the pilot, we'll offer a long-term contract to the company that best meets our needs."

Wow. Okay. This was completely out of left field. A head-to-head pilot? Things like that just didn't happen all that often. They were distant stories people told at cocktail parties. But Savvy hadn't lost the account, she reminded herself. So in a sense, it was good and bad news.

"When would we begin?" Mallory asked. She already had her game face on and was ready for whatever the next step would be.

"As soon as the ink is dry on the paperwork."

"Where do we sign?" Jessica laughed. A very professional, controlled laugh, she might add. It didn't sound like the laugh she remembered at all, and she'd be lying if she said that didn't unsettle her.

Jessica accepted the paperwork she was handed. Of course, she'd have her in-house legal team look it over before signing anything, but she was anxious to spend some time going over the feedback from the presentation.

On her way out, she paused next to where Brooklyn and Mallory sat at the table and extended her hand. "May the best team win."

Mallory accepted the handshake, followed by Brooklyn, who smiled up at her. "This could actually be fun."

It stuck with her, that comment. It was so incredibly Brooklyn. Here she was filled to the brim with tension and already trying to figure out how to steal this thing, and Brooklyn characterizes her own take in one simple word. Fun. And her eyes communicated the sincerity of the sentiment. Geez, what was it about this girl that always seemed to grab her attention and wouldn't let go? It was one damn night, and very little had actually happened between them. The allure was temporary, she pointed out to herself. Brooklyn Campbell was just a distraction. A novelty. Eventually she would get bored and move on to more important matters than the pretty competition with the cute quips.

"Wow," Bentley said, matching her stride as they spilled out onto West Seventy-third. The street was crowded with people moving in both directions, dodging one another to make it across the street before the light changed.

"I know. I didn't see that one coming either. But we can handle this. This account is ours, as they don't know what they're up against."

Bentley laughed as they crossed the street. "The pilot? Of course it's ours. It's laughable to think otherwise. But I was actually talking about the eye-catching Ms. Campbell. I see now why she caught your attention."

Tina offered her a curious glance, which she brushed off and focused hard-core on the street ahead of her. "It's a moot point. It's not even worth our energy to talk about it."

"Yeah, but still. She's a head turner, Jess. And so is her brunette friend. Maybe we could double-date." His eyebrows bounced and Jessica couldn't take any more. She stopped in the middle of the sidewalk and turned to him.

"So not appropriate. Yes, Brooklyn's an attractive woman. But that is not at all the main idea right now and not even close to what we should be discussing. Lots of work ahead of us, Bent. *Lots*."

They walked in silence for a moment before Tina finally chimed in. "Well, I for one don't care what they look like. They're going down."

Jessica stared at her. "Now that's the kind of fire I'm talking about."

❖

Someone was knocking at the door. It took Jessica a sec to register because she was so immersed in next month's budget laid out in front of her. She checked the clock. It was a little after ten. Geez, time had gotten away from her, which wasn't actually unusual. She'd started going over the numbers just before eight.

"Hiya, Jess," Ashton said when she opened the door. "Sorry about the time, but I had a feeling you were up." She was holding a bowl. The Colemans, a mother-and-daughter combo, were Jessica's next-door neighbors and the only other inhabitants of the floor. Ashton Coleman was fifteen and her most frequent visitor. Well, really her only visitor other than Bentley. In good news, she was pretty good company. She was a semi-trendy type who let her strawberry-blond hair fall where it may. Her fashion sense was laid-back teenager, which pretty much meant Chuck Taylors, scarves, and bracelets. Make that lots and lots of bracelets. She was like a mobile boutique.

"Hey, kiddo. What's up?"

"Just wanted to see if you had any milk. I was going to have some cereal, but I don't think my mom put in the grocery order. Sometimes she forgets. You know how it is."

She did. It was typical actually. Ashton's Mom, Karina, was the glamorous type who must have been independently wealthy, as she didn't seem to hold down any sort of job. She lived the high life 24/7 but had shown herself to be notoriously irresponsible and never there for her kid, who happened to be pretty great.

"Yeah, let's see what I can rustle up. Follow me."

Ashton lifted Jessica's file folder as she rounded the Silestone countertop. "I see you're having tons of fun per usual. You need a social life, Jess. You never do anything fun."

She snatched the folder back and bopped Ashton on the head with it. "Some of us have to work for a living. One day that will be you. Gear up."

"Should I do my backflip now or later?"

"Funny. You're very funny." She turned back. "Voilà. Your requested milk. Do you want to pour, or shall I?"

Ashton took the carton. "I got this."

As Jessica straightened the papers that cluttered the island, she stole a glance at Ashton. Despite the bravado, she seemed a little off. She had a sinking feeling and her heart ached for the kid. "Your mom out of town again?"

Ashton forced a smile. "Yeah. The Hamptons with her boyfriend. She'll be back in a couple of days, though. No biggie."

Unfortunately, this was standard. But it made Jessica furious. Yes, Ashton was mature for her age, but you don't leave a fifteen-year-old on her own for three days, even if the building is full service. The poor girl was lonely, that much was clear.

"You doing okay?"

Ashton nodded. "Oh, yeah. Definitely. Just, you know, the milk snag."

Jessica knew better but decided not to push it. "Wanna stick around and play a little one-on-one? I could use the distraction."

That did it. Ashton lit up instantly. "Okay. I mean, only if you have time."

"I do. You get it set up. I'll change out of my suit and into regular people clothes."

"Meet you on the floor."

For the next hour, she and Ashton went head-to-head in multiplayer Black Ops 2, complete with the totally necessary headsets.

"You're going down," Jess muttered. But Ashton's guy was slowly gaining on her.

"Only because you're screen cheating. Hey, watch it," Ashton called out.

"Seriously? You're calling me for screen cheating when you're the world's most notorious camper? Some of us play the game with skill factored in. I know that's hard for you to imagine."

"Move. Ahhh, damn it. You just wish you had my stats."

"I'd rather just be a good player," Jessica fired back.

"Keep dreamin'."

The game was intense, as always, and made Jessica forget the real world for a while. Carefree. That's how she felt. She had to admit, she loved their Black Ops sessions. Ashton had introduced her to the game once upon a time, and it'd stuck. Eventually, she'd even invested in her own system. It was a little-known secret about her and, okay, a tad out of character. But that's why it was fun. What would her employees think if they knew their take-no-prisoners CEO relished her time in front of the Xbox?

Once they'd both met their end, Ashton dropped the controller. "I'm out. School tomorrow, and English homework awaits. Thanks for the game. Oh, and the milk."

"Take the rest with you."

She paused and studied the carton. "Seriously?"

She ruffled the kid's hair, purposefully messing it up. "Yeah, I'll grab another carton tomorrow."

"Thanks. I'll pay you back."

Jessica laughed. "Not necessary. And Ashton?" She looked back over her shoulder. "Just knock if you need anything. I'm right here."

She smiled and this time it was sincere. "Thanks. You're a cool neighbor. I mean, nobody's ever…ah." She shook her head. "Just, you know, thanks."

And she did know. "Anytime."

❖

Brooklyn sat on a bar stool and studied Samantha from across the living room. "I have a What Would You Do for you."

She looked up excitedly from the issue of *Money Market Magazine* she was reading on the couch. Only Sam got jazzed about reading a bunch of financial projections. "Ohhh. I love What Would You Do."

"I know this about you."

"Okay, ask me. Ask me what I would do." She was grinning like a kid, which endeared her to Brooklyn that much more. Sam was a keeper.

"If you'd never met your mother and then, out of the blue, found out she was interested in getting in contact with you, how would you react?"

Samantha stared at her, her jaw slack as if she'd just told her the Republicans were surrendering the Senate. "I'm calling a Midnight Chocolate. I'll let Hunter and Mallory know."

Brooklyn drew in air and stood. "Totally not necessary. I just wanted to bounce the concept off you. See what you thought."

But Samantha was in front of her before she could argue further. "This is big, and that's what Midnight Chocolate is for. Your mother wants to meet?"

"Yeah, but I don't know if I'm ready—"

"Look at me. The three of us are your best friends. You don't have to be ready. You just have to be you. Midnight Chocolate can solve any problem life throws our way. Proven fact. Has it ever failed us before?"

Brooklyn considered the question. "No."

"Settled. I'm calling Mal and Hunter. Check the cabinet and see what we have in the way of reinforcements. And chocolate-chip cookies totally count. Ohhh, and ice cream. Grab the mint chocolate chunk because it's my favorite and I'm in charge."

Brooklyn was suddenly apprehensive. "So we're doing this? I don't want to make it a big deal."

Samantha met her eyes sincerely, in a way that communicated their years of friendship. "We're doing this. Because it is."

Brooklyn nodded and swallowed the further protest on the tip of her tongue.

Forty-five minutes later, Mallory and Hunter arrived, and not long after they were lounging around the living room in pajama pants, the absolute required dress code for Midnight Chocolate. Spread across the coffee table were malted-milk balls, chocolate-chip cookies, Oreos, the ice cream Samantha had requested, and, of course, extra hot fudge to top it with.

Mallory snagged an Oreo and took a bite, melting into its goodness. "God, we haven't had Midnight Chocolate in months. I think I really needed this. Not necessarily my waistline, but my soul."

"So what inspired this one, as in what's the dilemma du jour?" Hunter asked Samantha. "I ended a date for this, and damn it if I'm not going to solve a major crisis in the world to make that worthwhile."

Samantha slid Brooklyn a look. "I think you're on."

Brooklyn sighed and decided to just blurt it out as fast as possible. Rip the Band-Aid right off. "The woman who gave birth to me wants to talk. Or meet. Maybe both. I don't know where to go with that. There, I said it."

A pause as the dust settled.

"Oh, sweetie." Mallory moved to sit next to Brooklyn. "Are you okay? When did this happen?"

"Last week."

"Last week?" Hunter swatted Brooklyn's shin, incredulous. "And you're just now getting around to saying—" And then realization hit. "It was the day we were storyboarding, wasn't it? That was the call you took. You were white as a marshmallow."

Brooklyn quirked her head at the odd imagery. "Right. It blindsided me, hence the…marshmallow impersonation."

"What are you going to do?" Mallory asked.

"I go back and forth. What if she's horrible and I can't stand her?"

Samantha tilted her head. "What if she's not?"

Brooklyn thought about the very valid point, then raised her eyes back to her friends and made a decision. "When I was eleven, I was sent to my fourth foster home. The worst one. God, it was a horrific place." She covered her eyes briefly at the memory. "Kids everywhere. Very little food and lots of discipline. I would seek out any opportunity to sit by myself and daydream about what my real parents were like. My real mom was the PTA type, I decided. She'd send cookies and cakes for the school's bake sale like I saw other kids' parents do. She had blond hair, like me, and liked to watch *Days of Our Lives*. Sometimes she'd let me watch it with her and explain who the characters were. She was kind too. She helped me with my homework and made lasagna for dinner because she knew my dad and I liked it."

She stole a glance at her friends, who were all listening intently to the description. Their eyes held sympathy, which made her suddenly aware of the tears trailing down her own cheeks, but it wasn't like she could stop now. She was too far in. "In my world, my dad worked at an office and read the paper. He took our dog, a yellow Lab, for a walk when he got home each evening. Sometimes I'd go along and tell him about my day. He was a great listener. He'd call me Pumpkin and put one arm around my shoulders and squeeze. And for a little while, as I sat there by myself, I got to feel what it might be like to have someone love me."

Brooklyn raised her shoulder and let it fall. "Those kind of daydreams mattered to me. Do you understand? That make-believe family got me through the rough spots. And the beauty of it was, there was nothing anyone could do to take them away from me. Until now."

Samantha had tears in her eyes and she nodded, squeezing Brooklyn's hand. "You don't have to do this. There's no rule that says you have to upend your life."

"I know. But I also think I probably should follow through. There's a part of me that needs to know, that needs answers to questions I've always had."

"We're here for you, Brooks," Hunter said. "And whatever you find out isn't going to change who you are, or the fact that you're one of the best friends I've ever had, who I happen to love, by the way."

Brooklyn smiled through the emotion. She had a lump in her throat for a whole new reason, gratitude. She really did have some of the greatest friends ever. "I love you guys too. And ever since I've met you, I really do feel like I belong to a family. For the first time. And that's everything."

Mallory nodded. "Because you do."

"Yep," Samantha added. "And you're stuck with us. No matter how bossy Mallory is. Or how many women Hunter goes through in a year."

Hunter glared at her. "She forgot to throw in her obsession with puppy calendars."

Brooklyn laughed. "Right. Can't forget that." She took a bite of her ice cream as her thoughts shifted. "At least she's not in jail. My mother. I cross-referenced the phone number, a Connecticut area code, to all the nearby penitentiaries."

"Very thorough of you," Mallory said.

"I learned from the obsessive," Brooklyn answered, grinning.

Mal studied her. "There's bound to be a compliment in there somewhere. Will someone pass me the hot fudge while I attempt to find it?"

It had been a good idea, the Midnight Chocolate. Letting her walls down, even for a short time, felt like a much-needed release. She didn't talk about the details of her childhood all that often, and while she was a little shocked at herself for providing them with the details of her fantasy family, she was a little proud of herself for doing it too.

Brooklyn had gone through her entire life with one motto playing in the background as if it were on a recorded loop in her head: *Never let yourself need anyone*. And while she still hadn't found a way to shut it off, nor was she sure she wanted to, she was able to slowly start making exceptions.

Hunter, Samantha, and Mallory were necessary. She needed them.

It was a welcome revelation.

CHAPTER SIX

"Can I offer you some coffee while you wait?" the receptionist asked.

Brooklyn smiled. "No, thank you."

As she sat in the waiting room of Foster Foods, she wondered, once again, why she hadn't planned for the ridiculous cold of this place. Her knee bounced up and down in response to the chill and, well, maybe a little excitement.

She'd be taking this meeting on her own.

In what was shocking news to her, she was a favorite of the executives. According to their notes, her enthusiasm had been the highlight of the presentation. They'd found her competent and endearing. That had pretty much sealed it with Mallory, and Brooklyn was assigned to be their front person on the pilot. She'd never been the front person before. It was Mallory's gig. She, on the other hand, sat in a room and came up with ideas. That was her gig.

But she could do this. She was prepared to give them her best, and Mallory had prepped her well.

When Jessica joined her in the waiting room several minutes later, they exchanged a smile but nothing more. She wore a navy-blue suit today. A pencil skirt instead of pants this time. It was a good look on her. Wow. Really good, actually. Stop that, she chastised herself. Not appropriate.

The executives would meet with both of them that afternoon. At first together to go over the details of the first product they'd be working on and then separately for an individual consultation.

"How was your week?"

Jessica's question caught Brooklyn off guard. She didn't imagine they'd hang out while they waited. But yeah, okay. She could be friendly. Competition or not.

"It was great. Yours?"

"Busy."

"Yeah. I can imagine."

Silence.

This felt weird. Why were they being weird? Because when you make out with someone, tell them personal things about yourself and then try to revert to pleasantries while at the same time you're still wildly attracted to them, it didn't quite work. That's why. It was like trying to get toothpaste back in the tube.

Jessica must have felt the same way. "This is completely awkward, isn't it?"

She blew out a breath. "In the worst way, which is what we were trying to avoid."

"Can we just decide that it won't be? My guess is that we're going to see each other a lot in regards to this account."

"Aren't you supposed to be kind of cutthroat?"

"And ruthless. Don't forget ruthless."

Brooklyn couldn't help but smile because that just wasn't the vibe she was getting. "Okay, then. Let's tear through all of this right now. I've heard quite a few rumors about you."

"Try me."

"I plan to."

"Ready when you are."

"Amid the many Jessica Lennox tidbits circulating is the one about your rich husband who cherry-picks your accounts for you using his elite connections in the business world."

Jessica nodded, unfazed. "That one's my favorite, I think. It would certainly make my life less complicated. But as we've already discussed, I've never been married. I'm woeful and alone. See?" She pointed at her face, which she made appropriately sorrowful.

Brooklyn laughed. "Yeah. I don't believe that for a second. The lonely part."

"It's true. Why wouldn't it be?"

"Have you seen yourself?"

Jessica paused at the compliment and caught the blush that touched Brooklyn's cheeks after she'd said it.

"I just mean…" Another pause. She watched Brooklyn attempt to recover. It was adorable. She was. "I wouldn't imagine you have much trouble attracting the attention of others."

Jessica feigned confusion. "Hmmm. I'm not following you."

Brooklyn opened her mouth to speak and then closed it again, seeming to fumble with where she wanted to go. Finally, she sighed in defeat and sat back in her chair. "Okay, fine. You're gorgeous. You must know you are."

Jessica smiled. "Thank you. But, no, it's not something I hear all that often."

"If you say so."

Brooklyn went back to perusing the papers in her leather-bound portfolio, which gave Jessica a chance to study her. She wore mostly black today, but her pumps had this streak of bright green running through them. Edgy. She had her hair up in some sort of twist that she still managed to make contemporary and cool. If she tried something like that, it would come off serious and severe. She was definitely missing the hip factor.

But Brooklyn had it down pat.

It was sexy. Her vibe. Her look. The streak of green on her shoe. She pictured that hair tumbling down around her shoulders if she were to reach out and free it from the pins that held it in place. Now *that* would be a visual she'd carry with her the rest of the day. She'd push her hands into that hair and—

"What's that look for?"

Jessica blinked. "What look?"

"That faraway-in-dreamland thing you're doing over there."

She sat up straighter. "Groceries. Making a mental list." She pointed halfheartedly to her head. "It's a…thing I do."

Brooklyn nodded. "Those must be some pretty great groceries."

"They are. Most definitely."

"How'd it go?" Sam asked as they ate lunch at the office later that day.

"Great. They want us to start working up some ideas for Foster's Extra Crunchy Peanut Butter. I'm going to pitch Sandra, the exec in charge of all-things-peanut-butter, next week."

Hunter joined them. "They have an exec in charge of peanut butter?"

"They do."

"How do I get that job?"

"You don't need that job," Samantha said. "As the money girl, I'm sure we could arrange for compensation in peanut butter come payday."

Hunter looked skyward in contemplation. "I'm not against this."

Brooklyn shook her head. "I hate that you can eat whatever the hell you want and never gain an ounce."

"I hate you for this too, by the way," Samantha added. "Pencil me in on the hatred."

Hunter just shrugged and smiled, her fit frame and olive skin of beauty and wonder suddenly under the spotlight. Brooklyn got why girls flocked to Hunter whenever they went out. Today, she'd pulled her hair back in a tight ponytail that made her look tough and sexy at the same time. Brooklyn was taking notes.

"Well, as far as peanut butter goes, you're in luck because Foster sent me home with a case of the stuff. Good thing I drove there."

Samantha placed a hand on her forearm. "Good for who? Did you kill anyone on the way?"

Brooklyn deadpanned. "You really have to find a new joke."

In that moment, Mallory skated open the door to the loft and abruptly dropped her briefcase inside. "Anybody want a Hazelnut Macchiato masquerading as an Almond Latte?"

Hunter accepted the cup with the Starbucks logo as Mallory breezed past them to her desk, already flipping through the messages she found there.

Brooklyn followed her. "My God, Mal, you have to stop going there. It's just getting sad."

Mallory glanced up at her. "Then they win."

"News flash. This is not Russia. You're not in a cold war with Starbucks."

Mallory blew out a breath. "I wish someone would tell them that. I went to the one two blocks down this time. I'm pretty sure they've circulated my photo. How'd it go today?"

"Great. I e-mailed you the high points and the details of our newest task. Peanut butter. Extra crunchy."

"Yum. I read your notes on the train. Just wanted to hear from you. Who did The Lennox Group send over?"

"Jessica Lennox."

Mallory straightened. "Handling this one herself, it seems. Did she say anything to you?"

"We chatted while we waited."

Her eyes narrowed. "You guys are chatting now? About what?"

"I don't know. Her grocery list. The fact that we don't want things to be awkward between us if we're going to be sitting in a million waiting rooms together. It's possible I told her she was gorgeous. Total accident."

Mallory's mouth fell open. "You're flirting with her? Brooks, you cannot fall for her charm. She's playing you. This is competition, and when it comes to competition, she'll do whatever it takes. That includes distracting you. You cannot take checkers to a game of chess."

Ouch. The words hit hard. "Um, okay. But I don't think that's what I was doing. The checkers thing."

"Mallory's right," Samantha said. "I don't want to give you a hard time, but from a business perspective, it's not smart to let your guard down around her."

"No, that's true. I completely agree. But I need for you guys to trust me and understand that I can handle myself. Savvy is my number-one priority, and I'm not going to let anyone or anything get in the way of landing this account. Do you understand that?"

Mallory sat down. "We do trust you. That's not the issue. But sometimes you make reckless decisions, and that's a bigger concern."

Brooklyn was floored. Anger flared up within her. "Excuse me?"

"Did I or did I not have to take you to a car-impoundment lot in Queens last week?"

Brooklyn glared at her. "You didn't have a problem with it at the time."

"Because it's what I've come to expect."

"Wow. Okay. So I'm the screwup around here. Got it. Now I know my part."

Hunter chimed in. "She didn't exactly say that."

"Not *exactly*. No. But she didn't have to." Brooklyn turned and gathered her things from her own desk. "I think I'm going to work upstairs so I can screw up in the privacy of my own apartment."

Samantha stood as she passed. "Brooks, hang on a sec. What just happened here?"

"Well, let's see if I can recount it for you. Mal is getting her bitch on and I'm reckless. I think that about covers it. See you guys later."

As Brooklyn stepped onto the elevator, she was already experiencing the bubbling of self-recrimination. Damn it, why couldn't she stand strong?

Because she'd reacted badly. Correction, overreacted.

Where in the world had that come from? As her blood pressure descended from its crazy heights, she was left with the embarrassment one hated to be left with. Whatever. She would lock herself away in her room, work her ass off, and come up with the best campaign for peanut butter the world had ever seen.

A couple of hours later she was actually onto something workable. She was in the zone. And when she found herself in the zone, her thoughts sped up and the world around her disappeared. It was her favorite state of being. However, the sound of a sharp knock on the loft door brought her careening back to the land of the present. As she pulled the door back, she was met with a most puzzling sight. A paper towel on the end of a pencil.

And then she understood.

She peered around the corner to locate the waver. Mallory offered a tentative smile. "I thought it was creative."

Brooklyn nodded. "Definite bonus points." She drew in a breath. "I should have one of my own, though. Sorry for the royal freak-out earlier. Rough week. That's about the only explanation I have."

"We're all stressed. We just shouldn't take it out on each other." Mallory leaned against the doorjamb. "I trust your judgment. I didn't mean to insinuate otherwise, and the car jab was unnecessary. I like how passionate you are about your driving. As for Jessica Lennox, that's only me looking out for you. Sometimes, when attraction's involved, it's hard to see the forest for the trees. I'm just trying to offer you the perspective you might be missing. She doesn't have our best interest at heart. Of that, I'm positive."

Brooklyn nodded because it made sense and that was a perfect analogy for how she felt. "You're right. I can't see the situation as objectively as I'd like. I will make sure I never fully let my guard down around her, if you promise to cut me a little slack and trust me to handle things."

Mallory nodded. "I can live with this deal."

Brooklyn pulled her into a hug. "I think the referee rang the bell."

"Fight's over?"

She smiled. "Well, until the next round."

❖

Jessica passed a sideways look to Patrick, her doorman, as she waited in front of her building for her car service. "What do you call an alligator in a vest?"

He thought on it and answered in his typical monotone. "I give up, Ms. Lennox."

"Okay. But you didn't even try." She stared straight ahead but couldn't hold back the smile. "An investigator."

He took a minute, but his response was tepid at best. "That's a good joke, Ms. Lennox." He nodded but, in true Patrick form, showed very little emotion. It was as if he'd been an impassive doorman since birth, immune to even her best one-liners. She saw it as a challenge and was determined to break him. And she would one day, damn it. She just needed better jokes.

She glanced at her watch. Strangely, her car was late, which was going to make her late for her eight a.m. at Foster's. She didn't do late. It wasn't in her vocabulary. Especially not when competition was involved. "You're not going to believe this, Patrick, but I'm off to the subway."

"Have a good day, Ms. Lennox."

"You too. Don't smile too much."

He tipped his hat as she headed to the corner where she'd hop the C train and hopefully make it to Foster's on time. She might still be able to make this happen if the train arrived quickly.

In a stroke of fantastic timing, she found herself on the Upper West Side and climbing the steps of the office building with skilled precision for a girl in heels. She was only two minutes late as it stood. Not ideal but totally recoverable.

"Hold the elevator!" she called, but damn it, the doors were closing. "Excuse me, could you—" At the very last minute a hand caught the doors from inside and stopped them from closing. Thank God thoughtful people still existed in the world.

As the doors slowly opened again, her eyes landed on a pair of familiar blue ones. "Thanks," she said to Brooklyn. "I'm glad I'm not the only one who's late."

Brooklyn stared at her for a moment as if trying to assess if the comment was meant for good or evil. "You're welcome," she said finally, in a neutral tone, and then promptly shifted her focus to the climbing numbers.

Silence reigned.

Apparently Brooklyn didn't feel especially talkative this morning. Or friendly in the slightest. She could live with that. It gave her a chance to take a deep breath and regroup for the meeting. As the elevator ascended, she watched the numbers on the electronic window climb. The twenty-second story, the twenty-third, and the twenty-fourth, and then the whole thing shuddered abruptly.

Jessica gripped the metal bar behind her. God, she hated elevators. She exchanged a worried look with Brooklyn, who was kind enough to offer her an encouraging smile as the elevator once again began to move. "We're all good now. See?" She gestured with her head to the numbers above the door that continued to climb to the forty-second floor.

But Jessica hadn't released her death grip on the bar behind her, which was a good thing, as the elevator then let out a terrifying screech and ground to an abrupt halt between what seemed to be the thirty-sixth and thirty-seventh floors.

And then nothing.

The sound of the mechanisms, the hum of the climb, the little dinging sounds were all strangely absent, and in their place was a deafening silence. Jessica's stomach clenched and her vision went white with terror. Because that screeching hadn't sounded good at all, and now they weren't moving. Why weren't they moving? Oh, God, please get her out of this thing.

Brooklyn threw her a glance and began pushing buttons. Still nothing. No lights on the panel, no indication that the elevator was in any way responding. They were totally dead in the water. "I think we're stuck. I'll call security." She opened the emergency box and paused. "There's no phone in here. Where the hell's the phone? Isn't that an elevator requirement?"

Jessica opened her mouth to respond, but she was having difficulty forming any words. She'd always had an aversion to small spaces, but with elevators, it had always been a mind-over-matter kind of thing. They were a necessary evil in New York that she'd simply learned to live with. But being stuck in one was her worst nightmare come to fruition.

Brooklyn slid a concerned look her way. "You okay over there? It's not a big deal. We're just momentarily paused."

Jessica nodded.

"Hey, Jess, look at me. You're white as a sheet. We're going to be fine."

"How do you know that?" she finally managed.

"Because elevators hiccup all the time. Look, there's a call button on the wall." Brooklyn pushed it and waited. No response. She offered Jessica a nervous smile and tried the button again. Same result. "Okay. Not a problem. I have my phone with me. Brooklyn dialed and put the phone to her ear, only to pause and glance at the screen a few moments later. "Check your phone. Do you have a signal?"

Jessica pulled her phone from her bag and, thank the stars above, there was hope! "One bar." She dialed 911 and waited until a voice, a glorious, magical voice from outside of the elevator answered her.

"911. What's your emergency?"

"We're trapped in an elevator and aren't able to contact anyone in the building."

"Ma'am, what is your—"

But the operator's voice cut out and the signal dropped. Jessica stared at the phone. "Damn it. I lost her." She tried the call again but it didn't go through.

"That's okay," Brooklyn pointed out. "They can trace the call, and now they know we're here. It's only a matter of time before they arrive and have us out."

Jessica nodded, trying to reason with the part of her mind that wasn't totally freaking out. "Right. I'm sure you're right. I just, uh, don't do so great in small spaces." She flexed her hands and clenched them into fists.

Brooklyn's mouth formed a small O as she took in the information, then seemed to regroup, brightening. "But this isn't so small, and it's just the two of us in here. Not at all crowded. Lots of room to walk."

"Thanks, but it is. Small, I mean."

Brooklyn shrugged in concession. "It's not ideal. You're right. But it could be worse, there could be—"

The lights flickered above them before failing entirely. The elevator fell into complete and utter darkness.

"No lights?" Jessica couldn't see a thing. The hand she held in front of her face didn't exist. Her heart rate tripled and she descended to the floor. "I can't do this. I can't." She heard movement to her right as Brooklyn crawled the distance between them until she was sitting next to her.

"Yes, you can. I'm right here, and I'm going to get you through this." Brooklyn's hand found hers and held on. The warmth of it was comforting.

"Wanna hear a joke?" Brooklyn asked.

"How did you know I like jokes?"

"I didn't. But I'm filing it away. Wanna hear one?"

"Um. No, I don't think so."

"What do you call a person with no body and no nose?" A pause. "Nobody knows."

"Okay. That was horrible." But Jessica felt the fleeting smile across her face. Maybe she could tell it to Patrick.

"It was. It's a truly god-awful joke, but it's all we've got, that joke."

Jessica laughed at the lunacy of the comment, and along with that laugh, she felt a little of the fear fall away. "How long do you think it's been?"

"Not long. Maybe five minutes."

"That's it?"

Brooklyn squeezed her hand. "Try not to think about it."

"Tall order."

They sat in silence for what seemed like forever, but with Brooklyn's hand in hers she somehow felt safe, which was crazy because they were anything but. Hell, they were more than thirty stories in the air, capable of plunging to their deaths any time the elevator lost its grip. Yet, all she seemed to be able to concentrate on was the rich vanilla scent of Brooklyn's hair.

"What were you like as a kid?" she finally asked, breaking the silence that hung between them.

She felt Brooklyn shift next to her. "Me? I was quiet. Kind of moody. Pretty much closed off."

Jessica didn't love the answer and pressed on, looking for something brighter in Brooklyn's life. "What subject were you good at in school?"

"Surprisingly, science. I won the fifth-grade science fair and took all honors science courses in high school."

"Wow. You *were* good at science. Yet you work in advertising."

Brooklyn laughed. "It all goes together."

"Did you have friends?"

"Sometimes. I had a *best* friend when I was seven. Her name was Ziann, and she lived with the same foster family I did. We'd play all sorts of make-believe games together. She looked out for me. Would stroke my hair when I cried, that kind of thing." She took a moment. Jessica couldn't see her face, but she imagined she was lost in the memory. "I'd never had a friend like her before."

"Are you still in touch?"

Brooklyn pulled her hand away, and Jessica knew they'd ventured into uncomfortable territory. "No. The woman we lived with caught her sneaking food one night and knocked her around pretty good. I tried to stop her but…"

"But what?"

"A few well-placed fists and I backed down. I'd never been punched in the stomach before. It took the wind out of me. I was too scared to fight back after that."

"Oh, my God. What happened?"

"Ziann was taken to the hospital and I was removed from the house."

Jessica was shocked almost to the point of not knowing what to say. "Was she okay?"

Brooklyn was quiet for a moment. "I don't really know. I never saw her again. I asked about her, but no one seemed to have answers. Or maybe they just didn't want to tell me the truth. I didn't let myself make too many friends after that."

Jessica's heart fell at the concept of a seven-year-old Brooklyn alone and missing her only friend. On one hand, she felt guilty for bringing up what must have been a horrific memory for her. But on the other, something within her wanted to know more about this woman next to her.

Brooklyn was embarrassed. She wasn't sure why she'd shared so much with Jessica, yet again. Maybe it was her proximity. Or the fact that she had been holding Brooklyn's hand. But probably, it was the anonymity of the darkness around them that made it easier to go there. Not having to see the inevitable sympathetic look decreased the emotional risk. Still, she decided to change the subject. "What were you like as a child? You know, little Jessica racing around in a miniature business suit and heels."

Jessica laughed. "Pretty tame, actually. I was really into homework."

"Shocking."

"Don't make fun of me. I'm sensitive."

Brooklyn laughed. "That's not at all true, and you know it."

"You're right. But still."

"Get back to it, Lennox. What else?"

She heard Jessica blow out a conciliatory breath. "Ballet was a big part of my life when I was a kid. I was really into it."

"Ohhh, now we're getting somewhere. How much into?"

"I was good. Really good."

"So why didn't you pursue ballet over business? Turn yourself into a prima ballerina?" The idea of Jessica's sleek frame in a leotard was carrying her mind places already. It was a great visual. But when she thought about it, the dance thing made sense. Jessica moved with an inherent grace, an elegance that not many people were able to pull off.

"Too much risk involved. I wasn't the type who was willing to starve for my art and wait tables until the next big audition came along."

"So stability is important to you?"

"It's everything to me." It had been a quick answer, and that said a lot.

Brooklyn nodded, understanding a little bit more about what made Jessica tick.

"Plus, my cousin's the real dancer. We used to take classes together growing up in Boston. She wowed our teachers every step of the way."

"Where'd she end up?"

"She's currently dancing the lead in a Broadway show actually, *Elevation*. Have you heard of it?"

Brooklyn was shocked. "I've seen it. She's amazing. I had no idea."

"Why would you?"

They didn't talk for a little while. But it was a comfortable silence. And even though Jessica seemed calmer now, more in control of her fear, Brooklyn stayed next to her, shoulder to shoulder.

You know, just in case.

It was around half an hour later when the emergency lights at the top of the elevator popped on. Thank God. That had to be a good sign. Brooklyn stood because some sort of reaction seemed appropriate. "That's promising, don't you think?"

Jessica looked up at her with a weary smile. "It's progress, I guess."

As a preventative measure, Brooklyn pulled her inhaler from her bag and took a few puffs.

"Are you all right? Is there enough air in here?" Jessica asked.

Brooklyn smiled. "I'm fine. Sometimes I just need a little help in the breathing department. Nothing major."

"Hello, can you hear me?" came a voice from a speaker on the wall panel.

"Whoa." Brooklyn pushed the button to answer him. "Yes! We hear you," she practically shouted.

"Is everyone in the elevator all right?"

"We're okay. Just completely stuck and ready to get out of here."

"How many people are with you?"

"There's just two of us," she said, meeting Jessica's eyes.

"I apologize for the inconvenience. Maintenance is here and they're working on the problem. Sorry for the disruption in your day."

Jessica was up alongside Brooklyn and pushing the button. "How long?"

A pause. "We're working as fast as we can, but we've had to call out for a part. It's on its way. Could be an hour or two."

They exchanged a look. Jessica pressed the button with purpose this time, clearly in high-powered business mode. "Not acceptable. Call whomever the hell you have to and get it here faster. There's an asthmatic woman in here."

There was a pause before the voice answered. "We're doing everything we can, ma'am."

As Jessica shook her head and moved to press the button again, Brooklyn placed a hand on her arm. "Hey, look at me. They're on our side."

Their eyes met, and something in Jessica seemed to soften. "You're right. Of course, you're right." They sat back on the floor, opposite sides of the elevator this time. It was a given that they'd each missed their appointment with Foster, but it was starting to look like the rest of the morning would be shot as well. "Did you have anything pressing to take care of?"

Jessica shook her head. "Two in-house meetings and a client call this afternoon. Not to mention the mountains of work I need to tackle in between. You?"

"Just our regular weekly staff meeting. We bring in lunch and catch each other up on where we are with various clients. It's kind of a check-in."

"I know your firm's not big, but how many of you are there?"

Brooklyn smiled defensively as Jessica's tone seemed laced with judgment. "Four of us, and we're capable of a lot."

"Of course. I didn't mean to insinuate otherwise. Just curious. How'd you end up working at Savvy?" Jessica finally asked.

"We were best friends in school. Mallory, Hunter, Samantha, and I. We started working together in college on a small scale for the LGBT center on campus, and there was this synergy there I just can't explain. We knew we could do great things together."

"Tell me about them, your best friends."

"Well, you already know a little bit about Mallory. She's pretty much in charge of the world. She's organized, driven, and polished. Oh, and an obsessive list-maker. It's kind of mind-blowing, the number of lists she juggles. The great thing about her, though, is that in the midst of all that, she has the biggest heart. Not a lot of people realize that about her. She'd give a stranger the sweater off her back if they needed it."

"That's good information, you know, in case I'm ever cold."

"You're hysterical."

"Yeah, but I have to work at it. What about Samantha?"

"Right. Well, Sam is a money genius. She consistently amazes me with the way she cobbles together budgets for even the most meager of clients and stretches each dollar we have. She's probably the most pragmatic one in the group. And also the voice of reason to my crazy, more often than not. In case you haven't figured it out, I tend to be kind of a handful. Reckless even, and Samantha helps keep me in check. Oh, and we live together, so there's that."

"Let me guess. You're the messy one."

"Did she call you? It's important you know she lies."

Jessica gave her the sideways grin that showed her dimples. She liked the sideways grin. It was a favorite. "Just a hunch. And the fourth?"

"That would be Hunter. Her mother is Hawaiian and her father's from Rhode Island, so she has this exotic, beautiful thing happening. As a result, women and men alike throw themselves at her. For that reason, she's kind of a player. I don't like going out with her because it's pretty much ordained that she gets all the attention. Oh, but for Savvy she handles all of the graphic-design elements. She's a whiz on a computer, so we forgive the fact that she's late everywhere and pretty much does whatever the hell she wants at whatever time she wants to do it."

"Very interesting. Four lesbians working together in close quarters."

Brooklyn held up a finger. "Not exactly. Samantha is bisexual. She keeps her options open."

Jessica nodded. "Got it. So have any of you ever crossed the lines of friendship? It seems like it would happen somewhere along the way."

"Are you asking if there's been any scandalous interoffice romance in our history?"

"It did occur to me when I saw you with Mallory."

"No. Absolutely not. It's actually kind of a pact we made when we started the company." Jessica gave her a long look. "Okay, it's possible I made out with Sam our junior year, but it was like kissing my sister, and it never happened again by mutual conclusion. Total disaster."

"Aha. Busted."

Brooklyn couldn't help but smile at the look of triumph on Jessica's face. She relaxed back against the wall. "I like it when you're playful."

"You bring it out in me, I guess," she answered sincerely. A moment passed between them that Brooklyn felt all over. The sensation that came over her as Jessica's eyes held hers had her stomach doing a series of hard-core somersaults.

She liked it. She liked Jessica. Talking to her, staring at her. All of it.

And, damn it, it was a problem. She recalled her talk with Mallory, and feelings for Jessica weren't really an option. "What are we going to do?" she murmured.

Jessica blinked, her gaze dropping noticeably to Brooklyn's mouth. "About?"

"This. The fact that you're staring at me like I'm your next meal and all I want to do is kiss you into next week."

Jessica's lips parted in surprise. "Well, if you're just going to jump out there and say it…"

"I am," she said in frustration. "Because it's there. Every time I see you. And it can't be anymore." Brooklyn was up and pacing the small expanse of the elevator. "It causes problems with my friends, who are everything, and it messes with my head, and it's bad for business. Yours and mine. "

"What problems with your friends? Are you talking about Mallory?"

"Yes, actually. But that's just part of it. There are the texts. The business suits and that stupid top button. Seriously with the button? The way you do that little thing with your mouth where you bite your lower lip right before you say something thoughtful. That has to stop, by the way. The lip thing. No more of that. And that sleek, confident dancer walk you do—"

Jessica stood and held up her hands. "Whoa. You have to slow down. Half of that doesn't even make sense."

"It makes sense to me. It makes tons of sense, and that's why it has to end."

Jessica seemed to regroup. "So you're saying it drives you crazy when I bite my lip?" The small smile playing at the corners of that gorgeous mouth irritated Brooklyn to no end.

"Stop it."

"Stop what?" Jessica stood.

"Making light of this situation."

Her smile faded. "I'm not. In fact, I think I might have a solution."

"I'm listening."

"I think you should kiss me."

She studied Jessica. "Very funny."

"Except I'm serious." And Brooklyn realized she was. "Maybe it would get it out of our system if we just, you know, went for it, once and for all. One really good kiss might put this whole thing to rest. A kind of closure."

It sounded insane, but sometimes insane surprised you. Sometimes insane was the way to go when logical was no longer working. "And nothing comes of it?"

"Nothing comes of it," Jess said. "Of course not. It wouldn't work anyway. Can you imagine the issues we'd have, given our lives? Our jobs?"

"A proverbial laundry list of crazy."

"Exactly. But no harm ever came from one kiss."

The intelligent side of Brooklyn's brain was blaring warning signals like there was no tomorrow, but the physical pull she felt to Jessica was drowning them the hell out. Tentatively, she crossed the short distance between them until she was just inches away, close enough to pick up the scent of citrus and honey, which had her heart pounding and her head spinning. God, this woman was so many things, and intoxicating was definitely one of them.

Jessica was maybe an inch taller, but the difference felt minimal as they stood there, so very close. She could see every shade of blue in those beautifully expressive eyes, and there were several. They hadn't even touched and Brooklyn already felt that familiar stirring all the way through her, from the top of her head down to her toes, circling madly across her center. She wondered if Jess felt it too, because in that moment, her smile dimmed and those eyes went very serious.

She held Jessica's gaze and ran her hands slowly up her arms, across her collarbone to her neck until she cradled her face in her hands. Then, she gently tilted her face. It was achingly sensual to be so close to her. And she did mean achingly. It was becoming clear to her that their chemistry was maybe even more explosive than she'd first thought. And if this was her one shot to experience it, her only get-out-of-jail-free card, she intended to take her time. This would be a moment she would carry with her and access when other moments weren't an option.

Leaning in, she brushed Jessica's lips with hers softly, going in more fully after that because she simply didn't have a choice. Her mouth was warm, wonderful, and quickly awoke all kinds of unfamiliar yearnings Brooklyn was having a hard time categorizing. But she knew one thing for certain. In that moment, there was nowhere else she'd rather be, and she illustrated that fact by pressing closer and deepening the kiss, angling her head for better access.

And, man, could Jessica kiss.

Brooklyn let out a hum of pleasure because it was good. So good that she was struggling to keep her head about her. She could live in this kiss forever, drown there and be just fine. Jessica reversed their positions, settling Brooklyn against the wall and meeting her there as their mouths continued to dance with sizzling abandon. Jessica's breasts pressed against hers and brought forth a whole new onslaught of yearning. Plain and simple, her body was responding quickly. Too quickly. She was throbbing and needed more. She sucked on Jessica's bottom lip, then swiped it slowly with her tongue, gaining entrance. She needed to taste.

Jessica's mind went white.

With Brooklyn in her arms, up against her like this, she was lost, searching for a way to think, but nothing came. She answered Brooklyn's tongue each step of the way. In a new twist, the one-kiss agreement seemed to have bubbled into something off the tracks, and in that moment, she couldn't remember why that was a bad idea at all.

In fact, it felt quite the opposite, the best idea she'd had in weeks. Her rational side could take a few minutes off. The world wouldn't end.

And Brooklyn was everything she remembered and more.

A slow rhythm rolled between them, this give-and-take that was taking her places and fast. Jessica forced her hands to obey and not travel to areas they desperately craved to travel to. She was in torturous need, dying to explore more than just the kissing offered. She wanted to touch and be touched, and her restraint was fading to the recesses of consciousness. She moved her hands from Brooklyn's waist, down the outside of her hips and up again. The motion caused Brooklyn's pencil skirt to edge up her thighs to decadent heights, but that was more than okay because the skin there felt amazing beneath her fingertips. She lingered there a moment longer before tracing higher.

The ding of the elevator that interrupted that motion was like a god-awful alarm clock in the midst of the most wonderful dream. In jolted response, Jessica took a step back and attempted to catch her breath. Brooklyn gave her head a little shake and straightened her clothes. Two-point-two seconds later the door opened and a small group of workmen and office workers applauded their rescue, unaware of what they'd almost witnessed.

Brooklyn's eyes widened and she swore under her breath.

"Jesus," Jessica managed.

One of the workmen offered her his hand and helped her out of the elevator. "You okay? You look a little shaken up."

She stared at him, still reeling, hazy, and attempting to put her thoughts back in order. "Yeah, something like that."

"Thank you so much for your hard work in getting us out," Brooklyn said to a man with a hard hat and a walkie-talkie.

He tipped his hat. People still did that? Hat tipping? She couldn't remember. She couldn't think. "We're just glad everyone is okay," wrench guy said.

"We're fine," Brooklyn told him. She met Jessica's eyes in all seriousness. "Right?"

"We're fine." But she wasn't quite sure she believed it.

They were one spark away from igniting in that elevator, and it had stirred something in her that had been quiet for far too long.

She felt alive. And it was all kinds of exhilarating.

Chapter Seven

Two days later and Jessica sighed deeply before forcing herself onto the elevator in her building. "And here we go again," she murmured. Elevators had new meaning now, for a variety of reasons. She could never look at one the same way again.

It was a love-hate kind of thing, but a necessary relationship when living where she did. So she was just going to have to get past that "hate" aspect. Lofty, but since when was she one to shirk a challenge?

It was after ten when her car had dropped her off, as she'd worked late again. The day had kicked her ass, and she needed to eke out a little sleep so she could get up and do the whole thing over again tomorrow. That's just how her life went.

In celebratory news, the elevator delivered her safely to her floor, but as she approached her door, she caught sight of something, make that someone, slumped in the hallway just shy of the Colemans' door. Staring hard and then realizing it was her neighbor, Karina, she sprang into action.

"Karina, hey. Are you okay? Are you hurt?" She knelt down next to the woman and realized she'd either spent the day volunteering at a bourbon distillery or was drunk off her ass. Geez, that was strong.

Karina stirred and blinked at her a few times, her brow deeply furrowed. "Go away," she murmured. "Busy right now."

"Karina, you're lying in the hallway. Why don't we get you inside your apartment?

"Later. Sleepy."

Jessica smoothed the mass of hair from her face. "How about we find you some water, get you into bed, and you can go right back to sleep?"

"Fine. Okay. S'probably good." Karina, seemingly put out by the disruption, pushed herself into a seated position, and Jessica helped her up the rest of the way.

Then a thought occurred to her. "Karina, where's Ashton?"

"School. Ashton goes to school."

"It's after ten at night. She's not at school right now. Is she home?" Jessica tried the apartment door, but it was locked.

"Oh," Karina said, as if a magical thought had just occurred to her. "It's late."

Jessica held her tight as she stumbled. "Whoa. Yeah, it is. It's getting late." She knocked on the door. "Ashton, you at home?"

In only a brief moment the door opened, and Ashton in pajama pants and T-shirt stood before them, her eyes moving from Jessica to her mother. "Oh my God, Mom. I've been trying your phone for hours."

"I think she's had a little to drink," Jessica informed her conservatively.

Ashton's face flashed mortification, and she sprang into action. "Thanks, Jess. I got this." She ducked under Karina's shoulder and took Jessica's spot, helping her mother into the apartment. Jessica followed them in a few steps, but as soon as Ashton had her mother safely on the couch, she raced back, her palms up. "It's under control. I promise." Her tone was short. Clearly she wanted Jessica to leave.

"Why don't I stick around awhile? We should get her some water—"

"And three aspirin followed by more water. I know the drill. I can handle this. Can you just please go?"

A pause. Jessica didn't feel good about this. "Are you sure you don't want me to at least wait until—"

"Please?!" Ashton's eyes were wide with emotion. Clearly, her presence was making things more difficult for Ashton. She considered her options. Karina didn't look to be in any danger, until she woke up with a major hangover the next morning. And Ashton really did seem familiar with the scenario, which was upsetting for a whole separate reason. Deciding there was nothing she could do in the moment, she reluctantly moved to the door with plans to check up on them later.

"Call me if you need anything. I'm serious." When Ashton didn't answer, she stood her ground. *"Ashton."*

Ashton's eyes were filled with a combination of sorrow and embarrassment when she turned around to face Jessica. "Okay, fine. I promise."

"I'll check in with you in the morning."

Jessica had a hard time sleeping that night as she was consumed with genuine worry. She'd lived next door to the Colemans for a little over three years, and she'd watched as Karina's behavior spiraled into the land of questionable. How involved should she get? Where was the line between irresponsible and dangerous? Because it was feeling kind of close.

Brooklyn was in the homestretch of her presentation. This time, however, she was coasting, in the zone. "And this brings us to the last shot, which is the group of kids following young Tanner and his jar of peanut butter into the sunset. We watch them retreat in silhouette, as the camera pulls back to reveal the image on a movie-theater screen, and the audience breaks into thunderous applause." She smiled at Sandra and waited for her response. She was a tough cookie to read, this woman. She had her pegged in her early fifties, probably married with no kids and an impressive high-rise apartment in the upper West Fifties.

Sandra sat back and regarded Brooklyn. "I have to say, I think I like it."

"That's great." Would back handsprings the length of the hallway be too much? Because Brooklyn was considering them.

"No, I mean, I really like it. As you know, your competitor has already pitched their idea, but it feels to me like you have a deep understanding of our product and whom we'd like to market it to. And it's a very clever spot."

Brooklyn exhaled and let the compliment settle. "Thank you. I imagine you'll want to talk it over. I'll leave the storyboards with you and the CD with the art mockups."

"You lost the bacon project, you know." Sandra stood and came around her desk.

"Excuse me?"

"I don't know if they've officially announced that yet. But we're going with The Lennox Group's idea."

"Oh." She took a moment. "I hadn't heard that."

"So you're down by one."

"I see." Her spirit took a hit at that news.

"But the peanut butter is going to you." And suddenly they were back in it. "I don't need to discuss it with my team. This is a home run as far as I'm concerned, and I'm ready to move forward with Savvy on the concept."

"So that's it? It's ours?"

"It's yours."

Brooklyn suppressed the desire to hug Sandra eight thousand times and instead nodded once graciously. "I'm so happy to hear that. We will work night and day to get this campaign off the ground." In actuality, if they lost the account in the end, The Lennox Group would be implementing her ideas after the initial spot, as it was part of the signed agreement. She wasn't ready to let that happen.

Sandra shook Brooklyn's hand. "I'm rooting for you, Brooklyn. I'd like to work with Savvy in the future, and I hope the account eventually settles with your group." Sandra held up one hand and smiled. "Understand I'll deny having said that outside of this room."

Brooklyn laughed. "Of course. Your secret is safe."

She departed the Foster offices with much of the afternoon to spare, throwing a glance at the individuals in the waiting area, possibly on the lookout for one in particular. But she was in the clear. She hadn't seen Jessica since the scandalous elevator escapade, and she'd contemplated the best course of action for the next time she did run into her. She was trying to be more of a planner.

Avoidance was an option, but it wasn't incredibly practical. Their appointments at Foster were generally either on top of each other or in succession. They'd have many future run-ins. She decided breezy was the way to go. Friendly. On purpose. Make a point of proving that no crazy make-out session in a tight little elevator had affected her. No, it hadn't.

So when she caught sight of Jessica on her phone outside the office building, she made a beeline for her. Okay, so maybe it wasn't just Jessica she was trying to prove a point to.

As she approached, Jessica glanced up and flashed a smile, holding up one finger as she spoke a few directives into her phone.

Business, Brooklyn noted to herself. "Sorry about that," she said to Brooklyn after finishing her call. "How was your meeting?"

"Fabulous. Yours?"

"It was good. Some good news."

Brooklyn wanted to roll her eyes. "The maple bacon is yours. Congratulations."

Jessica paused and looked genuinely sympathetic, which only annoyed Brooklyn further. "I didn't know if they'd put that information out there yet, so I didn't want to lead with it."

"That and the fact that it would be incredibly rude to gloat."

Jessica winced. "That too."

It didn't sit well with Brooklyn that Jessica didn't seem to perceive Savvy as any kind of a threat. Her demeanor was way too serene. She minimized their competency, which was kind of infuriating. And that frustration motivated what she said next. "Sad about the peanut butter, though."

"In what way?" Jessica raised a perfect eyebrow.

"That job went to us. The little guy."

She stared at her. "What makes you so confident?"

"I don't know. The fact that Sandra just told me it was ours. I think the word she used was home run."

A pause.

A series of emotions passed across Jessica's face. Confusion, embarrassment, disdain, and finally that perfect professional mask settled back in place. "Congratulations. I'm sure Savvy deserves the work. And with that, I better run. You take care." With her attaché in hand, Jessica headed out across the plaza to the street.

"It kills you, doesn't it?"

Brooklyn's words stopped her progress and she turned back. Jessica was sensing some uncharacteristic aggression from Brooklyn that she didn't quite know what to do with. Yes, it was a definite blow to have missed out on the most recent project for Foster, a hit she hadn't seen coming, but why would that upset Brooklyn? She should be celebratory. "Kill is a strong word. I think I'll manage."

Brooklyn crossed the distance between them. She'd worn her hair down today and the wind caught it, lifted it as she talked. "You don't think we're as good as you are, the incomparable Lennox Group."

The fire in her eyes seemed to make the blue ever so vibrant and left Jessica momentarily fumbling for her words.

A foreign predicament.

Brooklyn had a way of disarming her in a way no one else ever had. "I've never said or implied anything of the sort. Why are you so defensive?"

"Don't call me defensive."

"Then don't come at me like I've committed some kind of crime. I'm doing my job."

"And so am I. So why don't we concentrate on doing those jobs and leave the rest of this bullshit out of it?"

Jessica flashed her most patronizing smile. "Fine by me, but the last time I checked, you didn't mind a little extra attention."

It was a low blow, even for her. Brooklyn met her gaze with an ice-cold stare. "Perfect. That's perfect." With a final shake of her head, she turned abruptly on her heel and headed off down Seventy-fourth.

Jessica sighed deeply at her retreat, because God, did she look good doing it.

❖

Brooklyn didn't know why she'd gone out of her way to pick a fight with Jessica. She could have easily let her walk away and found satisfaction in the fact that Savvy had outpitched The Lennox Group.

That should have been enough.

But for whatever reason, she'd let loose her inner bitch, and it had ended badly. At first, the exchange had felt good, and she'd walked away angry and triumphant all at the same time.

But several hours later and the unwelcome guilt was getting to her.

Why she couldn't just live with the little bit of animosity she'd infused into their relationship? It was good for them. And this feeling she had, it was annoying, the side of her that cared about her standing with high-and-mighty Jessica Lennox.

She was over it. Did you hear her, universe? *Over it.*

Brooklyn was meeting her friends for celebratory drinks at Showroom, the always bustling bar they frequented a block and a half from their building. When the place first opened, it had been a home to everything trendy, but the locals had quickly taken over, and it was now the epitome of comfortable and laid-back. The space was a converted warehouse from the 1800s. Very industrial but with the swanky perks of sculpted furniture and high-end lighting fixtures. It was way off the beaten path for tourists, so the clientele essentially consisted of neighborhood regulars. And for the Savvy girls, it was their go-to.

Brooklyn pulled open the door to Showroom and was met with the sounds of indie rock playing from the speakers. It was Friday, which meant lots more people and lots more music.

Thank God. She felt like losing herself tonight.

It appeared she was the last to arrive and easily located their table past the bar and to the right. As she walked by the dark mahogany bar, she made note of the fact that a new bartender was on tonight—a blonde with her hair pulled back partially, who seemed to be making crazy work of the drink orders in front of her with skilled precision. Brooklyn stopped to watch a minute, which earned her a smile. Very smooth, both the smile and the skills. And judging from the look of her, this new bartender was going to make a killing in tips.

"You look great," Hunter said as Brooklyn approached. "Hot date tonight?"

She'd worn her cute red dress because she felt like it. "If you three count, sure."

Mallory inched a martini her way. "We preordered for you. Cucumber, your favorite." Her friends raised their glasses.

"To Brooks," Samantha said. "And all the hard work she's put in."

Brooklyn joined them. "Okay, but I couldn't have done any of this without you three. It's pretty much a team effort around here."

"Then to all of us," Hunter said as they clinked their glasses. "Because we're all pretty fucking awesome for taking this one. I, for one, have never eaten so much peanut butter in preparation for art design."

They laughed and Mallory turned to Brooklyn. "But in fairness, this one is kind of your baby, and you've done a fantastic job. The news we got today is just further confirmation of what we already knew. You're a creative genius, a superstar of ideas."

Brooklyn didn't quite know what to say because geez, those words really mattered to her. She *had* been working really hard, and today, it had paid off. It felt good to hear the appreciation from her friends. "Thank you. Now, I think we could all use a night off. I, for one, am prepared to let off a little steam." She took a long drink of the cucumber martini as a waitress dropped an additional drink at their table.

Mallory looked to Hunter. "Undoubtedly for you." It was true that when a drink showed up, nine times out of ten it was from one of Hunter's fifteen thousand admirers.

"No. Actually, it's for you," the waitress said to Mallory. "Courtesy of our new bartender." As if programmed to do so, all four heads turned in unison toward the bar. The hot bartender nodded once in their direction and went back to taking the order of the girl in front of her.

"Whoa," Samantha murmured. "She's incredibly attractive."

"Nice job, Mal." Hunter nudged her.

Mallory sent her a look that said behave. "Please. It's one drink. She's just being friendly."

"That's one word for it," Brooklyn quipped. "Now if you'll excuse me, I think I need to dance like a crazy person. Anyone want to dance like a crazy person?"

"I'm in," Hunter said, taking the hand Brooklyn offered over her head and dancing behind her to the dance floor.

Sunday through Wednesday, Showplace was a mild-mannered bar scene, but come Thursday, the dance floor opened up and the place raged. It was exceptionally crowded that Friday, but she and Hunter found their own spot and let loose to the rapid beat from the DJ in the corner. Brooklyn closed her eyes and let the music flow through her, letting the stresses of the week leave her body as she grooved to bass that pounded the floor.

Several songs in and Hunter was no longer by her side. She'd been replaced with a sassy blonde who knew how to move. The dancing grew closer, and Brooklyn enjoyed the brushing of hips, hands, and thighs.

"What's your name?" she asked the girl once the music dipped into a slower number.

She leaned in close to Brooklyn's ear. "Sophie."

"It's nice to meet you. I'm Brooklyn. Want to get a drink?"

She seemed to consider the question. "Yeah. I could use a refresher."

They got to talking over cucumber martinis, and it turned out that Sophie was a hairstylist who worked for ABC News. She lived in the Meatpacking District with three roommates and loved New York.

And she was cute as well as seemingly intelligent. Definite bonus points.

"You should give me your number."

Sophie smiled. "And why is that?"

"Because I think you and I have lots more to talk about. And dance about."

Sophie reached for Brooklyn's phone and typed in her number. "I hope I hear from you," she said as she handed it back.

"Oh, you most definitely will." Brooklyn held her gaze and grinned.

"You're really beautiful, you know that?" And before she had time to think, Sophie's lips were on hers and she wasn't shy about reciprocating. It was a pretty good kiss too, and she felt that little sizzle that always comes when you kiss someone you're attracted to.

They danced the night away, she and Sophie, practically closing the place down. But it was the kind of fun she was looking for. The kind you didn't have to think about, agonize about, or feel guilty about later.

As she lay in bed that night, she played back the events of the evening. It'd been a good night. She'd had fun and met someone she'd see again. They'd kissed and it'd been good. Go her.

She closed her eyes and let out a deep sigh. Sleep didn't come easy. But in a twist she could have seen coming a mile away, Sophie's kiss wasn't the one she lay awake that night thinking about.

Chapter Eight

Brooklyn's routine had stayed pretty consistent since she'd moved into her place in Soho. Wake up, brush her teeth, and head to the gym two blocks down, where she'd spend the next hour sweating alongside Mallory while they looked out the giant picturesque windows at the city skyline.

The people-watcher in her enjoyed getting to see the city slowly wake up as pedestrians with briefcases began to populate the sidewalks. Businesswomen walked by in sneakers, their high heels stashed in their attachés until they reached their office building. Dog walkers zigzagged their way around the hustle and bustle, stopping at the coffee cart for their morning pick-me-up and a pastry. There was just something about New York City in the morning…

"You make the call yet?" Mallory asked from the treadmill next to hers.

"I make lots of calls. Which one were you referencing? I need specifics, Spencer."

Mallory shot her a sideways glance as she ran. "Only the most important call."

"Oh. Well, if you're referencing my wayward birth mother—"

"I am."

"—then no. I haven't gotten around to it yet. The past few weeks have been crazy. You know that."

Mallory turned the dial on her treadmill to the right, upping her speed. Automatically, Brooklyn's competitive spirit kicked in, and she was forced to follow suit.

"You're deflecting."

"Explain my deflection."

"You're coming up with all the reasons in the world to avoid your own life. It's what you do when things get tough. I'm not coming down on you, Brooks. I just want you to make sure you're doing things for the right reasons."

Brooklyn ran on, letting Mallory's words sink in as her calves burned and her heart pounded. They ran in silence for a stretch. She pushed herself beyond the usual, running until she couldn't catch her breath. But she liked the feeling, because as she ran, she didn't obsess or overthink or doubt herself.

As she brought the treadmill back down to a walking pace, Brooklyn watched raindrops begin to chase each other across the window. Several stories below, umbrellas sprang open and an array of colors now dotted the newly wet sidewalk.

"Would you say I'm emotionally unavailable?" They were in the midst of their cool-down, and the euphoric high from the run gave Brooklyn the courage to ask the question.

Mallory took a minute. "I think you take care of yourself, and I get why."

As they walked, Brooklyn wiped her forehead with a towel. "That's not what I asked."

"What's the longest relationship you've had?"

She did the math. "A couple of months."

"It was Tracy. And she was a decent fit for you, but the second things got close to serious, you bailed."

"I didn't *bail*."

"You did, Brooks. You ran. You let her calls roll to voice mail right in front of me. Canceled plans at the last minute. It was emotional withdrawal perfected. All because she got too close to you. To your heart."

Brooklyn turned the treadmill off and stared at the window for a moment. Suddenly, she felt very exposed. "It's not like I was trying to…" But then she couldn't quite find the words for the damn lump that formed in her throat. Because being called on what she knew was true of herself was hard.

"I know. It's a defense mechanism. You put it up with us in the beginning too. It took years for you to trust me. I just worry that you might miss out on something good because of it."

A moment passed.

She raised her gaze to Mallory. “I think I’ll call her tonight.”

“Tracy?”

Brooklyn laughed and it felt good, the tension falling away. “No, crazytown. Cynthia. My mother. There’s probably never going to be a perfect time. I should just go for it.”

Mallory put her arm around Brooklyn as they walked to the locker room. “Let me know how it goes, okay? I’m here for you. No matter what time of the day or night.”

She nodded and smiled. “I know. That’s why you’re Mallory.”

The lobby was silent, except for the distant sounds of thunder. Jessica had left her umbrella back at the office, figuring the morning storms had packed up and moved on. Bad move. Bad, bad move.

She glanced at her watch, noting that she still had a few minutes before her appointment with Royce to iron out some of the details for the bacon promos that would go into production in just a few weeks.

Across the room from her, Brooklyn studied her phone. Anything, she was guessing, to not have to talk to Jessica. They hadn’t run into each other the past few days, and it had given her time to reflect on their last exchange. She didn’t like the way she’d handled things. It was uncharacteristic of her to engage in such a basic argument, but Brooklyn had gotten under her skin. She seemed to have a way of doing that, and it was becoming a problem.

Finally, as the silence ticked on, Jessica couldn’t stand the cold war any longer. Because no matter how she sliced it, she liked Brooklyn, damn it. “We’re still fighting, aren’t we?”

Brooklyn glanced up, devoid of all emotion. “Yeah, I think we are.” And back to her phone.

A pause. Jessica pressed forward. “You know, I’m not enjoying the fight as much as I was hoping to.”

When Brooklyn sighed and her face softened, Jessica saw the girl underneath. “Yeah, it’s missing some of the, I don’t know, aggression. I’m trying to hate you. Really I am.”

“Ditto. And for the record, I shouldn’t have made the remark about the attention.”

"No, you shouldn't have. It was mean." She blew out a breath. "But I shouldn't have goaded you the way I did. It was less than professional."

"Or friendly."

"Or that."

"So we should go back to being corporate rivals who aren't so blatantly hateful to one another?" Jessica asked.

"Right. Standard run-of-the-mill rivals. None of the fancy stuff."

She felt the smile tug at her lips. "I'm agreeable to that."

"Excuse me, ladies," the receptionist said as she hung up the phone. "Unfortunately, an impromptu company meeting has been called, and Mr. Foster has asked that I reschedule all appointments for today."

Jessica sent a questioning glance to Brooklyn, who stood and crossed to the reception desk. "So we're canceled?"

"Unfortunately so," the woman answered.

Brooklyn shook her head in defeat. "Fabulous."

But it got worse from there, as once they reached the glass doors that led them out to the street, the rain was coming down like rapid gunfire. Pedestrians scurried for cover as if their lives depended on it.

"Now that's what I call a fall shower," she murmured.

Brooklyn tilted her head. "Or angry act of God."

"Are you gonna make a run for it?" Just then they watched as a powerful gust of wind flipped a woman's umbrella inside out. She struggled with it halfway down the street as the downpour soaked her through. Jessica stared on in shock. "Like a scene from *Mary Poppins*."

"You know, I'm not in an incredible hurry. At least you have a car. I took the A train."

"Not today, I don't. My driver had a dentist's appointment. So I'm on my own. I took a cab here, but it would be impossible to grab one now."

"And the subway's several long blocks away."

Jessica studied the coffee shop just off the building's main lobby. "We could grab a cup. Wait for a lull."

"What? You'd be willing to be seen with me? What would people say?"

"That a beautiful woman agreed to have coffee with me in lieu of death by giant raindrops."

Brooklyn seemed to consider this, finally meeting her eyes. "I can live with those rumors."

They snagged a table at the corner where they had the best view of the action outside and settled in with their steaming cups of joe. Brooklyn pointed at a pedestrian just beyond the window. "I feel bad for that guy. That newspaper over his head is going to disintegrate in three point two seconds. Not the most thought-out plan."

"But that little newspaper is all he has. Plus, he probably has some place to be. Oh, and now it's in two pieces. Sad times. We should invite him in."

"Definitely, Jess. You should run out there and bring him back right away."

"Oh, I'll get right on that." That's when Brooklyn licked a small dollop of whipped cream from the side of the cup. Jessica tried not to watch, but it turned out that wasn't really an option. *Christ.* The visual sent a flash of heat to her face and downward. Brooklyn licking things was…too much to think about.

Jessica tried desperately to shift gears. "How do you feel about rain?"

Brooklyn looked skyward. "Well, first of all, rain is good luck. And you know how I feel about luck. And when I'm tucked away like this, I love it. Give me a blanket and a good book and I'm in heaven. Something about it just makes me want to, I don't know, curl up. Stay in. Snuggle."

The image was a great one and brought a smile to her lips. Brooklyn had this way of driving every other thought from her head. Jessica was no longer interested in what she was missing at the office or the fact that she needed to send out her dry cleaning, things that had been in the forefront of her mind just an hour before.

Brooklyn caught it and leaned in. "What? What's that smile about? Are you judging me right now for being snuggly?"

She shook her head absently, trying to ignore the warmth of the tug in the center of her stomach. "I like the rain too."

"See? We aren't so different after all."

"No." They stared at each other for a minute before turning back out to the street.

Brooklyn glanced over at Jessica. She was enjoying herself and feeling brave. "So what's new in your life lately? And I'm not asking about work. I think it's best if we avoid that topic to preserve whatever mutual respect we're building upon. You and me are tenuous."

"At best. It's a good plan. Uh, let's see. Well, I've been struggling a bit with how to handle a next-door-neighbor situation."

"What? Loud music. I find it's best to just dance along."

Jessica laughed, and Brooklyn had to say it looked really good on her. She should do it more often. Then and there it became Brooklyn's mission to make that happen. "Not exactly what I'm dealing with." Jessica went on to describe her concerns for the neighbor, a teenage girl named Ashton. Once she finished the story, she sat back in her chair and regarded Brooklyn. "It helps just telling someone about it. It's been on my mind a lot."

"You know what I think?" Brooklyn said, once she finished. She had definite opinions on the topic and wasn't shy about expressing them. It was an issue near and dear to her heart. "I think that kid has to come first. You can't worry about whether it's appropriate for you to get involved. I've seen that happen way too often, and the end result is the suffering of the child." She shook her head in wonder. "Everyone's afraid to ruffle a few feathers. It doesn't make sense. Think of the big picture. If this girl's well-being is at stake, it's worth it to intervene. I wish someone had done that for me on more than one occasion. And trust me, there were opportunities."

The advice seemed to register. And Brooklyn was glad. She spoke from years of experience, both personal and observed. She'd had it rough, but in all honesty, she'd been one of the lucky ones.

"I think you've put it in perspective for me. Thank you. I mean that."

Brooklyn sat forward in earnest because this wasn't something she could just let go. "So you'll watch out for her?"

"I will. I promise."

A beat before Jessica scrunched up one eye. "I don't want to pry, but did you ever decide what to do with that phone number?"

Brooklyn took a deep breath. It sure was a popular question these days, but she was making progress with the situation. "I'm actually planning on calling her tonight."

"That must be terrifying. You know, you can call me if you need to talk. I mean that from a sincere place. No ulterior motives. I won't even hit on you, which would be hard."

Brooklyn smiled at the implication and took in the offer. "I appreciate it. I'm sure I'll be fine. It's a big step, but it's time."

Things were getting a little heavy for Brooklyn, and she decided to shake things up. She rested her chin on her palm. "Your hair is up today. I've never seen it this way." Then that familiar current of electricity hummed between them again. Jessica seemed to pick up on it too as color dusted her cheeks and her eyes softened.

"I'm not as creative as you when it comes to fashion, but I try my best."

"You don't have to try hard." Brooklyn had no idea why in the hell she was flirting with Jessica, but it seemed an inevitable part of their relationship. Her mind just naturally drifted there, and she'd be lying if she said she didn't enjoy it, enjoy Jessica and the little spurts of time they stole together. In fact, she found herself secretly looking forward to them and wondering when she'd next see her, even after an argument like the one they'd had.

"It's letting up a little out there," Jessica pointed out in a reluctant tone.

"It is. But, um, you know, I think I'll stick around and finish my coffee."

Jessica met her gaze. "Yeah, me too."

As the rain outside played on, so did one of the nicest mornings Brooklyn could remember having in quite a while. Lost in conversation and the laughter that she could always count on where Jessica was concerned, Brooklyn let herself relax and enjoy the connection that was still so very unexpected.

The real world could wait.

The Purple Post-it of Fate. That's what Brooklyn took to calling the square of paper in her hand. She stared at her own handwriting, the shaky curves reminding her how nervous she'd been when she'd taken down the number. She shook her head. They carried such power, those ten little digits written in blue ink.

She'd been holding the Post-it in one hand and her phone in the other for well over an hour now. It was humbling, really, for a slip of paper to have so much influence.

One last time, she ran through the possible series of events, prepping herself for whatever happened. She'd made a plan for what she'd say if she was routed to voice mail, and a plan for what she'd say if someone else actually answered the call, and a plan for what she'd say if it was Cynthia Mathis herself—which was easily the most daunting scenario of all.

Finally, she decided thinking was overrated. Turning off the rational voice in her head, she leapt without looking and dialed the number.

The individual rings seemed to last a lifetime, and just as she was losing her gumption and about to hang up, a female voice was there. She'd said hello. Brooklyn took a second.

"Hello?" the voice repeated. "Is anyone there?"

Her heart was pounding out of her chest, but it was go time. "Yes, I'm here. Um, I'm calling for Cynthia Mathis."

"This is Cynthia. Who is this?" She sounded distracted. Not rude, just busy. Maybe it was a bad time. *Now or never.*

"My name is Brooklyn Campbell. I was given this number by an adoption reunion registry."

Silence.

"It's kind of a crazy thing to say to someone, but I think you might be my birth mother."

More silence.

Brooklyn waited it out and stared upward at the ceiling.

And then she was back. "I…um. Oh, my. Your name is Brooklyn," she stated reverently.

"Yes."

"They kept your name."

She took a minute with that. "Oh. I wasn't sure where it had come from, actually."

"From me. It's what I picked out. I just figured your adoptive parents would have changed it." She took a breath. " I'm sorry. This call, it's caught me a little off guard. Let me sit down."

"I can try back another time."

"No!" she practically shouted. "No, please. I'm so glad you called. It's just…"

"A lot," Brooklyn supplied, standing up because she didn't know what else to do with herself. Movement seemed to help alleviate the extra energy so she paced the length of her small bedroom.

"Yes. Where do you live? I mean, if you don't mind me asking."

"New York City. I work in advertising. I'm a partner at a boutique firm."

"That's great. A partner? That's impressive." She heard the emotion in Cynthia's voice. Actual emotion, and it was doing a number on her.

"Where do you live?'

"Connecticut. I'm a nurse. Labor and delivery."

Kind of ironic, Brooklyn thought, given the last time they'd seen each other. It was a lot to take in, but she craved more information, like some sort of drug she wasn't proud of. She needed the details that she'd obsessed about for years. "Are you married?"

"Yes. I live with my husband. We have two children."

She'd known it was a possibility, but to hear for certain that she had siblings out there was enough to steal her next breath and force her to sit back down on the bed. She covered her eyes with the back of her hand as the information worked its way in. "Wow."

"So you have a brother and sister. Great kids. Ethan is twenty-two and just graduated from UConn with a degree in engineering. Cat, short for Catherine, is seventeen and about to be a senior in high school. Rambunctious."

"I don't know what to say."

"You don't have to say anything." A pause. There seemed to be a lot of those. But they were warranted. "I'd love to meet you."

And here we go. The panic alarms were ringing in her head, and she wasn't sure how to shut them off. "Maybe." It was all she could commit to.

"You could come to Connecticut. I live in a small town named Avon, near Hartford. We could have dinner. I'll pay for your expenses. Or I could come to Manhattan. You know, whichever is easier or preferable for you." She exhaled into the phone. "I'm sorry if I'm jumping the gun. Sometimes I do that. I'm just so excited that you've called, to hear your voice. I've imagined this moment…well, a lot."

"Can I think about it?"

"Of course. Yes. That's fair."

"I should go."

"Right. Okay. Thank you for calling, Brooklyn. You have my number. Please call again. Anytime."

Brooklyn felt a slight smile touch the corners of her mouth. It was small, what Cynthia had just said, but it meant something. "Okay. I will."

❖

"It was a short conversation. But I think I needed it to be short," Brooklyn told Samantha as they sat at a table in Bryant Park. They'd met with an up-and-coming candy company in midtown that morning so Sam could work up a potential budget for their account. It had gone well, and because they had to, they'd stopped at one of their favorite lunch spots in the park.

It was kind of their place, hers and Sam's.

As they ate from the cardboard containers that held their deluxe cheeseburgers and fries, Brooklyn recounted the phone call from the night before. "She was an actual normal-sounding person, Sam. That's what's so crazy. With a home and a job and kids. I just wasn't expecting that and still can't wrap my mind around it."

Sam popped a fry. "Did she say why she gave you up? Because who'd want to part with you? You're adorable."

"Right? But, no. We didn't go into it. Like I said, it was a short call."

"Seriously though, a monumental conversation like that? I can't even imagine what that must be like. For her *or* for you."

"I think it's safe to say that this is new territory for everyone."

Samantha sat back in her seat and regarded her, shaking her head. "I'm proud of you, Brooks. This was a big step and I wasn't sure you'd find the courage. I'm happy you did."

"Me too. But to be honest, if it weren't for you guys and Jessica, I'm not sure I would have."

Samantha held up one finger. "Slamming on the brakes for a second. Jessica Lennox knows about your mom?"

Brooklyn took a pull from her Diet Coke to buy some time, realizing that with that one little comment she'd showed her cards regarding the time she'd spent with Jessica recently. But in all honesty, she didn't mind doing that with Sam, divulging a little more. Sam was the sensitive one, the romantic. If Brooklyn could make anyone understand the unique relationship she had with their toughest rival, it was Sam. "I've talked with Jessica about all of this, yes."

"As in, recently?"

"As in yesterday. And also that first night we met."

"Whoa. That's a little unexpected, you have to admit. You don't open up easily. It took you two years to tell me your favorite color."

"That is so not true."

"Yeah, I made it up, but you get the gist. Trust is a huge process for you, which is why revealing intimate details of your life to someone you just recently met is entirely out of character."

"I know. That part is true." Brooklyn sat back in her chair and let her eyes brush the treetops as she thought through all the things Jessica made her feel. And the list was long. "It's crazy, Sam. I just click with her. And before you say anything, I'm beginning to think all the horrible rumors about her are false. She's not that person."

"Then how do they persist?"

Brooklyn shrugged. "Because I don't think she minds them and never puts them to rest. It makes her seem like some businesswoman-badass. In fact, I think she sees all the talk as a helpful leg up. In this scenario, she gets to be feared without having to be scary. Not a bad deal if you think about it. More fries?"

Samantha stared at her, her mouth falling open.

Brooklyn set the cardboard container back on the table. "What? What's with the look? You hate French fries now?"

"You're falling for her a little bit, aren't you?"

Brooklyn sighed. "It's not like that. Well, it is, but it's not. I would never let it go too far. Yes, I let myself flirt with her, and we spend time talking on occasion. You know, when forcibly trapped in elevators together. It's what people do. But come on, Sammie, I'm horrible at relationships, and one like ours has too much working against it already. So, to make a long story short, I'm indulging myself a little in the fun department. I like spending time with her. I like staring at her, lusting a little. Who does it hurt?"

"I just hope it's not you."

"Way to cloud the issue with logic."

"It's my job to look out for you."

Brooklyn accepted the sentiment and nodded. "I won't get hurt. Trust me." A beat. "I did make out with her in the elevator, though."

"And you're just now mentioning this?"

"Why would I ever bring something like that up, given everyone's well-known opinion? You guys would have freaked out. Mallory especially. She would have written a dissertation on all the ways it was bad for business and taped it to every wall in the loft."

"Look at me. I'm not Mallory. But I am one of your best friends and your roommate, for heaven's sake. I don't want to be shut out of your life. You hear me? There will be no shutting out." The fierceness in her voice said she was hurt, and it resonated with Brooklyn.

"I do. And I'm sorry."

She softened, leaning in. "So this kissing. It was good?"

Brooklyn closed her eyes. "Samantha, there aren't words. I've tried to find some. Trust me."

"I have to meet this woman one day."

"You won't have to wait long. Foster Foods is having a swanky cocktail party on Friday night, and we're all invited. The fancy invite came to the Savvy loft yesterday. They had some super-private meeting the other day and have now announced a new division that will focus solely on, get this, alcoholic beverages. The party is a sort of an unofficial kickoff. They rented out The Frick. I kid you not."

"The Frick? As in the museum, not some restaurant that knocked off the name?"

Brooklyn laughed. "No, that would be the museum itself."

"Oh, my sweet goodness, that is high-end. I get to wear my fancy clothes."

"I'm telling you, we need these people to be our clients."

"Yet, so does Jessica." Samantha smiled and batted her eyelashes flirtatiously.

"Stop it. Jessica is not a factor when we're talking business. And in case I haven't mentioned it, I'm taking a *date* to the party. So there will be no confusion on the issue."

"Wow. You're a busy girl. Who is it?"

"Sophie. The woman I met at Showroom the other night."

"Aha." Samantha smiled knowingly. "I spoke to her briefly. She seemed really into you. She'd have your babies."

"And I'm into her."

Samantha sent her a dubious look. "Of course you are."

"Shut up."

Sam considered this. "Pass those fries over here and we have a deal."

Brooklyn obliged. "One last thing."

"Try me," she said mid-fry.

"Can we not tell the others about the Jessica stuff? Mallory wouldn't understand, and Hunter would high-five me and then forget that she wasn't supposed to tell Mallory."

Samantha sighed. "They won't hear it from me."

"Fantastic. This is why you're my favorite."

"Well, I also let you hold the remote."

"That too."

CHAPTER NINE

When Jessica arrived at The Frick on Friday night, she was escorted to the Garden Court, a breathtaking indoor collection of plants and flowers complete with a stunning centerpiece fountain and towering Ionic columns.

A beyond-beautiful space.

The reception was in full swing, and she took a minute to assess the room. Well-dressed guests mingled over cocktails and appetizers among the symmetrical planters. It seemed Foster had invited all of New York's big players to help kick off the new launch. And they were all there, as who doesn't love an expensive party? As she perused faces, it was like a who's who of big business. Jessica was glad she'd forced herself to attend, despite the migraine she'd been fighting most of the day. Luckily, the new prescription her doctor supplied her with really seemed to be at least one step ahead of the problem.

She said a few hellos and accepted a glass of champagne from a waiter. She'd yet to see Bentley, who'd agreed to meet her there, so she set out in search of Royce Foster to properly greet her host.

A jazz band played just inside The Music Room, which, after a glimpse inside, stole Jessica's breath. The circular room, where the heart of the event seemed to be taking place, had a glass-domed ceiling, damask walls, and an open dance floor. It surpassed even her most opulent expectations for the night.

She immediately lamented leaving the fancy jewelry at home. She'd chosen an off-the-shoulder black cocktail dress and simple heels. She'd worn her hair down, which was less sophisticated, but a necessity when dealing with an impending migraine.

"You look stunning, Boss," Bentley whispered in her ear. She turned around and kissed his cheek, then ran her palms down the lapels of his Armani suit.

"And you're incredibly handsome in this suit. Very slick." And he was. His six-foot-two frame made him one of the more noticeable men in the room. If she wasn't a lesbian, she was pretty sure his debonair good looks would carry a different sort of weight altogether. At any rate, she was constantly on the lookout for the perfect girl to accentuate his arm. But Bentley and settling down didn't seem to go together.

"Thank you. You'll find Royce Foster at three o'clock."

"It's like you can read my mind."

"That's why we work so well together."

She grinned at him. "Meet me in the garden in fifteen minutes?"

"Deal."

Jessica circled the room once, saying a few hellos before making her way over to Royce Foster. He was definitely the man of the hour, with throngs of people to both his left and right. However, once she inserted herself into the mix, the crowd seemed to part just for her. Her reputation came with certain benefits, and she wasn't afraid to use it. He smiled widely as his eyes settled on her. "Jessica," he said, leaning in to kissing her cheek. "So good of you to make it."

"Thank you, Royce, for the invitation. The room is dazzling."

He looked around and met her stare intensely. "It is, isn't it?" The enthusiasm in his voice made her feel like she'd made the most innovative statement of the night. Geez, this guy had charisma. He inclined his head in the direction of her glass. "I see you've already snagged a drink, but before you leave tonight, make a point to try one of our summer wine spritzers. They're pouring three different flavors at the bar. A brand-new product that I'm confident you and your people are going to have a field day with. I can't wait to see what you'll come up with." Again with the intense staring.

"I'll be sure to do that. Enjoy the party." She knew better than to stay too long. There was a fine line between networking and schmoozing, and she was definitely not a schmoozer. She wasn't warm enough to schmooze. Now Mallory Spencer was another story. With her dazzling smile and melodic laughter on cue, she'd perfected the art. Jessica had to hand it to her, even if it was annoying from a competitive standpoint.

And speak of the devil in Prada, there she was. Right on cue. And already making her way over to Royce, where she would probably camp for the next twenty minutes. "Typical," she said quietly to herself as she accepted a glass of Foster's Pear Pinot Grigio.

"What's typical?" She turned at the sound of Brooklyn's voice. As she opened her mouth to answer the question, the words faded from her lips. Because the image in front of her was quite easily the most picturesque visual she'd seen in recent history. Brooklyn wore a midnight-blue cocktail dress that draped across one shoulder, dipping subtly at the bustline before falling just past her mid thigh. It was sexy and dignified all at once. Her hair was pulled back, but only partially, as soft tendrils touched her shoulders, curling ever so slightly at the ends. "Oh."

Brooklyn quirked her head. "Oh?'

"You just look…really beautiful."

Brooklyn grinned as the compliment settled. "Thank you. But I think you've shown me up. I realize now that I've never seen you out of business attire. It's kind of surreal."

Jessica thought about it. "You're right. You haven't."

"This is a whole new concept for me. It's…"

Jessica raised an eyebrow. "It's…"

Brooklyn gave her head a little shake. "Not important." It was then that a bouncy bottle-blonde landed at Brooklyn's elbow and handed her a glass of wine.

"Hello," Jessica said to the woman.

"Oh, hi. We haven't met. I'm Sophie Dean."

Brooklyn touched her forehead guiltily. "I'm sorry. Sometimes I'm rude. Sophie, this is Jessica Lennox. She also works in advertising. We're highly competitive and take every chance we get to make the other look bad."

Jessica laughed, understanding the jest, but Sophie just looked wildly confused. "She's kidding," Jessica assured her.

"Oh, okay." Sophie smiled again, all okay with the world. She was cute, which made Jessica start to wonder.

"How do you two know each other?"

"Sophie is my date. We met recently at a get-together."

"We danced at a club," Sophie supplied. "She's a fantastic dancer."

"Really?" Jessica enthused falsely. "I wouldn't know." A crop of total and complete jealousy was upon her before she knew it. It was childish and unattractive, but it was there all the same.

Suddenly Sophie was on her tiptoes and all sorts of excited. "Is that John Stamos over there? I love John Stamos. His hair started trends in the nineties that we're still learning from today. Excuse me a moment." And she headed off like a kid after a Santa Claus sighting.

Left alone, Brooklyn raised one shoulder. "She does hair for ABC."

"Wow," Jessica said dryly. "Ambitious."

Brooklyn stared at her, taken aback. "Okay. That was rude."

"Then I apologize." Her delivery was less than convincing. She was aware.

"Not everyone works in big business. Nor should they. The world wouldn't go round. Why are you being judgmental?"

Jessica forced a smile. "I'm just surprised you brought a date to a business gathering."

"The thing is, I'm not conducting *business* tonight, so I think we're in the clear."

Jessica took a breath and relented because she was acting like a jackass with no real sense of why. "You're right. And I'm out of line."

"Hey, Brooks. You look lovely this evening." A striking woman with auburn hair woven into a complicated French braid kissed Brooklyn's cheek before turning her attention to Jessica. "Hi. I don't think we've met. Samantha Ennis." Aha. The roommate.

"Jessica Lennox. A pleasure to meet you. I hear you keep your side of the apartment neat and orderly."

Samantha nodded in amusement. "My reputation is intact then."

Jessica smiled back. "If you'll both excuse me, I think I see someone I need to say hello to." It was a lie, an excuse to get her out of the conversation because no good was going to come of it. Brooklyn's date was already working her way back over, and she'd rather not stick around for the flirtatious display. Because really, who'd want to experience that? No one. That's who.

But after just a few steps, the world swayed violently in front of her. Whoa. As a result, she stumbled, almost to the ground if it wasn't for Brooklyn's quick reflexes. She was instantly there with a hand under her elbow to steady her. Her eyes flashed concern. "Hey, you okay? Jess?"

"Yeah, just, uh, dizzy for a second. I think I'm fine now." She blinked a few times to clear her vision.

"Are you sure?" Brooklyn didn't look convinced.

"Yeah. I should have eaten something. I skipped lunch."

"You should hit the hors d'oeuvre table. Better yet, why don't I get you a plate?"

Jessica flashed her most confident smile in an attempt to put Brooklyn at ease. "A nice gesture, but I got it. You better get back to your date."

Brooklyn released her and she headed off in search of Bentley, though she suddenly was having a hard time coming up with where he said they'd meet up. And oh, there were two of that man, which was kind of cool and frightening. She steadied herself on one of the fancy ornate columns. Oh, it felt kind of nice. Cool to the touch and sandpapery. Dizzy again. *Get it together, Lennox.*

"She's really attractive," Samantha said to Brooklyn once they were alone. "You were right about that part."

Brooklyn turned to her, frustrated beyond all measure. "Yeah, but why does she have to be? It would make things at least a tad bit easier if she were just more everyday. Is plain too much to ask for in a woman?"

"Who's everyday?" Sophie asked.

"Definitely not Jessica Lennox," Samantha said. The daggers Brooklyn shot her couldn't inflict enough harm.

Sophie beamed in amusement and pointed at Sam in a circular motion. "Oh, I think I'm picking up on something here. Somebody has a crush?"

"Oh, I think so." Samantha grinned back at Sophie as Brooklyn shook her head, silently sending Samantha death threats via roommate ESP.

Sophie linked her arm through Brooklyn's. "You should fix them up, don't you think?"

"Yeah, I don't think that's gonna happen."

"Why not?" Samantha asked sweetly, batting her eyelashes like the traitor she so clearly was. Oh, she was enjoying this way too much.

"You know what, Samantha?" Brooklyn inclined her head at a scene across the room. "Hunter is surrounded by a gaggle of good-looking women. And oh, look, a few men too. Bonus for you. Why don't you go see if she'll share?"

Sam shook her head, grinning. "No way. Too much fun over here."

"Speaking of your girl," Sophie said to Samantha. "She looks a little pale."

Brooklyn followed her gaze to Jessica, who was making her way across the room, and it only took her a moment to see that something was definitely off. Sophie was right. She was pale, and she wasn't carrying herself with her normal grace and confidence. She looked on as Jessica finally crossed to a chair and sat down, seemingly out of it. "Okay. She doesn't look good, you guys. I'll be right back."

"I'll come with you," Samantha said.

"I don't do good with sick," Sophie called after them. "Gonna hang back over there with, what was your friend's name? Hunter?" Brooklyn registered Sophie's words, but they didn't carry much weight. Her concern was firmly elsewhere in the moment. In a matter of seconds, Brooklyn was kneeling next to Jessica.

"Hey, Jess. You okay?"

Jessica stared at her absently. "Have you seen Bentley? My friend." She closed her eyes, regrouping. "My assistant. From Foster's, remember?"

"The guy you had with you that first day?" Brooklyn asked.

"Sure. Most days."

"This is unlike her?" Samantha asked Brooklyn under her breath.

"One hundred percent. Something's up." She turned back to Jessica. "Jess, can you tell me how you're feeling?"

"Strange. And the room is strange."

Brooklyn offered Jessica an encouraging smile. "Strange. That's a start. Are you able to walk?"

"Yes. I think so." And she could, just not especially well. Brooklyn escorted her to the women's restroom, and Samantha trailed after them. Once inside, Jessica was able to splash some water on her face as they looked on in concern.

Samantha took the reins. "Do you have any allergies? Could you have eaten something that set off an allergic reaction?"

"No, uh-uh. I'm not allergic to food. But I think I'll sit back down so the room will calm the hell down."

Brooklyn sprang into action. "Okay. Yikes. But maybe not on the floor. There's a chair over there. Let's get you into it." She helped Jessica from the floor to the chair. "Maybe you had too much to drink."

"I had one glass of champagne and a few sips of whatever the hell that Foster drink is. I'm not a lightweight, Brooklyn Campbell. It's sleepy in here. Are you guys sleepy? Let's all take a nap." Jessica lowered her head onto the arm of the chair.

She wasn't talking anything like herself, and Brooklyn was concerned. "Not quite yet, okay?"

Samantha knelt in front of her. "Jessica, I don't want to offend you, but have you taken any sort of substance?"

Jessica lifted her head from where it rested on the arm of the chair. "Drugs? No. I don't do drugs. Ever. Nancy Reagan, 'member?"

"I do, but I had to check."

"I think I should head home," Jessica said, pushing herself back up into a seated position.

Brooklyn held up a hand. "Not the best idea to head out alone when you're…not feeling well." She sent Samantha a questioning look, but she just shrugged in equal mystification.

Jessica frowned at them. "There was the migraine medicine from my doctor. I took that today, and it's good stuff too. Five stars. It got rid of my headache."

"Do you have it with you?"

Jessica gestured to the counter. "It's in my clutch."

Actually, it was all that was in her clutch outside of some cash, her phone, and some lipstick. Brooklyn turned the bottle and read the label. "Jess, it says not to take with alcohol, in big bold letters. I think you're having a reaction to the combination."

"The wallpaper in here is pretty."

"Yeah, okay, you definitely are."

Samantha took the bottle and did a little reading. "There's a number here. I'm going to call."

"Good idea," Jessica mumbled. "I'll sit here and politely ask the room to stop spinning. Stop spinning," she whispered to the wall.

A short time later, Samantha hung up the phone and confirmed what they'd suspected. Migraine medicine and champagne didn't mix well. “The pharmacist also said that if she hasn’t eaten, and she said she hasn’t, the effects would be intensified. She should be fine in a few hours, but someone needs to keep an eye on her just in case. Given the information, I think we should get her out of here before things get worse.” She turned to Jessica. “Did you come in a cab? Subway?”

“My car service.”

Brooklyn reached for the clutch. “I’ll call them for you. Is the number in your phone?”

“It’s labeled ‘car.’”

Brooklyn felt her mouth tug. “Very inventive of you.”

Jessica leaned back in the chair and closed her eyes. “I’m practical. We can’t all be charming.”

Samantha tossed Brooklyn a sideways glance. “I think there’s a compliment for you in there somewhere.”

“There is,” Jessica said, and then a thought seemed to occur to her. “Wait. First I need to go say good night to Royce. It’s good business and he has tall hair.”

“Yeah, I’m thinking that would be a bad idea,” Brooklyn said.

“Right,” Samantha agreed, wincing. “Even I don’t want the account that badly.”

Jessica waved them off. “I can pull it together. It’ll be fine.”

Brooklyn shook her head. “It won’t, so you’re just gonna have to trust me on this one, slugger. Let’s go.”

She smiled lazily. “I like it when you call me slugger. You’re coming too?”

Brooklyn and Samantha exchanged a look. “You go,” Samantha said. “I’ll make sure Sophie gets home. Or, you know, Hunter will.” She smiled playfully.

“All’s fair in love and war, I guess.” She turned to Jessica. “I’m coming with you. Someone needs to make sure you make it home okay.”

Jessica pointed to the door. “Let Bentley know I wasn’t feeling well?”

Samantha nodded. “I’ll find him.”

Brooklyn kissed Samantha’s cheek. “You’re the best, Sammie.”

Ten minutes later, Brooklyn was able to assist Jessica out of the party undetected, and they made their way down the stairs to the town car idling just past the entrance. As they drove to the apartment, Jessica turned to her. "It feels like the car is flying." Yep. They were still firmly in the land of magic migraine pills. "Is the car, in fact, flying? Can you confirm this?"

Brooklyn smiled. "Those are some good drugs you took."

"My head's so fuzzy. I'm sorry."

"Drink some more water," Brooklyn prompted her. "And let's roll the window down, get some fresh air moving through here."

Jessica closed her eyes and settled her head back on the seat. "That's nice," she murmured as the cold air rushed in. The car wound its way through the city before finally pulling up in front of a rather modern-looking high-rise in the West Village. A buttoned-up doorman stood out front looking rather serious.

"So this is you?" Brooklyn asked, staring up at the place. "Jess?"

Jessica's eyes fluttered a few times and she oriented herself a moment. "Oh. Yeah, this is home. Um, but you can just drop me."

"Right. Because that would be responsible. Give me your hand, Cinderella."

"Who?"

"Never mind."

She helped Jessica out of the car and steadied her when she swayed. Once the elevator arrived on the fourteenth floor, Jessica stopped them.

"Make sure Ashton's not in the hallway? My neighbor. She'll think I'm drunk, and that cannot be an image she has of me right now."

It was a thoughtful gesture, thinking of the kid. Brooklyn nodded. "I'll take a look first." Finding the walkway vacant, she returned for Jessica. "Coast is clear. Lead the way?"

Jessica's apartment was elegant. Tall ceilings and parquet hardwood floors covered with a fluffy lavender rug. But it was homey at the same time, which was an impressive feat. A sculpted beige sofa faced a wall-mounted television. A matching purple chenille blanket draped across the back of the couch. The room was open to the small, though stylish, kitchen with maple cabinets and stainless-steel appliances. It was a nice apartment, though it had to be out-of-this-world expensive, given the neighborhood. Brooklyn couldn't even conjure a guess without six zeroes tagging along. But it was very Jessica and she loved it.

Speaking of Jessica, upon entering the apartment, she had promptly deposited herself on the sofa, lying on her back and staring up at the ceiling. "I hate dizzy. It's the worst feeling. When I close my eyes, it just gets worse."

Brooklyn sat on the arm and looked down at her. "I think you should eat something. Maybe it'll take the edge off. Why don't you go get changed and I'll raid your kitchen. I'm no kitchen ninja, but I make a mean grilled cheese."

A small smile touched Jessica's mouth. "Like when I was a kid. My dad made me those."

"Mhmm. Just like that. Is it a plan?"

She seemed to run the words through again. "I get changed. You're gonna cook."

"And then we get you to bed."

A slow smile took over Jessica's face. "Yeah?"

Brooklyn felt the heat on her cheeks. "To sleep. We get you to sleep so you can wake up refreshed and recovered and the normal Jessica again."

She frowned. "Not as much fun, but okay."

The contents of Jessica's fridge were overwhelming and offered insight into the woman herself. Lots of raw vegetables, several different kinds of cheese, some organic orange juice, and in surprising news, tons of individual-sized pudding cups. Brooklyn smiled at the image of Jessica enjoying her pudding cup as she fed her addiction to reality TV.

Luckily, in the midst of it all, she was easily able to drum up the basics: bread, cheese, and butter. The essentials for any grilled cheese. The key to making it the *best* grilled cheese was the kind of cheese you used. Personally, she preferred chevre. But because she didn't know Jessica's taste just yet, she relegated herself to the old standby, American. Her motto was always extra, extra cheese, followed by more cheese. After the sandwich popped and sizzled in the butter, she pulled off a one-handed flip and congratulated herself on technique. Once finished, she transferred her masterpiece from the pan to the plate and called over her shoulder to the back of the apartment. "Order up, Jess."

It took a second and third call, but eventually Jessica ambled into the kitchen wearing a yellow T-shirt that came to her mid thigh.

Brooklyn swallowed at the expanse of skin on display. Her legs were long, toned, and bare. And did she leave out mouthwateringly sexy? "Did you forget your pants?" she managed to say.

Jessica ran a hand through her luxuriously thick hair, which only taunted Brooklyn further. "No. This is what I sleep in."

"Right. Okay." She could be an adult about this. Not a big deal. She was here to take care of Jessica and shouldn't be blatantly lusting after her anyway. Wasn't in the night's job description. She set the plate in front of Jessica, who sat in one of the tall chairs facing the island.

"I'm not sure I can eat anything."

"Oh, I need you to try." She used her most authoritative voice, which seemed to work as Jessica took a tentative bite.

"I like this."

"Told you."

"You're kind of a genius at grilled cheese," she said between bites.

Brooklyn laughed. "Sounds like somebody has their wits about them again."

Jessica offered a small smile back. She still looked pale, however. Brooklyn figured she'd get her settled in and wait until she fell asleep before sneaking home. It's what any decent friend would do.

Friend. She turned the phrase over in her head a few times. Because they were friends now, weren't they? Friends who were attracted to each other, she countered. But that was just semantics.

Jessica finished half the grilled cheese and obediently drank a tall glass of water. "Sleepy," she said to Brooklyn, then rested her chin on her hand in the most adorable fashion.

Brooklyn adjusted a strand of hair behind Jessica's ear. "Why don't you go tuck yourself in and I'll close up shop in here?"

She nodded and headed down the hallway to what Brooklyn presumed was her bedroom. She moved the plate and the pan to the kitchen sink and gave them a good scrubbing before putting them back in their respective cabinets, all the while enjoying all the little accents of character that made the kitchen uniquely Jessica. Her favorite was the magnet on the fridge that said, "Dinner will be ready when the smoke alarm goes off." She ran her thumb across it and smiled.

She turned off the kitchen light and a rather trendy-looking lamp on the end table, leaving just an overhead light in the entry way so she could see her way out.

Once she located Jessica's bedroom, she found her on top of the covers, sound asleep. For a moment, she just had to stare because she looked so angelically picturesque that it was impossible not to. Her hair fell in a swoop across her forehead, just shy of her eyes, which possessed the most attractively long lashes. As Brooklyn's eyes drifted down her body, the direction of her thoughts shifted, however, much to her own dismay.

The fabric of the T-shirt Jessica wore was rather thin and didn't leave much to the imagination. The generous curvature of her breasts, the nipples pushing against the light cotton, and then there was the expanse of leg so wonderfully on display. Jessica looked like a sexy ad in a magazine, right there in front of her. God. This was so not fair. Closing her eyes for a moment against the perfection in front of her, Brooklyn swallowed, ordering herself to snap out of it as she moved closer to do what she'd come there to do.

"Hey," she finally whispered, running her fingers gently through the hair on Jessica's forehead. "Let's get you under the covers, okay?"

Jessica's eyes opened and fell softly on hers. She offered a small smile in recognition. "Hey."

"Hey, yourself."

"I never thought you'd be here, in my bedroom."

Brooklyn glanced around, surprised by this turn of events herself. Just an hour ago, she'd been on a date. "Well, here I am."

Before she knew it, Jessica took her hand and pulled her down. Their mouths were inches apart, but the much more immediate issue was the curves Brooklyn felt pushing up against her. God, how she wanted to explore them. "Kiss me," Jessica breathed.

Brooklyn glanced briefly at the ceiling for mercy—to clear her head, to regain some kind of control of this runaway train. "You're trouble, you know that?"

"Mhmm. I've heard that before."

She stared down at Jessica, who seemed fixated on her mouth. Because it didn't seem like she was going to relent, Brooklyn placed a quick kiss on Jessica's lips in a move to sidestep what was about to be a potentially dangerous scenario. But Jessica overruled that sentiment and pulled her right back in, deepening the kiss with admirable determination and, okay, blatant skill. Brooklyn let herself enjoy it for a moment, sinking into the depths of wonderful that kissing Jessica always led her to. Jessica let out a soft little hum of contentment, which shouldn't have done anything to Brooklyn, but God, it so did. Her heart kicked in her chest. Her hands wanted to engage, to explore the body that was pressed up so sensually against her own. She pulled her mouth away. She wasn't sure how she found the strength, but she had to put a stop to things. Jessica wasn't herself. She stood and took a step away from the bed.

"You need some rest, Jess. Let's get you under the covers."

Jessica nodded and pulled her feet up so Brooklyn could extricate the sheet from beneath her. The action caused the T-shirt to ride up, exposing the barely there panties beneath. Christ, Brooklyn thought to herself, swallowing hard against the very powerful reaction her body had to the sight. Jessica slipped beneath the sheets, and Brooklyn pulled the covers up to her chin. There. Totally covered.

"Now go back to sleep," she said quietly, and placed a kiss on her forehead, lingering there for just a moment longer than casual. "Doctor's orders." As she pulled back, Jessica stared at her almost searchingly.

"Can you stay?" She pulled the covers down and indicated the spot next to her.

"Not a good idea. You know that."

"Just sleeping. I promise I'll behave. I feel so out of sorts that I don't want to be by myself."

It was hard to argue when she looked so vulnerable, her eyes now luminous, scared. It wasn't like she could say no. If Jessica needed her to stay, she couldn't say no.

She sent Samantha a quick text message and slipped out of her heels. She considered the impracticality of getting into bed wearing a cocktail dress and opted for the slip she wore underneath instead. As she lowered the zipper of her dress, she could feel Jessica's eyes on her. Her skin tingled in response, and the lust factor shot up into the dangerous zone. *She's not herself. She's actually sick, so stop it right this minute.*

Brooklyn climbed into bed, the sheets cool and soft against her admittedly heated skin. Jessica settled in and closed her eyes, accompanied by an endearing sigh. So as not to disturb her, Brooklyn took it upon herself to reach across Jessica and turn off the bedside lamp. She sank back against the pillow and tried to clear her mind from its over-analysis of her current situation, more specifically the fact that she was in Jessica's bed and in very close proximity to someone she was wildly attracted to.

It was one night and Jessica needed her here, she reminded herself.

She should just try to sleep.

But that didn't come easily either, and she watched the minutes tick by like hours. Forty-five minutes later, Jessica moved into her, resting her head beneath Brooklyn's chin and slipping her arm across her waist in a move Brooklyn wasn't sure had been intentional or not. She inhaled sharply at the unexpected contact, the warmth of Jessica's skin against hers, the wonderful scent of her hair. Some sort of berry. It was an onslaught of sensation and more than a little overwhelming.

But it wasn't long before she realized Jessica was breathing slow and deep. Out like a light. The kind of peaceful breathing reserved for those dead to the world. She smiled then, and something shifted in her. With Jessica sleeping soundly against her, she felt content, comfortable, at home. Instinctually, Brooklyn wrapped her arms around Jessica and pulled her more firmly in before giving in to the serenity of the moment and closing her eyes.

She remembered playing absently with Jessica's hair just before sleep claimed her. It had been a wonderful way to drift off.

Dear God, she'd slept hard. That much Jessica was clear on. Her limbs felt heavy and wonderful when she awoke the next morning. It took her several well-devoted blinks before the circumstances of her morning gradually floated back to her in fragmented waves.

But something else was different too. There was a warmth all around her, a kind of fantastic warmth that she reveled in for a moment or two.

That's when it hit her.

The wonderful warmth was Brooklyn. In her arms. Okay, so this was a little unexpected. As reality twisted into sharper focus, she understood that they were completely tangled up in each other, limbs intertwined.

In her bed.

And she wasn't wearing a whole lot. The sensation of skin on skin told her that much.

Okay, it was coming back to her more clearly now. The party, the car ride. She ran her fingers through her hair. The medication. The damn medication that she would throw away the second she got her hands on that bottle.

Now what to do?

She glanced down at a sleeping Brooklyn and hated to wake her. Maybe she could escape without having to. Just required a little finesse is all. But when she delicately tried to disentangle herself, Brooklyn stirred against her. And the effects of that movement stirred a whole lot more within Jessica. She took a sharp breath and closed her eyes against her body's very decided reaction. Oh, God. Okay. What to do here? She knew what she *wanted* to do here, but it was so not the right time. Brooklyn had shifted to where she was almost entirely on top of Jessica, her face pressed against Jessica's neck, a well-placed thigh wreaking havoc on Jessica's sense of control.

"Brook?" Jessica whispered, slowly picking up her hair and letting it drop softly against the back of her neck. "Hey, sleepyhead. You awake?"

Brooklyn took a deep breath and lifted her head, looking down at Jessica with those big blue eyes. She seemed completely content with the sight in front of her and blinked lazily. That is until those eyes finally widened in realization. "I'm totally sleeping on top of you right now, aren't I?"

"Not exactly sleeping anymore," Jessica pointed out.

"Right." She smiled and ran her fingers through her hair but made no attempt to move. And really, Jessica was one hundred percent okay with that. Brooklyn in her arms, up against her like this, felt amazing. Torturous, but in a good way.

Almost on cue, Brooklyn shifted against her again, and it was enough to unleash a whole new onslaught of sensation…everywhere. She closed her eyes momentarily to steady herself. "So good morning," Brooklyn said. It was the sexiest of sentences.

"Good morning," she whispered back. They stared at each other for what felt like forever. The heat rippling between them was off the charts, and her body was on fire. She'd never experienced anything like it and made every attempt to steady her breathing. In fact, she didn't know it was a possibility for her, to feel this overtly attracted to another human. Parts of her were beginning to throb in a way that she didn't think she'd be able to ignore for very much longer.

"I guess I should..." Brooklyn slid off her then, and she felt the loss almost immediately. In fact, it took a lot of restraint not to pull her right back to where she'd been and explore the morning and all it had to offer. And she had definite ideas on what she'd explore first.

Instead, she turned onto her side and propped her head up on her palm. With new perspective, her first observation was how great Morning Brooklyn looked. With her blond hair all tousled, she was downright alluring.

She looked up at Jessica from where her cheek met the pillow. Her brow furrowed in concern. "How are you feeling today? Better?"

It was a valid question and she took stock. The haze she'd experienced the night before seemed to have lifted. Her mind was clear. It was good news. Quite frankly, she felt alert and alive in the most wonderful way and knew from recent experience why that was and just who, specifically, was responsible. "Much better, actually."

Brooklyn's features softened. "Oh, good. I was worried about you."

"Really?"

"Mhmm. Really."

"You didn't have to leave the party because of me. I feel guilty for having dragged you away."

Brooklyn brushed the hair from Jessica's forehead, entranced. It had been surreal to wake up with Jessica this way, and she couldn't help but enjoy every minute of it, self-indulgent as that was. She pushed herself up onto her forearm and stared at Jessica, whose eyes were so very bright in the morning light. Fresh-faced and rested like this, she was breathtaking, more so than she'd ever seen her. Brooklyn's voice was soft when she answered. "I didn't mind leaving. You needed someone."

Jessica blinked and answered back quietly. "And you were there."

Suddenly, the honest exchange held a bit too much weight, and Brooklyn gave in to instinct. Pulling out her most basic tactic, she shook herself out of it with an upshift in energy. She sat up in bed, looked away, and resorted to playfulness. "C'mon. You'd have done the same thing, Lennox."

But Jessica's words were still laced in sincerity. "I would have, yeah. For you."

The comment landed. And the room felt smaller.

For you. Brooklyn heard the words again in her head, and they rocked her. Knowing Jessica's eyes were on her, she glanced back over her shoulder, their gaze locked. That link, that unshakable connection between them had never felt so apparent. It was there, all of it. The sexual energy coupled with the fact that she genuinely liked Jessica. She couldn't remember the last time she'd ached for a woman for more than just what she could offer her sexually. And she did ache for Jessica. It was a dangerous combination, enough to make her shift into panic mode. She threw the covers off and hopped out of the bed.

"You know what? I'm glad you're feeling better, but I really have to get going."

Jessica faltered. "Big Saturday plans?"

"Not exactly. I just can't stay…here."

"Oh. Okay." The light in Jessica's eyes dimmed. She'd gotten the message. Seeing that look on Jessica's face ripped right through her. Brooklyn knew, at least on some level, that she was purposefully running from the situation. From Jess, herself. And that was okay. Because she was terrified of the power Jessica carried. The power to make her *feel*. And that wasn't a state of being that she could entertain for long. *Nope. Never let yourself need anyone*.

She found her dress and heels and with a quick good-bye was out of the apartment in two minutes flat. It was cowardly, she damn well knew it, but that didn't matter.

Self-preservation was everything.

It was not to be undervalued.

If there was one thing she was familiar with, it was people letting her down. And if she allowed herself to go there with Jessica Lennox, that's what would inevitably happen, and that would hurt more than she was willing to think about.

Best to keep moving.

So she'd just ignore that she'd slept the soundest she could remember in her adult history. She would gloss over the fact that with Jessica's arms around her, she hadn't experienced a single nightmare, an incredibly rare feat. And she would definitely forget the wonderful way she felt when Jessica was the first thing she'd laid eyes on that morning. Yep. She'd just push those thoughts from her head.

Chapter Ten

A *Yard Crashers* marathon was on TV that afternoon, and though Jessica had a mammoth amount of work to tackle in order to stay ahead, she just didn't have the heart for it. Which was odd, because since when did she not want to work?

But the fact of the matter was, the past twenty-four hours had delivered a potent one-two punch, and she was dealing with the effects. It's what semi-depressed people did. Now, was it possible she was feeling sorry for herself and thereby indulging her penchant for Russell Stover's chocolate? Yes, that's exactly what was happening, and she didn't care what the repercussions were.

She'd face her trainer at the gym on Monday.

For most of the morning and into the afternoon, she let herself veg out on the couch with a blanket and her yoga pants. She tried not to think too much about all that had gone down and, instead, lose herself in the wonder of her TV set. But the truth was, she was mortally embarrassed about her behavior at the Foster event, some of which she wasn't even clear on. Whether it was her fault or not, who knew what the Foster people had witnessed? If it hadn't been for Brooklyn and her friends, the damage could have been so much worse.

As her mind drifted to Brooklyn, her spirits fell further. What a web of confusion she found herself in.

Waking up with Brooklyn in her arms had been so unexpected and gratifying that it was impossible to downplay the attraction any longer. She'd underestimated things. When Brooklyn was around, she was happy. Plain and simple.

It wasn't practical, it wouldn't be easy, but she could no longer just discard those feelings.

But apparently Brooklyn could, and that's the part that stung so blatantly. She'd torn out of there that morning like she was in some sort of race. The message was loud and clear. She wasn't interested, and if she was, she wasn't willing to go there. She popped another piece of chocolate into her mouth.

"Do you want some milk with that?" Bentley called from the kitchen.

"I'm good," she answered.

Four very concerned voice mails from him had been waiting for her once she'd showered and changed. She'd called him back and indulged his self-invite to her apartment. It wasn't all that unusual, actually. They'd bonded early when he first came to work at the agency, and because their working chemistry had been so intense, she'd quickly snatched him up and made him her assistant. He had a good mind for business but also knew how to complement her style with suggestions and feedback that only made the company better.

Over time, he became more than just her employee. He was her friend and they cared about each other. Bentley was the one person she could tell anything and everything to and vice versa. When the workday ended, so did their business boundaries.

"So what's your deal today? Why the cave dwelling?" He settled in on the couch next to her with a pint of ice cream from her fridge, nudging her feet out of the way like he owned the place.

"I already told you. I'm humiliated beyond all repair."

"And I've told you that nobody noticed. After you left, I made the rounds to all of the Foster VIPS and left things on very good terms. I sampled the drinks, complimented Royce on their delicious fruit flavors, and even danced with Sandra, who now has a wild crush on me. So we're all good."

She had to hand it to him. The guy had her back. "I'm lucky, aren't I?"

"That you work with a charming fellow such as myself? Yes, you most definitely are." She leaned forward and messed up his hair, always the surefire way to annoy and endear herself to him at the same time. "Knock that off. I have a date tonight. I need to look good." He flashed a killer Bentley smile. "Not that I have to try hard."

"With Sandra?" she deadpanned.

"With Svetlana, the leggy cocktail waitress from last night." He waggled his eyebrows. "She's also an actress, by the way. Or at least she wants to be."

She rolled her eyes. "Typical. One day, Bent, you're going to have to grow up and settle down with one girl."

"What, like you?"

"I'd kick you out, but that would require me leaving the couch. And I happen to love the couch."

"You're just upset because the girl of your dreams walked out of this apartment this morning before you could show her what 'good morning' really meant."

She threw a pillow at him. "You're such a guy. Who talks like that?" She paused. "We kissed in the elevator that day it was stuck."

He stared at her. "I don't give you enough credit. Was there tongue?"

She rolled her eyes. "Like I'm going to tell you that."

"It's an important detail. It says a lot about the kiss. The magnitude is everything."

She felt the workings of a smile. "You know me. If I'm going to do something, I like to do it well."

He whistled low. "This is a nice side of you." He took a moment. "I can't believe I'm going to say this, but I don't think you should let this girl get away, Jess. Rival agency or not. She's had an effect on you, and I gotta say, I like the end result. You're all snap, crackle, pop lately, and it works."

She set down the box of chocolate-covered caramels and stared at the wall. "It could cause a lot of problems down the line. Not just for me and her, but for the agency."

"Worse things have happened in the world. Earthquakes, hurricanes, mass shootings, and you're worried about a little lost revenue? Besides, you'd find a way to make it back. You always do."

He had a valid point.

"So you're saying I go for it despite the ramifications?"

"Yes."

"What if she's not interested?"

"Worst-case scenario? You crash and burn. You do that all the time when I wreck shop on you in Call of Duty."

Jessica ignored the insult of her gaming abilities and stared at the ceiling. "I'm going to tell you something I haven't said out loud to anyone. I *really* like her, Bent."

He softened. "I know. Which is why you're sitting here pouting. I'm gonna raid your fridge again."

She laughed at the lack of segue. "Have fun with that."

"If you have more ice cream, we're in business."

"I do. Peanut-butter chocolate-chip. You can't miss it."

"Peanut butter, seriously? After everything?"

"I know."

He hesitated, but only for a moment. "I'm eating it anyway. And when I'm done, we're going to war Black Ops style."

She laughed and sat a little taller, feeling markedly better about things. Maybe she'd even change into real clothes. "I knew there was a reason I let you come over."

It was an achingly beautiful day out, which only helped prove the point that Brooklyn loved autumn in New York. As she strolled through Central Park with Hunter and, as always, Hunter's dog, Elvis, all the necessary signs of its arrival were there. The air was crisp with the smell of changing leaves, jack-o-lanterns graced the outsides of street carts, and the smell of cider wafted through the air.

On the streets, everyone was in a hurry, but in the park everything happened at a slower pace. It was as if the world was excited for what was to come, enough to make her want to hug herself in gratitude for the season.

Hunter studied her. "Okay. You're doing that hipster Disney-princess thing again. All in awe of the world over there."

Brooklyn shook her head slightly, still smiling. "There's just something about this time of year that makes me want to skip. I love jackets." She did a little hop. "Don't you love jackets?"

Hunter pulled her leather one tighter around her. "I think they're necessary to brace against the cold, but I don't own sixteen of them the way you do."

"That's because you don't fully get it. I love you anyway."

They stopped for Elvis to sniff a nearby bench in case it had anything interesting to offer. He really was a pretty great dog. Hunter had picked him out from the city pound the day he was scheduled to be put down, saving his life by hours. That was three years ago, and they'd been best friends ever since. Though no one knew for sure, they had Elvis pegged as part terrier, part corgi. He had an extra-round body with short little legs, giving him a unique look all his own. Brooklyn had never owned a pet but jumped at the chance to accompany Hunter and Elvis to the park any chance she got.

After scoring a couple of hot ciders from a street vendor, they found a nice stretch of lawn and had a seat. Elvis danced all around them like it was the most exciting thing that had ever happened to him and not just their twice-a-week routine.

"Hey, Elvis. Is this what you're looking for?" Hunter asked, holding up his prized blue, fuzzy tennis ball. His response was to launch into a series of vertical leaps as if competing in the doggy high jump.

Brooklyn clapped her hands for him. "You're a good boy, Elvis. The best, aren't you? Look at that form." She turned to Hunter. "You know what? I think you should throw the ball for him after that. Pretty impressive skills."

"I should? I should throw it?" She imitated a throwing motion.

"I think you probably should."

"I might throw it, now that you mention it."

Elvis stared at one of them, then the other, listening intently to their conversation for any sort of confirmation that his wildest dreams were about to come true and his ball would, in fact, be thrown. After a few more impressive jumps, and a series of breathy whines, Hunter threw the ball into the distance and Elvis bounded off after it, short legs in flight, as if his life depended on it.

Hunter stretched her own long legs out in front of her and popped on her sunglasses. "So did you sleep with her?"

She sidestepped the question. "Who? Sophie? Shouldn't I be asking you that question?"

Hunter gave her a long look. "You know exactly who I'm talking about. When you didn't answer your phone this morning, I called Samantha's to ask her to wake you the hell up. She hemmed and hawed and said you were out. But here's the catch. Sam's a horrible liar. She's too sweet to lie properly. So, I repeat. Did you sleep with her?"

Brooklyn threw the ball for Elvis, who let out an amusing squawk as he tore after it. With the shift in conversation, she felt her good mood begin to float away. "No. I didn't."

"But you stayed over?"

"To make sure she was okay."

"Very noble of you. When are you going to sleep with her?"

Brooklyn turned her body to Hunter in mystification. "How do you seem to know so much? I haven't talked to you at all about this."

She shrugged. "I'm pretty good at picking things up, and you've been all out of sorts ever since the much-talked-about Jessica Lennox walked into your life. Which means one thing. You've got it bad, which," she held up a finger, "is new for you. I scoped her at the cocktail thing. She's smokin', Brooks."

Brooklyn had a couple of options here. She could balk—she was an excellent balker—and move on from this conversation. Or she could level with Hunter, who would see through her bullshit anyway. She decided to go with the latter. "Okay. So there has been some *flirtatious* interaction. Did you tell Mallory?"

"What, and have her kill the messenger?"

She covered her eyes in relief. "Exactly. Thank you. I don't see that conversation going well."

"No, me neither. But you have to understand, Mal means well. She just happens to think Jessica Lennox is Satan in high heels, and whether or not that's an accurate representation, she sees her as a threat to the agency."

"And she puts the agency first," they said in unison, because it was Mallory's mantra.

Brooklyn studied Hunter. "Can I tell you something?"

"Always."

"I didn't have a nightmare last night."

Hunter turned to her, clearly intrigued. "Nothing?"

She shook her head. "And it might just be a fluke, a coincidence. Or maybe when I'm with Jessica, I feel…"

"Safe," Hunter said.

"Safe."

"You're a big believer in signs, Brooklyn. This might be an important one. Maybe you should talk to Mallory."

Brooklyn nodded. "Trust me, I get that and will cross that bridge if I ever happen to encounter it. We're a little ways off. And then there's the fact that I've perfected the art of bridge avoidance."

"So that means all systems are not a go?"

Brooklyn pulled a doomsday face.

"All right. Out with it."

"It's possible that I acted like a lunatic this morning when things got a little too real. She may not be speaking to me."

"I've done lunatic and come back from it. What'd you do?"

Brooklyn explained the events of the morning and made sure not to skimp on the incriminating details. "I guess I just freaked out."

"Too much. Too soon."

"What?"

"That's what it was for you. I think in that way, we're kind of alike, you and me. I don't get attached because I'm not into drama. You have—"

"Some complicated emotional issues. Yeah, I'm becoming more and more aware of that."

"Right. So, if Jessica didn't fall into the important column, you'd have had no problem with this morning. In fact, you'd have probably taken things much further and had the best time doing it."

It was a valid point.

"So the moral of the story is this—when you find someone who really matters to you and you want it to have staying power, you're going to have to go slow. Baby-step the hell out of that thing to give it a fighting chance."

Brooklyn stared at Hunter for several long seconds before finally nudging Hunter's shoulder with her own, because what she'd just said was everything.

It gave her hope.

Maybe she *could* go out on an emotional limb for the right person, but for her it probably wouldn't be something she could do overnight. And she found comfort in that, because *someday* was better than *never*. "You're a smart chick, you know that?"

Hunter shrugged and flashed the killer Hunter smile. "I've been trying to tell you people."

"That's a cute dog you have there." Suddenly a guy was kneeling next to Hunter and petting Elvis rather enthusiastically. It wasn't uncommon for them to be approached in the park. Hunter attracted flirtatious attention practically everywhere she went.

"Thanks," Hunter said. "I think so too."

"I'm Simon."

"Hunter."

"Brooklyn," she said, unprompted, and raised her hand in greeting. Simon didn't seem to care. Yep, second fiddle when Hunter was around. No biggie.

"I don't mean to be rude, but I saw the flag sewn on your bag. Are you from Hawaii? I spent a year there in the service."

Hunter's gaze flicked down to her bag. "When I was a kid. I don't really remember it. My mom's a native, though."

"It's beautiful there."

"It is."

Mind if I join you?" He was one of those ultra-tan, super-confident fellows with the athletic sunglasses and energy drink in hand.

"You could, but Brooklyn and I were just in the middle of breaking up. She wants to see other people and I'm not taking it well. I mean, at all."

The wide-eyed look on his face was priceless, and he froze mid-sit. "Right. So I should leave you alone then?"

"Probably. I might cry at any moment." She grabbed his shirt. "How could she do this to me, Simon? *How*? After everything."

"Oh, I'm sorry. I'm sure I don't know." His gaze flicked nervously from her back to Hunter.

"And I'm pregnant. Now what am I going to do?"

His mouth fell open in mystification, and he shrugged apologetically as he practically sprinted for the nearby sidewalk.

Hunter dropped the emotion, turned back to the lawn, and casually drank her cider as if none of it had happened.

Brooklyn shook her head, unable to suppress her own chuckle. There really was no one like Hunter. "You're going to hell. You know this, right?"

Hunter threw the ball for Elvis. "But I'm gonna have fun getting there."

Chapter Eleven

Jessica didn't make it to the gym until late Monday night. She'd ended the workday in a brainstorming session with her top team of account executives. They'd locked themselves in the boardroom to go over some of the product stats for Foster's summer-drink line that would launch in the spring. She'd had a hunch it would be tossed their way as part of the pilot deal, and she'd been right.

It also most likely meant that Savvy was taking a crack at it too.

By the end of their session, they'd come up with some stellar ad ideas, but the team had a few more questions for the Foster folks before latching on to one idea and developing it.

All in all, it had been a productive day.

The hour and a half she'd finally squeezed in for a workout had made her body sing in all the right ways. The hot shower she took afterward eased her aching muscles. She was still on the tail end of an endorphin high as she turned the corner to the entrance of her building.

"Hey, Patrick."

"Good workout, Ms. Lennox?"

"Awesome, actually."

He took a step closer and lowered his head. "I don't want to overstep my bounds, but you might take a look to your left as you make your way into the lobby."

It was unlike Patrick to engage in any sort of real conversation with her, so this was clearly important. Jessica peered over her shoulder through the glass doors and was able to make out Ashton sitting in one of the couches near the center of the room. Her face was tear-streaked, and Jessica's stomach dropped at the sight.

"How long has she been down here?"

"A little over two hours now. I checked in on her, but she wasn't much for talking."

"Thanks, Patrick."

"Of course, Ms. Lennox."

It was probably best to approach Ashton casually when something was wrong. She embarrassed easily, and the last thing Jessica wanted to do was scare her away when she clearly needed help.

Jessica strolled through the glass doors and into the lobby, pausing a few feet from Ashton. "Hey, kiddo. What's new?"

Upon seeing her, Ashton sat a little taller and forced a smile, but it didn't take over her face the way Jessica was used to. "Just, you know, thinking. Introspection is in these days, and you know me. Trendy."

"That you are. I'm fresh from the gym and gonna make a smoothie. Healthy is also trendy. Ask your friends. Want one?"

She seemed to consider this. "Um. I guess I could go for a smoothie."

"Fabulous. Follow me."

Once inside her apartment, she gave Ashton the job of slicing the fruit while she prepped the blender.

"You'd think a high-powered businesswoman like yourself would have one of those machines where you didn't have to cut the fruit at all."

"And yet I have but a simple blender to offer our cause."

"You're livin' the struggle, Jessica."

"Don't I know it."

She opened the lid in order for Ashton to toss in the requisite fruit pieces. A dash of milk later and they were off and blending. She poured a glass for each of them and turned to Ashton. "Cheers."

Ashton offered the slightest of smiles. "Sure. Cheers." She strolled across the room and sat on the couch, still not offering up any information. As Jessica watched her, she decided she was just going to have to go for it.

"So, hey, where's your mom tonight?"

"At home." The fact that Ashton was instantly entranced by the contents of her glass signaled to Jessica that she was on the right track.

"You guys getting along okay?"

Silence.

"Ashton, you can level with me. We're friends, right?"

"I mean, yeah. We are."

Jessica perched on the side of the armchair across from her and dropped her head to catch Ashton's gaze. "Then tell me what's up. It's possible I can help."

Ashton took a shuddering breath, and that's when Jessica saw the fresh tears. "She's been drinking again. She promised she'd lay off the alcohol and it was fine for a few days. She actually stuck with it, but tonight she was upset about her boyfriend not calling or something. I think this guy's married, Jess, but she doesn't seem to care. When I got angry about the drinking, she started yelling at me and told me to get out. Locked the door."

Though Jessica's anger rose, she also knew it was important that she not react too strongly, for Ashton's sake. But seriously, who locks their teenager out of their own home?

"But what's really bad is that I have all this bio homework that's due tomorrow. I was able to grab my bag so I have the worksheets, but the book's in my room and she's not answering the door." The helpless look on her face was too much. The kid wasn't worried about where she was going to sleep; she was concerned about her grades, which spoke volumes about her character, her ambition.

Jessica stood up. "Then we get the super to let us in with his key."

Ashton paled. "God, no. We can't do that. Please. It'll make everything worse, and she'll never forgive me."

"Ashton, it's not okay that she won't let you in. Technically, we could call the police and they would force her to—"

"I shouldn't have come here." She set the glass on the coffee table and brushed the tears from her cheeks as she took off for the door. "Thanks for the drink. I gotta go."

Damn it all. She chased after her. "Ashton, wait. Hold on a second. Let's compromise." God, this was such a delicate situation. She wanted to do what was right for Ashton, but at the same time, she couldn't lose her trust or she'd never come to her again. And damn it, the girl needed someone in her corner.

"What compromise?"

"Stay here tonight. Text your mom and let her know where you are. I'll help you with your homework. Or Google will. But you have to agree to let me have a conversation with your mother tomorrow."

Ashton stared at the wall just past Jessica as she considered her options. "What are you going to say to her?"

"That I'm worried about you and about her. I think she may need more help than we're able to give her, though."

Ashton nodded, her eyes sad. "I think you may be right."

Jessica tossed an arm across her shoulders and offered a squeeze as she walked her back into the apartment. "So, biology?"

"It's really hard."

"Good thing I'm really smart."

It was just after nine when Brooklyn's phone buzzed. She and Sam were nearing the end of *Sleepless in Seattle*. It was Romantic Movie Wednesday at their place and her turn to pick the film. She glanced absently down at the new text message. "Remember when you said you were a science whiz? True or false?"

She stared at the random question from Jessica and typed back a quick reply. "True. You conducting a chemistry experiment over in the Village?"

"Something like that. Busy?"

She shot a look at Samantha across from her on the coach and Meg Ryan on the screen.

"Not overly. Why?"

"Fifteen-year-old neighbor and her crazy-hard bio homework."

"What do you need?"

"HELP. Cellular osmosis and diffusion. Not going well."

She thought it over and considered how much time was left on the film. "Give me thirty minutes." Who said she couldn't squeeze in both cinema and science? She was a girl of many hats.

When Brooklyn arrived at Jessica's apartment, she found her and a teenager huddled over a series of worksheets like cavemen trying to understand fire. The neighbor, Ashton, was a nice-enough kid who seemed grateful for the help. Jessica looked even more so. Her eyes communicated a silent thank you. But it was clear from the concern on her face that a lot more was going on here.

She took a seat at the bistro table off the kitchen and surveyed the first worksheet a few moments. "Okay. It's been awhile, but essentially, we're just describing how osmosis happens in a series of steps. See?"

Ashton tossed Jessica a look. "She's good."

"Told you."

Brooklyn pointed to the worksheet. "So this arrow is asking about the Law of Mass Action? Do you know what that is?"

Jessica looked to Ashton, who gave it a shot. "I think it has to do with dynamic equilibrium."

Brooklyn smiled, which made Ashton smile. "Smart neighbor you got here, Jess. Yes, let's run with that idea."

Ashton pulled up a chair and they got to work. Brooklyn calmly explained concepts, while Ashton helped fill in the blanks. Turned out she was a really bright kid, and likable too. Forty-five minutes later, they were finished, and Brooklyn was pretty confident they'd aced the assignments.

"Now why can't my biology teacher just explain it that way? It would save me a lot of time."

Brooklyn smiled. "Not as cool as me."

Ashton laughed. "Clearly. So you guys are friends?" She glanced from Brooklyn to Jessica.

"We are," Jessica answered, meeting Brooklyn's eyes. They stared at each other a moment as Ashton looked on, picking up on something.

She grinned. "Ah. Got it." She stood. "Now that my homework is complete, thanks to you nice people, I'm going to grab a shower. That okay?"

Jessica nodded. "Of course. You know the way. Feel free to borrow whatever you need from my dresser."

Ashton grabbed her backpack. "I got a few things with me. I just might need a toothbrush and something to sleep in, and I'm good."

"Medicine cabinet on the right and the third drawer down in my dresser."

"Thanks," she said, this time quite seriously.

The casual disappeared from Jessica's face. "Anytime. You know that."

Ashton nodded a few times and disappeared down the hall.

And then they were alone.

"Everything okay?" Brooklyn asked as Jessica rounded the island.

"Not exactly. Can I get you a glass of wine? You deserve it after the superwoman turn you did tonight."

"Love one. Wanna tell me about it?"

Jessica poured them a couple of glasses, and they adjourned to the couch where she explained the circumstances she'd come home to.

"Sounds like you did the right thing. She knows she can trust you now, but you've also got license to intervene on her behalf, which you most definitely need to do. It's one thing when she's passively drunk in a hallway, and another when she's raging and throwing her daughter out."

"Right. Ashton's the kind of kid who puts on a brave face. I just want her to know that she doesn't have to do that with me."

Brooklyn could identify. It's what she'd done her whole life. "I think it's going to take time. But she sees the good in you. That's step one."

Jessica's eyes sparked understanding and she interlaced her fingers with Brooklyn's across the top of the couch. "And what about you? What do you need from me?"

Brooklyn stared at their hands. *And here we go.*

She had a choice. She could face this thing with Jessica here and now, or kill it forever. Brooklyn knew what she wanted, but it wasn't as easy as simply reaching out and taking it. It never had been. But life was about growing and changing, she reminded herself. With change came improvement. So it was time she changed her bad habits and tried on a little courage.

She took a deep breath and asked Jessica for what she truly needed. "Time. I think I need us to go slow. And maybe a little bit of the control."

"Hence the disappearing act the other day?"

"Right. I guess you could say I freaked out a little."

"Because?"

She tilted her head as she tried to figure out how to explain. "It was a lot. Jess, I can do casual all day. I have a great reputation for casual. Ask the lesbian population of New York City." She attempted a smile, but it didn't take because the next part was somehow harder to admit. "But here's the catch, and it always has been. When things turn serious, the way they felt between us the other morning, my defense mechanisms kick in and tell me to get the hell out of there. It's childish, and probably counterproductive to me ever being emotionally mature, but it's who I am. I don't let a lot of people in. I just don't."

And that's when Jessica got it.

Brooklyn wasn't just concerned about their conflicting jobs, which was a big-enough obstacle on its own, but she was also fearful of the emotions that came with a real relationship. And really, if you thought about her life and the revolving door of her early years, it made a lot of sense.

So she could do what Brooklyn asked.

In fact, it wasn't such a bad idea anyway. "You know, if I'm being honest, I like the idea of taking things slow, seeing what this is. I think we agree that ours isn't the most ideal scenario."

"It's not," Brooklyn pointed out emphatically. "It's the opposite of ideal."

"Okay. So, let's not go crazy just yet."

Brooklyn took another deep breath and nodded a few extra times. "Okay. No reason to go crazy."

Jessica touched her cheek. "You *drive* me a little crazy, but in a good way."

Brooklyn grinned playfully. "So…I'm in charge? Of the pace?"

Jessica's stomach flip-flopped at how cute she looked when she said it. She laughed, shook her head, and studied the ceiling, wondering what she was getting herself into here. "Sure. For whatever time you need, you can be in charge."

"Super dangerous of you. Walk me to the door?"

Her spirits dropped. "You have to leave? But I like you here."

"Unfortunately, I do. I work tomorrow, you see." She led the way to the door and Jessica followed. "But I plan to see you soon, either in cut-throat competition for clients or, you know, to do a little of this, which is important." Brooklyn stepped in and kissed her softly. And she felt the tingles ripple through her as she kissed Brooklyn back. She was learning to expect them, the tingles, but that didn't seem to detract from their overall effect, which was shockingly dominant. Her arms, her legs, and more warmed in the most wondrous way when Brooklyn was close to her like this.

Brooklyn took a step back, and they stared at each other for one powerful moment. They'd kissed before. Passionately. With a kind of abandon. But this kiss had been different. Slower. Less hurried. It felt like a promise of things to come, and the understanding of that hung in the air between them in a kind of glow.

This was real.

And that's when it occurred to Jessica in specifics. They would have time in the future for more kisses in doorways and coffee in coffee shops and stolen smiles across lobbies, if she played her cards right. And she wanted to.

"'Night, Jess." Brooklyn said in a soft voice that communicated she was looking forward to those things too.

"Yeah." She smiled. "'Night."

Karina Coleman stared at Jessica blankly from the doorstep of her apartment, blinking several times to, no doubt, clear her head. "I'm sorry. What do you want to talk about?" she asked in annoyance.

Jessica's normally glamorous neighbor was anything but this morning. Her bleached-blond hair hung in limp sections, and her typically perfect makeup was smudged in dark rings under her eyes. Hangovers had a way of stripping the glitz right out of a person, and in Karina's case it wasn't pretty.

"Ashton, actually."

Karina glanced behind her, pulling her kimono tighter around her body as if trying to connect the dots. "I think she's in her room."

"She's not, actually. She's at school now, wearing jeans from yesterday, a shirt I let her borrow, and lunch money that I gave her because you kicked her out of the apartment last night."

Karina took a minute with that. "I didn't do that. I wouldn't have kicked her out. That's insane. Don't say things like that to me about my own daughter."

"But you did. You were drinking last night, Karina. Which is why you're hungover now. Ashton stayed at my place and left for school not too long ago. I'm here because I'm concerned for her well-being. She's too young to be on her own. She needs a responsible adult looking out for her."

"Ashton's a smart girl. She does just fine. I think I know my daughter."

"Then you know how scared she was last night, not just for herself, but for you. She's a kid, and this is too much for her to deal with on her own."

"So you're here to what? Threaten me? Try to take my daughter?"

"Absolutely not. You're her mother. Helping Ashton means helping you."

Karina's expression seemed to soften at that, point taken. "It's just been a rough week, you know? You've never had a rough week?"

"Oh, yes. I definitely have. But I'm wondering if it's more than that because weeks have come and gone. Months even, and things only seem to be getting more serious. I made some calls and got the number of a great alcohol counselor. It could make a big difference. For you and for Ashton." She handed her the slip of paper.

Karina scratched her head absently and stared at the number. "Maybe." A pause. "She really stayed with you last night?

Jessica nodded.

"I'll think it over, okay? But I'm not like some alcoholic." She looked back into her apartment in confusion. "Thanks for letting her stay with you. It won't be a problem in the future." She went to shut the door, but Jessica stopped it abruptly with her hand.

"Before I go, I need you to understand that I'll do whatever I have to do in order to make sure Ashton is safe and all right."

They locked eyes for several uncomfortable moments. Finally, Karina nodded and the door closed.

Jessica stared, not knowing how successful the conversation had been, but it was a step in the right direction.

❖

"Lucky Rabbit's Candy?" Mallory asked.

Hunter swiveled her laptop to face the table. "New logo and a full-page ad that will hit *Time Out New York* next month. I'm also working with them on a web redesign for their product page. We meet again Tuesday."

"Love it. Great use of color on the lower half," Samantha murmured as she studied the ad layout on the screen.

It was their weekly company meeting. Amidst coffee and blueberry muffins from Lulu's downstairs, the four sat around the conference table catching one another up on the state of their clients.

As always, Mallory kept them moving. "Evolution Boutique?"

Brooklyn consulted her notes. "Uh, we started their Internet push last week. We supervised a series of online giveaways that went well, and I think Sam is tracking the results."

Samantha took the reins. "They did okay. The numbers from the push that actually culminated in sales, however, were a little lower than we'd hoped. I think it's going to be a process, and the client is aware of that and onboard for the long game."

"Perfect. It's a step in the right direction." Mallory tic-tacked away on her laptop, taking down all the updates from the meeting. Later that afternoon, as she did every week, she'd send them each a full report in copious detail via e-mail. She turned to Brooklyn. "What about Foster? I was going over the product descriptions for the new summer drinks. Are you thinking outdoors for the TV spot? Fun-in-the-sun kind of thing?"

"If we have to," Brooklyn said. "It's kind of obvious, but I think it might be what Foster wants. In my opinion, it would be smarter of us to give Foster what they don't know they want."

Mallory nodded, clearly in thought. "We can assume The Lennox Group is going to go with something youthful. A beach party, some sort of luau. They're not that hard to predict."

"Right. So what if we pivot on that and capture summer, but do it with a twist of elegance? Hear me out." She studied their faces. Hunter seemed intrigued. Samantha and Mallory looked at her with guarded interest. "I'm thinking an outdoor wedding. Simple. Beautiful. Maybe a gazebo. The toast is heartfelt, the couple's in love. They raise their drinks, but instead of champagne, it's Foster's Pear Pinot Grigio. People are dancing under the stars. It's every girl's fantasy, the picturesque wedding. And who are these drinks geared to? Women."

Mallory sat back, smiling. "You're saying we should summer-romance it."

"It fits," Sam pointed out. "These drinks are light, simple. They're happy drinks. People in love are happy."

"I, for one, vote yes," Hunter said, closing her laptop. "I never would have come up with it, but I love it."

"Let's just hope Foster does," Brooklyn said. "I'll get more details from them this week and then you, me, and your computer?"

Hunter nodded. "It's a date."

"Anything else?" Mallory asked. They'd come to the end of the detailed agenda she'd passed out.

"That's all I got," Hunter said.

"Me too," Samantha said. Everyone began to pack up, intent on heading back to their individual projects. They had clients to call, meetings to make.

Brooklyn knew it was now or never. She stood. "Um. Before we all disperse, I'd like to take Friday as a personal day, if that's all right with everyone."

Mallory glanced up and seemed to check the calendar in her brain. "I don't think we have anything major on Friday. We're good."

Samantha scrunched up her forehead. "You just need a down day? Are you burning the candle at both ends?"

"Actually, no. I was thinking about visiting Connecticut this weekend. Meeting Cynthia."

Silence.

Brooklyn looked from one of them to the other. "It's not like someone died. You can say something."

Mallory smiled, came around the table, and pulled her into a hug. "I'm happy for you. This is a big step."

"Major." Samantha smiled. "Are you sure?"

"Yeah." Brooklyn nodded. "I've been thinking about it a lot. About her. And I'd like the chance to meet her. I called her this morning, and this weekend is apparently a good one for her and her family. She's actually really excited, which is, you know, maybe a good sign."

"This is cool, Brooks," Hunter said. "Take all the time you need. We got things around here."

"Of course we do," Mallory said.

"I appreciate that. But I'll be back by Monday. Lots to do on the Foster pitch."

"We're behind you. Just know that, okay?" Samantha said, and squeezed her hand. "But are you sure you want to go alone? I could move some things around. It's not a bad idea for you to have someone there with you for moral support. A familiar face."

Samantha was dubbed the sweet one of the group for a reason. It had occurred to Brooklyn that it might be a lot to take on her own, but at the same time she didn't know how she felt about involving her friends in these uncharted waters. They knew her history, but she'd held back the darker details of her childhood from them for a reason. She didn't want them to feel sorry for her or to let who she once was define the way they viewed her now. She'd worked really hard to break free of the past and didn't want to drag them into it now. And she had no idea what she would find in Connecticut. "That's all right. You guys have a lot on your plates here. I'll be fine on my own. Promise."

Samantha slid her a look of sympathetic understanding. "Let me know if you change your mind. We're here for you." Mallory and Hunter nodded in agreement.

"I know." And they were, just like always.

No matter what happened on her trip, she had her friends waiting for her back home. The family she'd never had. They'd pick her back up and dust her off and listen to whatever details she was willing to supply them with. Good or bad.

She was beyond lucky to have them.

❖

It was hotter than most days in autumn, and Jessica decided to go sans coat, which would have just given her one more thing to carry anyway. The morning had been crazy hectic, but she'd get a much-needed break after this planning session at Foster.

As she climbed the steps to the office building, she smiled as she spotted Brooklyn making her way down. Since she had a meeting scheduled at Foster, she was guessing Brooklyn had just finished one of her own.

They hadn't seen each other in a few days. A couple of text messages here and there, but it wasn't the same as seeing Brooklyn in person, taking her in. She'd missed her. And running into her in the flesh easily took her somewhere light, happy.

Brooklyn returned the smile as their gaze collided. "Well, what do ya know? The Lennox Group is here."

"Not a group today. Just me."

"That's how I like it. Time for coffee? Please say yes."

Jessica checked her watch. Damn it. "Actually, no. I have a meeting in five."

"Oh. Fun fact. The Foster people like it when folks are late. I'm positive about that. So coffee?"

"There you go trying to steal this account from me again."

"It's part of my DNA. But hey, how do you know it's not just my way of getting to spend a little time with you?" She smiled and Jessica felt the flutter. She loved that smile. And she was growing rather fond of the flutter too.

"I like that version better." She shifted her attaché. "What about this weekend? Dinner?"

Brooklyn paused and looked at her in apology. "I kind of have something to do this weekend."

A crash and burn. She felt the semi-embarrassed flush, which was also a new occurrence. "Oh. Okay. Well, another time. I better get to that meeting."

"Okay."

She made it about five more steps before the sound of Brooklyn's voice stopped her. "Jess?"

"Yeah?"

"Ever been to Connecticut?"

She stared at Brooklyn, not really understanding the trajectory. "Can't say I have."

"Wanna go?"

❖

As Brooklyn stood in line at Starbucks twenty minutes later, she was still shocked that she'd invited Jessica to go with her to meet her mother. It was the biggest day of her life they were talking about, not dinner and a movie. Who takes a date to something like this? The invitation had flown from her mouth on impulse. It wasn't like she'd actually thought it through. But the more she marinated on the concept, the more it didn't seem like such a horrible idea.

It would be nice to have a little moral support. And on the plus side, Jessica was close enough to her to know the story, but peripheral enough to not add any extra pressure. She was kind of the perfect person for the job.

And let's be forthright, she craved time with Jessica.

When they weren't together, she daydreamed about what she was doing, what her lips tasted like. But she already knew the answer to that one. Strawberry lip gloss and it was damn sexy. Brooklyn daydreamed about Jess during her downtime, her uptime, anytime really. Plus, her company would make the drive a little more fun. Maybe if she turned this thing into an adventure, it would feel a tad less terrifying.

She'd rented a cottage for the weekend on one of those rental websites, and now she was wildly aware that the sleeping arrangement could be an issue. Proper precautions might be in order. She wasn't planning to sleep with Jessica on the trip. It would be totally out of context, and they'd agreed to take it slow for her sake.

This weekend wasn't about figuring out how to maneuver the waters of their complex relationship, and she didn't want the temptation looming over her. And with Jessica, temptation was always present. They'd have time for all that wonderful romantic stuff down the road. And what Hunter said was true. Baby steps were the way to go.

She grabbed a table in the corner of Starbucks, logged onto the rental site, and changed the reservation to a two-bedroom on the same street.

Because, you know what? Better safe than sorry.

Chapter Twelve

It was just past lunchtime and Jessica waited in front of her building with Patrick. Brooklyn had been supposed to pick her up for their drive to Connecticut ten minutes prior. She checked her watch again, reminding herself that Brooklyn was often late. And okay, she had some extra energy and this little thrum of anticipation in the pit of her stomach for what was to come.

This trip was a big deal for Brooklyn. Huge.

She was surprised to be invited along, honored even, and okay, also a little nervous. It was important that this go well for Brooklyn, and she would play whatever part she had to help make that happen.

She'd only known Brooklyn a couple of months, but in that time, she'd crept up on her steadily, and now she felt important to Jessica in a way she wouldn't have guessed. Feelings were swirling that she didn't quite have a name for yet, but she was interested in figuring them out.

Brooklyn was a complicated person, she was finding, and so she had to allow for that. She'd been through a lot and that influenced how she handled things, took in people, situations. She hadn't planned on Brooklyn. But now that she was here, the world around her seemed to spark into color.

So when she was asked to go to Connecticut, of course she had to try. Her schedule wasn't the type that was easy to rearrange, but she'd managed to do it. Nothing too major should happen at the office on the weekend, and if it did, well, that's what cell phones were for.

She'd packed a small suitcase for the trip, not exactly sure what the requisite dress code would be. Casual should be fine. Right?

Patrick eyed her jeans and scoop-neck T-shirt. "No work today, Ms. Lennox?"

"Oh. I took the day off."

He raised an eyebrow.

"What?"

"Never seen you take a weekday off before."

"Never?"

"No, ma'am."

She thought on this and supposed he had a point. Not many things could make her shove aside an entire day of work. Not many people could either, for that matter. She took note of the fact that Brooklyn had.

That had to count for something, right?

As much as she second-guessed the logic of dating her biggest rival, this was yet another example that something different was at work here. And whatever it was warranted wading through the complicated details to figure out if they made sense.

Her thoughts were abruptly derailed as a lime-green VW Beetle sped to the curb in front of her and stopped abruptly, race-car-driver style. She raised an eyebrow at Brooklyn, who stepped from the vehicle.

"Hey, Andretti. Did you mistake this curb for your pit stop?"

Brooklyn's mouth fell open. "Is that commentary on my driving?"

"Absolutely not. The words reckless and scary didn't cross my mind at all." She punctuated with a smile.

"Oh, good, because I happen to take the way I drive very seriously. It's a source of pride." She reached for Jessica's suitcase and paused, seemingly struck. "Hey, you're in jeans."

Jessica glanced down. "I am. But so are you. Should I have dressed up more?"

"No. But Casual Jess is new for me. I didn't know you were capable of…" She sighed and rerouted, blowing out a breath. "You look good like this. *Really* good." Brooklyn studied her with obvious interest and then broke into a blush when Jessica answered with a knowing grin. Patrick pretended to study something on his glove.

"In that case, thank you. I accept the compliment."

But Brooklyn looked fabulous herself. She'd pulled her hair into a ponytail, and with a white T-shirt and baby-blue hoodie, her eyes popped with amazing color. The rip in her jeans was customary and thereby endearing. Kind of her signature. She looked fresh-faced. Youthful. Beautiful. But then she was always beautiful. She was Brooklyn. And, at that realization, a warmth flowed through her that manifested in a smile.

They loaded Jessica's suitcase into the backseat, and Brooklyn held the passenger door open for her. "Shall we?"

"Is this going to be a terrifying experience? I don't do good with terrifying."

"No way. I take my driving very seriously, and I plan to take very good care of you. The best."

"I'm going to hold you to that." She eased into the passenger's seat and popped her sunglasses on.

"You have Chanel sunglasses?"

"I do."

Brooklyn laughed. "Of course you do. I am so out of my depth with you. Are you sure you don't mind being seen with me?"

"Are you kidding? You give me hipster points."

"That's true. I do that."

And with a final wave to Patrick, they headed out of the city, top down, wind blowing their hair as Justin Timberlake sang about bringing sexy back.

Brooklyn couldn't describe the feeling she got when she realized it wasn't just a bunch of talk. Jessica was actually coming with her and doing it out of the goodness of her heart. It meant something to her. She wasn't sure what quite yet. But she'd sort it out eventually. When you had a gorgeous brunette in your top-down convertible, why rush to rationalizations?

But what Jessica didn't know was that trip almost hadn't happened at all.

When she'd awoken that morning, she had come very close to canceling the whole thing. Her stomach was churning, her palms were sweating, and horrible thoughts of all the ways this meeting could go disastrously wrong chased themselves around her mind like some sort of emotional haunted house. She should never have agreed to this, to meeting Cynthia. Way too lofty. She wasn't ready. What if it was awkward? And of course it would be. She didn't know this woman other than from the briefest of phone conversations. What if she wasn't nearly as together as she seemed? What if she was a drug dealer and lying about everything? Surely she was a drug dealer.

But it was bigger than just a prospective awkward meeting, and she knew it.

It seemed like her whole life was based around the fact that the people who were supposed to love her more than anyone else in the world simply didn't. They'd given her away, and that fact had colored every move she'd made since. And though she wished to God it didn't matter to her, she needed to understand why. And maybe if she could understand, the rest of her life might fall into place. The barriers she built up around herself would somehow become easier to dismantle.

She looked over at Jessica, who, apparently sensing her unease, reached over and ran her hand across the back of her neck in reassurance. Her heart did a little dip at the sentiment. There was so much to Jessica, more than the rest of the world gave her credit for. But for whatever reason, she'd let Brooklyn in, allowed her to see the softer side beneath the calm, cool exterior. Now if she could just learn to do the same. And the truth was, she wanted to lose those barriers. Maybe taking this big step in her life would help with that.

"Think we'll make it there by next week?" Jessica asked, surveying the gridlock in front of them on West Fortieth.

"Don't you worry, attractive business rival in my passenger seat. The one thing you don't know about me is my amazing ability to maneuver around the traffic of New York City. Sit tight."

"The phrase 'sit tight' sounds ominous. Do I want to see this?"

Brooklyn adjusted her rearview mirror and did some finger stretches. "Oh, I think you do."

When the light changed, Brooklyn veered them into the left lane, accelerating sharply and passing three cars to their right before cutting off the fourth. Horns honked in symphony, but they'd gained valuable ground. As the light in front of them clung to its final moment of yellow, Brooklyn snuck past, leaving the other cars stacked up behind them at the intersection. When they encountered traffic, Brooklyn zigged. When they ran into more gridlock, she zagged. She used back streets, took corners like she owned them, and did so without taking out any pedestrians in the process. Though it was close.

It wasn't until they were safely out of the city and onto the expressway that she sent Jessica her most winning smile. "Tell me you're impressed. We'd be sitting back there for another twenty minutes if anyone else had been driving."

Jessica shook her head slowly in mystification. "I don't know whether to be turned on or terrified of you right now. It's an interesting combination."

She considered this. "I could probably work with both."

"Let's not get off topic. You're kind of a menace. A skilled menace, because I've never seen anyone sail through the city like that, but a menace all the same."

"I like to drive fast and I'm good at it." Brooklyn shrugged. "Call it whatever you like."

"Death-defying. Let's go with that."

"I can get behind death-defying." She popped on her sunglasses and took them to I-91, where they cruised unencumbered for a good half hour. Brooklyn sang along with the radio as Jess bopped subtly in time to the beat. The vibe was peaceful, and the weather couldn't have been more picturesque if they'd ordered it up special for the drive. The sky was gorgeous, voluminous, creamy clouds playing against the backdrop of vibrant blue.

"Oh, look!" Jessica pointed in earnest to a billboard "There's a dairy out here. And they're open to the public. We should come back out here someday."

Brooklyn was intrigued by the reaction. "You have a penchant for milk and cheese that I don't know about yet?"

"I have a penchant for sweet, adorable cows. I never get out of the city. Cows are like leprechauns when you're a New Yorker. Heard about, but rarely seen in person. They have the kindest little faces."

Brooklyn stole another look at the light in Jessica's eyes and made a decision. "Okay then." She took the marked exit and steered them in the direction of the sweet, adorable cows.

"Wait. We're actually stopping? Oh, you don't have to do that. I don't want to put us behind schedule. This trip is more important."

"We have plenty of time. I think this is something I have to experience with you."

A grin crept onto Jessica's face. "Well, when you put it that way. Okay, I'm in."

They followed the winding road for a few miles before they pulled onto a smaller gravel road that took them to Heaven's Gate Dairy. It appeared they weren't the only ones interested in an up-close look, as the small parking lot overflowed with cars. The dairy seemed medium-sized and was comprised of side-by-side buildings, several large pastures, a main holding pen, and a large red house with a PUBLIC WELCOME sign in the shape of a cow hanging above the door.

"This could be educational," Brooklyn mused as she led the way into the house.

"I'm counting on it."

The front room served as a miniature gift shop with odds and ends all branded with the words "Heaven's Gate." Jessica held up a bumper sticker. "I think we need this for your car."

"Or your briefcase."

Brooklyn tried on a cowboy hat and turned to Jessica. "I could have easily gone into the cow business. Look how irresistible I am right now."

Jessica adjusted the hat. "I don't know why you didn't."

"You probably have to ride horses and know about milk."

"There is that. Maybe you could sneak by on your fashion-forward sensibility."

She thought this over. "I could. But then you'd land the Foster account and the universe would be upside down."

"Wow." Jessica laughed. "And I'm the one everyone thinks is cutthroat? But I have to agree with you about one thing."

Brooklyn sent her a sideways glance in curiosity. "And what would that be?"

"You are infinitely irresistible." Jessica smiled that smile that she seemed to reserve for very honest moments, and Brooklyn felt it tingle through her. She loved when that smile came out and would do what she had to in order to figure out how to see it more often. They held each other's gaze until Brooklyn slowly smiled back at the woman who could elicit so much in her so easily. Jessica stepped into her space and took the hat off her head. "Want to go see some adorable cows?" Jessica finally murmured.

"Such a sweet-talker."

"That's not even my best line."

"Wow."

"I know."

They stood in line at the counter and signed up just in time for the next departing tour. Dwight, their tour guide, seemed to take pride in saying everything in an overly loud speaking voice. "If you'll all step aboard the tractor trailer, we'll head out for our tour! Our first stop is the dairy barn, where we'll get our first up-close-and-personal look at a Holstein cow!" As he continued, Brooklyn shifted her gaze to Jessica in amusement of Dwight and his killer lungs but found her hanging on his every word, an expression of total and compete rapture on her face at the whole experience. It was so unexpected that it was endearing at the same time.

As the hour-long tour unfolded, they moved from one stop on the farm to another, learning about milking times, pasteurization, and care for the animals. They were escorted to a viewing platform, where they watched the milking process take place live and in person.

Through it all, Brooklyn found herself paying more attention to Jessica than the tour itself. A new energy overtook her that Brooklyn had never seen before, this kid-like enjoyment of the afternoon before them and all they were learning. When something especially interesting was presented to them, she'd look over at Brooklyn in excitement to gauge her reaction. Who would have thought? Take the sophisticated businesswoman out of her suit and the city she pretty much dominated, and you had a wide-eyed everygirl in jeans and a curve-hugging top. It was an intriguing discovery.

"Having fun?" Brooklyn nudged Jessica's shoulder with her own as they followed the group to the final stop on the tour: the nursery.

Jessica nodded, clearly swept up in it all. "Can you believe this goes on out here everyday? While we're juggling accounts in the land of concrete and high-rises, Dwight and the rest of these guys are out here under this blue sky moving the herd to the barn. At the same time, milk's being processed in the milk room and baby calves are being born. Each and every day."

"It's easy to get caught up and forget the rest of the world exists, isn't it?"

Jessica paused. "Sometimes I guess we need days like this one to remind us. I love how big the world is. How diverse the people in it can be."

"All right, all right," Dwight said, garnering the attention of the group. "This is usually most everyone's favorite stop on the tour, and I can't say I blame them! You'll be given a bottle of milk and the opportunity to feed a calf here in our nursery. Keep in mind that the calves are fairly zealous when it comes to their lunch, so you'll need to keep a firm grip on the bottle. They may nudge you with their head or shoulders as they drink, but that's just an instinct. Calves bump their mamas as a way of keeping the milk coming!"

Jessica couldn't remember the last time she'd enjoyed herself this much. As she kneeled down next to her assigned calf, she laughed at the way he wholeheartedly grabbed hold of that bottle and began sucking it down like there was no tomorrow. Good thing she'd been warned. As the calf drank, she stroked the back of his head soothingly and watched as his eyes slowly drifted up to hers. Right then and there, her heart melted. She was gone. She looked over at Brooklyn, who was studying her with interest from the fence.

"I want to take him with us."

"I can tell."

"He could be a city cow. He'd like the Village."

Brooklyn tilted her head from side to side in consideration. "Somehow I think he'd be happier out here."

Jessica nuzzled the back of the calf's neck. "You're probably right. There's half the bottle left. Do you want to try?"

"No, you finish. I like watching you with him."

"We are quite the pair."

Brooklyn snapped a couple of photos with her phone as Jessica smiled up at her, finishing up with her new best friend. Something warm attached to her and spread out as she fed that little guy. For the first time in a while, she felt totally and completely at ease. Relaxed even. In fact, she hadn't checked her phone or her e-mail once since she'd climbed into Brooklyn's car.

She reveled in this newfound ability to unplug. It turned out there were more pleasant ways to spend an afternoon than client calls and staff meetings. She smiled at the woman looking on from a few feet away because she was one of them. Next to her, the calf sucked the last droplets of milk from the bottle and trotted off energetically to join his buddies in the pen. Jessica stared after him fondly.

"Thanks for stopping. This was fun," she said to Brooklyn as she joined her on the perimeter fence.

Brooklyn tucked a strand of hair behind Jessica's ear. "It was, wasn't it? We haven't gotten to do too many fun things together. Yet."

"You just said yet, which I like."

Brooklyn looked skyward, playful now. "I did, didn't I?" She took Jessica's hand and threaded their fingers together. "I can be a lot of fun when called upon."

Jessica nodded, entranced by the way Brooklyn's eyes sparkled extra blue when she was happy. "I guess we'll find out."

"I don't want to pull you from your newfound second home, but we should probably hit the road. I'm supposed to pick up the key to the cottage by six."

"Want me to drive?" Jessica asked, overly hopeful.

"Not a chance."

As they walked leisurely back to the car, Jessica noted the way the fall foliage acted as a striking backdrop to the farm. The surrounding treetops burst forth with yellows, oranges, reds, and brown that blended together luxuriously. It really was a sensational display of autumn and, quite simply, breathtaking. She should make a point to notice nature more, she thought to herself and turned to Brooklyn to make that point. Instead, she found her studying the ground as they walked, pensive. And she understood that she'd drifted. "You're nervous, aren't you? For tomorrow."

Brooklyn stared straight ahead. "I think it's starting to hit me. Yeah."

"Don't overanalyze this. We're going to have dinner with a woman and her family, and then we're going to head back to the city."

"It sounds so simple when you put it that way."

"Then let's keep it simple. Can you do that?"

They climbed into the car, and Brooklyn studied the steering wheel before answering. "I'm glad you're here. I was nervous about it at first, bringing someone with me. But it was a good idea. You were a good idea."

Jessica sat back as the words sank in. Brooklyn didn't often let her guard down and allow her genuine emotion to show through. She was a fabulous flirt, an amazing kisser, and an adept conversationalist, but she rarely let things get sincere for too long. So the words carried weight with Jessica. They mattered. "Thank you for saying that. I'm glad you asked me." They stared at each other for a beat.

"Plus, you're not bad to look at, so there's that." And just like that, they were back to business as usual. The sincerity had been fleeting, but at least it had been there. It was okay. She could keep things light if that's what Brooklyn needed at this point. And this trip was all about Brooklyn, she reminded herself.

They drove for just over an hour before arriving in the quaint little town of Avon, Connecticut, their destination. And when she said quaint, she meant quaint. It was like something out of a sitcom. It had an actual Main Street, and was that a town library? Dear God, it was.

Brooklyn ducked her head and stared up at the buildings they passed through the windshield. "So this is the place. It's kind of picturesque, isn't it?"

"That's the perfect word for it," Jessica said, watching with fascination as a man disassembled his fruit stand from what seemed to be the lawn in the center of town. A woman turned the Open sign to Closed on the door to her flower shop. Dusk was falling around them and the town appeared to be tucking itself away. It seemed like the kind of place where things stayed the same. Stable. That was the word. And she liked that. She wasn't sure she could ever live in a place like Avon, but she'd sure enjoy visiting.

"So I did a little reading about this place before we came, and there is something I'd like to see before we lose light. Is that okay? It's kind of on my to-do list."

"That's more than okay," Jessica said, intrigued by the ongoing adventure.

Brooklyn drove them into a nearby park, where they parked the car and headed out on foot. The sky was holding onto the last bits of pink and orange. Because the temperatures were dropping, she shrugged into her green sweater jacket before following Brooklyn down a marked path. After a few moments, "Are you planning to tell me where we're going?"

"I'd rather show you. I don't think it's that much farther, actually. It should be—oh." And there it was, just around the bend in the sidewalk.

A beautiful covered bridge.

Underneath it, water cascaded down a series of stone steps into a stream. Jessica's heart sighed at the sight.

"Come on," Brooklyn said, taking her hand. "I've never actually seen a covered bridge in person, but I have this obsession with them. Samantha bought me a coffee-table book of them once for the loft."

As they made their way onto the bridge and looked out over the stream, Jessica was struck. "It's so peaceful out here. Almost like we're miles from any other living soul. Just listen." The air was crisp with the sound of only the water running beneath them and an occasional swallow call in the distance.

"It's called the Huckleberry Hill Bridge. It was built in the sixties for pedestrians to cross the pond. The lattice, there," she said, pointing, "isn't structural but, rather, decorative. It's a Town lattice-truss bridge."

"You know a lot about bridges."

Brooklyn lifted a shoulder. "I'm just really fascinated by them. Does that make me a dork? You can tell me if it does."

"Nope. It makes you even more interesting than I already thought you were."

Brooklyn studied her as if she was not quite expecting that response. "Thank you." She now looked about as serene as the landscape around them. With the sky purpling at the end of the day, they listened to the quiet for a few moments. It was the kind of easy silence that Jessica loved. After a minute or two passed, Brooklyn turned to her.

"As much as I love New York, and I do love it, there's something important about a place like this. There's, I don't know, a mysterious feel to it. It's romantic. I guess that's the word." And then she looked embarrassed as a blush dusted her cheeks. "That probably sounds ridiculous to someone like you. Hard-core city conqueror that you are."

Jessica shook her head slowly. "It sounds beautiful to me." She reached out and grabbed Brooklyn's hands, pulling her in and placing them behind her waist. They were face-to-face now, close. "In fact, *you're* beautiful, and I love that a place like this draws you in. I happen to like it here too."

"Do you know what I've wanted to do since I picked you up this morning?" Brooklyn asked. "When you looked so relaxed and sexy, wearing jeans on the curb?"

"I don't," Jessica whispered.

"This, right here. Wrap my arms around you, stare into your eyes. I could do this for hours and never get bored. It's the most intriguing thing."

"And that's all we'd do?" she managed, because she knew it wasn't.

"Nope."

Brooklyn inclined her head and leaned in slowly, hesitating just before she reached Jessica's mouth. It was the most wonderful yet torturous move ever. The buildup, the anticipation, the way they hovered, breathing in the same air, was more than intense. Jessica was helpless to the way her body trembled with Brooklyn so close. She craved the contact. She wanted that mouth on hers. Finally, Brooklyn closed the distance and seized Jessica's mouth in a searching kiss. The warmth of her was intoxicating, the way she tasted even more so. Jessica was lost, and that was perfectly all right. She skimmed her hands from where they rested on Brooklyn's waist up the sides of her body, across her shoulders until she cradled Brooklyn's face tenderly, returning the kiss that rendered her powerless, matching what she was given each step of the way.

She was totally and completely owned, and the realization surprised her to no end. She was used to being in control. She was known for her level head. But Brooklyn had a way of erasing all of that, and she'd be lying if she said it wasn't a little exhilarating.

As the sun made its final descent in the sky and the cold moved in around them, they continued to kiss slowly on the most romantic spot, this bridge, special to her now for an unforeseen reason. Not to mention, the kissing was some of the best she'd experienced and she lost herself in its unravel, in where it was taking her mind and her body.

When Brooklyn finally pulled her lips away, she blinked at Jessica, her eyes scanning her face, then the bridge, their surroundings. Jessica ran her thumb across Brooklyn's cheek softly. "What is it? What are you thinking?"

"I'm just memorizing this. You."

"Really?" Something about the sentiment warmed her and caused her to pull Brooklyn in tighter. It was one of those moments when she felt so ridiculously alive. The trees rustling, the water beneath them running crystal blue, Brooklyn in her arms all soft and amazing.

"Mhmm, really. Because being here with you, like this, is really nice. And if you don't agree, just fake it, okay?"

Jessica grinned at the concept. "But I don't have to fake it. That's the really good news. I'm a supporting player this weekend, though. This trip wasn't supposed to be about us, remember?"

"And it won't be. In fact, I got us separate rooms. I plan to behave really well. You'll be so impressed."

Jessica scrunched up one eye. "Probably smart of you. But I'm quite forgiving about slips in behavior. Just know that about me going in."

Brooklyn laughed and nudged her, looking playful and damn sexy as she did it. Maybe it was the fact that she'd pulled her hair out of the ponytail when they'd arrived at the park and it now fell around her shoulders generously. Or maybe it was the way her whole face transformed when she smiled.

Or maybe it was all of it.

It was everything.

Brooklyn stole another kiss and held it. "Let's take our photo before we go." She got out her phone and elevated it above them, leaning into Jessica. They smiled as Brooklyn took the picture.

And for good measure, they did a little more kissing under the Huckleberry Hill Bridge until the moon made its first appearance and ushered out the day.

Chapter Thirteen

It was just past three a.m. when Brooklyn bolted upright in bed, struggling to catch her breath. She looked wildly around the room, blinking against the darkness, trying to understand where she was and whether she was okay. She blew out a breath. It was just another nightmare. That was all. Only this one had been more powerful than any she'd had in recent history. She took another deep inhale, reminding herself from past experience that the best thing to do was to continue to breathe and wait for the dust to settle.

She was in the present.

She was safe.

And she was in control of her own life.

As life once again eased into the manageable square, she thought on the intensity of the nightmare. It made sense. As she'd drifted to sleep, she'd had a lot on her mind. Her overly loud inner monologue had been playing on a god-awful loop. So naturally her state of mind had exacerbated her typically unpleasant nightmare into a horrific one.

Tomorrow was, in all seriousness, weighing heavily on her mind.

This was the meeting she'd thought about, imagined, fantasized about on pretty much every difficult day of her childhood. Given, in her version, her birth mother had swooped in when she was still a kid to tell her that it had all been a horrible mistake. She'd then rescued her from whatever foster home she found herself living in and took her back home to live somewhere safe, secure, and happy.

Ironically, somewhere kind of like Avon, Connecticut.

She ran her fingers through her hair as she contemplated what to do with herself. She'd be so much better equipped to handle the next day if she could just work in a few valuable hours of REM. But there was no way she'd be able to sleep now. She was way too keyed up.

She looked to the wall to her right, knowing that just beyond it, Jessica slept soundly. She'd kept her promise and been good, keeping her hands to herself and opting for the second bedroom.

When they'd arrived at the little house on the lake, she'd been pleasantly surprised at its charm. While decidedly petite, it offered a cozy living room complete with soft quilts, a fireplace in the corner, and a set of rockers on the front porch. A small dock in the back extended a short distance into the lake. She'd sat on its edge with Jessica for a while before bed, talking, not talking. It had all been very peaceful. She appreciated Jessica's attempt to keep her mind off all that terrified her. And her presence and proximity definitely kept her mind moving.

Unfortunately, in that moment, there was no Jessica to save her from herself. And sleep wasn't going to happen. She could lie here for several more hours, twisting in insomnia, or do something she knew would be way more productive. So she made an executive decision, throwing the covers off her body.

Time for a late-night snack.

They'd picked up some groceries in town for breakfast in the morning, and she planned to take full advantage of them now.

She padded into the all-white kitchen and located a pan from under the countertop. A couple of eggs, onion, tomato, and pile of cheese later, and she was well on her way to a delicious three a.m. omelet.

There were noises coming from the kitchen. Jessica blinked against the dark. Why was noise coming from the kitchen? This couldn't be good. Her defense instincts kicked in. She checked the clock on her bedside table. It was still the middle of the night.

And someone was in the house.

She pulled on her silk robe, wishing to God it was longer and tougher looking, and grabbed the long umbrella she'd seen resting against the rear wall in the closet. *Think like a ninja. Think like a ninja*. Armed and determined to not show fear, she rounded the corner tightly into the kitchen. "Stop what you're doing right there."

But she paused, her heart thrumming wildly from adrenaline, because it wasn't an intruder at all. It was a scantily clad blond woman looking back at her from the stove in confusion.

"So I take it you're not hungry?" Brooklyn asked cautiously, raising her hands palms up.

She dropped the umbrella. "Thank God. I thought there might have been an intruder."

Brooklyn studied her curiously. "Because it couldn't have possibly been me? You know, the other person staying here? I was just unable to sleep."

Jessica felt somewhat defensive and tried to orient herself to the moment. "I don't know, okay? I'm half asleep and not thinking clearly yet. Strange town. Strange cottage. Strange noise. I leapt into action."

Brooklyn flipped whatever wonderful thing was in that pan, making the kitchen smell like heaven. She shook her head in wonder. "You're right about that. You totally leapt. It's kind of impressive the way you were ready to take me on. That umbrella isn't messing around either. I see why you chose it."

Jessica perched atop one of the stools at the island. "Mock at will, but you'd be extra grateful if I'd just saved your life."

"I'll give you that. Your valor scores points."

"Thank you. Now do you want to explain what's happening here, Julia Child?"

"Omelets are happening. They're all the rage in Avon, Connecticut." Jessica gave her a long look until she finally relented with a sigh. "Nightmare. Nothing new. And now I can't get back to sleep." The smile faded, and she pointed halfheartedly to her head. "Too much in here, you know? So I gave up. This is more fun anyway. Perfecting the great American omelet while the rest of the world slumbers? C'mon, time well spent. And I don't like to brag, but I'm getting pretty good. Generally, Samantha benefits from my talent. But tonight, you're the lucky soul. Want one?"

Jessica studied her, hating what she'd just heard and not wanting to do anything to make it worse. So she treaded lightly. "So that's pretty common for you? Nightmares?"

"I mean, only if you call 'all the time' common." She was smiling as if it weren't a big deal, which she was coming to learn was what Brooklyn did when she didn't want to go there. Pressing her to talk about it would just cause her to close up further. So she pushed past the issue. "Gotcha. As for the omelet, I think I have to have one. I can't say that I've ever enjoyed an impromptu middle-of-the-night meal before."

Brooklyn flashed a quick and wary smile. "Welcome to my world."

As they ate their omelets on the couch, Brooklyn managed to find a *Mary Tyler Moore* marathon on TV they could veg out to. As one episode merged into another, Jessica gently pulled Brooklyn toward her, so that her head lay in Jessica's lap. She allowed her hands to play softly with Brooklyn's hair, lifting it gently and letting it fall, the way she always found especially soothing when done to her. It wasn't long before she was met with the quiet sounds of deep breathing, indicative of sleep. She reached for the remote, careful not to wake the woman against her, and with a click brought the room to silence. She noticed the quilt on the back of the couch and pulled it over Brooklyn. Finally, she sank back against the cushion and closed her eyes, hoping against hope for a good day ahead.

Brooklyn watched each house number carefully as they slowly drove down the street of the picturesque neighborhood. Medium-sized houses that just screamed "New England" sat back from the street. They were accentuated with welcome signs, mature trees, and overflowing flowerbeds for that extra-added touch. It was a friendly neighborhood, but Brooklyn couldn't fully take it all in. It was as if she found herself in some sort of alternate universe.

"This is it," she said finally, double-checking the address with the one in her phone. Her heart thudded wildly away in her chest, and her mouth was exceptionally dry. "2902 Tanner Well Park." She eased the car up the long driveway and blew out a slow, steadying breath. Just push through, she repeated to herself internally.

Jessica squeezed her knee and gave her an encouraging smile. "Come on. Let's go."

"I need just a second." She checked herself briefly in the rearview mirror. "Are you sure I'm dressed okay? I shouldn't have worn jeans. I don't know why I did."

"Hey. Look at me. You're beautiful. We've been over this. It's a casual dinner in someone's home, and your outfit is perfect for that."

Brooklyn nodded, knowing Jess was right. But she couldn't resist a last glance in the rearview mirror. She moved several strands of hair around arbitrarily. You know, just for good measure. This was, after all, the biggest moment of her life thus far.

It was now or never.

With a deep inhale, she exited the car and walked steadily up to the front porch with Jessica just behind her. It didn't feel quite like walking, more like floating. Her mind felt empty like a blank sheet of paper, but at the same time it took in every detail. A strange arrangement she'd made with herself.

It was mid-November, and appropriately, a smiling Pilgrim stood just to the left of the charming blue door, and a wooden turkey hung in its center. A small stuffed scarecrow sat on a nearby bench, all homey additions. Before she allowed her nerves to bubble over entirely, she pressed her finger to the doorbell and waited.

And waited.

She exchanged a look with Jessica. They did have the time right, didn't they? Jessica held up one hand, signaling her to be patient. At last, the door opened.

And all Brooklyn could do was stare.

Cynthia was slightly shorter than she was, but the blond hair, the light-blue eyes were so eerily familiar, it was startling. She'd never seen anyone who looked so much like she did. But of course that made sense. She'd never met anyone who was biologically related to her before.

Time seemed to cease. In reality, it was probably only a moment or two that they stared at each other, but it felt like forever. Finally, Cynthia attempted a smile, but the tears that brimmed in her eyes overshadowed it. "Hi, Brooklyn."

"Hi. "

"I'm Cynthia. I don't know what to say. I had it all worked out and—"

"It's okay."

"It's just so nice to finally meet you." A pause, in which she brought her hand to her mouth and back down again. Brooklyn understood that she was just as nervous. "Would it be all right if I gave you a hug?"

Brooklyn nodded and braced herself against the feel of her mother's arms wrapping around her. For the first time.

It took her a moment to respond, to hug her back, but when she did, the tears she'd sworn she'd hold back filled her eyes automatically. She took in every moment of that hug, the one her childhood self would have given anything for. Her actual mother. It was the most surreal exchange she'd ever experienced.

Cynthia released her finally and stepped back, wiping the tears from her cheeks. Brooklyn did the same, and they laughed nervously at the mirroring of emotion.

Jessica hadn't said anything. But Brooklyn felt her there, just behind her, and it steadied her ship.

"Please come inside. Both of you."

"Oh, I'm sorry. This is my friend, Jessica. She was nice enough to come with me so I wouldn't have to make the trip alone." Reality was inching back into focus now, and her voice sounded somewhat normal. That was something.

"Nice to meet you, Jessica," Cynthia said, extending her hand.

Jessica accepted it. "Thank you for having us to your home. We've enjoyed what we've seen of Avon so far."

As Jessica and Cynthia made small talk, Brooklyn couldn't stop looking. Studying. Cynthia's hair was pulled up into a soft twist, but she guesstimated that it was just shorter than shoulder length when down. She had a freckle just beneath her left eye that reminded Brooklyn of the one next to her own ear. She ran her hand across where she knew it resided.

She also seemed young. But something, a look behind her eyes maybe, wasn't. It showed wisdom, scars. She could identify.

Cynthia turned to her tentatively. "I thought we could talk for a little bit, before you meet the rest of the family. They're not here right now. I asked them to give us time first."

"Okay. Sure."

Jessica gestured to the bench on the front porch, visible through the window. "Why don't I spend some time on that bench catching up on e-mail and give you two a chance to talk?"

Brooklyn grabbed her wrist and met her eyes. "Please stay." She turned to face Cynthia. "I'd like Jessica to stay, if that's all right with you." For whatever reason, it made her feel stronger to have someone from her own life there by her side. To center her. To remind her of who she was. And Jessica could do all those things for her.

"Of course. Whatever you prefer. Why don't we have some coffee? I have a pot brewing. I'm a big fan of hot beverages. Especially on cool days."

"Me too. The hot beverages."

She led them through the entryway and down a short hall. "What about you, Jessica? A coffee drinker?"

"An addict, actually. It's my favorite vice, though I've been trying rather abysmally to cut back."

Cynthia smiled over her shoulder. "I think you and I are going to get along well."

The hallway opened up into a sunken family room that was everything you'd think a quaint home would be. It sported an arrangement of two leather sofas and a comfy armchair, large paintings on the wall, a fluffy rug in front of a giant stone fireplace. Tons of natural light flooded in from three large windows, making the room feel cheerful. Somewhere a family might gather. It was a nice place. It hadn't escaped Brooklyn that there were photos on the wall of children, but she refrained from heading straight to them in overt curiosity. She would have time for that, she reminded herself. Don't get too far ahead.

While Cynthia prepared three cups of coffee, they chatted easily about the changing season and the peacefulness of Avon. Safe topics. But that didn't mean there wasn't an undercurrent of something so much more important in the air. It wasn't just an elephant, but a whole herd.

Cynthia seemed eager to accommodate, rushing around to make sure she got their coffee specifics just right. She'd also put out an assortment of breads all from the local bakery for them to snack on. Brooklyn took one out of courtesy but didn't know that she could actually eat, given the circumstances.

Cynthia also seemed kind, and smart. And while Brooklyn still felt herself very much on guard, she couldn't quite get past the fact that this woman was put together. Personable. When she'd always suspected such a different story.

As they settled into the sofas in the living room, Brooklyn and Jessica on one and Cynthia on the other, the mood seemed to shift. She wasn't the only one nervous, she could tell. But for whatever reason, it seemed they were both desperate to cover that up. Act like this was a normal occasion, when it was anything but.

Finally, Cynthia took control. "It couldn't have been easy for you to come here. Believe me, I get that." She paused. "I imagine you have questions. I'm not sure how much you know, so why don't we start there."

Brooklyn could do that. While she did have a lot of questions, she had one in particular that she needed to ask above all others. Because it wasn't just a question, it was *the* question. "I guess I'd like to start with why did you give me up?"

Cynthia nodded and studied her coffee before raising a thoughtful gaze. As her eyes settled on Brooklyn, she started to speak. "I found out I was pregnant when I was nineteen. A sophomore in college who knew nothing about life. I had just learned how to do my own laundry, if that helps put it in perspective. In order to pay for my tuition, I'd taken out student loans and was already in debt. At night, I waited tables at a pizza place to have enough money for groceries. I was barely keeping my head above water, and some days I wasn't even doing that. And then I got the results from an at-home pregnancy test. I was beyond shocked. At first, I thought I could find a way to make it work. To keep you. I thought I could drop out of school and work full-time. But I didn't exactly have any job skills, and waiting tables didn't come with medical benefits. And as my very vocal parents pointed out, babies need medical care."

"So your parents were against you keeping the baby? Me. I'm sorry, this is all very strange for me."

Cynthia managed a smile through the angst that telling the story seemed to bring about. "Trust me, I sympathize." She continued. "My parents were never easy people to get along with. And yes, they were big advocates of adoption. They pointed out all of the things I couldn't give you and made it clear that they weren't willing to help. At all. In fact, if I did keep you, they planned to cut me off entirely."

Brooklyn sat forward. "I see. Was my father in the picture at all?"

She nodded. "Yes, actually. The whole way. He was a student as well and a year ahead of me. We were in a relationship at the time. He was very supportive but didn't have a lot to offer financially. But it didn't matter. We decided we were going to make it work."

"Can I ask his name?"

She paused, and a glimpse of unease crossed her face. "Aaron. His name is Aaron."

Brooklyn blew out a breath as the new information settled. Her father's name was Aaron. "So what made you change your mind?"

"The further along I got in the pregnancy, the more real you became to me." Her eyes began to fill, the emotion taking over. "I was no longer wanting things out of life for just me. I was wanting them for you, and I had to consider that. Aaron and I broke up, and that was hard. Though he was still planning to help, I felt very alone at that point in my life. Brooklyn, it was the most difficult decision I've ever made, but in the end, I just thought someone else could do it better."

And there was the blow.

Because no one ever had. That someone never came along.

It wasn't Cynthia's fault. She'd made the best decision she could with the information in front of her. Brooklyn knew that on a rational level, but it still stung. Maybe because she sensed her discomfort, Jessica took Brooklyn's hand and held on tight. Brooklyn sent her a glance of gratitude and offered a squeeze to reassure Jessica that she was managing.

She turned back to Cynthia. "What happened next?"

"My parents put me in touch with an adoption agency. We agreed that it would be a closed adoption and I wouldn't have access to further knowledge about how you were doing or where you were. That part was hard, but it's what the counselors recommended. Open adoptions are more common now, but back then they were less prevalent."

Brooklyn opened her mouth to ask another question, but they were interrupted by the sound of the front door opening. Cynthia closed her eyes as if to brace herself. "I'm sorry. I thought for sure we'd have more time."

Brooklyn held out a hand to reassure her. "It's okay. We can finish later." She stood as a man, most likely Cynthia's husband, entered the room with a younger man and a girl trailing behind him. She focused on the older of the two men first. He was tall, with light-brown hair and a neatly trimmed beard. Smiling, she extended her hand in greeting. "Hi, I'm Brooklyn."

He accepted her hand and held on, fixated on her.

Cynthia stepped forward. "Brooklyn, I'd like you to meet my husband."

"Aaron Mathis," he supplied, holding her gaze. *Aaron*. She looked to Cynthia in question and saw the answer right there in her eyes. *Oh, God*. Finally, Cynthia nodded in response.

"I was planning to explain first. I thought we'd have time."

Brooklyn turned back to him, blown away. "You're my father."

He nodded, seeming just as mystified. "I can't believe I'm standing here looking at you. All this time and you're here." He was smiling, but there was a weight to it. He stepped forward and pulled her into a hug. Numb. That's how she felt as this man, her father, held onto her. His arms were strong and he smelled faintly of cologne. But that's all she was aware of, really. Those were the only two facts her mind seemed capable of comprehending. As he released her, she was introduced to Ethan, her brother, and Catherine, her younger sister. Apparently, she went by Cat. They were both friendly but forgivably nervous.

Her brain struggled to catch up.

It hadn't made the leap yet.

As these new people smiled and hugged her, she did her best to reciprocate, to go through the motions of how a normal person would conduct herself in this situation, but the details were all running together in her head, and the walls felt like they were somehow getting closer and closer by the minute. She felt a hand on her back and turned in time to meet Jessica's gaze. And she took a minute there, because those understanding eyes reeled her back in. If she could just focus on Jessica, everything would be okay. "I think it's time to eat," Jessica said quietly, redirecting her.

And that made sense because as she looked around, she saw a series of large containers laid out on the counter in the kitchen. They'd brought dinner with them. And Ethan and Catherine, Cat, she mentally corrected, moved easily about the room, getting the trays of food prepped and ready for everyone. She watched them and couldn't help but take in how comfortable they were in the space. They knew which drawer to open without hesitation as they brushed past each other in such an everyday manner. It was their kitchen. This was their home. And these were their parents.

And she was visiting.

She looked around. This should have been her family in some faraway parallel universe.

"Do you drink tea?" Cat asked, smiling as she filled the glasses in front of her. Brooklyn remembered Cynthia saying she was seventeen. Her hair was blond, but a darker shade than her own. She was a beautiful girl.

Realizing she'd been spoken to, Brooklyn blinked, trying to clear her head and remember the question. "I'm sorry?"

"I was wondering if you'd want iced tea with dinner. We're having BBQ from our favorite place in town, and iced tea goes really well."

"Oh, sure. That'd be great."

Ethan ruffled Cat's hair as he grabbed his plate and headed to the table. He was clearly a typical older-brother type. She remembered Cynthia saying on the phone that he was a recent engineering grad. He looked like the all-American frat boy and a lot like Aaron. As he passed Brooklyn, he paused a moment and dropped his voice. "I'm sure this has to be a head trip for you, but I'm really glad you came. Maybe when the initial stuff is out of the way, we can grab dinner sometime in the city. Talk one-on-one."

It was a nice gesture. "Yeah. Let me know when you're in town."

He inclined his head to the island of food. "Grab a plate and load up. We're pretty informal around here."

She did just that, attempting small talk along the way, but there were a lot of eyes on her, and the pressure to hold it together was crushing. It wasn't long before the six of them were seated around the long kitchen table, she and Jessica on one side, Ethan and Cat on the other. Aaron and Cynthia sat at either end.

"So Cynthia tells us you're in advertising?" Aaron asked.

She finished chewing a bite of brisket. "That's right. I work at a small firm in Soho with some friends."

Jessica raised one finger. "She's says it's small, but they're growing exponentially and landing some pretty high-end accounts. The company's garnered a lot of attention in the industry lately."

Brooklyn raised an eyebrow at Jessica, who smiled and went back to her dinner. It was an important compliment that she would file away for later.

"Well, that's very impressive," Aaron said. "You should be proud of yourself. Do you live in the city?"

"I do. In a loft a few floors above the office, actually. It's technically an artist's loft by zoning law, but that's not generally enforced. Plus, we like to think of ourselves as artistic."

Cat shook her head in awe. "That's so cool."

"It is a pretty cool space, yeah." She turned to Aaron. "What kind of work do you do?"

"I'm an engineer. I look at repair processes for the aviation industry, and Ethan, here, is coming to work for me starting this month."

Ethan nodded. "I'll try not to embarrass the old guy with my newfangled technology."

Aaron tossed his napkin at his son in playful revenge.

Brooklyn knew the day would be an emotionally taxing one, and she'd been ready for that. She'd be meeting her mother for the first time. But the fact that her parents were happily married, that they'd gone on to have other kids and live their perfect little lives was more than she'd bargained for. Because they'd done it all without her. The longer she sat with that information, the more cheated she felt. And while she smiled and nodded and tried to laugh at all the right places in the conversation, that's what she kept coming back to.

Cheated.

None of this was hers.

Her mother hadn't built some new life for herself after giving her up. That was a scenario Brooklyn could have come to terms with. It's what she had *prepared* herself for. But instead, Cynthia had gone on and lived the life that should have been theirs. She just did it on her own.

Brooklyn ate quickly. Not because she was hungry, but because the faster dinner concluded, the faster she could make a polite exit, because the clock was ticking on how long she was going to be able to hold it together.

"We haven't talked about your family," Cynthia said, covering Brooklyn's hand with her own. And there was that smile again. While it was a kind smile, the warmth of it taunted her now, given what she knew. Inherently, Brooklyn got that it wasn't fair of her to fault Cynthia. But with emotion running high, she wasn't exactly in a position to apply proper perspective.

"No, we haven't."

"What are they like? Your parents."

"I guess nonexistent is probably a pretty accurate descriptor." She stared at her plate, at the food she hadn't been able to eat after all. She couldn't sit there any longer with the perfect cookie-cutter family, straight off the cover of *Home and Garden* magazine, and describe to them all the ways she'd been unwanted from the time she was born.

Cynthia tilted her head in question. "What do you mean by nonexistent?"

"Oh. I mean I don't have any family. I lived in the system until I aged out at eighteen." She looked on as the color drained from Cynthia's face, but it wasn't like she could stop now. The information flowed out of her like some sort of broken faucet. "I went through five different foster homes, six if you count that first adoptive family that returned me because I was asthmatic, though at least they gave me a last name. I finally finished out my time in a group home. It was the kind of place where you hoped against hope that your roommate wouldn't steal what little you had to call yours. And I'm happy that you all have each other, sincerely, and I'm sure Christmases were great around here, but forgive me, because they were a little harder on me."

And then she realized herself and paused, gathered her composure. She looked around the table, at the shocked and sympathetic faces staring back at her, but that just added insult to injury. She didn't want to be pitied. She tried to make it better. "I'm sorry for that. I'm really very sorry. You have all been more than hospitable to me, but if you'll excuse me, I think I need to go now. I'm not feeling so great. Jess?"

She stood and without hesitation headed blindly down the hallway, scooping up her bag as she passed it. It was as if there were no air, and if she could just make it outside, she would locate some.

As she spilled out onto the driveway, she took a few deep, centering breaths. Whether she was experiencing a panic attack or asthmatic symptoms, she wasn't sure. For good measure, she took a couple of drags from the inhaler in her bag and placed her hands on the roof of the car, to anchor herself. She closed her eyes and continued to breathe, in and out, in and out until she registered footsteps behind her. She turned as Jessica's arms encircled her and exhaled slowly into the comfort they provided. She shook her head vehemently as Jessica released her. "That was rude, what I said to them. It was horrible of me, but I couldn't sit there anymore, Jess. I just couldn't." She covered her mouth in realization. "God, what they must think now."

Jessica shook her head. "Don't worry about that at all. I explained a little bit more after you left. They're upset to hear you weren't raised in the loving home they always imagined you were. But they're upset *for* you, for themselves, but not at you. See the difference?"

"I don't know."

"You need time and they get that. Come on. Let's get outta here."

She nodded. Jessica was right. She was smart. Listen to Jessica.

They drove back to the cottage in silence, and that time allowed Brooklyn to slip further into herself. But the more she thought about the facts in front of her, the more despondent she felt. When they arrived back at the cottage, she headed out the back door and found a spot for herself at the edge of the dock.

Jessica wasn't sure what to do, but leaving Brooklyn on her own to rehash the day over and over again didn't seem like the best plan. "Want some company?" she asked from a few feet behind her on the dock.

Brooklyn didn't so much as turn around. "Actually, no, if that's okay. I think I just need to be on my own for a while."

"Whatever you need. Maybe later we can watch a movie."

"Maybe." She turned then. "I'm just worried that I'd be horrible company."

"Good news, because there are no requirements for watching movies with me."

Brooklyn attempted a smile, but it wasn't even close to authentic, and it pulled at Jessica in the worst way. If she could just do something to make this easier for Brooklyn, who deserved so much better than life had given her, she would do it in a heartbeat. It was the most helpless feeling. "Okay. I'll be inside if you need me."

Brooklyn didn't answer.

She set up her laptop at the table in the kitchen that offered a perfect view of the lake. She tried to work, she really did, but her eyes drifted automatically to the dock and the woman who was hurting. Brooklyn had been sitting out there for over an hour now, and Jessica ached for her. She seemed so dejected. Raw.

An hour later when she returned to the dock, she didn't ask for an invitation. Instead, she simply sat next to Brooklyn and took her hand. They didn't talk for a while, which was fine. Sometimes silence was the way to go. After a long stretch of it, she turned to Brooklyn. "Catch any fish?"

Whether she wanted it to or not, the beginnings of a grin tugged at Brooklyn's mouth. Only slightly, but it was something. "Surprisingly, no."

"Might be your technique."

Brooklyn didn't say anything, just stared out onto the water. Jessica let a few moments pass before trying again.

"I thought your parents seemed like nice people."

"I agree. But let's not call them my parents. Seems kind of a misnomer to me. I think the requirement is greater, don't you?" The edge in her voice now hadn't been there earlier, and Jessica recognized it as a coping mechanism. Brooklyn was refusing to let them in.

"They didn't know, Brooklyn, what your life would be like when they made the decision to give you up. If they had, I don't think they ever would have gone through with it."

She laughed sardonically at that. "I kind of disagree. And it's not like they were alone in the matter. I was given up twice. Let's not forget." She held up the number two like it was a trophy. She was cavalier now, almost mockingly so.

"But that had nothing to do with you," she pointed out. "You have to know that."

She shook her head and turned to Jessica. The depth of emotion in her eyes spoke volumes. She might have sounded cavalier, but it turned out she was feeling anything but. "Didn't it, though? Think it over for a second. *No one wanted me*." She let those four words hang in the air, and it seemed like they were ripped from the deepest part of her. The tears now fell freely down her face. "In all that time. No one wanted me. Let's just be honest about that part. I need to be."

Jessica took a minute to recover from the gut-wrenching words Brooklyn had just spoken. What do you say to that? You don't say anything, she realized. She pulled Brooklyn into her arms, where she continued to cry as one uncontrollable sob after another overtook her. But she held on. She had Brooklyn and she wasn't letting go.

Brooklyn cried for several minutes until, finally, the sobs lessened in intensity before subsiding entirely. It wasn't long before her breathing evened out once again. But Jessica didn't let go. They stayed just like that, Jessica stroking her hair, letting her know she wasn't alone. Finally, Brooklyn pulled away and stared out at the water, her tear-stained face glistening in the waning sunlight. She wiped the tears from her cheeks and blew out a slow, steady breath.

"I'm sorry for that," she said quietly, still not looking at Jessica. "I don't know why I'm letting it get to me this way. I don't usually. I'm stronger than this."

"You're a human being, Brook, and you have feelings." She tried to make Brooklyn see things another way. "You were dealt a raw deal, and it's okay to acknowledge that. But at the end of the day, I hope you can find pride in who you've become despite the setbacks."

Brooklyn shook her head. "You probably grew up with a two-car garage and a dog. You couldn't possibly understand what you're talking about here."

"You're right. I did have a much easier time of it than you did. I would just hate for you to walk away from this day focused on the wrong information."

"I get that you're used to being in charge, Jess. I do. But this isn't your company and I'm not some doting employee, so please don't instruct me on what it is that I need to focus on."

Okay, that stung, but she could take it. "I know who you are. I also know that you're upset and you're angry."

"Thank you, Dr. Phil. I'll keep that in mind."

That's when Jessica understood that maybe she was just making things worse. "I'll be inside."

But she hadn't covered half the distance back to the cottage when she heard Brooklyn's voice. It was quiet, but it was there all the same.

"I'm sorry. That was uncalled for. I'm just in a weird space tonight. And I shouldn't be allowed to talk to anyone."

"It's okay," Jessica said.

"I just need a little more time to think."

"I know."

❖

It was dark outside.

And Brooklyn was cold.

She'd been sitting on the dock for a couple of hours now, as emotion after emotion took its turn with her.

A full moon painted the landscape around her with blue and white. It cast large shadows across the water, the trees, the cottage behind her. It really was a beautiful night, even if it didn't feel especially so.

She was hurt.

That's what it all came down to when she whittled her way to the core of her feelings. Not that she was given up for adoption; she'd come to accept that fact years ago. But that while she'd been completely on her own, they'd had each other. They'd celebrated birthdays, school dances, and family picnics. And when the holidays rolled around, they'd spent them as a family.

What was she supposed to do with that information? On a certain level, it would have been easier to find out that her mother had been struggling through life, addicted to drugs or moving from homeless shelter to homeless shelter. Because that was a woman who didn't have much to offer her. But the loss of this Disney Channel version of her parents, who were good-looking, and smart, and kind cut so much deeper.

The fantasy had been true. Her fictional family *could* have been hers. It just wasn't.

She felt a little like she was drowning. But the small piece of rope she clung to was the reminder of the people she did have. Mallory, Hunter, and Samantha had never let her down. She did have a family. They just came to her a little later in life.

She threw a glance behind her to the illuminated cottage. There was a woman in there who was beginning to matter to her more than she ever thought possible. Someone who made her heart stop when she smiled. Who was smart and witty and fun. And had a way of keeping her guessing, which she loved.

And Jessica might bring just as many questions to the table as she did answers, but tonight, that didn't matter. Brooklyn stared at her through the window. God, she was stunning. Her hair was down tonight, which wasn't a typical Monday-through-Friday occurrence. This was Weekend-Jessica, whose laid-back persona she seemed to like even better. As she watched her work at the kitchen table, a thought occurred to Brooklyn. If she had to guess, she'd say Jessica chose the spot so she could also keep an eye on her. Because Jessica did that. Looked out for her. That's who Jessica was.

And now the recriminations over how she'd treated Jessica earlier were out in full force. She'd lashed out at her, the woman who had traveled all this way, given up her time to be here for her. The woman who was still looking out for her.

She needed to make things right.

After sitting for so long, her muscles screamed out as she stood. She stretched languidly and headed inside. She hadn't realized how cold it had gotten, but the effects of the weather finally made it all the way to her brain. She would need thawing out. She flexed her fingers, noting that they were almost entirely numb.

Jessica looked up at her as she came through the door. Cautious. Brooklyn couldn't fault her for that. "Hey," she said softly.

Brooklyn shrugged. "Getting cold out."

"I was about to bring you a blanket, but—"

"You were afraid I might take your head off."

"I was going to say you came in before I could, but the head thing was a secondary fear."

"I'm sorry about my Sybil impersonation out there. This has nothing to do with you, and I wish I hadn't spoken to you the way I did."

"In good news, I'm a New Yorker. I can take it."

"Doesn't mean you should have to. I'm glad you're here. If I were on my own right now, I don't know how I'd…" She trailed off, but that was okay. Jess seemed to get it.

"I'm glad I'm here too."

A pause then as they stared at each other, still a bit on uneven ground. Jessica wanted to fix that and take Brooklyn's mind off the events of the day. There would be time for Brooklyn to deal with what she'd uncovered, but it didn't have to be tonight. She took the initiative. "Why don't I open some wine?"

Brooklyn offered the tiniest hint of a smile. "I can't think of anything on planet earth I want more than a drink to settle me down, but I'm frozen solid. I'm going to grab a hot bath first, if you don't mind, and attempt to turn back into a normal person."

"I don't mind at all."

It was just a few minutes later when Jessica heard the sound of running water. Brooklyn had seemed in better spirits when she'd come back in, but it was clear just by looking at her that the day had run her over.

She opened a bottle of merlot and poured two generous glasses into oversized globes from the cabinet. "Wine is ready when you are," she called. She took a deep inhale from the glass and let the aromas wash over her.

"Will you bring me a glass?" she heard her call back

"I can do delivery, I suppose," She carried the glass down the short hallway and knocked once on the door to the bathroom.

"Come in."

"Wine-delivery girl," she said as she entered, but then stopped short because Brooklyn was already in the tub. She felt the blush touch her cheeks, embarrassing as the reaction was. But it wasn't long before a whole lot of other somethings began to stir within her. "I'm sorry. I didn't realize you were already in the bath."

"Stop it. I'm covered with bubbles and completely decent." This was true. She was, but the knowledge that Brooklyn was completely naked beneath that thin layer of soap had her mind and body on high alert. It was an overly sensual image and had Jessica reminding herself to breathe. Her job was to be there for Brooklyn, to offer support, not to imagine her naked in a bathtub. Not that she could control the reaction she was having, because it was a powerful one.

Brooklyn stared back at her oddly, almost curiously. Had she missed a question?

"I'm sorry. Did you say something?" Jessica asked.

"I was just wondering about the wine? Are you planning to keep both glasses? Because in kindergarten, we learned to share."

"Right. The wine." She covered the short distance between them and handed Brooklyn the glass. But her mouth went dry and her brain stopped working properly as she glimpsed tops of breasts peeking out from beneath the bubbles. "Here you go."

"Thank you." Brooklyn took a slow sip from the glass and closed her eyes. And whether it was meant to be or not, Jessica found the move incredibly alluring, which also meant she needed to get the hell out of there. They had a "being good" pact that she was not planning to break.

"I'll let you soak for a while."

"Stay," Brooklyn said to her retreating form. "We can just talk."

Jessica turned around slowly. "That's not what would happen if I let myself stay."

Brooklyn met her gaze, and Jessica watched as recognition flared. Her eyes darkened and her lips parted in subtle response to the implication. The heat in her stare seemed to suck all the air from the space between them. It wasn't long before the quiet room was overflowing with sexual tension. Thick and potent.

"I'll let myself out," Jessica said quietly.

Brooklyn only nodded.

It was a testament to their relationship, the way they were able to get back on track after the sexy bathtub encounter. When Brooklyn emerged in shorts and a T-shirt awhile later, Jessica thanked God it was oversized. They cooked dinner together and found their way back to a light, friendly banter. The day had been killer, and a little everyday-casual was like water in the middle of a desert. They both seemed to zero in on the need for it.

"You're over-seasoning that chicken," Brooklyn said as she glanced into the pan.

Jessica let her mouth fall open. "I'm sorry. I thought I was in charge of sautéing the chicken and you were on mac-and-cheese duty. Did I misread the memo?"

Brooklyn pinched her side playfully. "No, Ms. Lennox. I'm just looking out for my dinner. I haven't eaten anything all day."

"Ouch. Then you shouldn't abuse the chef."

"I shouldn't. You're right." She closed the distance and kissed Jessica. "Sorry for the abuse, Chef Sexy."

Jessica exhaled slowly, enjoying the attention, the flirtation. "Totally worth it."

They had an easy dinner at the table and avoided the discussion of the day's events. Jessica thought her chicken came out a little dry, but Brooklyn didn't seem to mind.

"Who's your favorite superhero?"

Jessica stared at her in amusement. "Excuse me?"

"When you were a kid."

She thought for a moment. "Wonder Woman, I guess."

Brooklyn's eyes danced with an idea. "You'd make a perfect Wonder Woman, you know. Maybe for Halloween."

Jessica scoffed. "I don't dress up as characters. Ever."

"Yet," Brooklyn said happily.

They laughed and turned back to their dinner, eating peacefully, Etta James playing from the radio Jessica found in the closet. They'd be heading back to the city in the morning, and Jessica wondered if it had been a worthwhile trip. Maybe over time, Brooklyn would be able to put aside her feelings of resentment and forge an actual relationship with her parents.

"Jess?"

"Yeah?"

Brooklyn set her fork down. "I'm not exactly doing well with all of this, but you've steadied my listing ship. You let me lash out at you outside, and then you turn around and joke with me in the kitchen. So…thank you."

Sincerity from Brooklyn meant a lot.

And Jessica was learning to pay attention when moments like this happened. Brooklyn was letting her guard down more and more lately. "You're welcome. The thing is, I happen to think you're pretty great. More than that even. I happen to *like* joking in the kitchen with you. I'm also starting to realize there's very little I wouldn't do if you asked me."

Brooklyn wanted to answer, to say something back, but the lump in her throat stood boldly in the way because the words Jessica had just spoken were powerful. To have a woman like Jessica, who was smart, successful, and beautiful, say she'd do anything for her was a lot to accept. Though she was beginning to. The feelings that welled up inside as a result were unfamiliar. She didn't quite know what to do with them. So instead of lingering in the moment, of flailing any further, she nodded and cleared her plate.

Seeming to take the cue, Jessica assisted her and they put the kitchen back together in quiet silence. But a new heaviness pervaded the air now, as if that ever-present question mark were back. For Brooklyn, that wasn't the case. Though she'd just sidestepped the opportunity for a serious conversation about Jessica's feelings for her, it didn't mean she didn't feel those same things too.

And it felt nice to feel something for someone.

As she wiped down the counter, Brooklyn was hyperaware of Jessica's every move. The way her hair fell across her eye when she leaned down to put the last pan away. The faint scent of her apple-scented lotion. The fullness of the lips she'd explored thoroughly just the day before under the covered bridge. The sensations these things inspired, coupled with the sentiments Jessica had just expressed, had her head swimming. And it wasn't as if the day hadn't been full of head swimming already.

She tossed the rag into the sink and washed her hands. "If it's okay with you, I think I'm going to go to bed. It's been a tiring day, and I didn't exactly get a ton of sleep last night."

"Of course. We can pack the car in the morning and drive back to the city. We should try to be on the road by ten."

Brooklyn nodded and moved to Jessica, brushing her lips softly and backing away. "Good night."

"Sweet dreams. Oh, and Brook?"

Brooklyn took note of the shortening of her name. No one besides Jessica called her Brook. It was nice and communicated a familiarity that made something within her flare. "Yeah?"

"If you decide on middle-of-the-night television, wake me up. I'm in."

She offered a soft smile. "Deal."

As she lay in the darkened room, watching the shadows that the tree branches cast across the ceiling, she also saw the images of the day flash in succession in her mind. She curled into herself as the requisite sadness those images inspired was upon her instantly. She had a lot to wade through, but the underlying takeaway was that she was alone. She felt so hopelessly alone that it became impossible to feel.

And she needed to.

She needed that connection that she'd never really experienced. The risk had been too high. She'd held herself back. But tonight, that risk didn't matter. She needed to lose herself in sensation. She needed physical validation.

She desperately wanted.

God, did she want. That part she knew.

But for once, she needed to let herself feel what it was like to be wanted in return.

❖

The covers were too much against Jessica's skin and she shifted beneath them. The night was cool, but her body was acutely aware of even the slightest touch, which kept the bouts of sleep she managed short and ineffective.

As she lay there, floating somewhere between asleep and awake, her thoughts traveled in a direction all their own. They drifted languidly to her encounter in the bathroom with Brooklyn, her body wet and soapy. She felt it all over. The unmistakable heat in Brooklyn's eyes, the expanse of skin peeking out from the tub, the bubbles across its surface. She sucked in a breath, folded the offending covers back, and let the cool night air settle lightly around her. She ran her fingertips across her stomach, the outside of her thighs.

Better.

It had been somewhere after two a.m. the last time she'd checked the clock, but sleep hovered just out of her grasp. She closed her eyes anyway and heard the click of her door opening. Blinking against the darkness, she pushed herself up.

And there she was, Brooklyn. She came farther into the room and sat on the edge of the bed next to Jessica. The moonlight illuminated her face. Her eyes were wide, luminous, searching as she delicately brushed the hair from Jessica's forehead.

Jessica touched her cheek, because Brooklyn looked too beautiful not to. "Hi."

"Hey."

"Are you all right?"

Brooklyn nodded, a reassuring smile touching her lips, but her eyes communicated more. There was a hunger there, that much was unmistakable, and something else too. Something Jessica couldn't even begin to interpret.

She watched in captivation as Brooklyn grasped the hem of her T-shirt and pulled it slowly over her head. She sucked in a breath at the sight of Brooklyn topless in front of her, the visual more picturesque than anything she'd ever seen. She traced Brooklyn's jaw with her finger and watched as her lips parted in rapt response.

She understood Brooklyn's intentions. And now had a few of her own.

"Are you sure?" Jessica whispered to her. While she'd been ready to make love to Brooklyn for some time now, dreaming of it, in fact, she needed the reassurance that they were on the same page.

Brooklyn met her gaze. “Jess,” she said longingly.

Jess. The use of her name was a simple request, and Jessica understood. She slipped her hand from Brooklyn’s jaw, down to her neck and around the outside of her breast, never breaking eye contact. She circled underneath it, tracing the curve as Brooklyn hitched in a breath at the sensation, her eyes darkening. “Please,” she breathed. Jessica covered the breast with her palm fully, pushing against it, her thumb circling the nipple slowly. She eased her other hand into Brooklyn’s hair, pulling Brooklyn’s mouth to hers as intensity took over, spilling from her fingertips.

Brooklyn came willingly, her lips already parted in anticipation of the kiss, which seemed slow and fast at the same time. How was that possible? Jessica saw the world through a lust-induced fog. Her body thrummed with arousal, and a steady heat moved through her and sharply downward. But she was doing her damndest to keep control, to not get ahead of herself.

It was one of the harder tasks she’d taken on in her life, because this woman was so alluring it was impossible not to get carried away.

Brooklyn was on top of her now, kissing her with skilled precision, their legs intertwined. Brooklyn’s thigh was between hers. And that was good. It was what she needed. She pushed against it, a slow, addictive rhythm taking shape as the tension within her built steadily, climbing with each subtle movement.

Jessica wore only a tank top and panties, but Brooklyn was over it. She pulled her mouth from Jessica’s and tugged the offending shirt over her head. “God,” she breathed as she descended on Jessica once again. She placed open-mouthed kisses down the length of her neck, her collarbone, and settled decidedly on her breasts. She took her time, kissing, teasing, circling. Jessica ran her fingers into Brooklyn’s hair, but she was coming undone. She shifted beneath Brooklyn’s touch, seeking release from the wonderful torture. She rocked against her and a moan escaped her lips.

“I’ve got you,” Brooklyn murmured, glancing up at her before she continued her tantalizing exploration, looking damn sexy in the process. She kissed down Jessica’s stomach and slowly pulled the underwear down her legs, totally in control. She eased her hands behind Jessica’s thighs and parted her legs gently.

As Brooklyn kissed the insides of her thighs, Jessica attempted to steady her breathing, which was pointless because when Brooklyn's thumbs skimmed up her legs and across her center, she flashed white. She heard a quiet whimper and realized secondarily that it was hers. She began to move against the touch in more determined desperation. Seemingly encouraged, Brooklyn lowered her mouth to Jessica and allowed her tongue to play, explore, bringing her to the edge and then backing off purposefully.

Jessica closed her eyes and tossed her head against the pillow, helpless to the onslaught, but Brooklyn held her in place. Finally, she pulled her in more firmly, providing direct attention where Jessica needed it most. And with a direct swipe of the tongue, it all came undone. The orgasm ripped through her hard and fast, a powerful jolt of pleasure that overtook her entirely. It pulled a sound from her, a wordless cry that communicated the heights she'd just been carried to.

As her breathing evened out, Brooklyn lingered, bringing her back down again gradually, reverently. Jessica looked up at her as she moved back up the bed. She reached out, brushing the hair back from Brooklyn's forehead. She shook her head slowly as Brooklyn settled in alongside her, placing a kiss beneath her jaw.

"You continue to surprise me," Jessica said, still in recovery mode, her nerve endings tingling in the most wonderful way.

"I can say the exact same thing. I've never met anyone so beautiful. So sexy." Brooklyn skimmed an arm across her stomach.

Jessica stared at the ceiling, still reveling. "That was…I can't even think of a word. This requires a 'greater than' symbol from math class."

"Were you good at math?"

"I don't even know. My brain isn't giving me answers to anything right now." She kissed Brooklyn softly and felt her grin against her mouth. "What?"

"All of those business suits and finally."

Jessica laughed and cradled Brooklyn's face. "What does that mean?"

"Confession time."

"Excellent."

She propped her head up on hand and looked down at Jessica. "I used to stare at you in those ultra-sleek designer suits you'd always wear and imagine getting you out of them and having my way with you. Just like this. You made it very hard to concentrate on my job." She traced the outside of Jessica's breast with her finger.

"Yeah? That happened more than once?"

Brooklyn nodded most decidedly, her eyes widening. "You have no idea."

Except she did.

She remembered some very vivid fantasies of her own and was ready to experience them firsthand. She captured Brooklyn's mouth in a kiss that didn't take long to ignite them all over again. She'd relinquished control long enough, and she was ready to take it back.

But it wasn't long before Brooklyn gently grasped Jessica's wrists, halting their action. "Wait, wait, wait. Can we pause for a second?"

Jessica searched her face. "Are you okay?"

"I just…"

"What is it?"

"This is new for me."

Jessica felt like she was a step behind and her mind raced to catch up. "What do you mean? Are you saying sex is new for you?"

"No." A small smile flashed and then faded, replaced by what seemed to be trepidation. Brooklyn took a minute, her eyes searching Jessica's as she tried to explain. "I've had plenty of sex. But sex *like this*, I mean, is new for me." She held Jessica's gaze before closing her eyes against the vulnerability of the confession.

And that's when Jessica understood.

Brooklyn had never let anyone make love to her before. Feelings were involved this time, and that upped the ante. Her heart squeezed at the implication, and she brushed the hair from Brooklyn's forehead tenderly. She looked both incredibly beautiful and vulnerable, and that combination was a hit of something powerful. Brooklyn wanted to trust her. She was letting her guard down in a way she hadn't for anyone else.

And it was everything.

"Hey, look at me."

As Brooklyn's blue eyes settled on hers, she continued. "You know I would never do anything to hurt you, don't you?"

Brooklyn nodded.

"Let me show you something." She picked up Brooklyn's palm and kissed the inside of it before placing it over her heart. "Do you feel that? That's you."

"That's me," Brooklyn repeated, as if telling herself.

Brooklyn felt a lot of things in that moment. Excited, terrified, safe, loved. Whoa. Stop and rewind. That last word had popped into her head without preamble, but it resonated, smacking her squarely in the chest.

Jessica made her feel loved. She took a moment to revel in that realization.

And Jessica wanted her to be sure.

But the answer came to her easily. She closed the distance and kissed Jessica, tenderly this time, communicating feelings that she hadn't yet articulated with words. But it was a bold step all the same.

And that seemed to be all the encouragement Jessica needed.

They continued to kiss, only it wasn't long before the word tenderly slipped from the playing field altogether. As the seconds marched on, the level of heat between them escalated and took over. Jessica didn't hesitate and shifted them until she was on top. Brooklyn ran her tongue across Jessica's bottom lip, gaining entrance into the mouth that she never could get enough of.

As the tantalizing kissing continued, her muscles turned to liquid as Jessica moved against her, settling her hips between Brooklyn's legs, her sleep shorts the only thing left to separate them. The intense aching only grew as Jessica worked her magic with the ever-so-subtle movements of her hips. She heard herself moan quietly against Jessica's mouth and pushed her hands into silky, dark hair, gripping softly.

Jessica slipped a hand between them and into the shorts Brooklyn wore, closing her eyes in reaction to how ready Brooklyn already was. As she stroked her slowly, Brooklyn swore at the contact, at Jessica touching her for the first time. The effect was dizzying, and she was quickly swept into a tidal wave of wonderful need. She pushed back against Jessica's hand, desperate for more.

Jessica kissed the base of her neck. "You're overdressed," she whispered, and refocused her attention, pulling the shorts from Brooklyn's hips and settling herself back on top, a place she seemed very much at home. Jessica dipped her head and circled a nipple with her tongue, the effect of which was only magnified by the delicate tickle of her long hair across Brooklyn's stomach. She ran her palms down the smooth expanse of Jessica's shoulders, loving the feel of her skin against her own, the way Jessica's weight pressed her snugly to the mattress.

She wrapped her legs around Jessica, craving more contact, her body on fire. Taking the cue, Jessica began to move against her, but at an agonizingly slow pace. Brooklyn whimpered, pulling her in more, anything to accelerate the pace, but Jessica held strong. Jessica wrapped one arm all the way around Brooklyn and with the other reached between them. And then Jessica was inside her and the sensation was breathtaking. She dropped her gaze and found her eyes, the deep blue that reaffirmed their connection.

"Jess," she breathed, which earned her a reassuring smile. Little jolts of pleasure overtook her with each firm movement, and though it was her instinct to close her eyes, to let herself get lost in the sensation, she couldn't take her eyes from Jessica. She was too beautiful, the slashes of moonlight highlighting her features. The orgasm built steadily from her fingers and toes inward until she was flying uncontrollably, pleasure unleashed. She arched into Jessica, who pushed deeper, keeping them connected, pressed tight.

Brooklyn gasped for air, unable to say a word as she lay there, the feelings that swirled so raw, so new. Jessica rolled them onto their sides and kissed Brooklyn softly. "I'm falling in love with you," she finally whispered, stroking Brooklyn's cheek with her thumb. Brooklyn nodded and turned her face to kiss her palm because that sentence carried so much. She tried to answer, to say something in return, but the words simply wouldn't come.

So instead she turned on her side and pulled Jessica's arms tightly around her. That way, as they drifted off to sleep, she wouldn't see the tears that were already gathering in her eyes.

Chapter Fourteen

The number of voice mails Jessica had waiting for her at the office that next week was insane. While Bentley was good, he apparently wasn't that good, and the office had taken a hit with her off the grid for most of the weekend.

"Did you get the mock-ups to Preston over at Retro Records? They're not a major account, but they could be one day. We need to pay proper attention where they're concerned."

Bentley shuffled through the handful of papers on his desk. "Uh, let's see. Retro Records. Yes. Preston signed off and we're good to go with production."

"Fabulous. Make sure Nancy and her assistant know we're good to move forward." She rested back in her chair and rubbed the muscles bunched at the base of her neck. They'd been working for several hours, and morning had shifted into afternoon without a lunch break. "And with that, why don't we take thirty minutes and I'll inhale something resembling a salad from the deli?"

"I'll call it in."

"You're my favorite."

"You say that to all your assistants."

She tilted her head. "That's true. But you're definitely the most handsome."

That got her a smile.

He picked up their lunch from across the street and they ate together in her office. Bentley studied her throughout. "You haven't said a word about your weekend. I've given you every opportunity, but now I'm having to turn in my man card and ask for details."

She shook her head and moved the lettuce around in her plastic container. "There's not a lot to tell. I think it wasn't as easy for Brooklyn as she was hoping it would be, meeting her parents."

"What, are they crackheads? Criminals?"

"The exact opposite, really. Perfect. Kind. Together. I think it hurt her to see what she missed out on."

He considered this. "I don't blame her for that. I'd be so pissed I don't know what I'd do."

"Neither do I."

"Is she going to see them again?"

"I'm not sure about that part. Before we got back to the city, she already had a handful of voice mails from her birth mother. She called her back, but the conversation was brief and formulaic."

"She needs time to process."

"You're suddenly all-knowing over there."

He threw his sandwich wrapper across the room, sinking it perfectly in the wastebasket. His hands sailed into the air in victory. "And all-talented. Check that out. But the trip was good, you know, for the two of you?"

She got up to toss the rest of the salad in the trash. She really needed to stop frequenting that mediocre deli. "That's the thing. I think it was."

"I sense the word 'but' about to happen."

"It's early, and she's cautious." She sighed and sank into her leather desk chair. "And I might have jumped the gun."

"In what way?"

"I told her I was falling in love with her."

He froze as if not quite sure what to do with the information. "That's news. Did you mean it? Or was it just something to say in the moment? A carried-away-by-passion kind of thing? 'Cause I've done that."

"You are such a dog." She shook her head but moved past it, because it was a valid question and one she'd asked herself as well. She nodded. "I really think I did mean it." And then she amended. "No, I know I did."

"And that's even bigger news. Color me shocked over here."

She didn't want it to, but his reaction stung. "Because I'm not capable of adult emotion or—"

He held up a hand. "I know you're capable. I just didn't think you'd let it happen. You're so wrapped up in…I don't know."

She came around the front of the desk and rested against it. "Say it, Bent."

"The world of Jessica Lennox."

She nodded, absorbing the barb. They were talking as friends now, off the clock, and that meant he was giving it to her straight. "Okay, I'm self-involved generally. I get that. But do I have to be for the rest of my life? I see the value in how she approaches the world and who she is, and I just want to be a part of that." She ran her hand through her hair in frustration. "Do you know how badly I want to call her right now? Just to say hi. I'm resisting that urge because I don't want to send her running for the hills because I'm ahead of myself."

He shook his head at her.

"What now? What's with the head-shaking? Because I swear to God, I will tackle you, heels or not."

"Since when have you ever let anything stand in your way?"

She felt the smile tug as she straightened. "Valid point. Think I might need to actually leave at five o'clock today."

He nodded. "I'll alert the media."

❖

"Wednesday hates me," Brooklyn said as she dropped her head dramatically onto her desk.

"You know who else is going to hate you?" Samantha asked. "Your noggin, when you have to pop five aspirin for what you're doing to it over there. Maybe lay off the super histrionics? Just a thought."

She glared at Sam. "Histrionics are called for in some cases. And this would be one of them. I have two weeks to make this campaign pop and make Foster love us. Want to marry us. Have fantastic-looking children with us."

"What are you talking about?" Hunter said from where she sat atop the kitchen counter, her computer in her lap. "The stuff we have is unique, and they're going to be blown away."

"Lofty prediction," Mallory said, without even turning around from her desk. "As soon as we let ourselves get too complacent, that's when we lose the account. Let Brooks pout, it's part of her creative process." She swiveled around to face the room. "She panics, freaks out, and then comes full circle with a dynamite project."

"You're right." Hunter turned back to Brooklyn. "Proceed with the head-banging."

Ignoring the other two, Samantha pulled a chair up to Brooklyn's desk. "You've had a lot on your plate lately. Maybe knock off early today? Give yourself some time? You've had a big week."

"That's the last thing I need. I have several calls to return, a storyboard to dictate, and the final moments of the Foster spot to come up with. What I need is—" Her phone buzzed from where it sat atop her desk. She glanced at the readout and her skin tingled. How Jessica was able to do that via a text message still mystified her completely, but then again, much of how Jessica made her feel was uncharted territory.

"Is that who I think it is?" Samantha asked, her voice lowered on purpose.

She nodded. She'd told her friends about the weekend, about the meeting with her parents and how she'd fled the scene. But only Samantha knew about Jessica accompanying her on the trip, and only Samantha knew about the new turn their relationship had taken. And that was by design. She didn't want to upset the already-dicey waters if she didn't have to. It was better to bide her time and figure it out as she went.

It was also best to keep busy. Keep moving. It's what she did to stop herself from thinking too much. About meeting her family, about how unsteady she felt when she thought about Jessica and where things were heading.

Jessica, who seemed to come with a giant exclamation point as of late. Every feeling she elicited was that much stronger now, and that included fear. Brooklyn let her thoughts drift momentarily to the woman who'd occupied most of her daydreams since returning to New York.

The first thing she thought of was the dark-blue eyes that shimmered when Jessica felt passionately about something. She was smart and knew how to command a room. She was beautiful and her hair smelled intoxicatingly of strawberries. She was sexy for days, witty, caring, and had the cutest smile when she lost herself in a moment. It felt a little like waiting for the other shoe to drop. And wouldn't it? The other shoe *always* dropped.

"Are you going to talk to…?" Samantha inclined her head in Mallory's direction, keeping her voice low. "You can't keep dodging the issue, Brooks. That's not fair."

"So you think I should disrupt everything when we have this big account to worry about?"

"I'm thinking more about you. I think this whole thing matters to you a lot more than it used to, and it's time to face that. *Talk to her*."

"I think you should talk to her too," Mallory said, turning around in her chair.

Brooklyn opened her mouth and closed it again, as her heart thudded away. "You do?"

"I know the first meeting wasn't ideal and no one wants to walk into a surprise like that. But now that you've had time to process, maybe it's not such a bad thing to give it another go. You said the messages she left for you were all understanding, sympathetic. It seems like she's really trying to turn things around."

Brooklyn blew out the breath she'd been holding. *Cynthia.* Mallory was talking about Cynthia. Brooklyn blinked several times to clear her head and adjust. Relief really was a fantastic thing. The Mallory battle was not one she was in the mood to take on. And if she knew that Brooklyn was sleeping with their sworn enemy, it would be a battle indeed. "You know, I think I still need time. I don't know how I want to handle things on that front quite yet."

"That's understandable. If you need anything, more time off or—"

"Yeah, I know." She didn't mean to cut Mallory off, but it seemed like the stakes were growing moment by moment. Sam was probably right. She did need a break. She grabbed her bag. "I think I will take a few minutes after all."

Samantha squeezed her hand. "Good idea."

After the short elevator ride home, her phone buzzed again. This time it was an incoming call from Jessica. She smiled and clicked over.

"Hey."

"I hope I'm not bothering you."

Just the sound of Jessica's voice had the world slowing down for her, and she relaxed into it on reflex. "Just a little. But for some people I make an exception."

"What do you have going on?"

"This week has been crazy. We have this really intense competitor who keeps us on our toes over at Savvy. It's crazy."

"Sounds crazy. I don't know who she is, but I'm sure she would back off, sign all her clients away if it meant she'd get to lay eyes on you."

"If only I'd known it was that easy."

Jessica laughed, and Brooklyn sank comfortably into the couch at the sound. "Can we have dinner tonight?"

God, she wanted to see Jess, but she had a lot on her agenda for the day that she hadn't gotten to. She was planning a late-night work session. "I may have to work."

"Me too. But guess what's considered two birds with one stone?"

"What?"

"Have dinner with the competition. Scope them out. Surely, that's a good business strategy, no? Meet me at Puzzles."

She laughed. "Bad idea."

"You owe me, remember? The night we first met. You promised to reciprocate."

Brooklyn sighed. "Crafty. Very crafty making this about money when you already have so much of it."

"Come talk to me over wine. We can flirt. It'll be a good time."

The idea of going back to Puzzles, the start of it all, was tempting. She remembered the excitement of that first night. How taken she was with Jessica. How fabulous their conversation was and how off-the-charts attractive she found her. And those feelings had only grown exponentially since. She got a little shot of energy at just the thought. "Fine. One drink and then I really have a lot of work to get back to."

"That's all I'm asking for."

❖

Jessica walked to Puzzles from her apartment, taking in the sweet smell of the sugary nuts the street vendors always sold in the fall. The Village was bustling with folks wrapped up in jackets, moving to their end-of-day locations. She passed a group of twenty-somethings laughing and nudging one another before they headed into the restaurant across the street. Jessica stared after them, wondering what it was like to belong to a group of friends. She'd never really made time for much of a social life, and she felt the tug of regret now.

Brooklyn had that, she thought to herself, with the girls at Savvy. She didn't like that she was envious, but it was there all the same.

When she arrived at Puzzles, she blinked against the dim lighting of the bistro and scanned the tables, realizing she was the first to arrive. Jazz music played quietly from the sound system, and the place was quite a bit busier than the last time they'd been there.

She took the liberty of ordering a bottle of Chianti from the bartender and found a cozy table off to the side where they could talk. When Brooklyn walked in, her face was carefully blank. Her hair was pulled up today, and she wore a blue army-style jacket and jeans that made her look entirely too cool for Jessica and her black business skirt and heels.

Brooklyn's eyes settled on her and she smiled. And there it was, that little click that she'd been missing. Brooklyn leaned in and kissed her cheek before settling into the chair across from her. She was such a sight for sore eyes, it almost hurt to look at her.

"So, hi," Brooklyn said, resting her chin in her hand and grinning in the most endearing fashion. "How was your day?"

Jessica stared, still taking her in. It had only been a couple of days, but she'd missed her. "Better now. What about you?"

Brooklyn took a sip of wine and sat back in her chair, contemplative. "Getting there. This really is a charming little place." Her smile faded. "But if I'm being honest, it's really good to see you. I think that's a big part of it."

"How are you feeling, after the trip?"

"That's a big question. I think I need some distance from…my family. Regroup a little. Those words sound so weird. *My family*."

"I can imagine. And us? I was worried we'd moved too fast, that I might never see you again."

Brooklyn took a deep breath and shook her head. "I don't have answers. But I do know this. I want to sit here with you. And drink this wine. And ask you about your day. Because that sounds about perfect."

Jessica relaxed into her chair and let it all go—her worry, the lack of control that had her reeling. Because what Brooklyn had said made sense. There was no need to overthink it. "You first."

"Let's see. I walked with Hunter and Elvis through Central Park early this morning before work. We do that a couple of times a week. It's kind of our thing."

"I'm sorry, Elvis?"

"Elvis is our dog. Her dog. But kind of ours. The Savvy mascot, if you will. Does The Lennox Group have a mascot? I'm going to imagine not."

"No."

"Yet another disadvantage."

"I'm still learning."

"Well, clearly." Brooklyn snagged a crumble of manchego from the cheese tray. "What did you do this morning?"

"Straight to the office. I was there by six a.m."

Brooklyn nearly choked. "I'm sorry. Did you just say six a.m.?"

"I did. There's a lot to do."

"Yeah, but in my world it would still be there at eight."

"Yet another way we're different."

Brooklyn regarded her. "I like that about us."

It was a huge compliment, and Jessica let it settle. "Me too. Disorganized free spirit meets structured corporate rock star."

"Or creative race-car driver seduces uptight high-rise dweller."

"Or that." Jessica laughed.

They talked for the better part of an hour, nearly killing the bottle entirely, hitting topics as far-reaching as Jessica's weakness for anything sweet and Brooklyn's preoccupation with Anderson Cooper's wardrobe.

"I mean, it's always pristine." Brooklyn laughed. "Have you noticed that? He could be anywhere—earthquake, flood, a third-world country—but he's always perfectly coiffed. Prada adorned. How does he do it?"

Jessica finished the wine in her glass. "Must be a gift."

"You're kind of like that too, now that I think about it. Always put together. Dark hair always just so. Do you ever just lounge around your place in pajamas?"

"Not too often, no."

"Apropos of nothing, I just want to make out with you right now." Jessica laughed out loud at the non sequitur. "And if I remember correctly, your place is just a couple of blocks from here."

"Aww. Drunk-Brooklyn is kind of cute, I have to say."

"Not drunk. Tipsy, maybe."

"Well, Tipsy-Brooklyn. I'll find the bartender and pay the check."

Brooklyn scoffed and took out her credit card. "You will not. You have a short memory. This one is mine. And we're square now."

"Are we?"

Brooklyn paused, seeming to understand the double meaning. "I think we're getting there."

❖

The view from Jessica's balcony was one of the more picturesque views of the city that Brooklyn had ever seen.

Breathtaking. That was the word for it.

How had she missed this before? Jessica's condo looked out over the Hudson River, and the lights from the city reflected beautifully off its surface. It was the perfect contrast to the bustling city she could still feel all around them. It was approaching ten p.m., but the world still seemed so alive and awake. There was this sort of hum she felt, yet was somehow removed from. She liked taking it all in, tucked away like this in a West Village high-rise.

Jessica joined her outside, settling into one of the two cushioned chairs that faced out. Brooklyn turned from her spot at the railing and shook her head. "How do you not live out here? It's gorgeous. I don't think I'd ever leave."

"I do come out here after a long day to decompress. It helps me get my head together. I watch the water and feel myself coming back down to earth. It's cold out, though. So I don't last very long on nights like this." She wrapped her arms around herself.

"I have an idea for warmth. And I'm known for my ideas." Brooklyn walked to her and settled herself on Jessica's lap. "I like the thought of you out here all thoughtful and relaxed after a tough day of taking over the world. But you know what I like more?" She brushed the hair from Jessica's forehead and focused on the lips that had preoccupied her since she'd laid eyes on Jessica at the bistro. God, she could lose herself in this woman.

"What?"

"Being out here *with* you." She caught Jessica's mouth with hers and then sank into the luxury the kiss inspired. "Kissing you like this." Jessica wrapped her arms around Brooklyn's waist and pulled her closer. "For as long as I want." She went in again, this time tracing the bottom of Jessica's lip with her tongue until she was granted entrance and began to explore, to play. There was one thing she was more than confident in. She loved kissing Jessica. She could do it all night and never grow tired of it.

When they'd arrived back at her place, Jessica had shrugged out of the skirt's matching jacket but still wore the lavender dress shirt, and it turned Brooklyn on all the more. She unbuttoned the top button and ran her palms across the top of her chest up to her collarbone. Finally, pulling her mouth away, she held Jessica's face in her hands and looked down at her. The well of emotion that slammed her as she stared into Jessica's eyes was staggering.

And the expression on Jessica's face mirrored what she felt swirling within her. "Please don't be afraid of me," Jessica said quietly.

Brooklyn shook her head slowly. "It's not you that I'm afraid of. It's what you do to me, make me feel. It's like I'm free-falling, and while that's okay in life, I don't take a lot of risks with my heart. But I'm working on it. I don't want to run from you, Jess. I'm not planning to."

"Good."

She nodded, determined to find a way herself. After one last searing kiss that left them both breathless, she stood and offered Jessica her hand. Once inside, they kissed their way to Jessica's bedroom, where they took their time.

That night, Brooklyn let go of the fear she'd been clinging to since their trip and allowed herself to simply feel. As a result, each caress was more intoxicating, each kiss that much more potent. And at last, when she clung to Jessica in sweet release, she understood that there was nowhere else she'd rather be.

She watched the sun rise early that next morning as she lay in bed, Jessica sound asleep in her arms. As she stared out in reverence at the reds, pinks, and oranges that eased out from the water's surface, she understood that this was the start of something new and wonderful. She kissed Jessica's temple and stroked her hair as she stirred quietly beneath her touch.

And in that moment, she came to know the meaning of love.

Chapter Fifteen

Brooklyn burst into her loft apartment at the end of their workday completely out of breath. "We have to straighten up. Quick! Time got away from me."

Samantha stared back at her in skepticism from her spot at the island. "We do?"

"That's what I'm saying. Jump up. Give me a hand. Why aren't you jumping?"

But Samantha simply blinked back at her. "I can't jump until you explain yourself. Your hurricane impersonation is amusing, but it raises questions. Number one being since when do *you* want to clean up? Ever? Out with it, Brooks."

Brooklyn blew out a breath. "Jess is coming over. We made plans this morning for dinner, and since she's never seen our place, I thought why not here. But then I got caught up in all the Foster details and the clock kept moving. Damn clock. Bottom line. She doesn't fully know about my total lack of organization. I mean, I've hinted at it, but—"

"She's not aware that you have an aversion to hangers and their function in our society?"

"Right."

"And 'disorganized' is a total understatement, by the way."

"Got it. I can cop to that if you'll jump. I need clothes-hanging intervention, and you're the goddess of all things homemaking. There. Will you help me?"

Samantha relented and thank God for that, because she'd invited Jessica for dinner at seven and it was ten minutes until, and while

Samantha's half of the apartment sparkled, hers was woefully at a disadvantage.

Clapping her hands once, Samantha took charge. "Okay. Grab the pile of clothes on the floor, toss it into the closet, and close the door. That's step one. I'll make the bed because I'm not even sure you know how."

"That's not true. I can make the bed."

"Fabulous. I challenge you to prove it sometime."

Samantha was right. She should make more of an effort, and she would. If she could just get through this meet-my-apartment encounter with Jessica, she'd turn over a new leaf.

In the next eight minutes, they straightened. They dusted. They cleared off the things Brooklyn had strewn about in haste, and when they were done she hugged Samantha and kissed her cheek loudly. "You're the best roommate ever. Now, what will we have for dinner?"

"Really?"

"I know. I know. This is so not your problem, but just give me your opinion. I don't want her to think I'm a horrible cook—"

"Not horrible," Samantha pointed out. "Just limited. Just make her a grilled cheese. You rock at those."

"Right. But I've done that."

"Oh. Well, order takeout from China Moon. Everyone loves takeout. Especially during the workweek. It's workweek crack."

"Perfect. You're the smartest loftmate ever." Brooklyn hightailed it for the phone before glancing back over her shoulder at Samantha. "Moo shu pork for you with an egg roll cut in half?"

"I'm invited?"

"Of course you're invited."

Samantha studied her, and a slow smile started on her face and began to grow. "This is new. I don't even know what to do with all this. You're new."

Brooklyn paused mid-dial, curious. "Define."

"You raced around this place to get it all ready. You're nervous about what Jessica will think and are allowing the two worlds to overlap, which you never do with women you date. Ever. You're hard-core serious about her."

Brooklyn nodded a few times too many as something warm began to spread out within her. "I am. I really am. And I may be crazy and it may come back to bite me later, but I'm going for it, you know? Because I think about her all the time when I'm not with her, and I've had to stop myself from drawing little hearts on my brainstorming pad. Little hearts, Sammie. I'm twenty-eight years old and I'm drawing little hearts."

Samantha eyed her in approval. "This looks good on you, Brooks. Happiness."

Happiness.

That's exactly what this was. That's what Jessica inspired in her. And no, her life wasn't perfect, and Lord knows she wasn't either. But she'd found a little bit of wonderful here, and she planned to hold onto it.

An hour later, the three of them sat around the once-broken table she'd found at a secondhand store. The granite slab that acted as a tabletop had been another fantastic find at a junkyard in Queens. Brooklyn had spent a weekend with Hunter restoring it, and voila, they had the most perfect table in all of Soho.

She looked on, content, as Samantha and Jessica moved from the polite, get-to-know-you questions and were now firmly rooted in the land of mutual interest. Half-empty Chinese-food cartons dotted the table, and a bottle of merlot that Jessica had brought was nearing its end. The vibe was relaxed and comfortable.

Jessica tucked a strand of hair behind her ear as she chatted with Sam. "The show is sold out for the next eight months, but I'm positive my cousin would set aside tickets for us. She's offered several times. I've just never taken her up on it."

"Seriously?" Samantha said, leaning forward eagerly "You don't understand. *Elevation* is the one show I'm dying to see." She shifted her focus to Brooklyn. "Haven't I told you this? "

Brooklyn held her hands up in defense. "You told me several times. I can vouch."

Affirmed, Samantha bounced back to Jessica. "So your cousin, Jenna, who I may or may not have Googled several times in the past, is she older or younger than you?"

"She's several years younger."

"Likable?"

"Definitely."

"Single?"

Brooklyn shook her head in amusement but stayed out of it.

"In a pretty serious relationship," Jessica answered apologetically.

"Damn it." They laughed because Samantha was ridiculously cute sometimes, especially when she pouted. "But no worries," she said, straightening. "I'm actually in the beginning stages of seeing someone myself."

"Wait. How am I just hearing about this?" Brooklyn began the process of clearing the table, and Jessica jumped in to help.

"Because you've been a little preoccupied lately."

Brooklyn dropped her shoulders in defeat. "This is true and I'm sorry. But no more. Tell me."

"Remember Libby from 2B?"

"Libby from the building across the street? She's hot."

Jessica's mouth fell open in mock outrage, and Brooklyn answered with a teasing poke to her ribs.

"'Tis the one. She bought me a drink at Showroom, and we have plans for dinner on Thursday."

Jessica perched on one of the barstools at the island. "Dinner and not drinks. Means she's investing in the evening. That's a good sign."

Samantha pointed at Jessica. "I like her. Let's keep her around."

"I like her too," Brooklyn said, lacing her arm around Jessica and kissing her temple.

Jessica smiled up at her. "So I can stay?"

Brooklyn held up one hand. "There'll be a vote later."

"I'll vote yes," Samantha said as she rounded the island to the sink.

"What are we voting on?" a voice from behind them asked. Brooklyn turned to see Mallory closing the door and hanging her coat on the rack. As she swiveled back around and came farther into the room, her eyes settled on Jessica and she froze. "Oh. Hello."

"Hi, Mallory," Jessica said, standing. She was smiling, which meant she was making the effort. Brooklyn offered her hand a little squeeze before jumping into action, all the while trying to figure out the best way to handle this unexpected snag. She knew there'd be a moment when she'd have to explain things to Mallory, and she knew it would be soon. She'd just imagined it would happen on her terms, when she was prepared.

Mallory's eyes moved from Jessica to Brooklyn to Samantha. She seemed to be taking stock, a tiny smile plastered on her face. "I don't mean to interrupt. I was just finishing up downstairs and wanted to run something by you," she said to Brooklyn.

"No problem. We can chat. Are you hungry?"

Mallory eyed the containers, a bit too focused on them. "Uh… no. I'm fine, thanks. Tell you what. We can talk about it tomorrow instead. You're clearly in the middle of something."

Brooklyn saw the hurt in Mallory's eyes as she turned to go, and it stabbed at her. "Mal, I have time now. What did you want to go over?"

A coolness had settled over her by the time she turned back. "I wouldn't say this is the best time to discuss our clients, would you?"

As Jessica looked on, she felt bad for Brooklyn and annoyed at Mallory all in the same stroke. "I can take five," she offered, trying to salvage the scene around her. Brooklyn appeared guilt-ridden. Samantha looked shocked, and Mallory was bringing the temperature in the room down a good twenty degrees. These girls were best friends, and she was obviously in the way of that. She glanced at Brooklyn. "Or, you know, maybe we should just call it a night."

Mallory held up a hand. "No. It's clear your presence takes precedence here. Have a fabulous night, everyone. We can reconvene in the office tomorrow."

Brooklyn closed her eyes as the door to the loft closed with a thud.

"I'm sorry," Jessica said.

"For what?" Brooklyn attempted a smile, but it was halfhearted at best. "I invited you to dinner, you came. That's not exactly an infraction."

Samantha pushed herself onto the counter. "She'll get over it, Brooks. I mean, I think she will." She turned to Jessica. "Mallory's just not completely…sold on your intentions."

"Samantha," Brooklyn warned her.

"No. Sam's just being honest. That's fair." Jessica considered the facts. "I don't have a great track record with Mallory. I've behaved competitively in her presence in the past and probably didn't make the best first impression. And you know what? I'd probably feel the same way if the situation were reversed and Bentley were seeing someone from a rival agency."

"You're sticking up for her," Brooklyn stated.

"I guess I am."

Brooklyn stared for a moment before kissing her, catching Jessica by surprise, not that she was complaining. "What was that for?" she murmured quietly.

"For just getting it."

Samantha jumped down. "You know what? I'm going to give you guys some time. I happen to have a rather passionate romance novel in my room that requires all my attention."

"It was fun to hang out," Jessica said, meaning it one hundred percent. It had been the highlight of her week, seeing Brooklyn's place, getting to know one of her best friends.

Samantha paused at the door to her room. "I'm a little surprised to say this, but likewise." She smiled, tapped the doorframe twice, and was gone.

Once they were alone, she turned to Brooklyn. "Want me to talk to her? Mallory."

"Probably not the best course of action. I'll handle it tomorrow. It'll be fine." But the thing was, Brooklyn had the most expressive eyes of anyone she'd yet to encounter, and the concern they gave off spoke volumes over her words. She took Brooklyn's face in her hands and ran her thumb across her cheek gently.

"Thank you for inviting me over."

"It's nice having you here. Wanna stay?"

God, did she want to stay, but it probably wasn't for the best quite yet. She needed to give Brooklyn's friends a chance to maybe work through this new development, and apparently you never knew who could drop by. They seemed to have an open-door policy, which was a little overwhelming.

"I have an early morning tomorrow. Rain check?"

Brooklyn's face took on understanding. "Okay. But let's do a little of this first. It's only right." Warm lips found hers, and they spent the next few moments tangled up in each other, a common occurrence of late.

Finally, pulling her lips free, Jessica sighed with pleasure. "And on the eighth day, God created kissing."

"Damn right he did," Brooklyn murmured, going in for more.

❖

The following morning at Savvy brought with it very little conversation. Brooklyn kept her head down and her attention on her clients, but it would be impossible to say that she didn't feel the tension thick all around her.

Mallory only spoke to her in the course of "have to" moments, and Sam and Hunter had been snapping at each other over nothing. The office was out of whack, and she was probably responsible.

"All I'm saying is if you use the last of the creamer, say something. Then we can add it to the reorder list. It's really kind of simple."

Hunter flipped her laptop closed. "Fine. I can do that."

"See? Was that so hard?" Samantha asked in overly sweet voice.

"Don't push it."

Deciding to seize the moment, Brooklyn gathered her courage and turned to Mallory. "Want to chat about the final Foster pitch? Who's doing what? Get our ducks in a row. We're not that far out."

Mallory kept her eyes on her computer monitor. "Are you sleeping with her?"

"Way to get to the point, Mal."

"I'm not asking as your friend. I'm asking as your business partner because it matters."

"Well, as your business partner, I can assure you that I have everything under control. And as your friend, I would have hoped you'd show me the tiniest bit of support."

Mallory shook her head in disbelief. "You hid this from me for I don't know how long, and you're honestly playing the friendship card right now? She's our biggest competitor. You're jeopardizing everything we've worked for."

Okay, when she put it that way it didn't sound so fabulous. "I'm sorry, but I knew how you'd react, and I wanted to be sure that what was happening between us warranted the trouble. I needed to get my head sorted out."

"So you are sleeping with her then?"

Brooklyn sighed because Mallory wasn't giving an inch. "God, Mallory, yes. I've had sex with her. We're seeing each other. Legitimately."

"The same woman who would sell her grandmother to advance her career, that's the woman you're now pursuing a relationship with? Do you see the error in logic here?"

Brooklyn rolled her eyes. "You don't know what you're talking about."

"Ask her about how she got the City Shapewear account."

"Why would I do that?"

"Because she practically stole the account from Amy Davison's firm by pointing out an arrest Amy had for drug possession in college some fifteen years prior. Lennox knew the CEO was an anti-drug activist and used it to upend their relationship with Amy. It was something a mudslinging politician would do, not an advertising executive. Ask her, if you don't believe me. It was a shady thing to do. How do you know she's not in bed with you to find some way to neutralize us with Foster?"

"Come on, Mallory," Samantha said gently. "Let's not go there."

"I can handle this," Brooklyn shot at Sam, perhaps too aggressively, but she was fired up now. "Let her say what's on her mind."

Sam held up both of her hands in exasperation. "Excuse me for trying to help the situation. Carry on with your petty squabble."

Mallory wasn't deterred. "I'm only saying what we're all thinking. Even Hunter thinks it puts the business at risk."

"Don't bring me into this," Hunter said.

Mallory pushed forward, her eyes flashing. "I don't think you have your wits about you when it comes to Lennox. And I'm trying to save you some heartbreak."

"Wait." Brooklyn shook her head in feigned mystification. "I thought you were talking as my business partner. So confused right now." She turned to Hunter. "And if you have an opinion, I'd wish you'd express it directly to me next time."

Hunter tilted her head in acquiescence. "I think there's some validity to Mal's concern. Jessica has a track record for questionable business practices. We shouldn't just ignore that, especially now that she's a day-to-day factor in your life."

"There's no *we* in the equation. That's what you guys don't seem to understand. This is my life." She turned to Hunter. "And whatever happened to all that advice in the park? 'Go slow, Brooks. Baby-step the hell out of it.'"

Mallory sent Hunter a look. "So let me get this all straight. Everyone knew about this turn of events but me?"

No one said anything.

"Perfect. Wow. That's just wonderful. You know what? I think I'm gonna work from home today. I need a break from you three." But just before she reached the door, she turned back, her eyes holding fast to Brooklyn's. "Ask her about Emmaline Leos. That's a good story. And there's a lot more where that came from. I just think you should have all the facts before you embark upon corporate and emotional suicide."

Brooklyn watched Mallory leave, and the full brunt of the conversation settled over her. She wanted to hit something or cry. She wasn't sure which. She looked from Hunter to Samantha. "Thanks for having my back, you guys. Truly. Now that's friendship."

Jessica was just about to head to bed when she heard the knock at the door. It was kind of peculiar, that knock, the way it didn't really contain any pauses. What in the world had someone so keyed up? She swung the door open in time for Brooklyn to breeze past her, and it was clear from her expression that everything was not okay.

"I'm sorry. I know it's late, but I need you to tell me about Emmaline Leos and anything else you think I should know about you." She was wearing yoga pants and a white T-shirt. She looked cute and cuddly, and while Jessica wanted to touch her, Brooklyn's arms were folded across her chest with keep-your-distance vibes shooting off her like fireworks.

Forcing herself to focus on the question, Jessica ran the name over again in her head. "Uh, she's a former employee."

"Okay. I didn't know that. Can you tell me what happened with her?"

"Sure. As soon as you slow down and explain what's going on. Unless the whirlwind version of an inquisition is what you had in mind."

Brooklyn ran a hand through her hair and took a deep breath. "Right. This probably seems…" She quickly moved her hand across the air as if to erase an imaginary chalkboard. "Mallory and I had it out today and it was horrible and for whatever reason I can't stop thinking about some of the things she said. Things that make sense. A little. I'm rambling." She took a breath. "She told me to ask you about Emmaline. So here I am. I'm asking. And I'm hoping you'll answer."

"Do you want to sit?"

Brooklyn pushed herself onto the kitchen counter in typical Brooklyn fashion.

"Okay, that'll work. Emmaline was an account executive who worked for me several years back. She was good at her job. For whatever reason, she got tangled up with one of her married clients, who happened to be a big fish and the point person for the largest account on our books. When things went south with their affair, he refused to work with us as long as she was on payroll."

Brooklyn narrowed her eyes in accusation. "So you just fired her because some creep she was sleeping with told you to?"

"Of course not. I fired her for sleeping with him in the first place. We have a strict policy against it and always have. If she'd been honest with me, I could have assigned someone else to the account. Hell, I was even willing to work with her after the fact, but she continued to lie to me about it. I felt like I couldn't trust her. Plus, she'd placed us in a really compromising position with our client."

"I'm guessing that's not how she tells it."

"Yeah, well, I imagine she's still pretty ticked off. That tends to happen when you fire people. And Emmaline's always been into high drama, so I'm not surprised that she told Mallory all about it the second she was given the chance."

"I imagine that's exactly what happened."

Jessica nodded, already imagining the conversation. "So Mallory thinks I'm less than scrupulous and is not thrilled about you seeing me."

"Right. But she didn't use as big a word." Brooklyn attempted a smile, but it didn't make it past a flicker.

Jessica walked to her and placed her hands on Brooklyn's knees, looking up at her sincerely. "This is the thing. She's not completely wrong. I need to be honest with you about that. There was a time when I lost myself in what I was doing, and that time only ended very recently."

They stared at each other for a moment. "Did you land a client by exposing a competitor's police record?"

Jessica closed her eyes, hating what she was about to say. "Yes."

Brooklyn met her gaze, incredulous. "What else?"

"You need more?"

"I just need to know who I'm dealing with, Jess."

"I've never broken the law. I've never been dishonest, and I've never set out to be malicious to other people, though sometimes it came off that I did. But I have taken advantage of the position I've found myself in on occasion."

"Like preying on the weaknesses of others?"

"I'm not proud of it, but yes, like that."

"What about sleeping with your competitor to land the account you want? Is that in the realm of something you would do?"

Jessica stepped back and took a minute. She had to in order to steady herself against the force of the implication. She couldn't blame Brooklyn for wondering, but it still felt like she'd been slapped in the face. Finally, she raised her gaze to Brooklyn. "No. That's not something I would do."

She rested against the counter across from Brooklyn and tried to figure out how to explain. "When I met you, something changed for me. That's the best way I can describe it. My list of priorities was tossed into the air and everything was drastically reordered. Looking back, I don't like the way I've conducted myself. But the gist of it is this: the world looks different with you in it. With an *us*. It sounds like such a clichéd thing to say, but that doesn't make it any less true."

Brooklyn pushed off the counter, the serious contemplation still apparent on her face. "So what's the takeaway?"

"That I'd run away and start a bed-and-breakfast with you. Leave advertising behind, if that's what you wanted."

That seemed to resonate. "So I make that kind of a difference?"

Jessica ran a hand through her hair and nodded. "You make all the difference."

"But I don't want to start a bed-and-breakfast."

"I don't really either, but it was a cozy example."

Brooklyn blew out a breath and walked to just behind the couch where she could see the water, still trying to get her mind to reconcile what she knew with what she felt. "You cannot make underhanded moves anymore. Do you understand me?"

Jessica came up behind her. She knew this from the tingling sensation across the back of her neck, the way her body instantly hummed. "Yes."

"And you should probably volunteer at a soup kitchen or something to atone for your past practices."

Jessica chuckled quietly. "If you want me to ladle soup for strangers, that can be arranged."

Brooklyn felt her hair pushed aside, and warm lips descended softly on the nape of her neck and kissed slowly around to its side. She closed her eyes as a delicious shiver moved through her.

"And no individualized attacks. The personal lives of your competitors and employees shouldn't be any of your concern."

Jessica's arms circled her waist, and she kissed up to just below her ear. "So I should stay out of *your* personal life?" Her hands slipped beneath Brooklyn's shirt and moved upward, stopping just short of her breasts. "Because I'd rather not do that. God, you're warm."

Brooklyn hitched in a breath and locked her knees, as that was the only way she was going to stay upright. "I think there are exceptions. You know, um, extenuating circumstances between you and me."

"I do know." Jessica turned her around and slowly removed the T-shirt that encumbered her efforts.

As the air touched Brooklyn's skin, it was nothing compared to the heat she felt emanating from Jessica just inches away.

"We're supposed to be talking this out. Coming to some sort of understanding. Not taking each other's clothes off."

"Can't we do both?" With one arm around Brooklyn's waist, Jessica lowered her head and kissed her breast through the fabric of her bra. And with that, she lost track of everything. What it was they were discussing, the time of day, her name. All she knew were the wonderful sensations flying through her. She wanted, no, needed, Jessica's hands on her now.

"Take it off," Brooklyn managed.

Jessica lifted her head; her blue eyes shimmered a shade deeper. "Almost." She slid the straps of the bra from Brooklyn's shoulders to her elbows, trapping her arms there. Jessica dropped her head again, pulled the cups of her bra down, and set to work driving Brooklyn crazy.

Brooklyn heard herself moan and wanted desperately to glide her hands into Jessica's thick hair. Incapable of executing her plan, she instead pushed herself more fully into Jessica's mouth as little shots of pleasure coursed through her. Unable to take any more, and hyper-aware of the throbbing between her legs, Brooklyn waited until Jessica pulled her mouth away and then caught it in a kiss that had them both refocused and hungry.

They stumbled into the bedroom because in there they'd find room to explore, to luxuriate, and to finish what they'd so aptly started.

❖

It was the wee hours of the morning, but they'd yet to go to sleep. Jessica was too content right where she was to drift off just yet, no matter what the effects would be on the day ahead. Naked and tangled in sheets, they'd spent the last hour quietly talking and laughing about anything and everything.

Brooklyn traced lazy circles across the plane of her stomach. "The thing is everyone thinks Hunter's this hard-core player, but really she's just this total softie who loves to draw and play with her dog. I think she goes out with so many woman because she doesn't like to disappoint anyone."

"So she gets hit on a lot?"

"You have no idea. Gorgeous and Hunter mean the same thing, if you were to look them up in the urban dictionary. Who did you go to prom with?"

Jessica laughed. "I love your non sequiturs."

"Get used to it. It's how my mind works. Now answer the question."

"His name was Cruz and—"

"I'm sorry. Did you just say *Cruz*? Was this a soap opera? Did you go to prom on *Days of Our Lives*?"

Jessica tickled Brooklyn for that one and pulled her over until she was partially on top. "Do you want to hear the story or make fun of me some more?"

Brooklyn's eyes danced as she stared down at the body she'd never get tired of looking at. "I plan to do both. Please continue."

"He bought me a corsage, the wrist kind, and we went to the Olive Garden with two other couples. It was entirely fancy."

"Oh, I know. They have unlimited breadsticks."

That earned her another poke in the ribs, to which she laughed and squirmed and finally caught Jessica's wrists, pinning her down. "I'm sorry for making fun. Truly. I promise to behave and not mock the chain restaurants of your youth, but I'm highly ticklish, and if you continue your assault, I might die."

Jessica loved the playful side of Brooklyn. "I'll see what I can do. I'd rather you lived. Shall I press on?"

"Mhmm," Brooklyn said, and placed a slow kiss at the base of Jessica's neck as she listened.

"We danced the night away to Pearl Jam and the Backstreet Boys."

"Oh, this just keeps getting better and better," Brooklyn murmured, and continued to kiss up the column of Jessica's neck, which was pulling several notable reactions from Jessica. "Keep going. Then what?"

But it was getting harder and harder to concentrate. "We didn't have a curfew because of prom, so we made out in his car at one of those clichéd lookout points."

Brooklyn slipped her thigh purposefully between Jessica's and pushed upward. "Yeah? Were you into it?" She arched into Brooklyn automatically, needing more, her senses in overdrive.

"Not at all." At the answer, she felt Brooklyn smile against her collarbone before delving lower, pulling a nipple into her mouth and circling it slowly with her tongue. When she resurfaced, her eyes settled on Jessica's.

"Who were you into?"

"Anna Beth Thatcher."

Brooklyn raised an eyebrow, her eyes wide. "A girl? No!"

"Stop it." But she couldn't help but laugh at the overly shocked facial expression Brooklyn sported. God, she was cute.

"Did anybody know back then about your secret crush?"

"Nope. I've never told a soul about Anna Beth and her penchant for hair twirling during chemistry class."

"Ohhh, hair twirling is the worst kind of teasing." Brooklyn began to rock ever so slightly against her.

Jessica closed her eyes at the instant onslaught. "Oh, I can think of others."

"I like that I'm learning your secrets." Brooklyn's playfulness faded then, and her eyes held sincerity as she brought things between them to a stop for a moment. "Even the less-than-flattering ones."

"Me too."

"I want to know you, Jess. All of you. Promise that you'll always tell me the truth. Even if it's hard. Even if it's something you think I won't like."

Jessica reached up and brushed the hair back from Brooklyn's forehead so she could see her better, this woman that had come out of nowhere and changed everything. "I promise."

They made love again then and fell asleep shortly after, wrapped around each other in the most wonderful way. There was something cathartic for Jessica about the conversation they'd had that night. She wasn't a perfect person, far from it. But Brooklyn made her want to be better. And she would be.

❖

Brooklyn opened her eyes and took stock. The early signs of daylight crept in from the great big windows in Jessica's bedroom. She'd stayed over, she realized, blinking several times to orient herself.

And they'd ravished each other. Twice. A slow smile took hold and grew as she remembered the details one by one. Because it had been beyond good. Otherworldly was a better term. The best sex of her life, and that was a tall order.

She stretched as best she could without disturbing Jessica and closed her eyes as sleep once again descended. But it wasn't working fully as a noise was tugging at her from the here and now. In her still clinging-to-sleep state, she picked up on a very distinct knocking sound from the front of the apartment, and then she understood. Someone was at the door.

"Jess?" she whispered. "Baby, I think someone's at your door." Jessica stirred against her but gave no acknowledgement, no sign of cognizant response. Deciding to let Jessica sleep, Brooklyn took the initiative. She grabbed the thick white robe on the back of the bedroom door and headed to the front of the apartment, tying it around her as she went. The knocking only grew in tempo and intensity as she approached, inciting her to move quicker. She opened the door to find Ashton standing there, tears streaming down her face. She didn't wait for Brooklyn to speak.

"Something's wrong with my mom. She won't wake up."

The words were enough to jar Brooklyn fully awake and to attention mode without preamble. She could leap fast when called upon, a happenstance of living in volatile homes for a good portion of her life. Always be ready to defend yourself.

Ashton rushed back to her apartment with Brooklyn close behind her. As they entered the master bedroom, the undeniable scent of alcohol smacked Brooklyn in the face like a two-by-four. There, lying on the ground next to the bed, was Ashton's mother, seemingly asleep. Or passed out. She wasn't sure which. But her instincts kicked in and she knelt down next to Ashton's mother, took a pulse, and then listened for breath sounds. She was alive. Thank God. "What's her name?" she asked Ashton.

"Karina Coleman."

"Karina? Can you open your eyes?"

Nothing.

She tried again. "Karina. I'm here with Ashton, and we need you to try and open your eyes for us."

Karina's eyes fluttered slightly before closing again altogether.

She turned back to Ashton. "Do you know how much she had to drink?"

Ashton shook her head, and that's when Brooklyn saw what she'd missed earlier. Ashton sported a newly swollen left eye, complete with the customary red and purple discoloration.

Pieces of the puzzle were beginning to assemble themselves, and Brooklyn had a fairly clear picture of what the night prior had entailed. She was familiar enough with black eyes to know they don't happen on their own. But it was secondary to what they needed to deal with now, so she pushed past it, ordering herself to focus.

"What's going on?" Jessica asked from the doorway. After taking in the scene, she rushed over to them and knelt next to Brooklyn. "Oh my God. Is she okay?"

"Hopefully. But I need you to call 9-1-1. Can you do that? She's had way too much to drink, and she needs an ambulance."

"An ambulance?" Ashton asked, her eyes wide in terror. "Could she die? Oh, God. Please, no. She can't die." She was crying harder now, and Brooklyn wrapped both arms around her from the side in comfort, listening to Jessica on the phone in the living room.

"She's going to be okay, sweetie. We just need to sit here with her and keep her company until the ambulance gets here." But what she really meant was they needed to make sure that she continued to breathe on her own. Brooklyn had counted and she was taking fewer than seven breaths a minute, which was fairly shallow. She was trying desperately to remember what she'd learned about alcohol poisoning in that CPR class Mallory had them all take the year prior. Thank God for Mallory and her overly concerned side.

"They'll be here in five or six minutes tops," Jessica reported.

Brooklyn smoothed Ashton's hair and looked back at Jessica. When their eyes locked, she saw her own panic and fear mirrored in Jessica's eyes. The silent exchange was fleeting, however, as those were two emotions she did not plan to display in front of Ashton. She needed them to be strong for her and for whatever might be ahead.

"See? We don't even have that long to wait."

Ashton bent down next to Karina's ear. "Mom, help is coming, okay? Just hang in there. I'm right here." She stroked her mother's hair and continued to whisper words of encouragement. The move tugged at Brooklyn's heart with unexpected force.

When the paramedics arrived they collected as much information from Ashton as they could, but she didn't have a ton of details to offer. She'd heard her mother throwing up early that morning, and she was aware of her drinking heavily the night before, though she wasn't sure how to articulate how much.

"I found this empty on the kitchen counter," Jessica said as she entered the room holding up a bottle of Grey Goose.

The paramedic turned back to Ashton. "Was there a lot in the bottle before she started?"

Ashton nodded. "I think it was maybe half full. No, more than that." She shrugged helplessly. "I tried to get her to stop, but it just made her mad. It always does."

Brooklyn delicately traced the outside of the bruise around her eye. "Hey, look at me. It's not your fault, Ashton."

By this time, the other paramedics had Karina loaded and strapped into the ambulance stretcher. She was murmuring now, but her words were unintelligible as they wheeled her through the living room.

"Can I ride with her?" Ashton asked the paramedic.

He shook his head. "I'm sorry, ma'am. Only the parents of small children can ride in the ambulance. You can meet us at Bellevue." He handed Brooklyn a card.

"We'll take a cab," Jessica said. "Let me grab some shoes."

Brooklyn gave Ashton a squeeze. "Come with us next door, while I throw some clothes on." Ashton followed them like a lost puppy, and when Brooklyn turned back to check on her, she'd grown considerably pale.

"Ashton? Are you all right? Here," she said, steering her to Jessica's couch. "Let's get you sitting down."

Ashton looked up at her with the most haunted look. It shot a chill straight through her. "Honey, what is it?"

"I think that was the last time I'll ever see my mother."

CHAPTER SIXTEEN

From her seat in the waiting area of the emergency room, Jessica watched as Brooklyn, who was normally laid-back and fun, took control of the situation like she'd been through years of crisis training. It was impressive and a little shocking how she moved through what had been an incredibly difficult morning with effective calm. They'd been at the hospital for just under two hours. In that time, Brooklyn had called her friends and taken the morning off work. It was a testament to her character.

"I understand you have a lot of patients," she said to the nurse at the circular station, "but surely you could get us some sort of update. I'd be ever so grateful and will be filling out one of the questionnaires I see in this holder about how incredibly helpful you were, Marlene."

"Of course. I'll see what the doctor knows at this point."

"Who are you?" Jessica murmured to her as she sat back down next to her. Ashton was washing her face in the restroom, and she and Brooklyn had a brief moment on their own.

"Someone who wants to see this story have a happy ending. For Ashton's sake. But I'm starting to worry, Jess. They should have updated us by now." She ran her fingers through her hair.

In a stroke of fantastic timing, a balding man in a white coat consulted a nurse and came their way. "Are you the family of Karina Coleman?"

Brooklyn sent her a look as they stood.

"I'm her next-door neighbor. We found her unconscious early this morning."

"Are any family members present?"

"I'm her daughter," Ashton said, from just behind the doctor. Her face was devoid of emotion, almost as if she were too scared to breathe. Brooklyn held out a hand and Ashton moved instantly to her side.

Jessica wasn't sure how or when it had happened, but the two of them had a connection she couldn't quite name. But one thing was for certain: she was immensely grateful for Brooklyn's presence this morning.

"Your mother is stable. She's suffering from alcohol poisoning. We have her on oxygen and fluids to rehydrate her body. She'd had quite a bit to drink, and what we need to do now is offer supportive care while we allow the alcohol to leave her body."

Ashton stared up at him. "Is she going to be okay?"

"She should be. You did the right thing bringing her in. The nurses are with her now. You can see her shortly." He refocused his attention on Jessica. "We'll want Ms. Coleman to speak with a social worker before she's released and discuss possible options for treatment. Hopefully that's something she'll consider."

"I think it needs to be," Brooklyn said quietly.

"And if she refuses?" Jessica asked.

"That's her prerogative, unfortunately."

Jessica sighed inwardly. "I understand. Thank you."

He nodded and studied Ashton a beat. "A nurse will be by shortly with some ice for that eye. You'll also need to speak with the social worker when she arrives."

Jessica knew there was no guarantee Karina would be onboard with rehabilitation, but perhaps Ashton was the key to making sure it happened this time. She prayed the social worker would intervene, as this was the breaking point. The situation couldn't continue the way it was. Her gaze settled on Ashton, who looked relieved that her mother would be all right.

Jessica decided to seize the opportunity. "Ashton, let's talk about your eye."

Reflexively, Ashton's fingers fluttered to the bruise and she shook her head. "It was an accident. Not a big deal."

"Got it. Not a big deal. Can you tell me how it happened?"

Her eyes moved from Brooklyn to Jessica. "We were arguing. My mom and me. I was working on a project at Leslie's place, and when I came home she was drinking. She didn't used to drink so much when her boyfriend was around. But they broke up and she's been hitting it pretty hard. She promised me weeks ago she'd stop, so I was upset. When she wouldn't listen to me, I tried to take the glass out of her hand, but she refused to let go. We struggled over it and her elbow caught me here." She softly touched the bruise above her cheek, and her eyes brushed the ground in defeat. "She didn't seem to care. She went into her room and slammed the door. I didn't see her again until this morning when—" She broke off when the emotion hit. Silent tears streamed down her face.

Brooklyn took the reins, inclining her head to meet Ashton's eyes. "Hey, Ashton, I need you to listen to me for a minute. It's important that you tell the social worker exactly what happened. Do you understand? This is important."

"It'll get my mom in trouble. I don't think I can—"

"It will force her to get the help she needs," Brooklyn said gently. "And that's the only thing that will make things better at this point. It could have been so much worse this morning. Think about that. You have to be strong about this so there are no more mornings like today."

Ashton seemed to take this in but clearly struggled with a decision. She sat back in her chair, seeming desolate. "I don't know. If she goes away somewhere, to rehab, what happens to me? My dad isn't in my life. My grandma died last year. We don't really have any other family. They'd put me in some kids' home because I'm not eighteen."

Jessica didn't hesitate. "You could live with me."

❖

Brooklyn was in catch-up mode the entire next week. She'd already fallen behind on her projects, but the time she'd spent at the hospital and getting Ashton settled at Jessica's had taken yet another giant chunk of her scheduled productivity and tossed it out the advertising window.

Karina had been weak when they'd gone in to see her and was noticeably affected by Ashton's words. Perhaps that's why she'd reluctantly agreed to the three-month rehab program the social worker had outlined for them.

There was no way to know if she'd stay there, but it was a start all the same. Brooklyn couldn't articulate why she was so emotionally invested in the case, but perhaps she saw shades of herself in Ashton. The way she took care of herself as a kid when she really shouldn't have to. She also sensed a loneliness there, a fear, that she completely identified with.

She'd been shocked when Jessica had volunteered to take Ashton in.

But the good kind of shocked. The kind of shocked that made her realize that beneath that calm, cool exterior, Jessica Lennox had a much bigger heart than people gave her credit for.

"Brooklyn, do you have the latest version of the copy for the Foster spot? I want to go over it, make sure we're not missing anything."

Brooklyn threw a glance behind her to Mallory. "Um, yeah. It's here somewhere." She shuffled through the piles of papers and odds and ends and Post-its on her desk, wishing to God she were a bit more organized. "Here you go."

Mallory took the printed pages and headed back to her desk. "Thanks."

They were speaking now, but it was one hundred percent business. And it didn't feel good. Mallory was one of her best friends on the planet, and it was her warmth and leadership that had changed Brooklyn's life forever. She didn't want to fight with her.

But they were at an impasse.

If it were Mallory in her situation, Brooklyn would go out of her way to be happy for her. To find a way. However, Mallory clearly wasn't willing to do the same. She apparently felt betrayed, and Brooklyn didn't really know what she could say to change her mind.

And so they existed.

The normally lively office, always full of banter and brainstorming sessions, was now stark and silent, reminiscent of the study section of a library. Everyone kept her head down and her eyes on her own paper.

As the morning crawled into afternoon, the four-way tension was suffocating. When Hunter returned from her noon break, she stood in the center of the room and surveyed the scene around her. "Okay, that's it. I just came from lunch in a world where people actually speak to one another. Smile, on occasion. Remember what that's like? And now I'm back *here*, the land of bitter. I can't live like this. I'm calling a Midnight Chocolate. Tonight at Brooklyn and Sam's."

Mallory shook her head. "I don't see how that's going to—"

"You don't have to see anything," Hunter said, topping her in volume. She had all of their attention now, because Hunter was generally laid-back and never raised her voice. Brooklyn didn't think she knew how. This was sort of monumental. "You will wear pajamas and you will eat chocolate and we will find a way to fix this thing because it's killing us. And killing us is not an option. Does everyone here understand?!"

They nodded dutifully, because it was clear Hunter meant business.

"Good. See you tonight," she yelled. "I'll bring brownies." She grabbed her messenger bag, dropped her laptop inside, and headed for the loft door. "I'm going to work at Starbucks where people are *supposed* to ignore one another."

The loft door slid shut with a pronounced bang.

It was 11:47 when Brooklyn opened a bottle of red for herself and Mallory, and a bottle of white for Hunter and Samantha. It's what she always did for Midnight Chocolate. Her appointed job. But a lack of excitement surrounded the preparation this time.

The gap felt big and that made her nervous.

The Midnight Chocolate felt like a Hail Mary effort at this point. That's not to say she wasn't onboard to try. Because she needed those guys back.

Fifteen minutes later, they sat around the coffee table, which was covered in the requisite chocolate. Brooklyn sat on the floor, Mallory on the couch with Sam, and Hunter on the arm of the chair across from Brooklyn. It was clear who was in charge of the effort when Hunter began to speak. "We're here to sort this thing out once and for all, and that means putting everything on the table. Mallory starts. Tell us what's going on with you."

Mallory blinked and took a minute before speaking. "I don't trust Jessica Lennox."

"That's fair," Sam added. "She's done things that give me pause too."

Brooklyn suppressed an eye roll and Mallory pressed on. "But regardless of those feelings, one of you should have told me what was happening between her and Brooklyn."

"So what is happening?" Hunter asked.

Brooklyn opened her mouth to answer, but Sam beat her to the punch. "She likes her."

"I get that," Mallory said, reaching for her wine, loosening up a tad. "She's a beautiful woman. She's charismatic. You're hot for her, and why wouldn't you be? But at the end of the day, there are more important things in the world than sex."

Hunter held up a hand. "Now that might be a bit harsh. Sex is—"

"I'm in love with her." The words were out of Brooklyn's mouth before she could fully think them through, and three heads swiveled in her direction as if on a string.

Sam was the first one to respond, her eyes wide when she did so. "Whoa. You are?"

Brooklyn nodded. "And before you say anything, you should know that I get it. I see the strain this has put on our friendship, and I see the ramifications it could have for Savvy. But you should know I would never put those things at risk if what I felt for Jessica wasn't real. You guys, I get that I was a relationship train wreck. A one-woman demolition crew when it came to anything substantial. So I'm the last one who saw this coming." The words were tumbling out of her now without preamble. "I've never been in love before. I've never let myself get close enough to someone, because that's not who I am." She closed her eyes. "Correction, *was*. But I'm trying to be different. When I'm with her, I feel like I belong there, which is new and wonderful." Tears filled her eyes as she turned to Mallory. "And I don't want to walk away from that. Please don't ask me to."

Mallory held her gaze, and Brooklyn realized Mallory had tears in her eyes now as well. "You're really in love?" she asked weakly.

"I am. I haven't exactly said those words to her because it's me we're talking about and that's kind of terrifying, but I hope to be able to someday. "

Mallory nodded slowly as if turning over the concept in her mind. "And does she love you back?"

"I don't know." Except she did know. "Yes."

"Wow. Okay. I think that changes things a bit." Hunter blew out a breath and took a bite of a fudge-striped cookie. "So now what?"

All eyes were on Mallory, who studied her glass. When she raised her gaze, her green eyes were focused, calm, resolute. "We will have to set parameters. Information that you can't share over dinner, you know? We take things a day at a time. For Brooklyn's sake."

What did that mean exactly? Her heart pounded away at the prospect of Mallory's support. "So you're okay with me continuing to see Jessica?"

She offered what had to be hard for her, given the facts, a genuine smile. And it was a testament to their friendship. "I want you to be happy, Brooks. That's the most important thing."

Gratitude. Relief. Both flooded Brooklyn's senses in the most welcome way. She moved to Mallory and hugged her. "Thank you for trying. I know this isn't ideal."

"It's not. I'm doing this for you," she said in Brooklyn's ear before releasing her. "Because you deserve something wonderful. And if you've found that in Jessica, who am I to make it difficult?"

"I want you to get to know her. Some of what you had to say was true. She admits that. She hasn't lived a squeaky-clean existence, but there's so much more there, and I believe wholeheartedly that she's a good person."

Mallory sighed. "I can't believe I'm going to say this, but set it up."

Brooklyn couldn't have held back the smile if her life had depended on it.

"Wait." Sam pouted. "So Mallory gets to hang out with the new love of your life, and the rest of us don't get to witness it?"

"You already got to have dinner with her," Hunter pointed out.

"Yeah, but not with Mallory."

Brooklyn held up a hand. "You're all invited. We can do drinks some night at Showplace. Maybe next week."

Sam sat back with a thoughtful smile. "Mallory and Jessica forced to play nice in the sandbox. I can't even wait."

"Me neither," Brooklyn said.

"This is all well and good, and I'm thrilled you're happy, genuinely, but I should point out that I still very much want this account." Mallory turned to Brooklyn. "Are we all still on the same page about that?"

Brooklyn sat a little taller, charged up. "More than you realize. Nothing's changed on that front. Foster is ours." She glanced at her friends as an impulse tugged at her. "I know MCs aren't generally supposed to be work sessions, but I did have an idea I wanted to run by you guys for the commercial spot. With the not-talking and the tension, though, I was feeling fraught."

"Fraught?" Sam stared at her.

"Yes, fraught. People say fraught. Stay with me."

"With you," Hunter said. "And not at all fraught."

Brooklyn laughed but pressed on. "I have an adjustment I'd like to make to the storyline. If it's crazy you can tell me. I can handle crazy and we can stick with what we have."

"MCs don't have rules, and stop all the prefacing. Let's hear it," Sam said, popping a malted-milk ball. "And can I just say that whoever invented Whoppers needs to marry me."

"I'll draft a Craig's List ad," Hunter said, sending Sam a smile, which earned her an elbow to the arm. "What's your big Brooklyn idea this time?"

Here goes nothing. "Okay. Everything happens just as we've mapped out, but there's no groom."

"No groom." Sam repeated the words slowly, trying to understand the meaning.

Hunter was clearly intrigued. "Are you saying what I think you're saying? Because that's kind of awesome."

"A gay wedding," Mallory whispered, her eyes moving back and forth as if searching through the idea for drawbacks. "You know, that could be interesting."

"Hear me out," Brooklyn said, standing now because she was just too energized not to. "The world's changing. We know this. We've all seen it firsthand. Gay and lesbian content is everywhere. Books, hit TV shows, mainstream films. Gay weddings following the Supreme Court ruling are everywhere. Totally trendy. Taking on an ad campaign like this one for their product, their *new* product, I might add, puts Foster on the cutting edge. They seem hip. They seem open and with it. What do we know about the Foster family and their political beliefs?"

"Big donations to the left," Sam said. "Both at the state and national levels."

"Well, there you go."

"Yeah, but it's still pretty bold," Hunter pointed out. "We could crash and burn if they don't want to go there."

"Or," Brooklyn said, "we look like forward-thinking geniuses who are going to lead them to the big, wide world of generation next." She snapped her fingers. "And just like that, a whole new demographic of customers."

No one said anything for a moment. Brooklyn gave them time to work it through. It was no small proposition, and if they were going to move forward, they needed to be all in. One hundred percent onboard.

And so she waited. If there was a time for the *Jeopardy* theme song, this was it.

"I think we do it," Hunter said finally, raising her head.

Samantha looked over at her and nodded subtly. "It's a little terrifying, but I think we need to go big on this one. So let's go big. We need this account."

Only one opinion remained. "Mal?" Brooklyn asked.

She stared pensively at the floor before a wide smile took shape on her face. She raised her gaze. "I've examined it from every direction, and I keep coming up with the same answer. It's fucking brilliant. It's exactly the edge we need."

Brooklyn laughed in celebration. "Well, then I think we have a decision."

"How about a toast?" Sam asked.

They gathered their glasses and held them in a circle. "To bold moves," Brooklyn proposed.

Mallory met her eyes. "And good friends."

The evening ended much better than it began, and Brooklyn relaxed into the ease of being around her friends, her family. In their comfy pajamas, enjoying wine and chocolate, they slipped easily back into their usual rhythm. They laughed, talked, reminisced, and Brooklyn told them all the details of meeting her family.

"I don't think you should give up on them," Hunter offered.

"It's not that I want to. It's that I don't know quite where I'd fit in, you know? Their lives are already established, bound together. I'm like this extra little piece that doesn't fit into the puzzle."

Mallory shook her head. "I don't think they look at it that way. I bet, to Cynthia, you're the missing puzzle piece."

That resonated. And she wondered if it could be true, the thought of her being missed. She wasn't sure, but it was certainly something to think about down the line.

Not yet, though.

Not yet.

CHAPTER SEVENTEEN

Jessica blinked a couple times purposefully to force herself to refocus on the words in front of her. She was in the homestretch of her day, which had started a good twelve hours prior. She was exhausted, her muscles at the back of her neck bunched, and she was having trouble getting her mind to just hang in there a little longer. But if she could just get through some of the performance evaluations HR had been asking for, she might be able to sneak away before the hour turned ungodly. She'd checked in on Ashton, who seemed to be having a fabulous time at her best friend's place. It was Friday night, and though she'd sent Brooklyn a text, she'd yet to hear back about her plans for the evening.

It was likely she was with a client, she decided. She'd hoped they'd be able to connect later, decompress. If she could just push through a little longer.

"Hey, Bent," she called through the open door out to his desk. "Do you have the file HR sent down for me to go through? I can't find it."

She heard him close the door as he came in, shuffling through papers.

"My desk is taking over. There's too much stuff on it, and I can't find anything I need. The order I so desperately crave in my life is missing. Damn it," she said, still moving things around. "I hate it when I let myself get out of control like this. I need a serious break. When I'm done with the performance reviews I'm going to call it a night. But don't let me forget that HR wants—"

The file landed on her desk with a thud, and before she could reach for it, two hands found her shoulders and began to press, massaging gently. At the contact, she paused and instantly melted in surrender as her screaming muscles were silenced in the most soothing relief.

"Oh, God, that feels amazing," Jessica said, her eyes closed in concession as the tension of the day ran off her.

"It must. You're incredibly tense." At the sound of Brooklyn's voice, she opened her eyes and turned, smiling up at the most beautiful woman on the planet.

"Hey, you. How'd you—"

"I talked Bentley into letting me in." She continued to massage. "It's kind of a big deal, me being here, infiltrating enemy lines and all. It's very James Bond. You should call me that. Ms. Bond."

She tugged Brooklyn's arm, effectively pulling her into her lap. "Ms. Bond, the enemy happens to like you," she said, nuzzling her neck and inhaling the wonderful scent of peaches and vanilla that seemed to come with Brooklyn. "A lot."

"So I'm discovering. Not a hostile greeting at all." Brooklyn cradled Jessica's face in her hands and stared down at her. "So, hi," she whispered.

"Hey," she whispered back.

Brooklyn claimed her lips in a kiss that made the long day more than worth it, as it had led her to this moment.

When they came up for air, Brooklyn looked around in interest, taking in the room. "You're kind of sexy up here in your office. In charge of people. Making things happen." She strolled to the picture window. It was dark out, and the lights of the city twinkled brightly well into the distance. "I should have known you'd have this kind of view."

Jessica stared after her, already feeling infinitely lighter just to have Brooklyn in the room. "So what do you think of the place?" Was it unattractive that a small part of her wanted to impress Brooklyn with the company she'd worked so hard to build?

Brooklyn turned back around and nodded in approval. "I'd say you're doing very well for yourself. And that Bentley guy is charming. I have to give credit where credit is due. I think he might have been hitting on me, though."

She nodded apologetically. "He can't help it. He hits on all beautiful women. Something we're working on."

"It was good for my ego. I think Tina, on the other hand, is wondering what the hell I'm doing here. But while she glared at me, your receptionist had gone home for the day, so she was nice enough to take my jacket and attaché when I arrived."

"See? She's not all bad."

"I'm not conceding that entirely, but your endorsement matters. What are we doing tonight? Where's Ashton? We could all see a movie."

"She's staying at her friend Leslie's. Way cooler than me on a Friday night. She'll be back in the morning."

"Any word from her mom?"

"She called last night and they chatted. I think it's still a little strained between them, but Ashton seemed to think she was doing all right at the treatment center."

"So you're saying your place is empty."

"It is," Jessica said, liking where this was going.

"Do you want to hear what I'm thinking?"

"Desperately."

"You treat me to a fancy dinner and tell me all about your last couple of days and then listen as I tell you about mine. And there's a lot to tell, by the way. I should also mention that through most of dinner we flirt, because we're really good at that. My eyes spend a lot of time staring at the skin peeking out from beneath that top button of your shirt, and your eyes dip down to my bottom lip, the way they're doing right about now."

God, Brooklyn could push her buttons, and she meant that in a really good way. "And then what happens?"

"You take me back to your place and have your way with me. Or vice versa. I'm still deciding."

Jessica moved to Brooklyn and placed her hands on her waist and made slow circles with her thumbs. "Can I just say that I love that you showed up here? You have no idea what a sight for sore eyes you are after a boring, long work day." Jessica inclined her head to kiss her, but Brooklyn's eyes gleamed and she sidestepped the effort, crossing back to the desk. "Don't get ahead of yourself, Ms. Lennox. We have dinner to flirt through first."

"Of course, the flirtatious dinner."

"Do you have work you need to finish?"

Jessica glanced at her desk and back to Brooklyn. "I do, but it can wait."

"And so can I." In all honesty, Brooklyn really liked observing Jessica in her natural environment. She was getting a bit of a thrill out of it and was quite pleased with her little impromptu visit. "How about I sit on this comfortable couch over here and you finish whatever needs your expert attention."

Jessica eyed her as she sat happily on the couch. "If you're sure you don't mind."

"Do I look unhappy?"

Jessica stared at her. "You look hot."

Brooklyn laughed. "You're supposed to be working, Ms. Lennox, remember?"

"Right. Right. Working."

The room fell into silence, and Jessica refocused on whatever task came with the file she'd delivered. But it wasn't long before it was clear to Brooklyn that her plan had backfired. Because sitting in a silent office, with very little to do but stare at Jessica in her skirt, jacket, and heels as she concentrated, was turning out to be torturous. If one thing turned her on like nothing else, it was Jessica in contemplative mode, in the course of business. Okay, Casual Jessica in jeans and a T-shirt also turned her on in a whole separate way. And then, of course, Morning Jessica was crazy hot. Brooklyn paused, recognizing a theme.

But it didn't matter.

What did matter was the way her temperature was slowly inching up the dial as each second ticked by. As Jessica bit her bottom lip, Brooklyn imagined what her hands would feel like on her body. As Jessica tucked a strand of hair behind her ear, Brooklyn imagined Jessica slowly undressing her, one torturous button at a time. In response to the succession of images flashing across her mind, she shifted uncomfortably on the couch, drawing Jessica's attention.

"You hanging in there? I'm almost done. I promise."

Brooklyn nodded. "I'm good." A lie.

Jessica went back to work and Brooklyn continued to watch. Her mind was her worst enemy, and, try as she might, she couldn't seem to get the racy thoughts out of her head. She blew out a frustrated sigh, and this time when Jessica's eyes settled on her, she didn't disguise her emotions.

Jessica sat back in her chair and studied her. "I know that look."

"No, you don't."

"I do. I pay close attention. I'd tell you to come over here, but you seem to have strict rules. Something about dinner first."

Brooklyn tilted her head back and forth, considering her options. "Dinner's overrated. At least I've heard that."

A smile took shape on Jessica's face. "Who needs to eat? Come over here."

It wasn't like she could say no if she wanted to. She covered the short distance, stopping next to Jessica and leaning back against the desk. "You're really attractive when you work, Jess."

Jessica laughed quietly. "Yeah?" She eased Brooklyn back until she was seated on the desk and moved to where she stood in front of her. "I like figuring out how your mind works, what turns you on."

"I have a proverbial list. It's not overly expansive, but your name appears several times."

"Yeah?"

"You have no idea."

Jessica ran her hands from Brooklyn's knees to her thighs, stopping just at the hemline of her skirt. Brooklyn sucked in a breath, and as Jessica's blue eyes deepened a shade, she understood her intentions. That determined look only served to spike the need she already felt. "Does that door lock?" she asked Jessica in a shaky voice.

"It locks upon closing after five p.m."

"You think of everything."

"Mhmm." Jessica inclined her head and kissed just under Brooklyn's jaw. She'd worn her hair down today, and it tickled Brooklyn's neck in the most sensual way. She closed her eyes as her body responded in spades to the attention Jessica now paid it. And God, it was good attention, attention she was fantasizing about just moments before. Award-winning attention, if there were such a thing. There should be.

Jessica's hands inched up Brooklyn's thighs just enough to raise her skirt for access, and she slipped one hand in between. She pulled her face back enough to meet Brooklyn's eyes as she applied direct pressure to her center. They still had a thin layer of fabric between them, but the contact was enough to pull an audible gasp from Brooklyn, who craved more. "Jess," she managed to say as the onslaught of sensation tumbled down. Jessica continued, moving her hand in a slow, circular pattern, applying pressure and then easing back. Brooklyn closed her eyes, feeling her own lips part in rapture.

"Look at me, Brook."

And she did.

She found Jessica's eyes and held on, and that connection only heightened the allure, elevated the heat. She pushed back against Jessica's hand as the tension built slowly within her, continuing its climb. Jessica increased the pressure with which she touched her, and Brooklyn held on, her breathing a little erratic, outside of her control. It didn't take much before the orgasm ripped through her fast and hard. She had the wherewithal to stay quiet in light of their surroundings, but just barely, as she rode out the powerful waves of pleasure that barraged her every inch. She braced her arms on Jessica's shoulders and marveled at her, blinking several times as she floated back to earth. "Whoa," she said, steadying herself. "We just did that in your office."

"I don't think there was any way not to. Not with you looking at me like that."

"No, I don't either." She ran her thumb across Jessica's bottom lip and kissed her, doing her best to communicate all the feelings that were swirling inside of her. The fact that Jessica had just given her such pleasure without even needing to undress her was a testament to just how attracted she was to this woman. She'd enjoyed sex before, but she'd always had to work for the payoff, concentrate intricately on the process. But with Jessica, she could let go of everything and just feel, experience, revel in each touch.

When they broke from the kiss, Jessica shook her head in wonder. Brooklyn had the power to turn her day on its head without notice. An evening that felt burdensome and long had been transformed into something unexpectedly awesome in the course of thirty minutes.

Brooklyn made life spark into color.

"What? What are you smiling about over there?" Brooklyn asked.

"How much potential life has right now. It feels endless."

Brooklyn broke into a smile that could light up any room. "It does, doesn't it?"

The phone on the desk next to them rang. Recognizing its origin based on the extension, Jessica held up a finger and took the call. "What's up, Bent?"

"I don't want to interrupt, but did you still want to go over the performance reviews tonight?"

Jessica absently intertwined her fingers with Brooklyn's and stole a look at the beautiful woman in front of her. It wasn't even a choice. "Let's hold off on those until Monday. I have a dinner to flirt my way through."

Brooklyn kissed the back of her hand and raised a seductive eyebrow.

When they boarded the elevator to the lobby, they found themselves sharing it with two very buttoned-up businessmen. Jessica stared at Brooklyn, her thoughts tracking back to the day they'd been stuck in the elevator together. She marveled at how much things had changed. Brooklyn caught the look and smiled at her knowingly, holding her gaze the length of the ride down.

As they headed into the night, hand in hand, Brooklyn paused on the sidewalk.

"What is it?" Jessica asked, turning back.

Brooklyn studied her seriously. "I could get used to this. To all of it. Is that crazy?"

Jessica smiled at the sentiment. "It's not. In fact, it might be one of my favorite things you've ever said to me."

"Yeah?"

"Mhmm. So does this mean that you might want to visit me at work again?"

"I thought the first time went well."

Jessica smiled, her stomach tightening reflexively at the memory. "It did."

Brooklyn closed the distance between them. "But next time I'm in charge. Are you by chance free Monday?" Jessica took in air, the wheels in her head already turning. Suddenly Monday was her new favorite day of the week.

❖

It was snowing the next morning when Jessica woke. Not full-on accumulation caliber, but those were definitely tiny flakes floating past her window. A mid-season dusting, she thought. Well, at least it wouldn't cripple the city.

Her body felt warm and wonderfully sated after the night prior, and a smile crept onto her face at the alluring memories. Life was good. She stretched lavishly, enjoying the looseness of her muscles, and rolled over to find the spot next to her empty.

She was alone and it was disappointing.

But not entirely, she noted, because there was still stuff. And stuff, she was finding out, came attached to Brooklyn. She surveyed the scene. A glass of water by the bed. Lip gloss, two quarters, and a small wallet on the dresser. Several items of clothing leading from the bed back to the living room. Well, okay, that last part was her doing, but still. It was endearing, the stuff. Because, in contrast, she didn't come with much. Her life was streamlined, simple. The messy jumble Brooklyn came with was kind of refreshing.

She climbed out of bed and slipped into a T-shirt, hot on the trail of the wonderful aroma of coffee that wafted in. What she found in her living room was utterly adorable. Brooklyn, already dressed for the day, in *her* clothes, she might add, snuggled up on the couch watching what looked to be *I Love Lucy*.

Brooklyn's face lit up when she saw her standing there. "Hey, sleepyhead. Good morning. Lucy's on. Lucy's my favorite. Sam's too."

"She is, huh?" Jessica gave Brooklyn a once-over. "Those are my jeans. That is my Boston hoodie. Your own shoes, but I believe those are my socks. And I never sleep this late."

Brooklyn glanced down and pulled the hoodie tighter around her in a cozy display that caused Jessica's heart to do that little flip-flop thing. "They fit kinda perfectly. You may not get them back. And, yes, you seem to be making lots of changes lately," Brooklyn said knowingly. "Sleep looks good on you. You're all fresh-faced and radiant."

Jessica reflected on the state of things. How different her life seemed from just a couple of months prior. "Whoever would have thought I'd be in charge of a teenager? We're lucky she's still alive.

She is alive, right?" She sank into the couch. Brooklyn grabbed her ankle and proceeded to pull Jessica's legs across her lap.

"The teenager is not dead. She's doing great, in fact. I know this because I just said good-bye to her and Leslie, who I like, by the way. They went down to the deli for breakfast and are heading to the park with friends to enjoy the snow. She'll be back after lunch for homework. I hope that's okay. I didn't want to wake you to ask. You looked angelic."

"I never look angelic."

"You do. It's a fact. Can you imagine if the world knew the truth?" She leaned over and captured Jessica's mouth with hers. "And that's what I've been waiting to do since I woke up."

Jessica stroked Brooklyn's cheek with her thumb. "Wake me next time. We can do lots of that."

"Really?"

"*Really.* I wouldn't give up sleep for many things, but making out with you happens to be one of them."

"Good to know."

After a little more kissing, Jessica forced herself to focus on the day ahead and moved into the kitchen for the coffee that taunted her. "What's on the schedule for you today?"

"Work."

"That's vague."

"It is." Brooklyn sighed. She turned around on the couch to face her. "I never really know how to handle the topic of work where we're concerned. We're playing tug-of-war with a very important account, Jess, and one of us is going to lose. How's that going to go exactly?"

She sidestepped the inclination to make a playfully competitive remark because the look on Brooklyn's face told her she was sincere. "I think we have to agree to keep business just what it is, business. If the account goes to you guys, it'll be hard for me, yes. But if I know I have you at the end of the day, I'll be just fine. Trust me."

Brooklyn took in the words. Jessica was putting her first, making her the most important thing, above all else, and it flooded her with a feeling she couldn't name. "I do trust you."

"And to help matters, I've asked Tina to take the lead on the last pitch. I'll assume more of a background role. I think it's better that way. For all of us."

It made sense, and it would make things a tad bit easier if they weren't going head-to-head personally. Brooklyn flashed a playful grin. "You know you're going down though, right?"

Matching her, Jessica smiled sweetly. "Just know that my shoulder, and other parts of me, are here for you when that final decision is made."

"You're so generous."

"And sexy?"

"Generously sexy is what I meant to say." She stood. "I have to head out, but I was hoping you were free for a little get-together at Showplace tonight. It's a little bar in Soho."

"I have dinner with Ashton probably around six thirty. What about after?"

"Perfect. I'll set it up. Mallory's going out of her way to do this for me, so be nice."

Jessica pulled a face. "Am I ever not nice?"

"You've perfected the art of cool and aloof in Mallory's presence. I've seen it firsthand. And that's the only side she's ever experienced. I'd like her to see the rest." Brooklyn crossed the short distance for a kiss. "I'll see you tonight, Miss Generously Sexy. No pressure."

Once she was on the elevator, Brooklyn exhaled dreamily. The more they were together, the more she seemed to crave that time. She almost felt the need to shake herself awake, because she was having a hard time believing how well they fit together when they let themselves.

As she strode out onto the street in the late morning she paused. Tiny flakes fell from the sky and dotted the nearby surroundings with touches of white. It wasn't cold enough for the snow to stick, but its presence was just enough to make the world look beautiful. Brooklyn's heart sighed at the visual.

She reached instinctively for her phone and dialed. She needed to share this. Jessica answered on the first ring. "Forget something again?"

"Not exactly. You have to come down here. I need to kiss you."

There was a chuckle on the other end of the line. "You need to kiss me? Earlier wasn't enough?"

"In the snow. I need to kiss you in the snow."

"I have to say, I don't get a lot of kissing invitations inspired by weather."

"Thank God. Now get down here."

When Jessica emerged from her building, she tilted her head to the side and studied Brooklyn curiously. She wasn't wearing a coat and instinctively wrapped her arms around herself against the cold. The wind caught her hair and blew it back from her face, and her mouth, that generous mouth, quirked in amusement as she eyed Brooklyn.

"It's gorgeous out here," Brooklyn said without missing a beat. "It's not like we could miss it. Like I could let that happen to us."

Jessica moved to her and took in their surroundings. "I like that you see the joy in things like this. A simple morning that most people wouldn't notice. But you, you latch on, revel."

"How could I not revel? We're standing on a beautifully lined street in the West Village of New York City and delicate snowflakes are dusting anything and everything with the most perfect white accents ever. How can anyone not be excited about that?"

"Sometimes it's easy to forget to pay attention. I admit, I've been guilty of that."

"But now you have me to remind you to look around once in a while. The world is a pretty captivating place, Jessica Lennox."

"I'm beginning to understand that."

"Oh, good."

"You're a pretty powerful life force, you know that?

Brooklyn let the compliment settle. "I didn't, but I accept the challenge."

Jessica stepped into her, smiling, and grasped her by the lapels of her jacket, a move she admittedly found a little thrilling. Jessica turned her face up to the sky, prompting Brooklyn to do the same. The tiny flakes floated side to side before settling delicately on their shoulders, hair, and faces. Jessica's eyes found hers and the smile gradually faded. The kiss that followed was the kind of kiss that promised so much more. And God almighty, Jessica could kiss like no one else. It curled Brooklyn's toes and made her stomach do somersaults in the most wonderful way. She loved those somersaults. She loved Jessica.

Whoa. And there it was again. The ominous L word. But this time, she felt it all over. It moved through her in big warm waves. She knew the truth of her feelings and just had to find a way to properly express them.

She delicately plucked a flake from Jessica's eyelash. "I hope you have a fantastic day. And I can't wait to see you tonight."

"You too. Bye, Brook."

"Bye, Jess."

She backed away from Jessica before turning fully and heading off down the street to the train. There was an extra spring in her step that had never really been there before. And she knew why. A new door was standing open, and all she had to do was walk through it.

She smiled, loving the possibility in front of her.

CHAPTER EIGHTEEN

What had started out as a picturesque dusting had turned into a full-fledged snowstorm by the time evening descended on the city. And not just any snowstorm, Jessica thought, but an angry-act-of-God snowstorm.

"So I've set out some microwave popcorn and you'll find sodas in the fridge."

Ashton nodded. "Got it."

"We promise not to burn your place down," Leslie added. She was a perky little blond kid, always smiling.

Jessica tossed Ashton a sideways look. "That's a joke, right."

Ashton grinned. "Totally. Relax, Jess. Go have a good time and say hi to Brooklyn for me. Oh, and ask her what time she wants to go to the museum next Saturday."

"You two are making plans?"

"We are."

"Interesting. I'm a little jealous."

Leslie patted her shoulder. "It's good for you."

Jessica eased into her heavy coat, as lord knew she was going to need it. "What are you two planning to watch tonight?"

"*Notting Hill*," Ashton said. "Hugh Grant is my husband."

Jessica nodded. "And here I thought you were single. Lock the door behind me?"

"Roger that."

Thirty minutes later Jessica trudged her way up Lafayette Street toward Showplace, where she was set to meet Brooklyn and her friends. But it was no easy feat. Due to the traffic jams that snarled the city as a result of the weather, she opted for the train instead. Now, she found herself walking against the wind in a battle for the ages. Flurries were slamming into her face and eyes at such a rapid pace that it was impossible to see more than five feet in front of her. The horizon looked like a sheet of white paper. Mean white paper, in fact, that froze her cheeks and made her eyes water.

It was rough weather to be out in, but she was determined to make tonight happen. It was important to Brooklyn and thereby important to her. Plus, she didn't want to give Mallory any further ammunition. This was her shot to extend some sort of olive branch, and she didn't intend to miss it.

Hence, her trek. When she arrived at Showplace, she was surprised by how many people had also braved the weather for an evening out. The bar was fairly crowded, and what a cool place it was. She understood why Brooklyn liked it so much. She scanned the room for any sign of her. Though she came up short, she was able to spot Sam and Mallory at a table just past the bar. They were laughing at something the way friends did, clearly enjoying themselves.

She took a deep breath. She could do this.

She'd faced way scarier people than little Mallory Spencer. Who knew? Maybe given some time, she'd even like her.

"Jessica!" Samantha said as she approached. "You found us. And you didn't die on the way here." It was a warm greeting, which was helpful, as she was frozen solid from her trip. She unwound the scarf from around her neck and shrugged out of her coat to find herself pulled into an embrace from Sam. She wasn't hugged on a daily basis, she realized.

"Barely, but yes. How are you, Sam?"

"Fabulous."

"Mallory, it's good to see you."

Mallory smiled, but it was difficult to assess what she was really feeling, and Jessica did wonder. She didn't get up, which kind of said something. "Likewise. I'm glad we're all getting together."

She glanced around as she took a seat. "So no—"

"Brooklyn?" Sam supplied. "Generally, always late. I'm guessing you're starting to figure that out. She means well, but she has her own clock. I left her in her closet, where she'd created a mountain out of sweaters." She covered her mouth. "Not sure I was supposed to say that."

"It's okay." Jessica laughed at the visual, knowing how accurate it probably was. "So we may or may not see her."

"Oh, we'll see her," Mallory countered. "The question is, in which sweater?"

Okay, so they were relaxing into some conversation. This was good. Now if Brooklyn would just arrive, it would be even better. Jessica ordered a Scotch and water, then noticed Sam and Mallory were drinking martinis. How was it that she was still somehow that less-than-secure kid in high school, trying to keep up with the cool girls? Scotch and water was a perfectly acceptable drink, she told herself.

"A Scotch girl," Mallory noted.

"I tend to mix it up. The weather had a little something to do with this," she said, holding up the glass.

"Now you've made me jealous," Sam said. "It is a cozier drink. That'll be my next one." She was really beginning to like Samantha.

"So how's life at the office?" Mallory asked.

"Busy. As I'm sure you can sympathize with."

"Well, the final pitch is in two short days."

Okay. So they were going to go there. "It is."

"Do you all feel ready?" She said it like small talk, but the direction of the conversation was anything but.

"More than ready. What about you?"

"I think we're getting there."

Sam and Mallory seemed to zero in on someone behind her. *Please be Brooklyn. Please be Brooklyn. Please be Brooklyn.*

Sam inclined her head in the direction of the girl approaching their table. "Jess, I don't think you've met Hunter yet."

She stood and turned, coming face-to-face with a girl who could only be described as a stunning beauty with a hipster edge.

"So this is the famous Jessica," Hunter said with an easy smile. Her calmness put Jessica at ease. Almost a lack of judgment, a charm.

"Nice to meet you, Hunter. I've heard a lot about you."

"I'll buy you a drink and tell you the truth later."

"You will not," said a voice from behind them. Two hands snaked around her waist, and in that moment, all was right with the world again. "Promise me you won't fall in love with her like everyone else does," Brooklyn whispered playfully.

"I'll do my best."

And then softer, "Hey."

"Hey," she said, looking down at the smile that could end wars.

"I'm sorry I'm late. And I'm sorry for dragging you out in a blizzard." She stole a quick hello kiss that only steadied Jessica's ship all the more. As they turned to sit, she caught Mallory's gaze on them, which she quickly refocused elsewhere.

"It wasn't my easiest commute, but it was worth it."

"You're my favorite."

"That was the goal."

"Have you guys had a chance to chat?" Brooklyn asked, glancing from one face to the next. She still had her arm firmly around Jessica's waist, which Jessica happened to enjoy.

Samantha smiled widely. "Yes. In fact, we were just discussing the Foster account."

Brooklyn stared at Sam, clearly surprised by the news. "Then I got here just in time."

And she had, because with Brooklyn there as the commonality, things naturally fell into place. Over the next hour, Jessica relaxed into herself, getting to know the girls and taking in their shorthand. And there was a lot of it. The four best friends really were that, Jessica noted as she surveyed the easy banter and the familiarity of their exchanges. They teased each other, commiserated over dating issues, and were completely at home with one another.

She admired their friendship because she'd never really had anything like it.

Brooklyn turned to Jessica and felt infinitely lighter as she laughed with her friends. After a brief introductory period, in surprising news to her nerves, things seemed to be going pretty well. From the back pocket of her jeans she felt her cell phone buzz. As the conversation continued around her, she pulled it out and glanced at the readout.

The text from Hunter read, "Your girlfriend is hot and doesn't seem at all like an evil queen of all things business." She glanced up and exchanged a smile with Hunter before typing out a response with her thumb.

"Right? Thank you for getting that."

"The worst part, though," Sam remarked, "was when Mal finally got Starbucks to repeat her name back correctly only to have them spell it wrong on the cup in big bold letters. I spent the rest of the morning with the clearly labeled Mellory. It was tragic."

In response to Mallory's expression, the table erupted in laughter, because alcohol or not, it was pretty pitiful.

"Give them a fake name," Jessica suggested. "I do."

"What have you used?" Mallory asked, clearly amused.

"Julio." The table erupted again.

"Next round is on me," Hunter said. She signaled the waitress and offered Brooklyn a wink.

Jessica eventually excused herself to the ladies' room, which was much nicer than one would have expected for a bar essentially laid out in a warehouse. As she reapplied her lip gloss, the door opened and Mallory's image appeared in the mirror behind her. Jessica turned and stepped away from the sink. "All yours."

"I'm good, actually," Mallory said. "I'm sorry about earlier, when you got here. I was on hyper-alert mode. It's something I'm working on."

Jessica softened. She hadn't seen much sincerity in Mallory up until this moment. "No need to apologize. I get it."

"That's not to say I'm not intensely protective of Brooklyn."

"I can understand that."

"And while I'm supporting her and her decision to enter into this relationship, I'm not convinced it's the wisest move for either of you."

Okay, so that was less supportive.

"You should know that she comes first, Mallory. My intentions, where Brooklyn is concerned, are one hundred percent sincere."

She nodded. "That's good to hear. Because she's met her quota for rough times."

"I think we agree on that issue."

"I hope so. You should know that we all have her back and will hunt you down if you hurt that girl."

"Got it. I'd rather not be hunted, so…"

Something in Mallory's face softened. "You should know that I'm not as hard-core as I seem."

"No?"

She shook her head and shrugged. "I had to get that out of the way."

And then Jessica understood. A smile tugged. "That was the big-brother speech, wasn't it?"

Mallory laughed and tilted her head from side to side. "Something like that, yeah. I happen to have three big brothers and a little experience to draw from." And then her fierceness was back again but this time more endearing. "But that doesn't make the sentiment any less real. You break her heart and you answer to us."

"Those are terms I can live with."

"Good. Because the thing is, Brooklyn expects people to disappoint her. That's a given in her head, that's just who she is. But for whatever reason, she's pushed all that aside for you. Don't make her regret it."

"I won't."

Mallory nodded and turned to go.

"Mallory?"

"Yeah?"

"Are we going to find a way to be friends at some point?"

"One step at a time, Lennox." But the playful gleam in her eye when she said it meant something.

There was hope and it made Jessica want to celebrate a little. When she arrived back at the table, she took Brooklyn's hand and pulled her onto the dance floor. Jessica loved to dance. She always had, though it was unlike her generally conservative demeanor to slow dance in public, to put her softer side on display. But then there seemed to be a lot of new lately.

Something soft was playing from way back, and several couples were swaying easily to its beat. Soulful and bluesy. Billie Holliday maybe. She liked it. It was the kind of music you danced to in a snowstorm. She liked it even more when Brooklyn settled in against her and met her eyes.

"So you're a hit."

"Really? How do you already know?"

"Easy. They stopped being polite. It's a surefire sign, as it doesn't happen all that often when outside people are around. But after about fifteen minutes, they were totally and completely themselves. That,

Cinderella, means they like you. Which is not hard for me to believe at all. As I happen to feel the same."

Jessica tried to hold back the smile, but it was a losing battle. She was relieved and grateful and excited. "It's a good night, then."

Brooklyn placed a soft kiss along her jaw. "It's a very good night. And I'm going to enjoy it. The calm before the storm."

Jessica tilted her head to the side. "Are you referencing the one outside? I happen to like it."

Brooklyn took a deep breath. "Monday morning is kind of a big deal, wouldn't you say?"

Aha. The final Foster pitch. "Can I tell you something?"

Brooklyn tickled the back of her neck softly as they danced. "You can tell me anything, Jessica."

And she knew it was true. They had this ever-present connection between them, and it'd been there since that very first moment. She tucked a strand of hair behind Brooklyn's ear. "I am not worried about the Foster account. I probably should be, but I'm not."

Brooklyn's mouth fell open, and she poked her gently in the ribs. "That confident, huh?"

She shook her head, laughing. "No. I'm not saying it right. What I mean is—"

"Yeah?"

"I'm not worried about whether we get the account. If this were three months ago, I'd lose sleep, agonize over every detail. And while I'd still really like to land it, I'm not even going to be there Monday. Tina can handle this one on her own. I'll send Bentley to assist."

Brooklyn didn't understand. "Why?"

"Because that's not what I'm invested in. In case you haven't noticed, I've been really happy lately, and it has nothing to do with what goes on at the office. I'm in a place that I never thought I'd be, never imagined for myself, and I don't want to go back."

Brooklyn stared at Jessica and felt the smile on her face slowly fade as she took hold of Jessica's meaning.

The music shifted to something contemporary and fast paced, but they didn't move from their spot. Jessica took Brooklyn's face in her hands as she spoke. "I told you once that I was falling for you, but I think that moment has passed."

"It has?" Brooklyn's heart hammered away.

"Mhmm." Jessica brushed Brooklyn's bottom lip gently with her thumb, then placed a kiss in that very spot. "Because now, I'm so in love with you I don't even recognize myself. I'm planning vacations and Christmases and daydreaming about kissing you in the snow every winter you'll have me."

She drew in a breath because there it was. Jessica *loved* her. Hearing the words, Jessica's desire for a future together, caused something to stir within her. Something that had been long absent clicked into place. And the feelings it inspired washed over her now in great big wonderful waves, propelling her to act. She was on her tiptoes and kissing Jessica before she had a chance to think, angling her face for a better fit and sinking into the amazing warmth. Kissing Jessica had this way of satisfying her and making her want more at the same damn time.

It was a wondrous thing.

When she pulled her lips back, she found those dark-blue eyes and stared, knowing the ball was in her court. But somehow the words she needed failed her, and as she grappled, a crippling fear took over, sending a shiver through her entire body.

And she remembered who she was.

She took a step back, offering a reassuring smile through her struggle. Her eyes brushed the ground and she took a slow breath, wondering why she couldn't just function like a normal person and take that emotional leap. *God.*

"Hey, Brook. Look at me," Jessica said. So she did, and somehow the world felt manageable again. That's what Jessica did for her. "You said everything you needed to say just now in the way you kissed me."

It wasn't enough.

Brooklyn knew that much. But at the same time, Jessica understood. And that made her that much more wonderful. That's why she deserved to know the depth of the feelings Brooklyn had for her. And she would. Soon. If Brooklyn could just gather a little bit of courage.

Jessica placed a quick kiss on Brooklyn's open palm. "I'll settle the tab."

She went home with Jessica that night with a full heart, laughing their way through the brutal wind and stopping for an impromptu snowball fight, as you always must when snow's in supply.

And with an even fuller heart they found each other in Jessica's bed, the tender exploration shifting to lust-induced heights, the way it always did when the two of them were together. Jessica drifted off first, in the wee hours of the morning. Brooklyn watched her for a bit, captivated by how beautiful Jessica was when she slept, how peaceful. Long eyelashes and full lips and gentle breathing. She was quite simply an angel in front of her.

Jessica was hers, she reminded herself.

"I love you too," she barely whispered. She spoke the words into the safety of the darkness and not to Jessica, but that didn't make them any less true. She closed her eyes then and surrendered to sleep, enveloped in the knowledge that she was truly happy for the first time in the whole of her life.

Chapter Nineteen

"Nervous?" Mallory asked as they waited for the elevator to arrive and take them to the Foster offices.

Brooklyn pondered the question, taking note of the butterfly races happening in her stomach. "Yeah. But in an excited kind of way. Whatever happens, I'm proud of the work we've done. I think it's our best yet. In the end, these guys are going to go with the best idea. That's what this is about."

They stepped into the elevator, and once alone, Mallory checked her lipstick in her compact mirror. "True. But we have a pretty kick-ass idea, if I do say so myself. I agree it's our best yet, and all the credit goes to you. But we can't control the outcome."

"Right. I know. But I've worked so hard for this one. Like blood, sweat, and some definite tears, you know? Is it bad to say that I really, really want this?"

"Aww, I can't take that adorably hopeful look on your face." Mallory smiled and pulled her in for a hug. Mallory really did give the best hugs. "We're going to nail the presentation."

She exhaled slowly. "Positive thinking. I like it."

The elevator dinged their arrival, signaling go-time in Brooklyn's head. They strode with purpose into the lobby and checked in with the receptionist. The waiting room was empty, which meant that Tina and Bentley were already inside presenting.

Brooklyn liked the fact that Savvy had the second spot. Something about getting the final word resonated with her. She glanced at her notes again and ran her hand across the large, leather-bound carrying case that contained the amazing storyboards Hunter had crafted. It felt cool to the touch and somehow that was reassuring. She couldn't wait to show them off.

That's when the door to the conference room opened, and Tina, Bentley, and Jessica filed out quietly. But wait a minute. Jessica wasn't supposed to be at the presentation. She'd said specifically that she wouldn't be. So what was she doing here now? What had changed? They stood as the other team passed and nodded their professional hellos. Jessica met her eyes briefly and squeezed her hand as she passed. But she had a look on her face that Brooklyn couldn't quite decipher.

She shook it off.

"Ms. Campbell, Ms. Spencer," the receptionist said. "You may set up now."

Brooklyn nodded. They gathered their materials and headed into the conference room, which was now empty, allowing the executives a short break between presentations. Brooklyn oriented herself to the space and glanced at her presentation points one final time.

She was ready.

"Brooklyn, can you come here for a second?" Mallory asked.

But when she turned to join Mallory at the front of the room, what she saw as she approached stopped her short. "I don't understand."

When Mallory turned back to her from the storyboard on the easel, her face was pale. "I don't know. It was just sitting here. Probably from that last presentation."

Alarm bells were going off loudly in her head, and her mind went into overdrive trying to figure out what she was looking at. The storyboard in front of her showed the end-of-commercial spot. Their commercial spot. The beach. The wedding. A *gay* wedding. It was their concept to a tee. She reached for the remaining storyboards propped against the wall. The Lennox Group must have left them there for the executives to peruse.

As she studied the other storyboards, it only got worse. She felt the blood drain from her face as the realization settled. Not only had they stolen their concept, but they'd lifted their execution as well. The core of the work was much the same, the only differences being slight angle shifts or color replacements on the storyboard.

She stared up at Mallory. "This isn't a coincidence."

"No, I would say not. They're too similar." The look on her face communicated everything.

"You think Jess did this. She wouldn't have. Would she? No. No way."

Mallory hesitated, but only slightly. "I don't know. I'm just looking at the facts."

Brooklyn blinked effectively to try to clear her head, but the air in the room was feeling rather scarce. She held onto the back of one of the conference room chairs and closed her eyes.

"Here," Mallory said, handing her the inhaler from Brooklyn's purse. "It's going to be fine. Just breathe. In and out."

Brooklyn took a couple of puffs from the inhaler, and while her breathing might have settled, nothing else had. The world felt wildly upside down. It didn't make sense. How did the other team have access to their work? She tried to reason her way through it. "Let's say it was Jessica. She would have had to—" And the understanding slapped her in the face as she turned solemnly to Mallory. "The laptop. I had my laptop with me when I visited her office." She covered her mouth. "Mallory, I'm so sorry. This is my fault."

"It's okay." She moved to her then and ran her hands up and down Brooklyn's arms in reassurance. "And this is *not* your fault. But do you know what happens now?"

Brooklyn shook her head. She was at a total loss.

"We give the presentation we came here to give. Present *our* ideas, because they are ours."

It seemed like a ridiculous thing to do at this point, but she didn't see a lot of options, short of wandering out of there with their tails between their legs, which she wasn't prepared to do.

They would have to be impressive, but they could do that. A bigger issue was looming, though, one she couldn't quite face just yet. She'd think about what all of this meant later, because if she did that now, she'd come undone.

The executives filed back in, and after a few pleasantries, they were underway. Brooklyn took the floor. "Imagine if you will the most picturesque, balmy day. Love is in the air. It's the perfect afternoon for a wedding, and who doesn't love weddings?" She smiled confidently at Mallory, who smiled back. Once she got started, she fell easily into the zone. As she discussed the spot that had become near and dear to her heart, she felt that passion bubble to the surface all over again.

While a few glances were exchanged once the duplicate concept was clear, she could tell that they were pulled in further and further as she spoke. It was because her connection to the concept was strong, and that was something The Lennox Group didn't have, couldn't have.

The presentation went by in a whirlwind, and before she knew it, Brooklyn was met with applause and a series of handshakes from the team in front of her.

"An interesting series of events today," Royce said as he approached. "And while I may have a few questions about that later, I enjoyed your presentation very much. We'll be in touch with a decision soon. We're eager to move forward quickly with this."

They didn't speak on the ride down. But once they spilled out on to the street, Mallory turned to her. "You were on fire in there. I've never seen you that good. The presentation couldn't have gone any better."

She nodded. "Thanks."

"You know what? Why don't we get a drink? It's close to five, and I think the universe owes us. We can talk it out."

"You go on ahead. Call the others. I need to take a walk."

Mallory shook her head slightly. "Brooklyn, don't. You need to be around your friends right now. And you know what? Maybe it was all just a big misunderstanding that we'll laugh about one day."

The anger, the hurt, it was all building now, slamming into her like the most brutal tidal wave. "Do you believe that? That this was some misunderstanding?"

It was several long seconds before Mallory answered. "No."

"Me neither, which is why I have to go."

"Wait, Brooks. I'll walk with you." She reached out a hand to touch Brooklyn's arm, but she effectively sidestepped the touch. The look of helplessness on Mallory's face was too much. She didn't want anyone feeling sorry for her, and she certainly didn't need to be taken care of. By anyone.

"I just need to do this on my own for a while." She backed away from Mallory, who nodded solemnly, before turning and losing herself on the crowded sidewalk. As she walked aimlessly, she took comfort in the nameless faces that enveloped her. People she expected very little from, but people who didn't have the power to hurt her either.

Tears spilled down her cheeks as night cloaked the city. Couples strolled past, hand in hand, en route to dinner or home after a long day.

Good for them, she thought, battling the gut-wrenching pain that accompanied the truth. Good for them.

❖

The day was coming to a close, and Jessica was going crazy wondering how the big day had gone for Brooklyn. Her text messages hadn't been answered. She'd left a voice mail too, but perhaps Brooklyn had gone out with her friends after the presentation and hadn't heard her phone.

She grabbed her office receiver and dialed five for Bentley. "Do I have any messages?"

"Three. I forwarded them to your inbox."

"Personal?"

"Nope."

"Okay. Thanks."

She swiveled in her chair and watched for a few minutes as the lights of the city began to flare in contrast to the darkening sky. It was beautiful, and she let it wash over her a minute.

She paid more attention to those kinds of things now.

And that understanding made her smile.

She thought back on the afternoon. Brooklyn had looked surprised to see Jessica exiting the boardroom. She wanted to stop and explain why, fill her in on how strange the whole day leading up to the meeting had seemed. But at the same time, she also knew it wasn't the time to treat Brooklyn like her girlfriend. And while she hadn't planned to attend the final pitch session, something about the way Tina was acting that morning had worried her. The normally confident account executive seemed nervous and unsettled. Something was up, and Jessica had decided to tag along just in case she needed to take the reins.

In good news, everything had gone swimmingly, and the Foster team seemed really interested in their concept. It was odd to root for herself at the same time she was rooting for Brooklyn, but as complicated as it seemed, that's exactly what she was doing.

She tried Brooklyn's phone again. Maybe she'd be free to join her and Ashton for dinner. They planned to try the new sushi place across the street from their building, be adventurous.

But again, her call rolled straight to voice mail.

❖

Two days later and Brooklyn was on automatic pilot. She went through her day checking the boxes, answering e-mails, smiling at her friends' jokes, but the world just looked gray. Winter had lost its charm, and she just wanted the holidays firmly in her rearview mirror. Leave the turkeys and the fa-la-la-la-la to someone else. Seriously.

She felt foolish.

Embarrassed.

And no matter how many times Sam told her it was all right, or Hunter explained that she didn't have anything to apologize for, it didn't make a difference. This was all her doing. They'd warned her about the complications of involving herself with a competitor, and she'd scoffed. And whether they landed the account or not couldn't take the place of the guilt she felt.

But that was just the surface-level stuff.

Those feelings didn't touch what hurt the most. She'd opened herself up to Jessica, trusted her with parts of herself she'd never trusted to anyone. And that's what gutted her most. The betrayal. No matter how happy she'd been just days prior, nothing was worth what she was feeling now. She'd take it all back if she could. An all-consuming emptiness haunted the place where her heart had been. And what's worse was her mind hadn't caught up. She still found herself reaching for the phone to call Jess at the end of her day, or somehow worked her into the weekend plans. God, it felt like the rug had been pulled out from under her in another cruel blow from the universe.

Never again, she told herself. Lesson learned once and for all.

She glanced warily at the clock. It was after eight p.m. and she rarely worked this late. Mallory generally closed the place down, but today Brooklyn might edge her out. "Hey, you," Mal said, coming around to her desk and perching on the side of it. "Wanna grab dinner in midtown? I'm starving."

"Can't. Going to the gym."

"At night?"

"What can I say? I'm suddenly a fan of two-a-days. I might try a yoga class next week."

Mallory nodded and offered an encouraging smile. "Trying to outdo me."

"Please. Like that's even possible." She tried to seem playful but wasn't sure how successful she'd been. She grabbed her attaché and slipped it onto her shoulder. "See you tomorrow. Don't work too late."

"Brooks?"

She turned back reluctantly. Lately she craved time on her own and the comfort that independence afforded her. People kept getting in the way. Walls were in place and weren't about to come down. "Yeah?"

"You okay?"

"I will be." She was convinced of this. She'd survived worse times. Hunger. Loneliness. Even the occasional smack across the face. She could survive a broken heart. She could also lie to herself rather effectively when necessary.

❖

Jessica knocked on Brooklyn's door a second time and waited. No answer. She glanced up and down the hallway for any sign of someone she knew. She was at a loss. Something was definitely wrong.

In the past they'd gone days without seeing each other, but not without talking. Brooklyn hadn't returned her phone calls or answered her text messages. Either she was purposefully avoiding her or had been abducted. And since no one at Savvy had contacted her, she was imagining it was the former. More determined and worried than ever, she returned to the building's rather no-frills lobby and scanned the directory for the Savvy offices. After riding up to the sixth floor, she didn't bother knocking.

The rather striking office was open and trendy, and seemed to match its inhabitants quite accurately. But the space seemed deserted tonight, with the exception of Mallory, who turned at her desk as the door slid open.

"Hey," Jessica said. "I'm sorry to bother you, but I can't seem to get ahold of Brooklyn."

Mallory stood and regarded her calmly. "No. I would imagine you couldn't."

Okay, what the hell did that mean? "You're kind of freaking me out right now. Is she okay?"

"She's fine. Or she will be. What is it you want, Jessica? You've done enough, wouldn't you say? Mission accomplished and all?"

"Okay, you're going to have to explain whatever's upset all of you. Is this about Foster? Have you heard something I haven't?" Maybe they'd been given the account and she hadn't been notified.

Mallory shook her head and returned to her desk as if she refused to dedicate much of her attention to Jessica. "Let's start with, you stole our work and presented it as your own. Sound familiar now?"

She took a minute with the accusation because it was a big one. And it wasn't even close to accurate. "Okay, where did that come from?"

"The storyboards you left behind after your presentation. They were near duplicates of ours. Surely you knew we'd see them."

Jessica retraced the series of events in an attempt to decode what Mallory was saying. Royce Foster had asked them to leave the storyboards for further reflection. That part was true. She'd seen no problem leaving the artwork. Tina hadn't been wild about the idea.

"Right. And you're saying they were similar to yours?"

"That's an understatement."

"Can I see them?" Mallory stared at her blandly. "Please, Mallory. This is kind of important."

Mallory sighed and turned to her computer as Jessica came to stand behind her. After clicking through a number of windows, Mallory produced a series of images in Photoshop. Jessica studied them, and a heavy feeling of dread washed over her. They weren't identical, but the similarities were striking. The close-up of the first bride's face, the bubbles in the drink.

She straightened. "I don't have an explanation. I didn't do this."

Mallory turned to face her. "Then who did?"

"I don't know. The idea for the wedding was Tina's. It came late in the game. We were originally focused on a tropical-vacation theme. Fun in the sun. "

"Until Brooklyn brought her laptop to your office. Then suddenly a new concept appeared. Am I close?"

And then it all clicked into place. She stared at Mallory. Brooklyn's bag. The *laptop*. She closed her eyes as the horrible understanding knocked her back a few steps. "Can I sit down?" But she didn't exactly wait for a response and sank into the nearest chair. It was Brooklyn's desk, she realized, recognizing the handwriting on the Post-its along the bottom of the computer monitor. Somehow it felt wrong to be sitting there now.

"You okay?"

"It had to be Tina," she said half to Mallory and half to herself. "My account executive. She's the one who took Brooklyn's coat and bag that day. Brooklyn even commented on it. Tina was also acting super keyed up the morning of the presentation. And she didn't want to leave those storyboards behind." Jessica shook her head. "I knew she was cutthroat, but I had no idea."

Mallory was watching her with obvious interest. "I'm shocked at what I'm about to say. And understand that I mean *really shocked.* But I think…I believe you."

Jessica looked up at her, her composure breaking a bit at the unlikely show of support. "I promise I'm telling the truth. I wouldn't have done this to her. To any of you. I know I've made some less-than-scrupulous calls in the past, but this wasn't one of them."

"I think I get that." She leaned against Brooklyn's desk. "So now what?"

Jessica fished in her bag for her phone. "I call over to Foster and bow out, explain what happened, and tell them the concept was yours." She started to dial.

Mallory extended a hand. "There's no reason to do that. Royce called thirty minutes ago to congratulate us. The account is going to Savvy."

Jessica sat back in her chair and exhaled slowly. "Thank God." And then she moved on to bigger matters. "Where can I find her? Because I need to, Mallory."

"Let me talk to her first."

CHAPTER TWENTY

Jessica handed the double mocha to Ashton and accepted the black coffee from the Starbucks barista in exchange for her credit card.

"This is awesome," Ashton said, going in for a second sip. "How have I gone this long without coffee in my life?"

Jessica raised one shoulder. "I didn't think kids drank coffee. Are you sure it's okay that I bought you some?"

Ashton passed her a look. "I'm hardly a typical kid. Plus, you've met my mother, yes?"

"Touché. I talked to her briefly this morning."

They sipped and strolled casually down Thirty-fourth Street, window-shopping after the shopping excursion to beef up Ashton's winter wardrobe, Jessica's treat.

"You did. What about?"

"You. She wanted to make sure you were doing all right. She mentioned your father in Colorado. He wants to reconnect."

"Right."

"So you and he have talked?"

"About moving in with him? Yeah. He offered. Kind of out of nowhere. I haven't talked to the guy in years."

"And how do you feel about that?"

Ashton shrugged. "Mom's got another couple of months, and I can't keep putting you out."

Jessica steered them to a bench in front of Macy's and they took a seat. "Here's the thing. You're not putting me out. You happen to be exceptionally good company. You do your homework. You run around with your friends, but you're always home when I ask you to be. I like having you around. You're an amazing kid."

Ashton was staring at the sidewalk, but when she raised her gaze, a smile pulled at the ends of her mouth. "You think so?"

It wasn't something she heard a lot, Jessica realized, and she instantly wanted to shake the people responsible for that. "Not a doubt in my mind. And while it might be nice to explore Colorado, ski, get to know your dad more, you're also more than welcome to stay with me. I'm by no means an amazing cook, but I think I can manage a passable Thanksgiving dinner. We can go down and watch the parade that morning. I can get us some pretty decent seats too."

Ashton's arms were around her before she realized it. She hugged her back and held on, doing her best to swallow the emotion that threatened. Ashton needed her, and she would be there for her for however long she needed.

Ashton released her and they watched the shoppers brush past each other, bags in hand. "You're different lately," Ashton said.

Jessica tossed her a look. "In what way?"

"I don't know. Less serious." She gestured around them. "You're out doing stuff, enjoying yourself. Not staring at papers and files. It's, I don't know, pretty cool."

Jessica smiled. "Well, a few key people are responsible for that shift." She touched Ashton pointedly on the nose.

"Speaking of key people, where's Brooklyn? I haven't seen her in a while."

"Me neither. It's been close to two weeks. We're having dinner tonight, though. Some things happened that I need to sort out with her."

"Uh-oh. Her fault or yours?"

"Mine, I guess. And I need to make it right."

"Women like flowers."

"Brooklyn's not exactly traditional."

"Then a candy bar."

"Really?"

"Buy her some Peanut M&Ms and Mountain Dew. You can't lose."

Jessica had to laugh. "Noted. I think I'm coming to you for any and all dating advice."

"Well, duh."

They spent the next twenty minutes taking in the whimsical Christmas windows at Macy's. They took photos with the Christmas trees, gingerbread houses, Santa Claus, and his many elves and reindeer. While it was hard to get excited about the impending holidays until things were right again with Brooklyn, a part of her hoped that by the night's end, they would be.

Because it was everything.

Brooklyn exhaled slowly. She didn't know what she'd say when she saw Jessica. If the right words would come. She'd thought about it in detail on the car ride over but was coming up short and hoping she'd somehow know when the moment was upon her. She pulled into a no-parking zone, confident no one would notice, but upon further reflection moved her car to the garage three blocks down.

Perhaps she was maturing after all.

She'd let Jessica select the restaurant, which was one she'd never been to. She checked her watch under the lamplight as she approached Casellula in Hell's Kitchen. Only ten minutes late, due to the parking escapade. It could be worse. She caught sight of herself in the reflection of a nearby window she passed, adjusting her black sweater and pulling her white coat tighter around her against the cold. The streets were bustling the way they always were on Friday night, full of theatergoers dashing to make curtain and locals trekking their way to hipster nightspots. She was trying to push down her nerves, but it was hard, because there were things she needed to say tonight, and they wouldn't be easy for her.

She and Jessica hadn't seen each other since before the presentation from hell. Yes, Savvy had landed the account, but the damage had been vast and this dinner felt uneven as a result. How were they supposed to behave to one another?

Brooklyn took the steps to the door of the restaurant and surveyed the place upon entering. It was tiny. Maybe ten tables or so dotted the dimly lit room surrounded by high ceilings and exposed brick. Jessica was sitting by the window appearing as uneasy as she felt. Brooklyn sucked in a breath at the image of her, so soft yet so complicated. It was what drew her to Jessica innately.

Her hair was partially pulled back. She was wearing jeans she'd tucked into stylish boots and a green cashmere sweater. Her eyes met Brooklyn's and held on. And whatever questions Brooklyn had were answered in that moment.

Jessica stood as she approached but made no move to touch her. It was probably best, given the uncertain nature of their meeting. "Hi. I'm glad you came."

"Me too."

They sat, a distance looming between them. Brooklyn studied the menu of small plates, but it was just for show. Her appetite had left her days ago.

"Wine?" Jessica indicated the bottle on the table.

"Sure."

"I know you're upset," Jessica said quietly. "You have every right to be."

She nodded, accepting the glass Jessica poured for her. And then, "Mallory believes you didn't know. That it was our concept."

"What about you?" Jessica asked, leaning back in her chair.

It was an important question and one she'd asked herself a million times. "I believe you too. Now."

"Now. What convinced you?" Jessica tilted her head to the side, and the candle from the table flickered a glow across her face.

"To be honest, I don't think I was sure until I walked in the door tonight. When I saw you in front of me, I remembered who you were. You wouldn't have done this."

Jessica felt the world lift from her shoulders. Everything could be okay again if Brooklyn truly felt that way. She reached across the table and threaded her fingers through Brooklyn's and exhaled. "You don't understand what it's been like these past couple of weeks. Not knowing how you were doing, what you must be thinking of me."

Brooklyn ran her thumb across Jessica's hand in reassurance. "You're a good person, Jess. I just needed reminding. So what happens for The Lennox Group now?"

"I fired Tina, though she'll probably just open up her own firm and put us both out of business." Brooklyn shook her head in exasperated wonder and sipped from her wine. "For good measure, I also placed a call to Royce to explain the series of events, so they had no question of integrity on your end."

"You did that?"

"Mhmm."

"I don't know what to say. Thank you." Her eyes dropped. Suddenly Brooklyn was incredibly interested in the grooves on the bread plate in front of her. Jessica had a sinking feeling.

"Is there something else we should talk about? What's up?"

Brooklyn raised her eyes, which were so full of emotion, Jessica found it difficult to breathe. "I can't."

"You can't," Jessica said slowly. Two incredibly simple words that carried such weight when said in conjunction. "Please tell me that means you can't figure out what to order. Or you can't stay over tonight. Or better yet, that you can't wait to get out of here with me."

But none of those things were true, because the eyes that had once sparkled and danced were now closed off to her in a way she couldn't handle. Dread spread through her like wildfire, and she squeezed her napkin absently.

Brooklyn shook her head at Jessica's nervous smile, knowing what she was about to say was for the best in the long run, even if it didn't feel that way now.

The two weeks since the presentation had been excruciating. The feeling of loss she'd experienced was too consuming to risk ever running into again. Deviating from what had worked so well for her all of these years had been a mistake. The joy they'd found in each other surely had an expiration date, and she couldn't stand around waiting for it all to be ripped from her at any moment.

Brooklyn pulled her hand away slowly. "I'm not cut out for this—a relationship. I'm out of my depth here. Especially with someone like you who's thoughtful and attentive and has given me everything I've needed, including time. You're the best kind of person, Jess, and you deserve someone who can give herself back to you. I thought I could be that person, but I can't. It's too much."

"You're running away because you're afraid of getting hurt," Jessica stated matter-of-factly. "That's what happened, isn't it? When you thought I'd sold you out to get the account—"

"Yes, okay. It was eye-opening, and it was a lot to deal with. So the account stealing was a false alarm, but maybe down the road you'll meet someone else, or become disinterested in me, or gradually the competition with our careers will eat away at us. I don't know what it will be, but something will happen, and the concept of that loss is too much to take. I feel like I'm standing under this house of cards and at any point it could come tumbling down, and I can't be there for that, do you understand? And it's true. The past two weeks were a horrific sneak preview, a wake-up call."

"What if none of those things happen? There are no guarantees in life, Brooklyn. But you have to be willing to take a little bit of a risk when it matters, or you drift through life without experiencing the best parts."

"But I'm not willing. That's the thing. So I'm not the bravest person in the world. That doesn't change my decision." She stood and placed her napkin on the table. And because she had to, she leaned down and kissed Jessica on the cheek one last time. "It's better this way. Trust me."

"Don't do this," Jessica whispered, touching her cheek. "I love you."

The words that once meant everything were painful now because they weren't hers to keep. "And because of you, I finally know what that feels like."

They had nothing left to say. She walked to the door of the restaurant and took one last look back at the woman who'd come to mean everything.

And then she walked blindly away.

The bitterness of the cold outside was nothing compared to the pain in the center of her chest at what she'd just turned her back on. Tears burned her cheeks as she walked to the garage, but she wiped them away systematically as they fell. And her guard, the distance she placed between herself and the rest of the world, moved slowly back into place.

CHAPTER TWENTY-ONE

The line at Starbucks was kind of insane, but Brooklyn and Mallory had decided to brave it anyway. The winter weather definitely had the customer count at an all-time high, making the store cramped and uncomfortable.

They'd made it through Thanksgiving. She'd gone home to celebrate with Samantha's family in Maine, the way she had for the past eight years. It was nice to have somewhere to go, and Sam's mom made the best stuffing she'd ever tasted. But she'd be lying if she said her thoughts hadn't drifted several times to the Thanksgiving that was surely taking place in Avon, Connecticut. Or the smaller one, tucked away in the West Village.

And now, the constant playing of Christmas carols everywhere she went served as an annoying reminder that Christmas itself was now less than two weeks away. They paid the barista and moved off to the side to wait for their order.

"So the party's kind of crept up on us this year," Mallory said. Ah, yes, their yearly Christmas party. It had started back in the day as a warm, rather professional gathering to which they invited all of their clients, a total Savvy event. But in the coming years, the party had morphed into something a little more social, to which they invited their friends and neighbors in the building. They converted the office loft into a Christmas happy place and let the bubbly flow. It was festive and fun and often went late into the night. In fact, they had a reputation for throwing the most fun Christmas party in town.

"I haven't forgotten," she answered. "Hunter wants to go with more of a winter-wonderland theme this year. Lots of blues. Serve arctic martinis with a miniature candy cane as a garnish."

Mallory turned to face her. "I can get behind blue."

"Samantha wants to do Santa hats again this year."

Mallory offered a smile. "She's kind of adorable at Christmas. We probably have to oblige."

"Agreed. Like one of those wide-eyed kids waiting for Santa. She doesn't ask for much in life."

"What about you?" Mallory asked.

"What about me?"

"Any special party requests? You've been noticeably less opinionated lately."

Brooklyn shrugged. "Nope. Just doing my thing."

Mallory studied her. "It's been a rough couple of months for you. I just want to see you happy again."

She turned to Mallory and flashed her a playful smile. "I'm always happy, you know that."

"That's not what I mean."

"I have a peppermint mocha for Brooklyn and an almond latte for Mowery," the bored-with-life guy behind the counter called out. She was saved by the bell, or in this case the 'Bucks.

Mallory sighed as she retrieved their drinks.

"At least they're getting closer," Brooklyn offered good-naturedly.

Mallory rolled her eyes and sipped from her cup. "Either I got your peppermint mocha or the cold war continues."

Brooklyn tested her own drink and shook her head. "Nope. It's your move, Russia."

"You know what? Let's just go. It's too crowded today to fight back."

Brooklyn stared at Mallory in mystification. "How is it that you're so in charge everywhere you go in life except here? What does Starbucks have on you? Naked photos? Take it back to the counter."

"You think I should?"

"Mal, you're killing me."

With eyes of steel, Mallory nodded and moved to the drink counter. "Excuse me. I ordered an almond latte and this is a peppermint mocha."

The eighteen-year-old boy at the bar stared back at her blankly. "The order I was given said peppermint mocha. I just made it."

"Yes, you indeed made one for my friend. But you made one for me too, which I did not order."

"So why did you take it? Give it back."

"Because you said Mowery."

"And you're Mowery?"

"No, I'm Mallory."

"Then you shouldn't have taken a drink that didn't belong to you."

"It did belong to me, but I ordered an almond latte."

"I made what you ordered. I don't see the problem."

Brooklyn couldn't take it anymore. The carols, the crowds of people, the barista who'd perfected the opposite of customer service. Her coping skills were at an all-time low, and this kid and his ignorant power trip nudged the scale in the wrong direction. She snapped into action, stepping forward. "Listen to me, you little coffee asshole. You got the order wrong. This shouldn't be news. You always get the order wrong. It's the only thing you're good at. I know because I'm in here daily. It's not cute anymore. I'm sorry you never get laid, sincerely. That must suck. But that's not reason enough to ruin everyone else's day. So push past it and make my friend the best almond latte you've ever made. Because it's the holidays, for fuck's sake!"

His eyes were as big as saucers when she finished. "Yes, ma'am."

"And make sure it says Mallory on the side. You know what? I'll help." She reached across the bar for his Sharpie and an empty cup and scrawled Mallory's name in large letters. "Now you'll never forget it again. See?" She turned the cup around for him.

He nodded. "Mallory. Okay. Got it. I was just confused before about the order."

"I mean, clearly," she said, softening. "But I think you have it now, right?

"Right."

Mallory looked on in wonder until she was handed a piping-hot almond latte with her name correctly spelled across the cup.

"Merry Christmas," Brooklyn said sweetly to the barista.

They spilled out onto the sidewalk as a blast of winter smacked them straight in the face in the form of sideways sleet. At least snow was pretty. Sleet was just downright painful. Mallory didn't seem to care and danced her way across the street to their building.

"I can't believe you just did that. That might have been one of the coolest moments of my life."

"It did feel pretty good."

"You just went for it. No holding back. Bam!" Mallory said, miming a punch.

"I kind of don't think he'll forget your name again."

Mallory pressed the button for their floor in the elevator and laughed. "No, I would think not. And this is what I'm talking about. I miss this fun, fiery side of you. It's been noticeably absent lately. Welcome back."

"Thanks," Brooklyn said, understanding the sentiment. And also feeling a lot more alive, now that Mallory mentioned it. Maybe she should lose it on people a little more often, she thought jokingly to herself. She'd been on automatic pilot the past few weeks. Admittedly. It was a coping mechanism to get her through the days that had been, well...rough. The break-up itself had been hard to get through, but the aftermath had been so much harder.

But she was learning some tricks.

Number one was not to let herself think about Jessica and how great the past couple of months had been, because when she did, it snowballed into much more. She was getting good at it, rule number one.

Rule number two was to occupy her life with as much mundane activity as she possibly could. If the file drawer needed alphabetizing, she was the girl to do it. Staying busy was the name of the game, and she was reaping the rewards. Life had floated back into the manageable column. And though the world seemed to have dulled significantly as of late, it was also a place she feared less.

"Brooklyn one, Starbucks zero," Mallory declared loudly as they entered the office. "You should have seen it, you guys. She was awesome. In charge and a little frightening, I have to say. But look!" She displayed her cup in all its glory.

"Seriously?" Sam asked, clearly impressed.

"Aww, look at that. Your name is even spelled correctly," Hunter said from where she sat atop her desk. "A monumental day for Mal. And Brooks too, apparently."

"Not that big a deal," Brooklyn said, downplaying the outburst. She still wasn't sure where it had come from.

"I'm surprised the place didn't break into the spontaneous slow-clap after the way she tore into that blank-staring barista."

"I'm a little bummed I missed it," Sam said, coming around the desk to Brooklyn. She seemed a little preoccupied.

"I wish I'd gotten video," Mallory said, still on cloud nine over the whole thing.

Hunter shot Sam a look. "Hey, do you think you ought to—"

"Yep. Brooklyn, can I steal you for a second? I need to discuss something with you."

"Sure, what's up? Someone you need me to lay into for you? I'm apparently on a roll."

But before Sam could answer, the bathroom door clicked, and Brooklyn turned in time to see her younger sister standing there.

"You have a visitor," Samantha said. "That's what I wanted to tell you."

"Hey," Cat said nervously. "I hope this is cool. Your friends said I could wait."

Brooklyn threw a glance at her friends as her mind struggled to process the series of events. "Hi. I don't understand. How did you get here?" It wasn't the warmest of greetings, but it was all she had.

"I took an Amtrak to the city. You told us where you worked when you visited, so I hit up Google."

"Oh. Okay. Does your mom know where you are?"

Cat shrugged. "Not exactly. I wanted to see you on my own. I thought maybe we could get coffee or something, but uh…" She gestured to the cup of coffee already in Brooklyn's hand. "I should have called first. I'm sorry. I'll go." Cat reached for her bag on the floor.

"Wait a sec." Brooklyn didn't know where to go with this. Her sister was seventeen and had just crossed through two states on her own. She couldn't turn her out onto the freezing streets of New York just as night was falling. Who knew what would happen to her. "Well, have you had dinner?"

"Not really."

"Tell you what. Why don't we grab an early bite and we can talk. Sound good?"

Cat nodded.

"I take it you've already met Hunter and Samantha."

"Yeah, they're awesome. Hunter explained how the grid system works in case I get lost."

"They are pretty great. And this is Mallory, one of my best friends and also my colleague." Mallory stepped forward and shook her hand.

"Nice to meet you."

"Mallory, this is Catherine. My sister."

❖

Cat sat back in the booth and stared in awe at her plate. "That stuff is amazing. What do you call it again?"

"Gnocchi. Specifically, potato gnocchi in asiago cream sauce."

Cat hadn't been especially confident when looking at the menu, so after a few well-placed questions, Brooklyn had guided her to something she might like. She'd taken her to Il Pozzo, a cozy little Italian restaurant on Spring Street that she frequented whenever possible. It was early enough that the place wasn't too crowded, and that gave them a chance to take their time.

"I'm glad you liked it. They also have a pesto version that's to die for."

"I've never even heard of gnocchi until today." Cat shook her head in awe. "I can't believe you live here, that this is your life. It's so cool."

For whatever reason, Cat's elevated opinion of her resonated. She liked that she was able to impress her little sister so easily. And it was still startling to her how much they resembled one another. Genetics was a wondrous thing. "So are you going to tell me why you're here?"

"Is that entirely necessary?"

"No. But I'm asking anyway."

"We had a fight," Catherine explained, rolling her eyes. "Me and my mom. Which isn't that unusual lately."

"What was it about?"

She hesitated a moment. "You."

The information hit Brooklyn squarely in the chest.

"It's not your fault. I don't want you to think that."

"What about me?"

"She's pulled away again. Ever since you came to visit, she's just been sad."

"And that upset you?"

"I don't like seeing her that way. I wanted to do something about it. Call you. See if we could all try again. Not just for her, but for me too. She said she'd done enough to you and should give you space until you're ready."

"So you thought you'd run away to New York City? It's nice to see you, but don't you think coming here on your own was a little dangerous? Think what your mom must be going through."

"I just wanted the chance to get to know you. I've always known I had a sister. They never kept that from us. And even though you weren't there growing up, it's like you were. There's always been this empty space, you know? I think my parents felt it the most. We knew where their heads were on Christmas or your birthday. They always had this distant look in their eyes."

Brooklyn dropped her gaze to the table, and the emotion she'd kept in check began to bubble to the surface once again. "I didn't realize. After I met you guys, I just kind of imagined a really perfect household. Something from a sitcom tied up in a neat little bow."

Cat shook her head. "Mom was never fully ours. Something was missing for her, and it's like nothing we could do could change that. No matter how many A's I got, or awards I won, I could never fill the void you left in her life. Do you know how frustrating that is?"

"She loves you, Cat. I saw that in just the short time I was there."

"I guess so." But the tears in her eyes made Brooklyn's heart clench. "Listen. You may never want to see us again, and I get that. But I thought you should know that it wasn't like anyone just forgot about you. If anything, you were on her mind more than we were."

Brooklyn blinked back at her because she hadn't known that. "I feel like I should say I'm sorry, but that doesn't really fit, does it?"

Cat shook her head. "I think that's the problem. Maybe we all have to get past thinking someone should apologize." They were wise words coming from a seventeen-year-old. But Brooklyn had a feeling Cat had been through a lot.

"You might be right. But enough with the serious stuff, if that's okay with you." She flashed Cat a smile. "We should order dessert."

Cat dabbed her eyes and sat forward, smiling back at the invitation. "Choose for me. Something I probably haven't tried before."

"An adventurous type. I like it." As Brooklyn reached for the menu, she noticed her: their mother. It was strange to see Cynthia out in the real world, in her very neighborhood, to be exact. She was speaking to their waiter, who was gesturing in their direction. She turned and crossed quickly to their table.

Brooklyn inclined her head to Cat. "I think we have company."

Cat turned just in time for her mother to arrive. Without hesitation she slid into the booth next to Cat and pulled her into a tight embrace. "Do you know how terrified I was?"

"I'm sorry," Cat mumbled, but she was hugging her back and that was something.

"I'm so glad you're okay. I had all these visions of something happening to you, never seeing you again." She was holding Cat's face in her hands. "Please don't do anything like this ever again. I felt like my blood pressure—"

"Mom, mom, mom," Cat said, trying to slow her down. "I'm sorry. I shouldn't have taken off, but I'm fine. We were just having dinner."

She turned to Brooklyn then and her eyes softened further. "Thank you," she said. She reached across the table and took her hand, squeezing. But she didn't let go. She stayed just like that, one arm around Cat and one holding onto Brooklyn.

"It was a surprise," Brooklyn managed to say. "But it gave us a chance to get to know one another."

"I tried gnocchi," Cat reported proudly. And then a thought seemed to occur to her. "How did you find me?"

"You weren't answering your phone, but I was still able to track you with the lost-phone app. I was only a couple of hours behind you. Technology can be a wonderful thing sometimes."

"Wow. Who knew?" Cat asked.

"And don't think you're off the hook. Just because I'm thrilled to see you alive doesn't mean we're not going to discuss this later, with repercussions."

Cat sighed deeply. “Gotcha.”

“Since you’re here, do you want to join us for dessert?” Brooklyn asked. It felt like an olive branch in some way. They hadn’t ended their last visit on the best of terms. It was only then that Cynthia released her hand, and a warm smile replaced the touch. She held Brooklyn’s gaze for several beats.

“I would like that very much. I’m starving actually.”

“We could order some more gnocchi,” Cat suggested.

Brooklyn signaled their waiter.

Two hours later when Brooklyn glanced at her watch, she was shocked at how quickly the time had passed. They’d killed the second round of gnocchi and a half a tray of Sicilian cannoli and were now on to their second cup of coffee. The ice had been broken fairly easily this time around, and something about the combination of the three of them just clicked. The conversation flowed; they laughed together and swapped stories with ease. Maybe it was the impromptu nature of the meeting, with no stressful buildup first. Whatever it was, she was genuinely having a good time.

Brooklyn gestured in a circle with her spoon at Cat. “So I think we’ve established that you’re a little boy crazy.”

“How so?” Cat asked, her mouth hanging open at the assertion.

“Three possible prom dates you can’t decide between is kind of telling.”

Cat shrugged. “What can I say? I’m a sucker for fluffy hair.” That pulled yet another laugh from Brooklyn. She really was a fun kid.

“So what about Jessica?” Cynthia asked. “How is she?”

“Oh,” Brooklyn said, faltering for a moment. “Um. That’s a good question. I’m not really sure. We stopped seeing each other a few weeks back.”

“No way,” Cat said. “You guys seemed so perfect together. What happened? Her fault?”

“Mine, actually.” She set her coffee down. For whatever reason, she felt strangely at ease with the two of them, like she was among friends, and that brought on an uncharacteristic dash of candor. “I don’t do well with relationships.”

“Why is that?” Cynthia asked with concern.

"Um. I guess I don't let people in easily," Brooklyn admitted. "It's just not something I'm ever going to be successful at. It terrifies me actually."

Cynthia tilted her head to the side as if trying to assess the situation. "Answer me this. Do you love her?"

Brooklyn took a deep breath and studied the portraits on the wall across the room. This felt like a blatant breaking of rule number one, but she allowed herself to go there temporarily. "Yes. And that's part of the problem. The stakes were too high. I need my life to be simple."

Cynthia sat back thoughtfully. "I could sit here and nod my understanding and support at what you seem to feel so strongly about, or I could give you the advice I missed out on giving you all these years."

Brooklyn didn't hesitate. "What's the advice?"

"Sweetheart, you can't hide from life. You're depriving yourself of the most precious gift this world can offer you. Love."

Cynthia opened her mouth to continue but had to pause, as something was clearly tugging at her. She stared at the table for a moment, but when she raised her eyes back to Brooklyn's, the emotion they held was jarring.

Brooklyn's heart pounded away in anticipation of what Cynthia was about to say.

"You may have felt like you were unloved most of your life, and that devastates me more than I can ever articulate. But you have to know that wasn't the case. My heart was bursting with love for you, and so was your father's. We didn't know where you were, or what you were doing on a given day, but we did know that we loved you. So you see, you've always had love. You just didn't know it."

It was a new way of looking at things that she'd never considered. She took the words and turned them over again in her mind. Coupled with the stories Cat had recounted, it seemed that she did have a place somewhere, in a strange way. And then and there, something lifted. She felt lighter. "So what you're saying is—"

"That you, Brooklyn, are entirely deserving of love, and that—"

"The brain freeze is worth the ice cream," Cat artfully inserted.

That pulled a look from Brooklyn. "I'm sorry. A brain freeze?"

"That's what Mom always says. I've heard it a hundred and nine times."

Cynthia tilted her head from left to right, mulling this over. She turned to Cat. “That’s true. I was just trying to say it a little more eloquently for Brooklyn.”

“Why? Isn’t she part of the family technically? Shouldn’t she hear it the way the rest of us always have to?”

Cynthia held up a hand, palm up. “You know what? You’re right.” She turned back to Brooklyn. “The ice cream is worth the brain freeze. And isn’t ice cream everything?”

“It is.” Brooklyn smiled at the concept. “Ice cream is everything. I’ll keep the brain-freeze thing in mind. But for now, I think I’m doing okay. Now that I have you here, however, would you mind telling me about my name? I’ve always wondered.”

Brooklyn couldn’t be sure, but she thought she saw a twinkle in Cynthia’s eye at the mention. “You were named after our first date.”

Cat narrowed her gaze. “Your first date with dad?”

Cynthia bopped her playfully in the head. “Of course with Dad. He finally asked me out after I’d waited months for him to notice me, and I desperately wanted to go. The only problem was that neither of us had any money. So he came up with the idea that we would hold hands, walk across the Brooklyn Bridge, and get to know one another better. He proposed that if it went well, when we made it across the bridge, I would let him kiss me.”

“And how did it go?” Brooklyn asked.

The blush that touched her cheeks was endearing. “It was the best conversation of my life. Followed by an off-the-charts kiss.”

Cat raised one shoulder. “That’s kinda sweet.” She turned to Brooklyn. “You were named after a date. You have no choice but to be a romantic.”

“The cheeky kid has a point,” Cynthia said, wrapping her arms around Cat.

Brooklyn had to admit it. She liked the story.

Chapter Twenty-two

"There's got to be somewhere better for you to be right now."

Jessica didn't turn around at the sound of Bentley's voice. She kept her eyes on her computer monitor and the verbiage from legal that would go into their revamped proprietary agreements. "That sounds like judgment," she murmured.

"Very astute of you." He came farther into the room and stared at her. She could feel his gaze overtly and finally swiveled to face him.

"Something you need, Bent?"

He shook his head. "I left my wallet. I thought I'd come back to the empty, dark office and retrieve it. But what to my wondering eyes should appear?"

"A workaholic and eight tiny Red Bulls?" Jessica asked, smiling sweetly.

"That's one way to put it." He perched on the edge of her desk. "It's Friday night, Jessica. Christmas is four days away. You shouldn't be at work at 9:23 in the evening. You should be with friends, family. Where's Ashton?"

"She's spending Christmas with her dad in Colorado. I encouraged her to go. She should spend time with him. She'll be back after New Year's."

He considered this and switched directions. "Come to dinner with us. Me and Deidre."

"I'm happy here. On my own. Besides, I have no interest in crashing your dinner date du jour. That's actually a more pathetic option, thank you very much."

He grabbed a stack of mail from the corner of her desk. "What about these, huh?" He sorted through the pile. "Invitations galore, Jess. Hit up one of these fancy holiday parties."

She shrugged and rubbed her eyes, weary from staring at the screen for so long. "It's all corporate stuff. Just another form of work."

"But it would get you out and into a nice dress and drinking some pink champagne and—" He froze mid-shuffle and held up a brightly colored invitation, turning it around to face her. "Bingo. I think we just found what you're doing tonight."

She stared at the green-and-red invite, the one she'd studied once an hour since it had arrived two days prior. "No way."

"Why not? It's not a corporate party. In fact, it looks entirely social."

She met his eyes. "She wouldn't want me there, Bent."

"And how do you know that?"

She stared at the wall as the lump she'd become all too familiar with presented itself in her throat. "She couldn't have been any clearer when she told me good-bye. It's not worth it to her. Correction, I wasn't worth it to her. End of story. We all move on now." It hadn't been as simple as she'd made it sound. The past few weeks had been disastrous.

"And yet her friends have taken it upon themselves to invite you to their Christmas party. Interesting."

She rolled her eyes. "Three names are signed there. Take a look. Not four. That's kind of telling, don't you think?"

"Then don't go for Brooklyn."

"What do you mean?"

"Go for you. Enjoy yourself. Wear designer jeans and a sexy top and get to know some people. You might make a new friend. And if in the midst of it all, you happen to get the chance to wish Brooklyn a Merry Christmas, well, what's so wrong with that?"

Jessica blew out a breath and weighed her options. She'd considered going to the party on and off since the invitation had presented itself so surprisingly. An actual Christmas party where friends mingled and music played and no one wanted to talk to you for purposes of upward mobility. How long had it been since she'd been to one of those?

And let's be honest, she'd get to see Brooklyn.

It would hurt like hell and feel entirely strange, but it was a big draw just to see her face again. To at least give herself that. Self-inflicted torture was apparently her new thing.

She snatched the invitation from Bentley's hand and stared down at the handwritten note at the bottom. "Hope you can make it!—Mallory, Hunter, and Samantha." Maybe Bent had a point. This was an opportunity. What was so wrong with taking it?

❖

Brooklyn looked around the winter wonderland that used to be their office, sipped her blue martini, and bopped her head in time to the music. The place was packed with their friends, acquaintances, neighbors from various floors, and quite a few people she'd never seen in her life. But you know what? The more the merrier. The room was in a collective good mood and partaking in a variety of activities one would partake in at a party. Dancing, eating, carousing, and okay, even some holiday smooching were all in full effect. She glanced away, not needing to see the romantic bliss play out in front of her and her martini.

They'd chosen to have the party downstairs at Savvy so they could comfortably accommodate more people. The annual shindig just seemed to grow bigger each year. They'd cleared the floor of desks and pulled together some makeshift seating areas. Samantha had handled the majority of the food. Hunter and Brooklyn had worked together on the decorations, and Mallory had compiled a guest list from their combined friends and sent out the invites.

"Rockin' Around the Christmas Tree" played loudly from built-in speakers as the awesome hors d'oeuvres Sam had cooked, ordered, and plated were consumed in large quantities to rave reviews.

"Where do you get these?" a girl asked Sam, holding up a round piece of chocolate.

Sam glanced up from the fruitcake she was slicing, though her hips never stopped sashaying to the music. "Oh, those are truffles from this cute little bakery I visited in Illinois. Have you ever tasted anything more amazing?" The girl shook her head in awe through her next bite. "They're called Mollydollys, and you can order them online from the bakery's website. I'll write down the information for you if you want."

"Definitely," the girl said. "Because I'd sell my five-year-old for a box of these things."

"Right?"

As Sam scurried off, Hunter took her place and bumped Brooklyn's hip with her own. "You don't look like Good-Time-Brooklyn, and she happens to be my favorite. How do we get her here? Does someone need some mistletoe to get the party started? Because I could find you some."

Brooklyn sent her friend an easy smile. "Not necessary. I'm taking a laid-back approach to the party this year. Laid-Back-Brooklyn, an interested observer."

"Not in the Christmas spirit?"

"I'm working on it." Something was missing, and she knew exactly what it was. Who it was. She was just going to have to wait for enough time to go by—that was all.

"Can I just say that these people love Christmas," Mallory said, emerging from a group a few feet away. "And the old Christmas cocktail. Miniature candy cane?" She held up the small offering to Brooklyn.

"I'm good," Brooklyn said. She turned in time to see Hunter communicating something silently to Mallory, who, when she swiveled to look, seemed to be shaking her head subtly.

"Okay, superspies. What am I missing?"

Mallory's eyes widened slightly. "Hunter was trying to hit on the woman in the corner, but she's taken. Can you believe that? I've told her ten times already."

Brooklyn squinted at the extra-older woman in the corner—and she did mean extra. "Mrs. Mayo from 2B? Wow. I didn't know she was your type, Hunter."

Hunter stared at Mallory blandly. "I'm branching out."

Interesting, Brooklyn thought, and straightened. "Well, you two have fun. Off to mingle like the hard-core partier I am," and with that she left her two entirely weird friends. She located Sam at one of the food tables, refreshing the sugar cookies. She picked up a stalk of broccoli and examined it. "Nobody ever eats the vegetables. So what's the point?"

Sam tossed her a glance. "Vegetables make us classy."

"They do?"

"Proven fact. Without the tray of untouched vegetables, we're just a bunch of animals."

"I feel bad for the veggies, almost like—" But the words died in her throat. She blinked to clear her vision, but it did no good. Jessica was still standing in front of the door, taking off her coat, looking drop-dead beautiful. So against rule number one that it wasn't even funny. She wore dark blue jeans and a black cashmere sweater. And at the sight of her, Brooklyn's heart began to kick right on cue. Sam must have followed her gaze.

"Whoa. She looks nice."

"I don't understand." She turned to Sam. "Did you invite Jess?"

She held up her hands. "Not guilty." And then came the very telling double blink. "But maybe talk to Mallory."

Brooklyn blew out a breath. "I can't believe she did this. She should have talked to me first." She had an urgent need to rearrange the broccoli so that all the stems faced inward. But in between arranging, she stole glances at Jessica, who'd been handed a glass of wine by that crazy girl Serena who lived down the hall and drooled over Hunter whenever she came over.

It was whatever.

Oh, look. The celery should probably go from green to greener. She could take care of that. Who was Serena introducing Jessica to now? What were they laughing about? A twinge of irritation shot through her. Too many carrots in the carrot compartment. Some of these should definitely go on another tray. She'd find one in the kitchen. She also found Mallory there.

"You invited Jessica to the Christmas party? Isn't that something you might have checked with me about first?"

"What are you talking about? I didn't invite her. But…"

Brooklyn narrowed her gaze. "But what, Mal?"

"I think Hunter might have."

She blew out a breath. "Seriously?"

Mallory folded her arms. "I'll throw her out if you want. Jessica, I mean. Not Hunter. I don't think we're allowed to throw Hunter out."

Brooklyn straightened, tray in hand. "Of course we're not throwing her out. Don't be ridiculous. I'm fine. Did you hear me? *Fine*."

"You look fine. Especially that crease right between your eyebrows. What's the tray for?"

"The carrots need room."

"I'm sorry. Room?"

"To do carrot things, Mallory. Don't look at me like that!"

The music had shifted to "Baby, It's Cold Outside," and people were singing the song to each other as Brooklyn returned to the vegetables. It should have been charming except that it wasn't.

"Need any help?"

She raised her eyes to Jessica's, and the room seemed to slow down around her. "No, I think I got it." She straightened and offered a halfhearted smile. "Hi, by the way."

"Hey. I hope it's okay that I'm here. When the invitation arrived, I wasn't sure it was the best idea."

She shook her head, as if it were the most casual thing in the world. "Of course it's okay." She hadn't seen Jessica in weeks, and the idea that she was standing in front of her now had her nerves in overdrive. And was she crazy, or did her face feel hot?

"I just wanted to come over here and say Merry Christmas."

Brooklyn held her gaze for what felt like longer than casual. "You too. I mean that."

Jessica nodded and turned to go. But it hadn't been enough for Brooklyn, the exchange. She didn't want Jessica to walk away again and laugh with Serena and smile at other people in the confines of this new world where they didn't mean anything to each other. Yes, it was all her doing, and it was a good decision, but it still felt wrong. "Are you headed back to Boston for Christmas?"

Jessica paused when she heard Brooklyn ask her a question. She wanted to answer, but when she turned back, she found herself wildly distracted by the way Brooklyn's hair fell just shy of her left eye and the glossy quality of her lip gloss. God, it was good to talk to her again, to see her again. The red sweaterdress and boots she wore might have been her best look yet. The dress seemed to have been made for her subtle curves and was perfect for a party like this.

But there was a question on the table, so she mentally shook herself out of it. "No, actually. My parents are taking a holiday cruise, and my brother and his wife are going along. I was invited, but the timing didn't work out with things at the office."

Brooklyn nodded. "So a West Village Christmas it is. How's Ashton?"

Jessica smiled. "Having a blast with her dad in Vail. She'll be back after the New Year. She texted me that the ski instructor's hot, so I think she's in teenage-girl heaven. What about you? How have you been?"

"Oh, you know. Okay. Staying busy. Keeping the pedestrians of New York on their toes."

"I have no doubt about that." There was so much more Jessica wanted to say, so much she wanted to know. But that sadly seemed out of bounds now. "Well, I'll let you get back to your—"

"Carrots." Brooklyn supplied absently as her eyes drifted down Jessica's face, settling on her mouth. Was Jessica imagining it, or was she a little preoccupied herself? That was something, at least. That it was hard for her too.

"Right. Your carrots."

"Have a good time, Jess."

She backed away and flashed what she hoped was a good-natured smile. "Already happening. Your neighbor is friendly."

Brooklyn's eyes narrowed at the mention. "In that case, don't have too much fun. I'm thinking of you when I say that."

"So noted. And Brooklyn?"

"Yep?"

"The sweaterdress is a really good look."

The song crossfaded to "All I Want For Christmas is You" as Jessica crossed back to the heart of the party. But she wasn't very far in before Hunter was at her elbow.

"Jess! You made it." She found herself pulled into a warm hug, which she happily returned. Hunter was wearing slim-fitting gray jeans and a dark-green top with a Santa hat, and was easily the coolest-looking one there.

"I did. It was nice to get the invitation."

"Let me introduce you around." With that, Savvy's exotic beauty escorted her from group to group until she felt like she had a whole new slate of acquaintances. Hunter really did seem to know everyone in the entire world. And everyone seemed to love Hunter. It was an intriguing dynamic.

Time flew as she chatted with the artist who did studio work across the hall from Savvy, Mallory's attorney, and Samantha's accounting buddy. She took stock. She was out of her house and having an actual good time. Imagine that. Of course, she was noticeably aware of Brooklyn's location in the room at any given point, and that was entirely distracting, but she was proud of herself for doing something social. It felt…nice.

"So how do you know Hunter?" Serena asked, popping up yet again. She'd somehow tailed her around the room with adept skill.

"We both work in advertising."

"Truly? I have to tell you. I find the corporate world incredibly sexy. Brunettes too."

Jessica raised an eyebrow. Serena clearly had an agenda and had no plans to go home alone that night. She tried to steer the conversation elsewhere. "What is it that you do?"

"I'm a masseur. I have fantastic hands." She wiggled her fingers. "You should set up an appointment. I can work wonders on a body like yours, the motivation being so high and all."

Brooklyn watched from across the room as Serena stepped into Jessica's space and ran a slow hand up her arm. She noticed then that she was clenching her jaw. She was really starting to dislike that Serena girl. No more small talk in the elevator for her.

Hunter handed Brooklyn a glass of champagne. "Looks like Serena has a new project. You can't blame her. Actually, everyone I've introduced Jessica to has taken a noticeable interest in her. So you're welcome. You're off the hook."

"Best news of the night." A total lie. She hated every moment of it. She'd never thought of herself as a jealous person before, but that had been a mistake because she definitely was. The most jealous, in fact, and that just angered her further. She turned to face Hunter. "Thanks for the heads-up that she'd be here, by the way."

"I didn't know myself. From what I hear, Samantha's the one to blame. She invited her."

Brooklyn glared as her annoyance bubbled over. "Okay. Enough of the games. The pointing fingers. I'm calling a meeting in the kitchen in three minutes."

"You can't call a meeting during a party."

"Can too. Doing it. Party-meeting in the kitchen."

Hunter sighed and skulked her way there. Brooklyn took a lap and wrangled the other two, herding them into the kitchen like reluctant sheep. The room was open to the party but still private enough to give them a minute.

Once they were assembled, she surveyed the lineup. Three overly innocent faces stood there, blinking back at her.

"I've never heard of a party-meeting before," Sam murmured to Mallory.

"That's because she made it up," Mallory whispered back.

"Well, it's a thing now, okay?" Brooklyn shot. "And don't stand there looking so innocent. You're a meddlesome group of girls, and you know it."

Hunter squinted one eye. "What are you getting at, Brooks? I think I speak for all of us when I say we're confused on what you're upset about."

She rolled her eyes. She had to hand it to them. They'd perfected the art of playing dumb. "Who invited Jessica?" They looked at each other helplessly, no one saying a word. "Exactly. Suddenly everyone's very quiet. Listen, I get that you thought you were doing what's best for me, but only I know what's best for me."

Mallory took the initiative. "You've just been so sad lately. And we only wanted to see you get the spark back. We invited Jessica because we thought if you saw her again, in person, that maybe the Christmas spirit would—"

"Make me realize I made a horrible mistake? "

"Well, yeah," Sam said. "Because I think maybe it was."

Brooklyn's frustration tripled. "Well, that's not going to happen. I ended things with Jessica because it was the right thing, not a mistake. And of course I want her to be happy, but not at *my* Christmas party, do you get that? I don't want her a part of my life."

"It's not a problem. I'll go."

They turned at the sound of the voice. Jessica stood a few feet away at the counter, empty plate in hand. "You were out of cookies," she said quietly. "I was just going to refresh the tray." She placed the large plate on the counter and headed off, as Brooklyn's stomach dropped reflexively.

"Shit. I'll go after her," Mallory said warily. "This is our fault."

"No," Brooklyn said, holding up a hand. "I did this. I'll go."

But she wasn't fast enough, and Jessica beat her to the elevator. The look on her face when Brooklyn had turned around to see her there replayed itself in her head on some kind of horrible loop as she took the stairs two at a time. Her heart was beating out of her chest, and her emotions refused to settle. She didn't know what she'd say to Jessica, but she couldn't leave things this way. When she hit the bottom step in the lobby, she caught sight of her as she turned left out of the building. Brooklyn was on the sidewalk in no time.

"Jess, wait!" she called. But she didn't. She continued walking, which only made Brooklyn feel that more helpless and out of control. "Please, Jessica. Just talk to me for a minute." She'd raced outside without a coat and the cold air accosted her skin immediately, but she didn't care. The only thing she cared about was the way she'd just made Jessica feel, and she couldn't live with it. She doubled her pace, catching up to Jessica, who shot her a sideways glance as she walked.

"You don't have a coat on. You're going to freeze."

"I'll live. Will you talk to me for a minute?"

"Go back to the party, Brooklyn. It's fine. I shouldn't have come."

With a final step, she passed Jessica and turned around in front of her, stopping her progress. "This is not your fault, and I'm sorry you heard that."

"Don't be. I probably needed to. You meant what you said, and you're entitled to your feelings. You don't want me around. I get that. I'm leaving. See? So what is it that you want?"

Brooklyn covered her eyes with her hand. "It's not that I don't want you around. It's that I do. And that's the problem and that's why I need space. So I'll stop the wanting."

"That doesn't make any sense." Jessica sidestepped Brooklyn and continued walking.

"It does to me," Brooklyn said, suddenly desperate to make Jessica understand. She *needed* her to understand or she couldn't move forward. "I think about you all the time." Jessica paused a moment and then turned back, listening. "I wonder what you're doing—if you're working late. Or if you've remembered to take time for yourself. I wonder if you're sitting on your balcony staring out at the lights reflecting off the Hudson. If you're thinking of me. I'm trying to find a way not to do that anymore, and seeing you tonight just makes me miss you that much more, okay? And I can't do that anymore. I have to *stop* doing that. Do you understand? I can't. So you have to—"

"Why?" Jessica shot.

"I just explained why."

Jessica aggressively closed the distance between them on the sidewalk. "Why do you feel those things?"

"I don't know."

"Yes, you do." Jessica had a fire in her eyes. "Answer the question."

"What's the point?" she said helplessly.

"That's not an answer."

"It's all I have."

"Try again. Why do you think about me?"

The words were coming so fast. Brooklyn shook her head as the tears threatened, but her walls were crumbling. "I can't."

"Yes, you can. For once in your life, Brook, take a risk and say it."

"No."

"Why do you miss me? Say it."

"Because I love you." The words were out of her mouth before she could tamp them down. She closed her eyes momentarily and blew out a breath at her own visceral reaction to hearing them out loud. "Is that what you wanted to hear? It's true. I love you more than I ever thought possible, okay? But that doesn't change who I am. What I'm capable of taking on."

As Jessica stared back at her, her eyes brimmed with tears. Brooklyn had never seen Jessica cry, and it sliced through her now. She dropped both hands in defeat. "Then I guess there's nothing left to say. Merry Christmas, Brooklyn. I hope you get everything you want."

Brooklyn stood there, rooted to her spot, as she watched Jessica walk away from her into the night. She wrapped her arms around herself and went slowly back to the party.

Inside, people smiled, laughed, and carried on with their friends. How easy it looked for them. Brooklyn played her role, dancing and toasting and singing with her friends to the music, but inside something had come loose and she couldn't quite get it back in place.

Chapter Twenty-three

Jessica took a step back from the Christmas tree in her living room and admired her work. Oh, but wait. She stepped forward again and turned the Frosty the Snowman ornament so he faced the front. An important touch.

The decorated tree was actually quite beautiful. White lights, simple ornaments, and even a star on top for good measure. Not bad, if she did say so herself.

It was Christmas Eve, and Jessica was slowly slipping into a semblance of holiday spirit. She'd been late decorating because she just couldn't get herself excited about the holidays. But you know what? That had been stupid and unfair to herself. No, things weren't the way she wanted them to be, but she had to find a way to make life manageable again. One of the things Brooklyn had taught her in all of this was that it was important to find beauty in the little things. And she was right.

So she was trying.

She'd had to pull a few rather expensive strings to have a last-minute tree delivered on Christmas Eve, but she'd done it. And now here it was in her living room, twinkling brightly back at her. There was hot cider on the stove, and Pandora had her favorite Christmas songs on a rotation. She was determined to enjoy this thing if it killed her. And it's not like it had all been on her own. Bentley had taken her out to a nice early dinner before heading to his parents' house. The two of them had toasted their friendship and the success of the year they'd shared together.

Now, she'd have a quiet evening to herself, maybe snuggle up with a good book, a luxury she rarely took time for. And tomorrow, she'd go to her cousin Jenna's place for the Christmas dinner her girlfriend was preparing. Adrienne was a fantastic chef and would pull out all the stops to make the day an impressive one.

Not exactly her perfect Christmas, but not so bad either.

❖

It was the worst possible time for the elevator to break. Seriously. Dragging her giant suitcase down what felt like fifty thousand flights of stairs was so not on Brooklyn's list of things to do on her time off for the holidays. On floor five thousand and fifty-three, she paused and turned to Samantha.

"Just how badly did you want to spend Christmas with your family? Because I'm thinking we may never get out of this stairwell. Christmas in a stairwell. How does that sound? I think I have trail mix in my bag. Could be festive."

Sam seemed to be having a worse time of it, however, as she lugged her oversized bag one step at a time. "At least you work out. I may die from this, do you understand? Death by suitcase is imminent. Remind me again why I felt the need to pack every outfit I own? I don't need to be cute for my family. They have to like me. It's in the rulebook."

"Exactly. Plus, you're naturally precious. We all know this. Now channel your inner Jillian Michaels and let's do this."

But to be honest, the words were meant just as much for herself as Samantha. Brooklyn was having second thoughts about their trip to Maine this year. She loved Sam's family and they always made her feel so welcome, but something was holding her back. And she knew exactly what it was.

Her heart was in New York.

Though she tried to push past it, it was like this little knocking sound in the back of her head that wouldn't let up. It felt like she was teetering on the brink of something big.

With an exaggerated sigh, Sam grabbed her bag and tackled the final flight of stairs. When they finally reached the bottom step and headed out into the fresh cold, Brooklyn turned to Sam. "I don't know if I can do this."

Sam tilted her head in contemplation. "What are you talking about? We just did it. Rock stars. Both of us."

"I meant the trip to Maine. I don't know if I can go this year."

Sam blinked back at her. "But it's our tradition."

"Right. I know, and I'd hate to miss your mother's Christmas turkey. It's the highlight of my year, but I think I need to spend Christmas in the city."

"No. Uh-uh. Absolutely not. You're not staying here alone. The holidays are important, and you need to spend them with the people you love."

Brooklyn felt the slow smile take shape and grow as she recalled the words she'd spoken on this very sidewalk just a few nights ago. "Yeah. I think that's what I'm gonna try to do."

As understanding hit, Sam's eyes widened in delight. "Does that mean what I think it means?"

"I need to get her back, Sam. I don't know if she's still speaking to me, but I need to put myself out there. My mom offered me some advice that—"

"Wait. You just called Cynthia your mom." Sam shoved her hard, like you would a football player.

Brooklyn laughed as she stumbled back. "I don't know where that came from, but I guess I did. Yeah."

"Who are you?" Samantha asked happily. "And how are you so awesomely evolved? This is my favorite Brooklyn in life right here."

"Well, I'm glad I'm living up to your standards."

Sam perched atop her suitcase dreamily. "In love, huh? I'd shove you again, but I'm all warm and fuzzy."

Brooklyn nodded. "In love." What excited her was that she only grew more and more sure of that fact as the minutes unfolded. It was like saying those words out loud three nights prior had punched this tiny little hole in the universe that only seemed to grow bigger and bigger as time went on until it was something she couldn't look away from anymore. And you know what? She didn't want to look away anymore.

"And where has this newfound courage come from?"

"That's what I was trying to tell you before you went all linebacker on me." Brooklyn shook her head slowly as she reflected. "Sometimes you gotta go through the brain freeze to get to the ice cream. That was the first piece of parental advice I've ever received, and I think it'd be wrong not to take it."

"Ice cream *is* pretty great. You come from wise people."

"I guess I do."

Sam checked her watch. "As much as I'd like to stay here and celebrate all of this awesomeness with you, I suppose I need to catch a cab before I miss my very lonely train home. Who's going to check my crosswords for accuracy?"

Brooklyn smiled and took a step toward her. "The really attractive woman you're going to find a way to sit next to. Plus, you won't be lonely for long. All of Maine is waiting in anticipation."

Sam's eyes lit up and she made a circular gesture. "I like the sound of that. All of it."

Brooklyn held up one finger. "And I have a better idea, because who needs to pay cab fare? I'll drive you to the station."

Sam hurled her a look of terror, and Brooklyn grinned back wickedly. Christmas was starting to shape up. Now if she could just make the next part of this work in her favor. As she drove Sam to the train station, her heart kicked noticeably in her chest.

She just hoped she wasn't too late.

Why did all Christmas romances have to end happily? Jessica closed the overly sweet novella she'd just concluded. While heartwarming and okay, a little tingly, that kind of perfect romance was an unobtainable ideal and made people expect that kind of thing out of real life. And it wasn't realistic. Not everything ended with a nice little bow tied around it.

She could attest to that.

As Judy Garland advised her to have herself a merry little Christmas, she poured herself a cup of cider and took stock. The year behind her had been full of ups and downs, but regardless of the brutal couple of weeks, she wouldn't trade it. Brooklyn, and Ashton, and even the derisive Tina had taught her some very important life lessons that she wouldn't soon forget. She knew what life was capable of offering her, and she would remember that as she moved forward.

The bell rang and Jessica checked her watch. Right on time. Every year on Christmas Eve, Patrick delivered a gift basket from the building to each of the tenants, complete with wine, cheese, fruit, and snacks. It was actually a nice touch. She grabbed the Christmas card she had for him containing a generous monetary thank-you for his service and swung open the door with a smile.

Except it wasn't Patrick.

Brooklyn stared back at her, wide-eyed and shifting from one foot to the other. At the sight, her heart sped up. "Um, hi," Jessica managed to say and glanced into the hallway, trying to piece together the turn of events.

Brooklyn took a deep breath. "I'll probably forget to make the bed."

Jessica attempted to understand the context and tilted her head curiously. "Okay."

"And I'm not playing that shoot-'em-up game you like. I'm not that into video games."

"You're not?"

"No."

Jessica nodded as she began to understand.

"I can be annoyingly spontaneous, but I try to make up for it with thoughtful gestures."

Jessica felt the inklings of a smile tugging.

"I suck at organization."

"You do. But I'm a great organizer."

"I drive like a crazy person, but I'll work on being more conservative."

Jessica laughed out loud through the tears that were now fully present in her eyes. "No, you won't."

"No, I won't. But I'll try to consider my passengers more."

"That's good," she murmured, settling decidedly on the eyes that had dominated her conscious thought for the weeks she'd gone without them.

"But despite the fact that my clothes might reside on the floor more often than you'd like them to, I promise that if you'll let me, I will love you with everything I have. Because I do, Jess. I love you. I'm saying it all on my own this time because it's the most important thing there ever was for me."

The silence that seemed to hang in the air forever had Brooklyn's heart beating out of her chest, her knees wobbling, and her palms itching. She'd just laid it all out there, and she was waiting for some sort of reply. And while Jessica hadn't slammed the door in her face and had even smiled at the admissions she'd laid out, she still hadn't said what Brooklyn needed so desperately to hear.

Jessica leaned against the side of the door in contemplation and finally weighed in. "But will there be kissing?"

The sentence alone made her body warm. Brooklyn flashed a smile infused with the relief she felt all over. She stepped into Jessica's space and cradled her ridiculously good-looking face in her hands. "Oh, a lot of kissing, I'm afraid. Way more than what others consider normal. I need to be honest about that up front."

Jessica gently brushed a strand of hair from her forehead. "I think I could get behind those terms," she said quietly.

"Best news ever. Maybe we should start now."

"Yeah?"

Brooklyn angled her head and sank into the kiss that would start it all, their life together, the promise of more to come. Everything. When she pulled back from the kiss, there were tears on Jessica's cheeks, and she took her time wiping away each one.

"I love you," Jessica whispered.

"I love that sentence. Never stop saying it."

"Excuse me," a voice said from just behind them. They turned to see Patrick staring back at them like a deer in headlights. "I'll just leave this here," he said, placing the gift basket on the floor a few feet away.

"I think it's going to be a very Merry Christmas, don't you, Patrick?" Jessica handed him her Christmas card, and he smiled genuinely this time.

"I certainly do, Ms. Lennox. As you were."

Snuggled up on the couch with wine and cheese and a roaring fireplace, she and Jessica talked for hours, catching up on the time they'd lost. In the wee hours of the morning, she led Jessica by the hand to her bedroom, where she undressed her one piece of clothing at a time before lowering her to the satin sheets and joining her there moments later. As their bodies connected, skin on skin, Brooklyn closed her eyes and sighed at the sensation.

"Christ," Jessica murmured against her neck.

"God, I've missed you. This."

And as they began to savor, to explore, and to luxuriate in each other, Brooklyn tumbled to a place she'd never been. It was warm and wonderful there. It was a place she felt safe and loved. That's when she understood. She had found what she'd been seeking her whole life, and it was better than she'd ever imagined it could be.

She was, at long last, home.

EPILOGUE

Five minutes to midnight," Cat called out to the group.

Brooklyn accepted a fresh glass of champagne from her father. "Thanks, Aaron."

"My pleasure."

The invitation to spend New Year's Eve in Avon had been a nice one, and the town certainly went all out, celebrating together in the ballroom of a historic hotel in the center of town. The room looked magnificent, with round-looking ornaments reminiscent of champagne bubbles floating to the top of a glass hanging crisply from the ceilings. Brightly colored centerpieces decorated the tabletops, with lemons and silver balls interspersed in a creative jumble. A live orchestra underscored the party, which had consisted of dinner and dancing in a place where everyone seemed to know everyone. Cynthia had stayed close to her side, making sure she felt comfortable but also taking pride in introducing her to friends and neighbors.

While she wasn't entirely at ease just yet, this was a definite beginning of sorts. And that mattered. She wanted a relationship with her family, and they seemed to feel the same way.

Over time, they'd get there.

"Four minutes," Cat yelled over the swell of the music.

Ethan had his arm around his girlfriend but inclined his head to Brooklyn. "While my first dance of the New Year is booked, I'm hoping you'll do me the honor of being my second."

Brooklyn smiled. "The honor will be mine."

Cat scoffed and pointed to herself in an obvious fashion.

"Relax," Ethan said. "You, little sister, can be twenty-seventh."

Brooklyn laughed. "Excuse me, guys. There's someone I need to snag before midnight."

The hand on the small of her back brought a smile to Jessica's lips. She wrapped up the conversation she was having with one of Aaron's coworkers and turned to Brooklyn happily. "It's almost midnight."

"That's right, Cinderella."

"You ever going to explain that one?"

"Someday. For now, I just want to stare into your eyes and envision the incoming year stretched out in front of us. I think I want to take up race-car driving. What do you think?"

Jessica laughed. "Dangerous. But maybe if you wore a cute little helmet."

"I would. And black leather. Think that through before you say no."

The comment sent Jessica's mind to new places.

Brooklyn laughed. "I don't think I'll ever get tired of you looking at me like that."

"Like what?"

"Like you want to have your way with me."

"I did that just a few hours ago."

"Don't distract me with steamy memories."

But Jessica loved the twinkle in her eye at the reminder. "Sorry. Back on track. I don't know how the incoming year can beat the last. Mysterious identities, corporate espionage, ambulances, break-ups."

Brooklyn held up a finger. "Sexy kissing, covered bridges, elevators, falling desperately in love with one another."

She looked skyward at the mentions. "Ohhh. I think I love your version."

"And I love you.

The crowd began to chant. "Ten. Nine. Eight. Seven. Six. Five. Four…"

But Jessica didn't wait. She captured Brooklyn's lips in advance of the New Year and kissed her right into it. As partygoers broke into "Auld Lang Syne" all around them, Jessica smiled and took in the scene. This was what life was supposed to feel like. "I still can't believe you're mine," Jessica marveled to Brooklyn.

"Get used to it," Brooklyn whispered into her ear.

As they joined her family outside for the fireworks over the lake, Brooklyn's heart had never been so full. They stood together as the blues, reds, and greens burst forth in the sky. She squeezed Cat's hand and relaxed against Jessica's arm, wrapped snugly around her. A year ago, she'd never have imagined that she'd be where she was now. She had three of the best friends on the planet, the love of her life at her side, and the family she'd never known opening their hearts to her. Though it had taken a long time to get here, she really was very lucky.

Life had endless possibilities, she realized.

And she couldn't wait to explore them.

About the Author

Melissa Brayden is currently at work on her master of fine arts in directing in San Antonio, Texas, and enjoying the ride. She is a three-time Goldie Award winner for her books *Waiting in the Wings* and *Heart Block.*

Melissa is married and working really hard at remembering to do the dishes. For personal enjoyment, she spends time with her Jack Russell terriers and checks out the NYC theater scene several times a year. She considers herself a reluctant patron of the treadmill, but enjoys hitting a tennis ball around in nice weather. Coffee is her very best friend. www.melissabrayden.com

Books Available From Bold Strokes Books

Kiss The Girl by Melissa Brayden. Sleeping with the enemy has never been so complicated. Brooklyn Campbell and Jessica Lennox face off in love and advertising in fast-paced New York City. (978-1-62639-071-3)

Taking Fire: A First Responders Novel by Radclyffe. Hunted by extremists and under siege by nature's most virulent weapons, Navy medic Max de Milles and Red Cross worker Rachel Winslow join forces to survive and discover something far more lasting. (978-1-62639-072-0)

First Tango in Paris by Shelley Thrasher. When French law student Eva Laroche meets American call girl Brigitte Green in 1970s Paris, they have no idea how their pasts and futures will intersect. (978-1-62639-073-7)

The War Within by Yolanda Wallace. Army nurse Meredith Moser went to Vietnam in 1967 looking to help those in need; she didn't expect to meet the love of her life along the way. (978-1-62639-074-4)

Escapades by MJ Williamz. Two women, afraid to love again, must overcome their fears to find the happiness that awaits them. (978-1-62639-182-6)

Desire at Dawn by Fiona Zedde. For Kylie, love had always come armed with sharp teeth and claws. But with the human, Olivia, she bares her vampire heart for the very first time, sharing passion, lust, and a tenderness she'd never dared dream of before. (978-1-62639-064-5)

Visions by Larkin Rose. Sometimes the mysteries of love reveal themselves when you least expect it. Other times they hide behind a black satin mask. Can Paige unveil her masked stranger this time? (978-1-62639-065-2)

All In by Nell Stark. Internet poker champion Annie Navarro loses everything when the Feds shut down online gambling, and she turns to experienced casino host Vesper Blake for advice—but can Nova convince Vesper to take a gamble on romance? (978-1-62639-066-9)

Vermilion Justice by Sheri Lewis Wohl. What's a vampire to do when Dracula is no longer just a character in a novel? (978-1-62639-067-6)

Switchblade by Carsen Taite. Lines were meant to be crossed. Third in the Luca Bennett Bounty Hunter Series. (978-1-62639-058-4)

Nightingale by Andrea Bramhall. Culture, faith, and duty conspire to tear two young lovers apart, yet fate seems to have different plans for them both. (978-1-62639-059-1)

No Boundaries by Donna K. Ford. A chance meeting and a nightmare from the past threaten more than Andi Massey's solitude as she and Gwen Palmer struggle to understand the complexity of love without boundaries. (978-1-62639-060-7)

Timeless by Rachel Spangler. When Stevie Geller returns to her hometown, will she do things differently the second time around or will she be in such a hurry to leave her past that she misses out on a better future? (978-1-62639-050-8)

Second to None by L.T. Marie. Can a physical therapist and a custom motorcycle designer conquer their pasts and build a future with one another? (978-1-62639-051-5)

Seneca Falls by Jesse Thoma. Together, two women discover love truly can conquer all evil. (978-1-62639-052-2)

A Kingdom Lost by Barbara Ann Wright. Without knowing each other's fates, Princess Katya and her consort Starbride seek to reclaim their kingdom from the magic-wielding madman who seized the throne and is murdering their people. (978-1-62639-053-9)

Season of the Wolf by Robin Summers. Two women running from their pasts are thrust together by an unimaginable evil. Can they overcome the horrors that haunt them in time to save each other? (978-1-62639-043-0)

The Heat of Angels by Lisa Girolami. Fires burn in more than one place in Los Angeles. (978-1-62639-042-3)

Desperate Measures by P. J. Trebelhorn. Homicide detective Kay Griffith and contractor Brenda Jansen meet amidst turmoil neither of them is aware of until murder suspect Tommy Rayne makes his move to exact revenge on Kay. (978-1-62639-044-7)

The Magic Hunt by L.L. Raand. With her Pack being hunted by human extremists and beset by enemies masquerading as friends, can Sylvan protect them and her mate, or will she succumb to the feral rage that threatens to turn her rogue, destroying them all? A Midnight Hunters novel. (978-1-62639-045-4)

Wingspan by Karis Walsh. Wildlife biologist Bailey Chase is content to live at the wild bird sanctuary she has created on Washington's Olympic Peninsula until she is lured beyond the safety of isolation by architect Kendall Pearson. (978-1-60282-983-1)

Windigo Thrall by Cate Culpepper. Six women trapped in a mountain cabin by a blizzard, stalked by an ancient cannibal demon bent on stealing their sanity—and their lives. (978-1-60282-950-3)

The Blush Factor by Gun Brooke. Ice-cold business tycoon Eleanor Ashcroft only cares about the three Ps—Power, Profit, and Prosperity—until young Addison Garr makes her doubt both that and the state of her frostbitten heart. (978-1-60282-985-5)

Slash and Burn by Valerie Bronwen. The murder of a roundly despised author at an LGBT writers' conference in New Orleans turns Winter Lovelace's relaxing weekend hobnobbing with her peers into a nightmare of suspense—especially when her ex turns up. (978-1-60282-986-2)

The Quickening: A Sisters of Spirits novel by Yvonne Heidt. Ghosts, visions, and demons are all in a day's work for Tiffany. But when Kat asks for help on a serial killer case, life takes on another dimension altogether. (978-1-60282-975-6)

Smoke and Fire by Julie Cannon. Oil and water, passion and desire, a combustible combination. Can two women fight the fire that draws them together and threatens to keep them apart? (978-1-60282-977-0)

Love and Devotion by Jove Belle. KC Hall trips her way through life, stumbling into an affair with a married bombshell twice her age. Thankfully, her best friend, Emma Reynolds, is there to show her the true meaning of Love and Devotion. (978-1-60282-965-7)

The Shoal of Time by J.M. Redmann. It sounded too easy. Micky Knight is reluctant to take the case because the easy ones often turn into the hard ones, and the hard ones turn into the dangerous ones. In this one, easy turns hard without warning. (978-1-60282-967-1)

In Between by Jane Hoppen. At the age of fourteen, Sophie Schmidt discovers that she was born an intersexual baby and sets off on a journey to find her place in a world that denies her true existence. (978-1-60282-968-8)

Under Her Spell by Maggie Morton. The magic of love brought Terra and Athene together, but now a magical quest stands between them—a quest for Athene's hand in marriage. Will their passion keep them together, or will stronger magic tear them apart? (978-1-60282-973-2)

Rush by Carsen Taite. Murder, secrets, and romance combine to create the ultimate rush. (978-1-60282-966-4)

Homestead by Radclyffe. R. Clayton Sutter figures getting NorthAm Fuel's newest refinery operational on a rolling tract of land in upstate New York should take a month or two, but then, she hadn't counted on local resistance in the form of vandalism, petitions, and one furious farmer named Tess Rogers. (978-1-60282-956-5)

Battle of Forces: Sera Toujours by Ali Vali. Kendal and Piper return to New Orleans to start the rest of eternity together, but the return of an old enemy makes their peaceful reunion short-lived, especially when they join forces with the new queen of the vampires. (978-1-60282-957-2)

How Sweet It Is by Melissa Brayden. Some things are better than chocolate. Molly O'Brien enjoys her quiet life running the bakeshop in a small town. When the beautiful Jordan Tuscana returns home, Molly can't deny the attraction—or the stirrings of something more. (978-1-60282-958-9)